THE
NATURALIST
SOCIETY

ALSO BY CARRIE VAUGHN

The Kitty Series

Other Books

THE
NATURALIST
SOCIETY

CARRIE VAUGHN

47NORTH

Text copyright © 2024 by Carrie Vaughn, LLC
All rights reserved.

Published by 47North, Seattle

www.apub.com

Amazon, the Amazon logo, and 47North are trademarks of Amazon.com, Inc., or its affiliates.

ISBN-13: 9781662519031 (paperback)
ISBN-13: 9781662519024 (digital)

Cover design by David Drummond
Cover image: © Eric Isselee, © Lukasz Szwaj, © Sur / Shutterstock; © Canon_Bob, © mikroman6 / Getty

Printed in the United States of America

*To my grandfather Dr. Allan D. Linder, who gave me
my first field guide and binoculars*

Zoölogical Nomenclature is a means, not an end, of
Zoölogical Science.

—From the 1886 *Check-List of North American Birds*,
by the American Ornithologists' Union

A note about scientific names: Scientific names, like nature itself, are not immutable. Names given to species can change when scientists learn more about them and reclassify them. The taxonomic names some of these species had in 1880 are not the names they have now. I've used the modern scientific names to make referencing them easier for a modern audience.

ONE

Aix galericulata

August 1877
Manhattan

Beth wondered why showing her journals to Mr. Harold Stanley felt more risqué than stealing a kiss. Her heart raced; her hands shook. She rushed down the stairs from her room back to the parlor, worried that he might have vanished while she'd been gone. That he might have decided this was all nonsense, retrieved his coat and hat, and left.

He had not. He was waiting on the sofa right where she'd left him and stood when she entered the room again. A handsome man, he was well turned out in gray trousers and a dark coat over a pressed shirt and burgundy waistcoat. Fashionable without being showy about it. His dark hair swept back from a slim, clean-shaven face. Aristocratic, she liked to think, but that seemed a cliché. His smile was kind, and she liked that part of him best. He smiled now, and she smiled back. Her cheeks were burning; she glanced away and wondered at her own ridiculousness. They were just going to talk about birds.

"I've brought three from the last year," she said quickly. "There's lots more, of course. I've been doing this for years—"

"When did you start?"

She had known Harry Stanley—the very first day they met, he asked her to call him Harry—for four months, and she knew he wouldn't make fun of her journals, where she kept a record of the birds she saw: the species, the number, the place, the season, the time of day, behaviors, and what hints of Arcanism she might have felt accompanying the observation.

Others might tease her. Her brother certainly had. Her mother called it a waste of time and implored her to take up more ladylike pursuits. Her father chuckled indulgently and said that every young woman ought to have hobbies.

This wasn't a hobby.

Harry might mock himself, society, or the stuffy professors delivering the lectures they sometimes attended. But he had never once made fun of her, not for her obsession, not for knowing the name of every single bird in Audubon's paintings without looking at the labels. She had told him about her journals; he had asked to see them. And here they were.

"I was fourteen," she confessed. Eight years' worth of journals.

"You must have dozens."

"I've lost count." She kept them in her room, in a box under the bed; if she kept them anywhere else, they might disappear, thrown out as nonsense.

"Well, bring them over, let me see." He made space for her next to him on the sofa. She held them out to him like an offering.

Opening the first clothbound volume, he sat back to read. He turned each page slowly, his eyes roving. She had drawn grids on the pages, listed names, temperatures, weather, with hatch marks for each sighting. The charts recorded her walks in Central Park, of course, but also a trip to the Hamptons and another to Cape May this past spring, catching part of the migration season and the thousands of birds traveling north along the coast. That had been the single best observation day of her life. All she'd had to do was sit, and dozens of species of warblers flew into view, too many to count. But she had tried. Blackburnian and black-poll warblers, redstarts and ovenbirds. So many, all brilliant and singing. She had made sketches of various plumage patterns—splashes of color, the caps and bibs, lines over the eyes, streaks on their breasts, bars on their wings—to keep them all straight. Harry was looking at that page now.

She reached for a cup of tea from the tray set out on the table. She fumbled a bit but didn't spill.

Finally, he looked up. He seemed astonished. "Beth . . . I have some naturalist friends who would commit actual crimes to get their hands on these."

Harry had studied natural history at Harvard under Professor Agassiz. She was insanely jealous. And while he wasn't an Arcane Taxonomist himself, he knew many. This was likely as close as she would ever get to that world. She cherished the chance.

"It's just notes I got in the habit of making." She wanted to find every bird, to see them all, to learn everything about them. Whenever she could, she fled the parlor and her mother's luncheons, stayed outside as long as possible. When she finally had to return, to sit nicely in the parlor and be amiable, the journals and sketches helped her remember.

Harry spread his hand on the cover of the book. "These are more detailed than the logs of men at Harvard right now. Beth. Will you marry me?" He held up the book the way another man making a proposal would hold a ring.

He was joking. Surely he was joking. "Are . . . are you serious?"

He blinked, as if startled at his own words. "You know, I think I am. Odd." He set the book aside and took her hand, pressing it between both of his, and this seemed much more like a proper proposal. Her stomach turned as if she were at sea, and she leaned into his touch, hoping he would keep her steady.

"Beth Clarke. You're one of the most brilliant people I know. I'm not at all smart. Not like you, or the Naturalist Society men. The way you all talk. Profound mysteries. All of you are profound mysteries to me, and . . . and I love that." He spoke with a sense of subdued awe, the way one did inside a church. "If I could somehow be closer to that . . . I'm sounding foolish."

"Not at all," she said breathlessly. "I will. I mean, yes. I'll marry you. If you're really serious?"

"Why wouldn't I be?" They were clinging to one another now. "I hadn't planned to ask right now, like this, but the more I think of it . . ."

The girls she knew all talked about getting married—some of them, it was all they talked about. They dreamed of romantic proposals, and Beth had gotten caught up in it as much as the rest of them. She must marry someday, of course she must, and she'd wondered who he would be, what he'd be like, and she'd heard all the stories of men getting down on their knees and making declarations of undying love—

Harry had done none of that, which was just exactly like Harry, and she preferred this, and the reverent way he treated her work. The look of wonder in his gaze. But she had never thought about what came after the breathless declarations. *Yes, I will marry you. Yes, my life has just irrevocably changed.* What now?

"Would you like some more tea?" she said absurdly, and blushed even harder. "I'm sorry, this is . . . but my mouth's gone dry. Oh, Harry."

"Yes. Tea. Let's catch our breaths."

She took hold of the pot and poured. The tea had gone tepid; the cups weren't even a little warm. She started to apologize, to find the bell for the maid, and he touched her arm. An electric, thrilling touch, even through the sleeve of her gown. Maybe he'd never let go.

"It's fine, Beth. No need to call," he said.

"I . . . I think I can warm it back up."

"Oh? Let's see."

Anyone else would have scoffed at the idea of her working Arcane *practica*. Maybe even been horrified at a woman doing such a thing. But not Harry. He raised a brow and watched attentively, wearing a crooked, anticipatory grin.

She held the cup in both hands and gazed at the brown liquid, translucent, jostling against the porcelain—her hands were still shaking a little.

Review the catalog, then, of all she had seen, and what of their aspects she had taken into herself. What of heat, what of fire. Freezing water was easier—that was taking energy away. This would be adding it back in, to increase the temperature . . . and only a little. Hot but not boiling. Think of a desert bird, like the roadrunner, *Geococcyx californianus*. Sun, heat—saguaro cactus, *Carnegiea gigantea*, iconic for that environment. But she had not seen them for herself, and their influence was abstract. Think instead of a waterbird with fiery plumage; use its brightness rather than literal heat. She had seen a mandarin duck once, an escaped pet on the estate of one of her father's business associates. *Aix galericulata*. A dainty thing, yet magnificent to look at, with its curling tail, red bill, bright-orange beard swept back from its face—like flames. Now, send that into the water.

The tea in the cup shuddered, and steam rose up. The porcelain grew almost too warm, and she hissed at the sting.

Harry collected the cup from her. "You amaze me. Constantly." Cradling the cup, he breathed in the steam. "Imagine, never being without a hot cup of tea."

She imagined herself doing this for Harry—heating up cups of tea, lighting candles, everything—for the rest of their lives. Secretly, she might have dreamed of more. A life as a naturalist, traveling and publishing her surveys and observations. But maybe it was best to hope for what was possible rather than what wasn't. Harry would get her away from her parents, and there was some freedom in that.

He sipped, and his brow furrowed. "I've just had a strange idea."

Please don't take it back, she prayed. *Please don't change your mind . . .*
"Oh?"

"I've told you about my friend from Harvard, Brandon West? Right now, as we speak, he's in the Arctic somewhere, counting seals and birds off the ice sheet in Greenland. Hopefully not freezing to death. But I worry. I'd help him if I could, but I know myself well enough to know I'm not cut out for that kind of work. Never had a scrap of Arcanism in me. I'm more at home in parlors. But you . . . your research, your knowledge. I'd bet my hat you know just as much about Arcane Taxonomy as he does."

She laughed a little. "I don't see how that's possible."

But he was serious, so intense he was frowning. "You publish your work. Write up a few surveys to start, then an essay or two. Move up to monographs. Arcane Taxonomists like Bran use that work to increase their own abilities. The more he knows, the more successful his expeditions—that's how it works. You could help him. *We* could help him."

"Oh, he wouldn't want my help. They won't let me into Harvard, or the Naturalist Society, or anything." She had known better than to even dream of such a thing.

"So we don't tell anyone it's you. You'll use my name; I'll be the front. If you're Mrs. Harold Stanley, we'll just be leaving off the *Mrs.*, so it wouldn't even be a lie. Sort of." He gave an uncharacteristically shy shrug.

She needed a moment to think through the implications of what he was saying. A career. She could take the next step, do serious work, and whether Harvard or Columbia or Princeton ever let her in wouldn't matter. Whether the Naturalist Society ever acknowledged her didn't matter—they'd recognize Harry.

"What if someone found out?" Her heart raced at the thought. To be exposed, her reputation tarnished . . . and what did that mean anyway? "I had a cousin, a distant cousin. She wore trousers and hunted with a rifle, and her family finally had her declared hysterical, locked away, and I never saw her again." There had also been whispers that she'd been an Arcanist, altering the weather and causing leaves to fall from trees. Beth never had the courage to ask what had really happened to her.

"That won't happen," he said, so confident. His smile turned sly. "And if they do find out, well, we'll cross that bridge when we get to it. I promise you, I'll never have you locked away for anything. What do you think?"

Beth took a moment and weighed Harry's words, building up her courage. "Yes," she finally said. His confidence was infectious. What could she do but trust him?

"This will be a partnership. In all things—"

"I understand. They wouldn't listen to me, but they'll listen to you. And my work . . ."

"People would see your work."

She could compile her thoughts, ideas she'd hardly dared examine when she was the only one looking at her journals. But with Harry's help . . . a hope rose up in her. A fevered thing, deep in her rib cage—a bit of stray fire from the mandarin duck.

"Yes," she said, determined.

"God, this feels more serious than the marriage proposal."

"I'm still saying yes."

He touched her chin, leaned in, and kissed her. Lightly, chastely, just on the corner of her lips. She closed her eyes, held her breath, and still felt fire.

The cup jostled, and this time some of the tea sloshed out. They giggled, patting their laps dry with handkerchiefs. She was giddy. She was *happy*.

"I suppose I should go talk to your father," he said. He stood, and she stood with him, clinging. She didn't want to let him go.

"You know him. Flatter him and he'll say yes to anything."

"I'll tell him he has a brilliant daughter." He kissed her lightly again, and she held his arms, keeping him there. Just for a moment. "This is good." He murmured low, as if he had to convince himself. "This is right."

After a last urgent glance back at her, he left the parlor to go see her father in the study.

All she had to do now was imagine racing forward into the rest of her life.

TWO

Cepphus grylle

August 1877
North Baffin Bay
West coast of Greenland

Brandon West was just as eager for the chance to try out this *practicum* as he was to catch a *Pusa hispida*. The sequence would take perfect attention and timing. Which he had, he was sure.

He sat on the crusted-over snow next to the narrow opening in the sea ice, a hole not more than a foot across, where he'd seen a seal emerge for air an hour before. This region was crowded with seals; one of them would come up sooner or later. He balanced his rifle across his legs, noted the coiled rope at his side, kept his vision soft. Rubbed his gloved hands together.

He breathed in, then out, reveling in the stabbing cold. He made the air still, his hearing sharp as an owl's. His clothing was as warm and insulated as the reindeer it had been made from. He accessed what he'd gleaned from the wild to make himself *more*.

Time slipped out of joint to his advantage, and he heard the splash in the water just before the seal emerged: a naked doglike face, thick whiskers and shining black eyes, sliding up from the water. The animal blew out a heavy breath, sucked in another, and—

Bran froze the world. Or at least the few yards around himself. Stopped time, just for a few seconds—a few seconds were all he could manage, but he didn't need more. The seal was suspended, framed by bluish ice, peering up from the liquid metal shine of the sea. Drops of water fanned away from it, frozen in space. Its nostrils had stuck, flared open, showing the pink flesh inside. Its eyes stared unblinking—he could see himself reflected in them. The water on its shining coat was already starting to freeze. He scrambled to drop a loop of rope over its head—

—and time unstuck, flashing dizzily. He hauled back on the rope, and the seal was caught, unable to sink back underwater. It grunted, no doubt confused, but not for long. Bran aimed the gun and fired through its neck. A sound to break the world, against the stillness of the ice.

The shot echoed. A bit of red splashed out, stark against the sparkling white, hot enough to melt the ice under it. Bran dragged the body out of the water.

He pulled down his goggles and leaned in to study the animal's face. *Pusa hispida*, ringed seal. Warmth in the cold, a map of fisheries along this coast. Through this creature he could almost smell schools of fish in the water. *There, drop your nets there,* he'd tell the captain of a fishing boat. More useful at the moment to draw on the power of the seal's blubber. Summer in the Arctic Circle and Bran's eyelashes were freezing from the vapor of his breath. He was breathing too hard. But he'd gotten another specimen, and its power, for his collection. The boys back at Harvard would weep with envy. Sitting back, he reveled in the moment and caught his breath. Coming out of the spell, he pawed at his belt, searching for his knife to skin the seal.

He should have been paying more attention to the world around him instead of his own power.

Something—a huff of breath, a rumble on the ice under him, or maybe the instincts of the seal he had just taken into himself—made him look up.

Ursus maritimus. Polar bear, charging right at him.

Normally, Bran wouldn't put himself in a position to be attacked by a raging predator. He didn't make a habit of carrying raw meat around in the wild, knew not to put himself between a mother and her cubs. He hid in blinds to conduct observations and made plenty of noise to scare off the shy creatures when he traveled.

Yet here he was, butchering one of the bear's favorite meals, right in the open, making himself an irresistible target. Earlier, he'd searched the ice pack; it had been clear, but that was the problem with polar bears, wasn't it? Their white coats matched the ice. They were so perfectly suited to their environment. And Bran wasn't, no matter how many traits of the seal he could catalog. He should have focused more on the creature's instincts for survival.

The bear's big foot pads crunched, a racing beat, and Bran's mind froze before he could think of what to do. He could camouflage himself, create some distraction, make himself appear large—or maybe make himself seem small. Generate some noise, like the scream of an eagle or the roar of a lion, startle the thing enough to make it stop. Blind it with a flash of light. Stop time, except he was sure he wouldn't be able to do that again so soon.

Too many possibilities, so he did none of them.

Two rifle shots cracked. Bran flinched back to himself.

The bear stumbled to its chest, struggled to get its legs back under it, then fell dead.

Anton Torrance stood a couple dozen paces off, his brown face just visible past the fur-lined hood of his parka. His stance was wide, confident; he handled the rifle like some hero in a painting. The gun's mouth smoked; the shots still echoed. He waited a moment, to see if another shot was needed, but the bear didn't move again. He wore slotted goggles to protect against the glare, like the native peoples did. He took them off now to look at Bran. "Are you all right?"

Bran was certain he fell madly in love with Anton in that moment. His worried squint, his shaggy black beard along his jaw, the way his lip started to curl in a wry smile when he saw that Bran was in fact all right.

Bran's heart decided to race with fear only after it was all over. Fear, longing. One or the other.

"God. Yes," he gasped. "Thank you."

"Arcane Taxonomy still can't solve everything, can it?" Anton, smiling fully now, said in his aristocratic English accent, rounded with a touch of the Bahamas, where he'd been born. A very long way from here. How did he manage to be so at home in the cold? Well, Bran was grateful for him. And definitely in love with him.

Nodding in satisfaction, Anton trotted out to his kill.

Bran glanced at the *Pusa hispida*, which wasn't going anywhere. Huffing a sigh that fogged thickly in the cold, he pulled the hood of his own parka more firmly over his head, retrieved his knife, and followed Anton out to see the bear.

Bran pulled back its eyelids, studied the shining dark of its eyes and considered the sheer overwhelming bulk of the animal. A perfect hunter in the cold, traveling such distances. Take in that skill, that stamina. The ease of it. How it was made for the cold. Another specimen, cataloged.

Anton waited until Bran sat back and sighed.

"Ready?" Anton asked patiently.

Still full of the wild, Bran simply nodded.

Together, they got to work skinning and butchering both animals and loading them on the sled to haul back to camp.

A week later, they hiked along the edge of the ice. Their ship, the *Indomitable*, was overdue picking them up. Bran wasn't worried—yet. Too early to start panicking. And, well, Anton never panicked. The pair had been set down to collect, catalog, take measurements, and observe while the ship pushed on until the ice turned them back. But if something had happened, as had happened to so many expeditions before them . . .

Beyond the jagged ice the sea was a field of gray, crowded with floes that seemed oddly still and solid. The landscape appeared empty, but it was in fact teeming. Fish, crustaceans, mollusks, the myriads of near-microscopic life that supported them, on up to seals, whales, birds that swam, birds that flew. Fulmars and terns were born on these winds and could soar on them for miles. Bran wished for their eyesight, the views they had, to look for their missing ship. Felt for a pattern in the world that meant something artificial, some presence of man, moved through it.

He found a wall of dark clouds growing in the northwest. "Storm's moving in," he said. Anton nodded in acknowledgment.

As for searching for the ship, Bran had to resort to using a spyglass like anyone else.

They took turns with the glass, and Bran counted every bear, seal, and whale they spotted. But no ship. On a lone bare patch of ground, they built a cairn and left a message.

Bran tried Anton's patience, lingering to chase after a guillemot he was sure he had spotted swooping low over the waves. Might have been a murre instead. Both birds were dark, fast, and direct in flight, hard to spot against the water. Neither had been recorded much this far north, and he needed a positive identification to log the sighting. He kept asking for the spyglass back, only to catch another unsatisfying glimpse through it. He was almost certain the bird was a black guillemot, *Cepphus grylle*, off course from its colony—but not sure enough to put it in writing, alas. Anton was very patient with him, right until he wasn't.

"West. It's snowing."

Bran lowered the glass and blinked into the cottony gray sky; bits of falling ice pelted his face. So it was. Anton stowed the spyglass in his pack, and they set off, trudging back to camp.

The storm caught up with them, wind coming up, bringing a wall of driving snow with it, wiping out their prints behind them. Bran again thought of fulmars and terns, which used the wind instead of being buffeted by it, and was able to keep the worst of it off them. Couldn't do a thing about the dwindling visibility, though.

The distance back to their camp seemed twice as far as when they'd set out. One step in front of the other, on and on. No other way to finish any journey. But walking soon became painful, knives driving up through Bran's feet with every step. He was determined to keep on, to not say a word. He didn't want to slow Anton down.

"You're limping," Anton shouted over the wind. Of course he noticed.

It's fine, it's nothing, he almost snapped back. But they were alone in the Arctic, hundreds of miles from anywhere, potentially stranded—it wouldn't do anyone any good to lie. As much as it hurt his pride, Bran needed to tell. "Frostbite."

Anton hitched a breath. Frostbite was death if not taken care of. They both knew that. Bran didn't need the lecture; he just needed to keep walking no matter how much it hurt. Wasn't anything they could do about it out here, so there was nothing for it but to get back to shelter.

Anton pulled Bran's arm over his shoulder, and they stumbled on together.

At last, the humped dome of their ice hut emerged through the blowing snow. Anton brought them unerringly to it. The man never got lost, even here, where the sun didn't move and compasses were unreliable. Didn't even need his Arcane Taxonomist to do it.

They collapsed at the entrance. Bran crawled in, Anton urging him on from behind, and finally they were out of the wind. Bran's ears hurt from the sudden quiet. The howling went on, whistling past the entrance. But inside was peace. Bran fell over.

"Can you get the lamp?" Anton asked, arranging their guns and gear out of the way.

The oil lamp sat on a storage box off to the side, a makeshift table that also held a pan, tin cups, and their boxes of tea and biscuits. He had a feeling he ought to be hungry, but he couldn't be bothered just now. He touched the wick and it ignited, a spot of buttery flame. Fire, the first technology, a bit of civilization among the ice and furs. Smoke rose up through the venthole. A small light against the storm outside, but it was enough for now.

Anton said, "The man who can light a fire in any weather. I'll bring you along on all my expeditions."

"That's a deal." He would like to go along on all Anton Torrance's expeditions. The man was a wonder.

The hut would grow surprisingly warm from this small flame, their own bodies in the closed space, and their labored breathing. Maybe not comfortably warm, but this wasn't supposed to be comfortable, was it?

Bran lay back to catch his breath and must have dozed, because he jolted awake to find Anton, bare handed, pulling off his boots and peeling off his socks. All Bran could feel of his feet was a stabbing, paralyzing burn. They felt swollen. He started to imagine a life without feet, sure that amputation was the only solution. Being crippled would be terrible, but right now he just wanted his feet gone so the pain would go with them.

His Arcane abilities, however impressive, couldn't do anything about it.

Anton held up a sock and glared accusingly. "You let them get wet."

"I think I was sweating. Got too warm, I suppose." *Pusa hispida.* Insulation in the face of extreme cold. He'd been keeping himself warmer than he should have.

"Well, bet you'll never let that happen again."

Anton carefully examined both his feet, including every single toe, moving them to look between, then nodded in satisfaction. "No black at all. Cold, but they'll thaw. It'll hurt like hell."

"Yes, I'm aware of that," Bran said through gritted teeth.

"You don't need to solve everything with your Arcanist ways, my friend." Far from being angry with him, Anton seemed amused.

Anton gathered Bran's feet inside his coat, holding them against his own body for warmth. Body heat wouldn't burn, unlike flames. And then the damned extremities started to thaw out and somehow managed to hurt *even worse*. Bran splayed flat on his back, unable to move.

"Guns and warm hands, that's all we need, is it? Oh God that hurts—" He clenched his jaw. He *wouldn't* cry out—he'd never hear the end of it.

"Just give it a moment," Anton said soothingly.

He was right; the intense burning faded to a million stabbing pinpricks, which then faded to horrible itching, which he couldn't scratch lest he damage the skin. Bran groaned with annoyance and relief, and Anton had the gall to chuckle at him.

Anton drew Bran's feet away, and by then the interior was warm enough Bran didn't feel the difference much. Anton kept hold of one foot, rubbing it almost absently. His hands were dry, warm. The gentle touch was heaven after the pain and itching.

Bran sighed appreciatively. "You can just keep on doing that."

In an instant, the mood changed from genial survival to something more insistent and luxurious. Bran's heart went a little quicker, and he met Anton's gaze across his own body, anxious about what he would find there. Wishing he could take the words back while also nurturing a hope that he wouldn't have to.

Anton's strokes up and down his foot slowed; his hand slipped up the cuff of his furred trouser to rub his bare calf. Bran melted a bit more and didn't dare move. Then Anton raised his foot and kissed his ankle. Such a simple, prosaic thing, so unlikely in the middle of an Arctic storm, hundreds of miles of travel between them and another living soul. Or maybe it was perfect.

Bran pulled off his gloves and held out his hand; Anton took it so Bran could draw him up between his legs to lie on top of him, to kiss him, and Anton kissed back, their hands searching for hair and skin to grab hold of but only finding the fur of each other's coats. Anton tasted like seal meat and old tea. Like someone who'd been living on hard rations for the last couple of months. They both did. It was terrible. But his lips were warm, pliant, eager.

They paused, drawing back to meet each other's gazes, a moment of wonder. Bran murmured, "I wasn't sure . . . if you . . ."

Anton chuckled. "You haven't noticed me gawking after you like a schoolboy these last weeks?"

Well, that was a revelation. His brow furrowed. "No?"

"Ah, behold the observation skills of America's next great naturalist."

The teasing should have been annoying, but Anton was looking at him so fondly and stroking the fur over his shoulder. Bran touched his face. "You are magnificent and I want you."

The fondness became deeper, warmer, like embers, and they kissed again, their unkempt beards tangling. Anton sighed. "I'm too damn exhausted to do this properly."

Bran laughed, a wheezing chuckle betraying his own exhaustion.

Anton settled himself on the furs next to Bran, his weight pressing against him. Somehow, they got themselves nestled comfortably together, foreheads touching, hands wound around the other's collars. The storm outside felt very far away.

"I have a proposal," Bran said. "As soon as we get home, we do this properly."

"I promise." Anton kissed him again, lingering, and Bran was right on the edge of persuading him that surely he had some strength left for just a *little* more . . .

"I think sometimes . . ." He furrowed his brow.

"What?"

It was a silly thought, but what better time for silly thoughts? "Part of me doesn't want to go back at all. This world here is so much simpler. We could . . ." He shrugged a little, letting the thought drift off unfinished, and hugged Anton hard. Here, they could do whatever they liked with each other and not worry about anyone finding out.

Anton hugged back, just as fiercely, and kissed Bran's brow. "I know what you mean. But I would like to eat something other than seal blubber someday."

"There's that," Bran admitted. "Drink something other than stale tea."

"A big steak. Medium rare. Chased by a good bourbon."

"Ugh, stop talking about it, it's torture!" They giggled together like boys.

"After the storm we'll go looking for the ship again," Anton said. "If we don't manage to meet up with it in the next week, we'll walk south. There's a Kalaallit village, two hundred miles down I think. We can resupply there."

Bran murmured appreciatively. His legs still ached, and he didn't dare try moving them, but he'd rarely been happier than he was right at this moment.

"You're not worried, are you?" Anton asked.

"Not at all. I'm with you, and you're invincible."

"Let's hope so."

Bran considered the movement of birds' wings, and the lamp's flame blew out. He listened to the wind pummeling outside the entrance for a while longer, and thought of fireplaces, down-filled coverlets, and Anton naked beside him.

He murmured, "'Carry me when you go forth over land or sea; for thus merely touching you is enough, is best, and thus touching you would I silently sleep and be carried eternally.'"

"Whitman," Anton murmured back, half-asleep. Bran somehow fell even more in love.

That part of the expedition never made it into the lectures they delivered, in the years to come.

In 1732, Carl Linnaeus made a six-month-long expedition to Lapland, exploring, observing, collecting, and recording details about the region and its people. Here, he performed the first recorded instance of the practice of Arcane Taxonomy. Night had fallen, and so had rain. Linnaeus found shelter but no fire or warmth. He had collected fresh specimens of the flowering plant that would become known as *Linnaea borealis*, sometimes called the twinflower, and had hoped to prepare them for preservation. He would say later that a great many feelings converged in him in that moment: eagerness to preserve and record the specimens, uncertainty regarding the overall success of the expedition, homesickness, and sheer physical exhaustion from facing the elements. He hoped for light: knowledge, understanding, and also literally light so he could see what he was doing.

The plant in his hand began to glow. Some force—not electricity, not magnetism, but something like both—passed from him to the plant and burned. Several nights later, he successfully repeated the *practicum*.

To name a thing is to know a thing, he would write in his journal. And to know a creation of the natural world is to take some of its power into oneself. With his studies and the publication of his *Systema Naturae* in 1735, he meant to organize the natural world, to find the laws and structure that governed creation. He did more than that, revealing a heretofore unknown realm of knowledge that he named Arcane Taxonomy.

Linnaeus is also credited with inventing the index card, to better organize his classifications.

Some would say Arcane Taxonomy is still largely not understood—its practice so difficult, the ability to access it so rare, that it isn't a science at all but a kind of art. A religion. Around the world, universities train up naturalists, botanists, zoologists, and physicians, hoping to find among them men with the talent of Arcane Taxonomy, but not one in a hundred reveals any potential.

THREE

Piranga olivacea

July 1880
Manhattan

After her first sighting of a scarlet tanager, *Piranga olivacea*, Beth could light fires. Just a candle, but it was a start, the beginning of a path that she'd fairly run down, in secret, until she arrived here, in a chair by a deathbed. Harry was still breathing, somehow. She changed the dried-out cloth on his forehead for a freshly damp one. He didn't stir.

She'd seen a snowy owl, *Bubo scandiacus*, two years ago, upstate. Murmuring the name, she recalled what she felt—the hard cold and the white ghost flying silently across a field—and made the cloth cooler, as if that would help. Encouraged some movement in the air, hoping he would be more comfortable. She had no idea what he was feeling. Whatever else she could do, she couldn't read minds or speak to the dead.

Species: *Homo sapiens*. Type: Caucasian. Individual: Harold Stanley, average height, pleasant features, charming demeanor. Her husband.

Beth Stanley could name him but not the thing that was killing him. Nothing could save the last bit of his life slipping away, but she would stay to witness it.

Germ theory stated that tiny organisms were swarming through his bloodstream, killing him. If she knew their names, if she could identify, describe—label them as thoroughly as she had all the specimens in the room—maybe she could stop them. But she couldn't. Books were stacked on the nightstand and on the floor beside it, along with notepads and pencils. Treatises on the microscopic world, engravings of magnified bacteria, and speculation, so much speculation that these tiny beings caused disease, caused so much death. But no one had yet found a way to stop them. She made notes, sketches, lists of Latin names, hoping to kill the thing that was killing Harry. But she didn't have a microscope and wouldn't know what she was looking at even if she did. She couldn't stop them if she couldn't see them with her own eyes, and she had no power here. Her education had been inadequate, a hodgepodge of whatever she could manage to gather.

If she could go back in time, prevent the injury that caused this—

To name a thing was to know a thing. Beth could name thousands of creatures and didn't know anything.

Last night, she'd locked the bedroom door to keep everyone out while she pored over the books one more time. Buttoned up in a nightshirt, Harry lay neatly arranged under the coverlet, hands resting on his chest, with a deceptive appearance of peace. But he shuddered with shallow breathing, desperate little gasps. He hadn't moved in more than a day. The last time he'd opened his eyes, he hadn't seen her, not really. His face was pale, gleaming with sweat and fever. The damp cloth was useless, a mechanical gesture.

Exhausted yet still restless, she stood to stretch her back, to wander the few paces along the bed. Their room, their bed, had stopped feeling familiar. Shelves above her vanity held seashells collected on outings to Long Island, feathers from hawks and egrets, interesting rocks, different pine cones. On the walls hung paintings of seascapes, mountains, the places they had visited or talked of visiting, botanical drawings of flowers, dissected sea creatures. The whole natural world packed in here, or at least as much as would fit. They would lie together at night, barely able to see the artifacts in the dark, and talk.

Harry had never discouraged her studies, as everyone else in her life had done. In fact, he'd encouraged. Nurtured. Used what she knew, even, and she was happy to let him. They were partners. She was going to lose all that. Harry was dying, and she was standing on the precipice of a dark life she didn't want to lead.

From a shelf, Beth picked up a fossil trilobite, *Ogyginus corndensis*, running her thumb along the ridges of its back. Harry had collected it on a trip to England when he was younger. Fred, he'd named it—a very unscientific label—and speculated about what life for Fred had been like in the primordial mud of its original home. A pet of a long-ago alien age, as if he could put a little leash on it and stroll through Central Park. She had laughed at the image. He hadn't been interested in the science so much as he was in the stories. The stone was heavy in her hand; she set it back down, and the clunk it made on the shelf seemed particularly loud. She glanced at the bed—but no, Harry still didn't stir.

Should she pray? Which of the hundreds of names of God and prayers to him would do any good here? That was the problem; so many things could not be accurately named despite the quest of so many people to do so. The more was discovered, the more waited to be discovered, and no one had yet found a way past death.

She didn't pray.

The room smelled sour. The heat of his fever seemed to press out. Beth opened the window to let in some air, but the summer morning was already hot and sticky. The sky was gray—dawn, already. She had thought it was still the middle of the night, but light had somehow crept across the sky, and the birds were awake, the chattering calls of house finches filling the garden below. *Haemorhous mexicanus*, a familiar species. Bright song, busy. And flight—if only she could fly, steal that power from them to get away and fill her lungs with clean air. No Arcanist had yet learned to take that trait for themselves.

But she could thank them for singing. Better than the quiet.

Listening to them meant she missed the moment when the rattling breaths stopped. She glanced back at the bed, a habitual movement over the last week, checking, *What does he look like now? What is happening now?* And saw that there was no movement. There was nothing at all.

She thought she might have felt it, the moment his life slipped away. That some . . . power would have struck her. But it was all so very quiet.

Beth leaned in to kiss Harry's forehead one last time, then unlocked the door and called for Ann.

The maid stood as soon as the door opened. A chair was in the hall, a basket of mending sitting beside it. She must have been waiting this whole time. Murmuring voices came from the parlor downstairs, where everyone else must have gathered. Beth supposed she ought to call the doctor up to make the final pronouncement. But her brain was sluggish.

"Ma'am?" Ann clutched her hands together, her expression strained.

"Ann, go and stop the clocks, would you?"

FOUR

Megascops asio

One month later

The pair stood on the front stoop of the brownstone for what seemed an interminable length of time. Neither reached for the bellpull. Bran West stared at the door. It was a simple thing: just reach out and ring the bell. He'd faced down charging polar bears; the bell at an uptown brownstone should be easy.

He preferred the Arctic to uptown brownstones. The rules of survival were clearer.

Anton took a step back. "We don't *have* to do this. The proper thing to do would be to send a letter—"

"I already tried that." Mrs. Stanley had not replied. Properly, they shouldn't be here at all. But this was important. Finally, determined, he pulled the bell before he could stop himself yet again. The brass rattled, and they were committed.

Brisk footsteps sounded on the other side of the door. A pause, the turn of a lock, and the door opened to a fresh-faced maid in a prim gray dress standing at attention. To her credit, her eyes only widened a little at Anton's brown skin, then settled back to the detached interest of a servant.

Bran smiled thinly and offered cards. "Mr. Brandon West and Mr. Anton Torrance, here to see Mrs. Stanley."

Appearing unsurprised but skeptical, the maid regarded them. The two men towered, and Bran hoped his smile didn't seem too fixed or leering. He had every expectation that she would declare Mrs. Stanley indisposed and close the door on them.

But she didn't. "Just a moment, sirs. If you'll wait here?" She vanished back into the house, even shutting the door on them, which seemed a definitive answer. Time ticked over for a minute, then another.

"She's never going to see us," Anton said.

"Have a little faith." At this point he didn't know which would be more nerve racking: if she turned them away or if she actually agreed to see them. He idly thought of what Arcanist *practica* he might deploy to shift the situation to their favor—

Absurdly, they both flinched when the door opened again. One would think a gun had been fired. The maid, her bearing almost military, announced, "Come in, sirs." She stepped aside and opened the door fully. Closed it behind them, then held out her arms for their coats and hats. The whole time Anton was giving him this look, a smirk full of blame. A reminder that they had walked into this voluntarily, of their own free wills, and Anton would never forgive Bran for making them do it. "If you'll wait here, sirs." The girl gestured them through a doorway that separated the tiled foyer from the parlor, then briskly went off, presumably to fetch the mistress of the house. The two men chose chairs and perched at the edges uncomfortably.

The parlor seemed typical, nothing particularly distinctive about it. A sofa and armchair were arranged for conversation before a fireplace, along with a table for a tea service. Another table held fresh flowers in a plain vase. *Zantedeschia aethiopica*, calla lilies, creamy white, with swooping graceful curves. Funereal. They seemed to be warning him away. On the walls hung several paintings of landscapes—Bran recognized a scene of Mount Marcy, in the Adirondacks. The drapes over the windows were open, the sunlight soft. The grandfather clock against the far wall was silent, the hands stopped at the hour of Harry's death a month before. Just before six in the morning. It had been an illness, Bran had heard, but no one seemed to know the details. Well, Mrs. Stanley did, if he dared ask her. But that wasn't why they were here.

Bran supposed he would have to stop thinking of this as Harry's house. No longer Harry's foyer, parlor, study, or anything. What a waste.

Anton stood first, and Bran rose after him as Mrs. Elizabeth Stanley entered. She was a tall, poised woman dressed all in black, a gown of a stiff, unrufflable fabric with a draped skirt, the collar buttoned high. Her hair, the brown of some drab sparrow, was drawn back and pinned up, not a lock out of place. Full mourning, a shadow given form. To be fair, she really did seem gutted, her face pale, gaze downcast, just as she had seemed at the funeral. Bran had no idea how long recovering from such an event as the loss of a husband should take. Maybe Anton was right, and they should have waited another month, but he worried that she would pack up all Harry's things and dump them onto the street without a thought. He could not trust that she would know what was valuable.

Bran hadn't spoken to her at the funeral. His mouth went dry now; he didn't know what to say. His gaze was drawn back to the lilies.

"Mrs. Stanley, I am so sorry for your loss," Anton said, his accent giving the sentiment an especially gentle polish. He'd grown up in parlors like this; he knew just what to do. They both wore good suits, didn't look at all out of place here. But Bran had had to learn the manners that belonged in places like this, and he wasn't sure he'd learned them all that well. He'd *wanted* to learn Latin and biology, and they'd come much easier to him. He was feeling his Pennsylvania farmhouse roots. He didn't belong here.

Mrs. Stanley gave a shudder, something a statue coming to life might do. "Thank you. And you as well—you were Harry's dear friends;

you must feel this deeply." Her voice was soft, precise, though she did not look at them. She kept her gaze on a spot on the carpet.

Bran felt a kick in his gut at that. Yes, he did feel it. He hadn't been sure she would notice, if she would declare herself the only one with a right to grieve Harry's loss. He forged ahead. Charging polar bears, he reminded himself. This was nothing compared to that.

"Thank you for agreeing to see us under such difficult . . . well. Harry left a few unfinished matters, and I was hoping, we were hoping . . . I wondered if we could see Harry's study? He'd spoken about an essay he was finishing."

"He was also assisting us with preparations for our next expedition." Society connections, Anton meant. Those lists of well-to-do clubs and organizations with deep pockets and a wish to advance the cause of exploration. They were definitely going to miss Harry's help in those efforts. Given her silence until now, Mrs. Stanley seemed disinclined to take his place.

"Yes, I'm aware," she said softly.

Bran had come to rely on Harry's work. His observations, identifications, speculations. He had added to Bran's own knowledge and therefore his abilities. "You must be wondering what to do with his specimens and field notes. I'd be happy to take charge."

"No," she said. Quick and curt as a knife cut. Now, she met his gaze straight on, and he felt himself go pale. "No, I will be keeping Harry's specimens and notes. All of it."

Bran glanced at Anton, who was gazing at him warningly. *Thin ice, mate.* Bran spoke carefully. Maybe too carefully. "Mrs. Stanley, I don't want to upset you, but maybe you don't understand the importance."

"I understand it very well, and I will be keeping it."

Just a touch of influence. Use charm, use enticement. Not overt manipulation but rather encouragement. The way a person was drawn to touch a clump of wildflowers growing along the path. "I could finish any essays he left incomplete. Harry was doing such good work, and I hope to extend his legacy—"

"No," she said, even more forcefully. "I'm sorry you've come all this way for nothing."

"It's no trouble," Bran murmured. He'd thought she would be relieved to have the work cleared out. His persuasion seemed to have no effect, and he didn't know what to say to her now. "I should have come sooner to pay my respects."

"You're so kind," she said curtly.

Somehow, the lilies once again drew his gaze. They seemed to be getting larger. He wanted nothing more than to leave the room. Did Anton feel it? Anton's gaze was narrowed, studious.

What sentimental value could there be in a cabinet full of dead birds? Did Harry's will say anything about it? Surely he would have wanted his work to go to his colleagues. If she would only listen . . .

He wished for a ticking clock to break the silence.

Clever Anton saved him. "Might we at least see his study? To say one last farewell. Then we'll leave you in peace."

She relented—broke, even. The ice in her eyes melted as she glanced away. The stiff fabric of her gown scraped and rustled. "All right."

And the lilies were only lilies again. Bran suddenly felt queasy.

Out the parlor, a short hall led to a locked door. She wore the key on a band around her wrist. How sentimental was she about Harry's study? Bran was never going to get any of Harry's work away from her, was he? He was at a loss as to what else he might do. Exert his power to make threats? He wouldn't go that far.

She opened the door.

This room was full of power. Packed with it. He could almost smell it; it pressed against him like the humidity of a greenhouse. He nearly stumbled. Anton put a steadying hand on his elbow. Something was happening here, something he couldn't see. Harry had never practiced Arcane Taxonomy, he had no Arcanist abilities, but his investigative work these last couple of years had been good enough that Bran had used it to develop his own skills. Harry had been so proud, and had promised more, whatever he could—

He studied the room with his eyes instead of that instinct in the back of his mind.

Here again the drapes were pulled back from the windows, spilling good light across the desk and shelves. Bran had expected the room to be shut up and dark, like a tomb. Wasn't that traditional in houses of mourning? Bran had never paid much attention. But this room seemed oddly, strangely alive. As if Harry had just stepped out and not been in the ground for a month. No smell of dust or neglect lingered. The shelves were packed with all the expected volumes, Linnaeus and Lyell, Darwin and Gray, as well as what seemed to be an entire set of the *Pinfeather*, the quarterly journal of the Manhattan Naturalist Society, which published many of Bran's own articles. On display in a pair of cabinets were a variety of fossils, bird eggs, shark teeth, turtle shells, and small skulls, as well as a claw or two from some reptile and the entire wing of a colorful tropical bird—a parrot, probably, though the red had faded. Odds and ends collected on various trips, a museum in miniature.

On another wall was Harry's famous migration map. This was the centerpiece of his scientific work: a detailed map of the eastern United States, covered in pins with colored glass heads, labeled with slips of paper. These marked sightings of a number of different species of birds, all over the country. After several years of observations, a sweep of color traveled up and down the coast, changing with the seasons as birds migrated from north to south and back again. It was an illuminating trove of information. An engine to fuel an Arcanist's power.

He must convince Mrs. Stanley to part with all this. Bran needed it.

Inexplicably, he thought again of the calla lilies. The cabinet held what seemed to be the skull of a barracuda; Mrs. Stanley was studying it. Bran backed toward the door. They ought to leave now; they didn't belong here.

Ursus maritimus. He must be relentless. He couldn't indulge in pity.

The wide oak desk in the center of the room was scattered with work: a stack of journals on one side, letters in a tray on the other, and between them, pages of writing. A blotter was spattered with ink, an inkwell and well-used pens arranged beside it. Several preserved warbler specimens, tags tied to their curled-up feet, were lined up for study. Harry might come in at any moment to natter on about plumage patterns.

Bran was missing something important. "Is this just how he left it?"

She hesitated, folding her hands together, fingers squeezing tight. "No, I've been here, arranging his work." A tone of challenge touched her voice.

"It would have been better if you had left it how it was until one of us could look at it."

"I have a right to go through Harry's things."

"I beg your pardon, Mrs. Stanley. I only meant to say we might better understand what all this means."

She gave a little sigh; when she looked away, tears gathered at the corners of her eyes. She brushed at them quickly.

Anton had caught his mood and studied her closely. Bran couldn't very well ask him what he was seeing, with Mrs. Stanley right here, but he was thinking hard. Next, Anton turned his considerable attention to what had caused Bran's disquiet—the desk—and leaned in to get a better look at the skins: a black-throated blue warbler, a cerulean warbler, a black-and-yellow warbler, all males in summer plumage. Delicate birds, only a few inches long. Their colors—blue, sharp lines of black and white, yellow—shone incongruously on the brown and cream of the desk's disarray. They were migratory. Travel, flight, quickness. Beauty.

"Here," Anton said, drawing out one of the pages. "The essay you were looking for, I think."

Anton's fingers guided him along lines of writing. And yes, here it was, written out in a neat hand. A list of observations of osprey on Long Island, detailed descriptions of habitats, dates, times of day, along with information provided by correspondents in Florida last winter. The article speculated that by identifying individual birds, one could track whether the same birds returned to the same nests, and the patterns would become even clearer. Bran was thrilled. Such good work Harry was doing . . . had been doing, rather.

Next to the essay draft sat a field notebook, open to a page that included a sketch of a warbler's nest. Anton tapped the essay, the notebook, and the tag on one of the warblers, and Bran drew back, startled. "This isn't Harry's handwriting."

Mrs. Stanley's whole manner was stiff as iron, her expression unbending. A bit of the flash of a barracuda's scales shone in her eyes— defending her territory.

Bran went to the specimen cabinet and opened a middle drawer, which was filled with woodpecker skins, two dozen, five different species. He turned up the label on one, then another, then another. The same handwriting as the tags, the essay, the journal. And not Harry's.

He stared at the widow. "Mrs. Stanley, this is your handwriting."

She wiped away another stray tear.

He tried to make sense of it. "You took notes for him. You . . . you were his secretary."

Anton shook his head and tapped the notebook. He'd been turning pages. "These latest observations are dated after his death. Good lord, was this at the cemetery? You were recording observations during his funeral?"

Her voice shook a little. "There was a screech owl in the ash trees to the west. It called through the whole service. Did you hear it?"

Bran had. "It seemed like an omen. Some haunting choir." *Megascops asio*, a hunter, at home in the night, unseen in the day. From the moment he met her, Bran had hardly paid any attention to Mrs. Stanley. He paid attention now.

"I had to write it down. I've been writing down the birds I've seen since I was a girl."

Harry had published; he'd lectured; his essays about bird migration had been about to make his career as a naturalist, along with his ideas promoting the use of Arcane Taxonomy. "What here is Harry's?"

She said, frustrated and fond, "Do you know he could never reliably tell the difference between a downy and a hairy woodpecker, even when I was holding specimens right in front of him and pointing at their bills?" She reached out her hands as if she held the birds, and Bran could see it, clear as anything, her pleading with him, *Look, just look at them, see their bills, the size of their bodies, these are not the same species.* And Harry staring back at her, good-naturedly shrugging in confusion. Bran had had conversations like that with Harry himself. However clever he was about wider scientific concepts, he'd always needed a bit of encouragement with detailed fieldwork. It was part of why he'd never made the leap to Arcane Taxonomy. Or so Bran had always thought.

Anton retrieved a candle and its holder from a shelf in the corner and showed it to her.

"Mrs. Stanley. Can you light that for me?"

"The matches are—"

"No matches."

The silence seemed loud, grating. Bran was choking on it.

"I—I've never done this with someone watching. Someone other than Harry, I mean."

"Take your time," Anton said gently.

Her hand trembled until she drew a deep breath and settled herself. She touched the wick lightly, fleetingly, and the flame sparked with a hiss. The glow was lost in the sunny room, but the flame was clear, steady.

Anton smiled at her. "Well then. Here we are." He blew it out and set the candle on the desk.

"You're an Arcanist," Bran exclaimed stupidly. Lighting candles was the first *practicum* most Arcanists learned. She'd hardly had to think about it; it came easily to her.

He didn't want to believe it, but it was all so clear now. The room, the lilies—she'd been trying to keep them out. He'd been in an Arcanist duel without realizing it.

"She mouths the Latin under her breath the same way you do when you're working," Anton said.

One of Mrs. Stanley's tears escaped, slipping down her cheek. Anton drew a handkerchief from his pocket and handed it to her; she nodded in thanks and wiped her eyes more successfully this time.

Over the last three years, Harry had published a variety of good articles on nesting behavior, speculation about birdsong across different species, observations on migration patterns—and was Bran to simply accept that Elizabeth Stanley had written all of it? And that she had somehow learned Arcane Taxonomy besides?

Be a good observer, a good naturalist, and look at the evidence. Bran had dozens of Harry's letters, he'd known Harry since their days at Harvard, and nothing in this study was Harry's writing. None of it. She might have served as a secretary, might have written the labels for him if she had the neater hand. But the articles, the journals, the observations—none were Harry's. They were hers.

"Harry knew?" he managed to get out, more roughly than he intended.

"Of course he did. It was his idea."

"Does the Society know? The Naturalist Society, someone there has to know." Every Arcanist was a member of some professional organization and granted a government ranking. It was how they got work and advanced their studies; it was the only way to track and regulate their abilities.

"I am not allowed in the Society, Mr. West," she said evenly. Her voice was ice. Barracuda's teeth.

"I'm astonished," Bran murmured. His plans to take Harry's final essays and finish them, get them published as a tribute, turned to ash.

"Astonished that I did the work or that Harry lied about it?" she said.

The sample drawer was still open, the woodpeckers lying before him, black backs spotted with white, stuffing coming out of their eyes. The hairy woodpeckers were larger and had longer bills, the downy had shorter, no bigger than a finger joint. And she was right, Harry had been useless at telling the difference. He'd done a very good job of disguising it, though. Bran remembered being in the field with him when they were just starting their careers. Harry would show Bran the bird he'd just shot, the bloody thing right there in his hands, and ask, *What do you think, Bran? What would you say about this one?* And Bran would answer, *It's a yellow-shafted flicker, it's a hermit thrush, it's a brown creeper*, or whatever the bird was. Harry would chuckle and agree with him like he was a teacher giving a test. *Ah, very good, well done, Mr. West.* And God help him, Bran would glow at the praise.

It's yours, he would say next. *All this power is yours.* And Bran had taken it.

Then Harry had married and stopped bringing him anything. Instead, he took the specimens—and the power—home to her. She did all the work, and Harry put his name on it. No wonder his career had finally taken off these last few years.

This felt like waking up in the morning of an Arctic summer and finding the sea ice all broken apart, the whole world changed.

They had been shocked when Harry announced he was marrying. They hadn't known her at all. Her family was good, she had a bit of money, but Harry had his own and didn't need hers. Back in school they had all declared they would devote themselves to their studies, they didn't need the distraction of domestic life. They had their work and each other, didn't they? But he'd gone and gotten married. He had seemed happy, but his wife had remained an enigma, quiet and downcast, just as she seemed now.

Harry hadn't married because he wanted to be married. He'd married because of *her*. And what of Harry's legacy, now?

"You see, Mr. West, why you cannot have Harry's work." Mrs. Stanley was full of resolve. If Bran didn't have his own store of power to draw on, he'd have fled already.

She was right; that had been a screech owl calling incessantly, a sort of stuttering whinny, at Harry's funeral. He'd had some poetic notion that nature itself was mourning him. But it was only nature doing what it did.

He closed the drawer as gently as he could, but the knock of the edge against the chest still seemed loud. Anton arranged the pages on the desk just as he had found them.

"Mrs. Stanley, I'm sorry. We'll leave you in peace." Bran made an awkward bow and moved to the door. Anton followed, expressing his own more eloquent sympathies.

"Please don't tell anyone." She spoke urgently, a tightness in her voice. He didn't understand why she should sound so desperate.

"Of course," he answered, and she nodded grimly.

"I'll see you out," she said.

"That isn't necessary."

But she was already in the hall, walking briskly to the foyer, kneading Anton's handkerchief. What could they do but follow? The maid was waiting with their hats and coats, which they accepted without a word.

They reached the front stoop, and Mrs. Stanley stood across the threshold, hands folded and resting on the stiff fabric of her skirt.

"Good day," Bran said, tipping his hat. "Again, we're so very sorry for your loss."

And what, exactly, was it she had lost? Not just a husband.

The maid shut the door on them.

Bran and Anton walked the ten blocks back to their flat in silence, not daring to look at one another. If they looked, caught the other's eye, then one of them would have to say something. Bran felt like a cad.

The sky had grown overcast in the short time they'd spent at the Stanleys' brownstone. Less than an hour? It had seemed much longer. Amid the soot and muck of the city, Bran smelled an approaching storm. He prayed for it, and for an evening of sitting with a book while the sound of rain pattered on the windows. He could fall into other thoughts than these.

The doorman at the building let them in, they climbed to the second-story flat they shared, and that last door between them and the world shut. Bran turned on the lamp while Anton locked the door, rattling the handle to be sure, as he always did. Bran drew the drapes over the pair of windows, confirming that they were alone and could do what they liked. The ritual of habit and necessity. The silence folded in, and they couldn't not speak.

"I don't believe it," Bran blurted. "Do you believe it?"

A ridiculous question. They had no choice but to believe the facts they had witnessed themselves. Observation above all.

"After all that, I didn't ask about that schedule of lectures he'd promised to put together. That was a very unsuccessful expedition, my friend."

Bran took off his hat, tossed it on the nearest chair, and rubbed a hand over his face. "So what do we do now?"

"Do we tell?" Anton said. He drew off his coat and hung it on the tree by the door. Made a come-along gesture at Bran, who peeled off his own coat at the request. Anton hung up his hat, then collected Bran's from the chair and put it in its place. "She's a good Arcanist, if she could stand up to you."

She *had* stood up to him, however much he hated to admit it. How had she learned without any schooling? "She asked us not to. If she had wanted anyone to know, she'd have told already."

"Would anyone believe her?" Anton said, his brows raised, the practical voice.

There were stories about women Arcanists. A few here and there. Hardly worth mentioning, so no one did. Mrs. Stanley wielded power without anyone the wiser.

"She'd want to protect Harry's reputation. Wouldn't she? *We* want to protect his reputation. So we don't tell." This was the correct decision, he was sure, and yet it felt like lying. It *was* a lie. She had called Harry a liar without a twitch, and she was right. To name a thing is to know a thing . . . she'd named Harry true and mislabeled herself. Mislabeling was a weakness; it reduced one's power. But Mrs. Stanley lived with it, somehow.

Anton stood before him again, closer now, and smoothed the lapels of Bran's vest. Smiling wryly, he loosened the knot of Bran's tie and pulled away the strip of fabric. "You never do look right with that on."

His touch calmed Bran, who let himself be comforted. Anton was a few inches taller, the right height so that Bran could lean his forehead on the other man's shoulder. "That went even worse than I'd feared."

Anton held him. "No, it didn't. I was sure she would burst into hysterical tears."

"Why? Is that based on evidence or preconceived assumption?" Bran drew back. "She barely cried at the funeral, now that I think of it. Did she even love him?"

"Did he love her? Or was he using her?"

Bran had loved Harry, but he wouldn't put it past the man. "God."

"I am going to pour us a couple of glasses of far too much bourbon," Anton said, kissing Bran's lips lightly before turning to the sideboard.

Their front room was a parlor, a library, a study, and a trophy room all together. A monument to all they'd done and all they wanted to do. A rack of rifles and pistols, along with Bran's specimen cabinets, lined the walls, next to shelves full of books and their field journals.

Bran's desk was a storm of letters and notes, the contents of his mind given physical form. In another corner, out of place in an otherwise comfortable setting, lay a pile of Anton's gear: pickaxes, coils of rope, a bundled blanket, thick snow boots, and a set of snowshoes needing repair. All of it so busy, speaking to ambition and accomplishment. Over the mantel, in pride of place, was a photograph from the Greenland expedition that had made their careers. The *Indomitable* had finally found them, only three weeks overdue, and the various field groups reunited. The members of the expedition lined up behind the skin of the polar bear Anton had shot, draped over boxes and crates to show its immense size. Bran; Anton holding his rifle over his shoulder; the nine others who'd spent a year in the Arctic, including two Inuit guides; all of them bundled up in furs and squinting through slotted goggles, their beards overgrown, their faces chapped, and grinning happily like fools. Except the bear, reduced to a hulking mound of fur.

Anton had made good on his promise to Bran in a hotel room in Boston the same night the *Indomitable* returned to port. The two had rarely been apart since. After spending a couple of years with the expedition, neither had had a place to live, so they found one together. Temporarily, only until the next trip. To the rest of the world, they were professional partners, the adventurer and the scientist, perfectly matched to conquer the world. In private . . . well, that was their own business.

They were planning an Antarctic expedition next, hoping to leave next summer, to reach their destination by autumn—the South Pole's spring—giving them almost a full twenty-four hours of daylight to explore that world. It would be a collecting trip, though Anton was arguing for a push to the South Pole—to put a flag there, mark it, and claim it for science and his own sense of achievement. Bran wasn't sure that was possible and preferred selling the trip as a chance to collect specimens, to hunt for fossils on rocky shores, and to seek out whatever other wonders they could discover. A whole new taxonomic world. And to write a book or three about the trip, of course.

They were scraping together the last of the funding. Harry had been a large part of that plan—he moved so easily in society. He got them invitations they might not get on their own, even with their reputations. All that was gone now.

Harry had been trying to talk them into bringing him along. He didn't have the cold-weather experience, but they thought his scientific work made him a good candidate. That decision was out of their hands, now. For the best, maybe, given what they'd discovered.

They had a lot of work ahead of them, and perhaps it was just as well they hadn't taken on sorting through Harry's work. "What are we going to do?" Bran asked again as Anton handed him a glass that was, as promised, full of too much bourbon.

"About Harry's work? Mrs. Stanley's work, I mean. I suggest we do nothing." Anton raised his glass in a toast and drank. "I believe we have a series of lectures to plan. And we'll have to do it without Harry's connections." He went over to the desk to find the appointment book.

Bran tasted the bourbon and turned inward, stewing. He thought back—Harry had attended one of their lectures just last April, at Columbia. They hadn't really had time to speak after, and he regretted that now. He'd thought there'd be many more chances. He'd given so many lectures, and Harry had been to so many of them, Bran struggled to remember the particulars of this one event. Was he only imagining that Mrs. Stanley had accompanied him? Had there been a quiet, meticulously turned-out woman clinging to his arm?

"Do you remember that lecture we gave at Columbia back in April?" Bran asked suddenly. "Harry was there, wasn't he?"

"I think so, yes."

"Was Mrs. Stanley with him?"

Even Anton had to stop and think a moment. Had she really been so invisible? Bran was shocked, thinking that neither of them had noticed her. Or that they had so completely disregarded her.

"She was, but we didn't speak to them," Anton said finally.

"Ah. I wish now that we had."

"Bran," he said, looking up, frowning. "Let it go."

Yes, that would be best. He drank the glass down and poured another.

FIVE

Poecile atricapillus

When the door finally closed on Harry's friends, Beth Stanley thought she might faint or melt or turn to air, her relief was so profound. She slouched and sighed, no longer having to hold herself up so carefully. When the letter from Brandon West arrived asking for a visit, she had felt physically ill. She had known exactly what he intended and hadn't known how to reply. She suspected he might appear unannounced one day, and then he'd brought along the famous Mr. Torrance as well.

She feared they might try to physically carry out the books, papers, even the specimen cabinets. When it had only been the pair of them and no wagon—no workmen to carry out furniture and no way to haul it—she had felt hope. But they had still asked. They had still assumed she would let it all go. She'd still had to argue, and she wasn't sure what she'd have done if they had not relented. If they had not believed that the work was really hers in every way that mattered.

If she had not been able to draw upon her Arcane *practica*.

She had given herself a fierceness that wasn't innate to her, a determination she desperately needed. She'd had to use it all, hoping to have this confrontation once and never again, because West had used *his* first, trying to persuade her. He must have been so shocked when his power crashed into hers. She'd been ready for it; he hadn't. That might have been what saved her.

Ann lingered, waiting. Worried, no doubt, but everyone around Beth had looked worried for a month now, and she wasn't sure she could see anything else anymore.

"I'll have tea in the garden, I think," she said, trying to give the girl a comforting smile.

"Yes, ma'am." Ann hurried off to the kitchen, and Beth went to the back of the house and outside.

She still held Anton Torrance's handkerchief. It had been very kind of him to give it to her. It had no embroidery, no monogram. But then, he was a bachelor, wasn't he? No one to do the monogramming for him, and he likely hadn't thought of it. She was a little angry that she was thinking of it. What use were monograms? She knew little of him, only that he had come from the Bahamas and his family had some status there. She knew just as little about Brandon West. He and Harry had met at Harvard; Anton had come along later, when he and Mr. West had gone on that famous expedition. Harry had always spoken about them with such pride. How fortunate for him, to have such friends.

He had kept her from them, Beth now realized. Mr. West might have learned what she was and exposed the secret.

In the small walled-off alcove behind the brownstone was a lush garden. The space got just enough sunlight to support a row of flowering shrubs along one side, some honeysuckle, a pot of strawberries, as many flowers as could be persuaded to grow in as many planters and pots as could be crammed along the sides and into the corners, with overgrown ivy tangled around it all. A whole collection, and the more she possessed, the more she could use. Near the door to the house was a tiled table and a pair of chairs. Enough space for a woman to sit with a tea tray, a notebook, a pencil, and her thoughts.

And there were birds.

Along with the shrubs and flowers, she had put out trays of seed, a bit of jam on a plate on one of the windowsills, and another plate full of nuts. Finches, chickadees, and three different species of sparrows were feeding. An oriole devoured the jam. A large potted thistle had just started shedding its fluff; several goldfinches swarmed, harvesting seed there. A robin explored the ivy. Beth wrote down the number and species, as she did every day, then sat back to watch and listen, sipping her tea, trying to leave behind the memory of her visitors, which continued to intrude.

One of Harry's oldest friends, Mr. West was a noted naturalist and a famous Arcanist. He taught at Columbia. In hindsight, Mr. Torrance accompanying him should not have been a surprise, but she had been startled to see him standing in her parlor. West was the naturalist, not Torrance. She probably should have expected a whole contingent of Harry's science-minded friends demanding that she turn over his work. She should have been grateful that she had only to contend with two of them, but she would have rather they'd left her alone entirely.

She had not expected them to discover the lie so quickly. Harry had been so sure no one would ever learn the truth because no one would even question it. As long as she could have her journals, her studies, and her questions, she had been satisfied to leave the career to him. Their trips together had been a true joy: tromping about New England and the Appalachians, staying in remote cabins, searching out birds and wondrous rare flowers, trees, and creatures. Trips she never would have been able to make on her own but that no one questioned when she accompanied her husband. *How brave she is,* people said. *How devoted they must be to each other. Look at them, they can't bear to be apart, and she puts up with wilderness without complaining for his sake.* It was the other way around, really.

Already she desperately missed mornings in deep unpopulated forests, listening to the chaotic weave of the birds' dawn chorus as mist rose. The creak of swaying trees, the rich smell of growth and decay. She could close her eyes and imagine herself at the beginning of the world.

The little city garden where she drank her tea was better than nothing at all. All the things she ought to be grateful for, so at odds with all the things she longed for.

The buzz of a chickadee called from one branch, then another. Finally the little thing flew to the tray of seed, a masked feathered fluff on stick legs, pecking, tilting its head, turning shining black eyes to her, pecking again, and flying off with a beak full of seed to eat at its leisure.

The door opened very softly; Ann peeked out cautiously. "Ma'am? Mrs. Stanley is here. The other Mrs. Stanley, I mean." She held out a little tray with a card, very proper, just the way the other Mrs. Stanley liked it. Mrs. Agnes Stanley, Harry's mother. In her house, sitting in her parlor. Another person believing she had some claim of possession over Harry's things, which of course included Beth.

She didn't bother looking at the card. "Please tell Mrs. Stanley that I am very sorry but I am indisposed." Such a useful word, *indisposed*, requiring no further explanation.

Ann pursed her lips; they both knew that Mrs. Stanley would argue anyway.

"But, ma'am. If I may."

Beth tilted her head, inquiring.

"She might . . . interpret that a certain way. Make assumptions."

Ah. Of course. And how many months before Mrs. Stanley could be made to understand that Beth was not carrying Harry's child? Probably the full nine-month course, and another month besides.

"Let her assume," Beth said, because nothing would stop Mrs. Stanley from making assumptions. She'd deal with the consequences later.

"Yes, ma'am." Ann slipped out. Her expression was calm, professional, no doubt masking a raft of opinions.

Ann returned a moment later. "Ma'am. Mrs. Stanley asks if she should send a doctor."

Beth put her hand to her forehead. All the garden's calm, destroyed. "I think you know the answer to that."

"Well, yes, of course, ma'am. But I had to at least pretend. You know Mrs. Stanley." She curtsied a little, flashed a smile, and went away again.

Ah, yes. Mrs. Stanley would not be satisfied with being told off by the maid, so they must go through the motions. Beth resolved to stay in the garden until she could be sure Harry's mother was gone.

Meanwhile, the tea had gone cold, and Beth didn't have the heart to warm it back up.

Benjamin Franklin was an avid man of science who, while not an Arcanist himself, encouraged others in the study of Linnaeus's work and was particularly interested in potential applications of the practice of Arcane Taxonomy in warfare, especially during the American Revolution. Popular stories suggested that both Daniel Boone and Francis Marion either had Arcanists in their company or were practicing Arcanists themselves, though no proof supporting these claims survives. Nevertheless, the American revolutionaries' familiarity with their own territory and willingness to engage in unconventional tactics—Arcane or otherwise—no doubt contributed to their victory in the war.

What was documented without a doubt is the first example of a dynasty of Arcanists, knowledge and abilities passed down from father to son. Charles Willson Peale knew and painted Franklin and many other prominent figures of the American Revolution. He also founded the Philadelphia Museum, one of the first natural history museums in America and an early adopter of the Linnaean system of taxonomy for organizing its collection. His son, Rembrandt Peale, followed in his father's footsteps as an acclaimed naturalist, curator, and painter. The younger Peale's portrait of George Washington remains one of the best-known likenesses of the president. Whether their portraits conveyed powers of protection and strength on their subjects is, as with so much Arcanist practice, difficult to verify. But both men helped establish a respectable foundation of artistic and scientific endeavors in the young country.

The early European Arcanists were secretive. At first, Linnaeus trusted only his immediate students and correspondents with what he had learned. The feeling persisted that Arcanist teachings were dangerous, too easily abused and exploited. But he published, his books traveled, and the knowledge of Arcane Taxonomy couldn't be restricted.

The Americans were different. The Peale family, through its association with and encouragement of other Arcanists such as Alexander Wilson and John James Audubon, set a pattern for American academics wherein naturalists came together in organized schools and societies for the benefit of knowledge and to nurture those among them who had the talent for Arcane works. Businesses took an early interest in potential commercial applications of Arcane Taxonomy in surveying, prospecting, mining, security, and manufacturing. Initially, a proposal was made that Arcane Taxonomists should be drafted into the military and organized for the benefit of national security. After several court hearings, the proposal was declared a violation of the Fourth Amendment to the Constitution, prohibiting illegal searches and seizures. This reinforced the pattern of Arcanists operating independently, under the auspices of mutually beneficial organizations. Eventually, a system of rankings for Arcane Taxonomists was developed by the Department of the Treasury to assist business concerns wishing to hire Arcanists. Association with a university or academic society, rather than an individual patron, was a requirement.

In contrast, the European tradition continued to rely more on direct apprenticeship, finding patronage and employment through personal networks tracing back through academic lineages. Unsystematic and full of favoritism, this situation often made establishing the knowledge and abilities of individual Arcanists difficult. The Arcane Taxonomists of Napoleon's army had been political appointees based on personal recommendations, which had dire consequences during the Russian campaign. By the middle of the nineteenth century, many European universities had begun shifting toward a more American system of ranking and certification, but the old apprentice networks lingered. In a country like Britain, this could determine, for example, which scientists were invited to join the Royal Academy or receive knighthoods and which were not.

SIX

Pinguinus impennis

Anton and Bran arrived at the polished double doors of the Naturalist Society, housed in one of those lurking gray piles of a building in Midtown, the kind with lots of brass fixtures and bits of classical statuary, full of offices, clubs, and men of business and consequence. *Ex Natura Veritas*: the motto was gilded ostentatiously above the entrance. "From nature, power" would be closer to the reality of things.

Bran kept tugging at his tie and wincing until Anton couldn't stand it anymore and reached over, unknotted it, and pulled it off entirely, shoving it in his own pocket. In most respects Bran was so capable, so impressive. And then sometimes he seemed to lose himself. The contradiction made Anton protective of him. If he had to be the one to keep Bran from walking in front of a carriage someday, so be it.

"Better?" Anton asked. Bran sighed.

"People are going to ask about Harry. What do we say?"

They'd been over this. "We will raise a toast to his memory."

"*Veritas*," Bran muttered sourly.

Anton pushed open the doors.

The vestibule beyond was crowded with people, what seemed like dozens of men waiting for meetings, for access, for messages traveling back and forth. In another world, these halls would be subdued, a stuffy enclave of scientists and explorers discussing minutiae of fish scales and latitudes. In this world, they were all subtly fighting for access to power.

It created just a bit of mayhem, and the board of directors seemed to like it that way.

When Anton and Bran entered, the talk and shuffling stilled. Everyone stared. Anton basked in the attention while simultaneously pretending not to notice. The whispers started quickly enough: "It's Torrance and West . . ." "From the '76 Greenland expedition . . ." "Spent months on the ice and lived to tell about it." The admiration fairly glowed.

Anton could have gone to London and become a lawyer, as his father wished. He could have done anything, really. And in London, no matter what he accomplished, in every room he walked into he would have been "Sir Archibald Torrance's half-breed son."

He liked it much better here, where he was Mr. Anton Torrance the adventurer, admired on his own merits. He could be first to reach one of the poles. To summit any one of a dozen peaks that remained unconquered. Anything.

Bran was still fidgeting. He was one of only a handful of First Rank Arcanists working in the northeastern US, a wonder all on his own. But he didn't like the attention so much, poor man. He hadn't been born into paneled halls and status. Harvard had taken him on the basis of his talent, an achievement in itself, and he'd done well there. But he came into rooms like this with his shoulders bunched up, like he expected a fight.

They made a striking picture, the two of them. Anton cultivated the image, striving to project the platonic ideal of an intrepid explorer. Which, really, ought to have meant simply being himself, but there were certain expectations. He kept his beard in a mild state of disarray, his hair slightly untrimmed. His jacket was a good hardy tweed that looked like it could withstand a storm, though still neat and well tai- lored, as befitted a man who knew how to move in society as well as across wolf-infested tundra. The head of his walking stick was a piece of undecorated walrus tusk. At six foot, two inches, he was taller than every man here and gazed over them with a look of imperious unconcern, as if his mind were elsewhere, pointed toward more fascinating horizons.

The one thing he couldn't control was how they looked at his brown skin: the raised eyebrows of skepticism, the stares of curiosity, the occasional flash of anger that he stood here at all, even after all he'd accomplished. That was why every other detail that he could control had to be perfect, presenting a picture of authority no one could deny.

And then there was Bran. His jacket really had been through a rainstorm or two, and without the tie his collar hung loose and naked, which, rather than making him appear disheveled, served to make him seem beyond ordinary mortal cares. He'd brushed his hair back and shaved but had missed a spot on his jawline. He was probably thinking more about the nesting habits of peregrine falcons than the connections he ought to be cultivating.

Bran looked every bit the wild naturalist and mysterious Arcanist, and he didn't even know it—it was just the way he'd always been. Anton looked like the man in charge.

Anton desperately wanted to reach out and muss up Bran's hair, just to see the look of surprise on his face, those hazel eyes blinking back at him in confusion. He enjoyed the thought of it instead, and grinned.

Teddy, a middle-aged man with a smart suit and implacable manner, was on duty at the porter's desk this afternoon. How gratifying when the crowd parted to let them through and Teddy immediately ignored the rest to take Anton's and Bran's coats and hats from them.

"Good afternoon, gentlemen. Here, let me get those for you; then you can go right in."

"Thank you," Anton said. He nodded at the men milling behind him. They were awestruck.

He and Bran had started toward the back set of doors when a voice called, "Hold up! Mr. West!" A man in glasses marched up to them, eyed Anton warily, then grinned at Bran. "What would it take to hire you away from Mr. Torrance here? I work for a company that has mining rights in Juneau, Alaska—we're putting a survey-and-prospecting team together. Plenty of opportunity to explore and stake a claim. No man's ever set foot in some of those valleys, you know."

"No white man has ever set foot there," Bran corrected, an edge in his voice. This seemed to throw the gentleman off his script; his grin froze. "I've got my hands full, and I'm not looking to jump ship." He lifted his brow at Anton and continued toward the doors.

The man persisted. "We can pay top dollar!"

Bran turned on him, fists clenched. "Do I look like someone who can be bribed?"

The man's eyes widened, and he drew back.

Anton had never seen Bran take a swing at a man indoors, but he wouldn't bet against it happening someday. "Let's go, Mr. West. We've got more important work inside, yes?"

He touched Bran's shoulder, which relaxed just a little. Bran swung around and marched through the doors.

Anton nodded at the stranger and offered a fox-like smile. "Good day, sir."

They passed into the sanctum, this unparalleled organization dedicated to knowledge and exploration, the city's greatest gathering of men of science. Naturalists, explorers, travelers, writers, thinkers, professors, and fossil hunters. And of course the masters of the grand tradition of Arcane Taxonomy. On its best days, this was the vanguard of human knowledge of nature in this part of the world.

Its members were also scrambling for glory and fortune, every single one of them.

Three wide halls were linked by archways. Packed bookshelves reached to the high ceiling, with rolling ladders on hand to assist. On display were endless trophies: the taxidermy head of a wildebeest; rifles and sabers arranged on racks above a fireplace. Paintings of gold-tinged landscapes in far-off places, along with a couple of genuine Audubons, depicting magnificent birds of prey. Persian rugs, leather armchairs, mahogany desks and tables, crystal decanters—collected from around the world, illuminated with gas fixtures.

One wall was reserved for a collection of portraits, a field of honor: Wilson, the Peales, Humboldt, Cuvier, Audubon, Darwin. The botanist Asa Gray, whom Bran and Harry had studied with at Harvard. Carl Linnaeus, the founder of them all, reckoned the first practitioner of Arcane Taxonomy. "If you do not know the names of things, the knowledge of them is lost too," Linnaeus had written. Names were everything. Arcanists collected names. And then they *used* them.

These serious, esteemed men gazed out of their portraits with far-seeing eyes. Anton sometimes caught Bran staring up at them, perhaps wondering if he would find his place among them. But it often seemed there was much less in the world left to be discovered than when these men had worked. Discovery fueled their abilities, so what happened when nothing remained to be discovered?

Not every naturalist became an Arcanist. It was a talent—an art, even. One couldn't be afraid to dirty one's hands, Bran liked to say. To collect one's own specimens. To continue questioning beyond all reason.

Anton himself was only a fair-to-middling naturalist. As for Arcane Taxonomy—he thought it unreliable. There were always gaps in one's knowledge of a thing that could cause the *practica* to fail. Hard-won and oft-practiced skills were more reliable. He had observed the Inuit peoples of the North, at home on the ice in a way that seemed almost magical to outsiders, and they didn't need to know the Latin names of anything to accomplish it. Bran thought the Kalaallit people practiced their own version of Arcane Taxonomy, they moved so easily in their environment. He might have been right.

You brought an Arcanist on an expedition, relied on his skills—and if he was killed by illness or injury, what then? Bran earned a place on expeditions for his science, not his metascience.

Another wall held a second field of honor, one that better captured Anton's attention: a tall blackboard painted with a grid, listing geographic achievements. The board was filling up. Anton eyed the blank spaces with longing. The North and South Poles. The headwaters of the Amazon, the summits of Mount Kilimanjaro, the great monstrous peaks of the Himalayas and Karakoram. Some of the freshest chalk, the latest triumphs: the Englishman Whymper, who'd conquered the Matterhorn, had summited Chimborazo just this year, as well as a handful of other Andes peaks. Last year, Nordenskiöld had crossed the Northeast Passage, from Karlskrona in Sweden to the Bering Strait. The Northwest Passage still waited to be traversed.

The *Indominable* expedition had very briefly held the title of farthest north ever traveled, past the eighty-second parallel. But the Arctic was so busy these days the record had only stood a month, beaten by the HMS *Challenger*.

Anton felt like he was running out of time. He wanted to see his name on that board as much as Bran dreamed of seeing his portrait on the wall. They were a good match.

The rooms smelled of pipe smoke and alcohol. Some of it drinkable, much more of it in jars of specimens lined up on shelves, everything from a fetal shark to a mass of tapeworms to a human brain, complete with the label naming the former Naturalist Society member it had belonged to. No one Anton had known, thank God. He could do without so much mortality staring at him through glass. At least the brain in the jar was quiet, beyond having an opinion about anything.

"Once more unto the breach," Bran muttered.

Anton chuckled. "This isn't a battle."

"You sure about that?"

Well, he might have a point there.

"Ah, here they are, our very own Ross and Hooker! Gentlemen! Come, have a drink . . ."

Men approached; the greetings went on. Bran found one of his own, a fellow Arcanist—O'Connell, who'd been making collecting trips to Cuba. The two fell to talking in their own professional dialect.

Anton found himself standing before Hubert Andrews, the Society's current secretary, an older man, professor at Columbia. He was a superior fisherman who had written monographs on three different species of salmon.

"Professor Andrews." Anton took the offered hand and shook. "What's the gossip, then?"

"Charles Sternberg in Kansas," Andrews said brightly. "You remember him? The governor out there hired him to go look for gold, but the man's digging up fossil beds instead."

"Good finds? There's a market for good fossils."

"Indeed, and these are supposed to be very good, but try telling the governor that."

"And who's the gentleman outside looking for prospectors to go to Alaska? He tried to poach West right in front of me."

"We're seeing more of that. All these commercial interests—"

"West!" a voice called; the man it belonged to appeared, a sunburned gentlemen with a notebook in hand, interrupting Bran and O'Connell without a thought. "I'm told you're the man to go to for seabirds."

Graciously, Bran studied the sketches made in the notebooks and offered suggestions on identifications. And so it went, but Anton had come here for more than idle chat.

"By any chance do you know who's arranging lectures at Princeton these days?" he asked Andrews.

"Oh, I think you'd know about that better than I would," Andrews replied, and Anton reviewed his list of names, surreptitiously glancing around the room to see who else might be able to help. O'Connell was a Princeton man, he recalled, but Bran wouldn't remember to bring up the subject.

By some accounts Anton Torrance was wealthy; people must wonder why he had to chase after money for an expedition. But a wide variety of circumstances existed under the label "wealthy." Anton had never gone hungry outside of an expedition, had always been able to replace shoes that wore out. While his father had rank in British society, he lacked a fortune, and the family had never been able to spend with the freedom associated with their rank. Sir Archibald had offered to pay Anton's way—as long as he came to England and went into law or the foreign service or some appropriate profession. The family had been just wealthy enough that Anton got it into his head that he should be able to do whatever he liked. Anton had money enough for a roof and a good suit; he didn't have enough to outfit an Antarctic journey. Alas. On the other hand, he had some of that British aristocratic charm that Americans who *did* have that kind of money seemed very fond of. He was just poor enough that he'd learned how to use it.

Anton was getting ready to politely duck away and use that charm to drum up some lecture opportunities when Andrews said, "You were friends with Harry Stanley, weren't you?"

"It was my honor to be so."

"Did you go to the funeral, by chance?"

"Yes," Anton said. "It was a quiet affair."

"His death was such a shock. He'd seemed so healthy. Have you heard anything?"

This was exactly the sort of talk Bran had worried about. "No, the family's been very quiet."

"Such a shame. Such a bright career ahead of him. And now it's all over."

Anton said neutrally, "One might hope an unpublished essay or two might turn up."

Bran was watching them. Mention of Harry had caught his attention. His expression had gone stony.

"I need a drink, if you'll excuse me." Bran ducked away from his conversation, raising a hand to summon a uniformed attendant. He ordered whiskey.

"Yes, such a shame," Andrews repeated, and wandered off.

Anton did the rounds, noting who was present, who seemed to be holding court and who seemed to be making inquiries. He got the name of an entomologist at Princeton who could help arrange lectures and had an actual pleasant conversation with a botanist who'd been making collecting trips up the coast of Newfoundland. He fielded another three questions about Harry and how he'd died. Bran, making his own rounds, intercepted him briefly to say he'd gotten six questions about Harry, who would have been pleased to know he was such a topic of conversation.

Men, even naturalists and explorers, died at home of illness all the time. It was no great mystery except to a group of men obsessed with investigation and discovery. Anton imagined himself asking Mrs. Stanley exactly what Harry had died of—and no, he wasn't brave enough for that.

In an opportune moment, Anton found his next target, a government cartographer. "Jennings! You still have your man at the Signal Corps?"

"If you're about to hit me up for your next Arctic trip."

"Antarctic, rather," he said, ready for the pitch.

Jennings made an appreciative noise. "It's a good time for it, but you'll have to move quick. More folks than you are looking to the south."

Anton was afraid of that. It shouldn't have been a race, but it was. "Any idea who?" he prompted casually.

"Well, Montgomery Ashford, for one. Interesting plan he's got too."

Ashford's a fraud was right on the tip of Anton's tongue, but he managed to hold back. "Does he, now?"

He found the man himself in the next room over, holding court at the armchairs before a fireplace. Annoyingly, several of the more senior members of the Society, including Hubert Andrews, were listening. The group made room for him at the back, and Ashford glanced over. He nodded warily but didn't miss a beat of his patter.

"But my friends, it is high time to push *past* the boundaries of what is possible! We are scientists, are we not? We propose a hypothesis and then search for the evidence that will prove or disprove it. Until that moment of proof, all things are possible."

Montgomery Ashford had gained admission to the Society on the strength of work he had done cataloging specimens for the American Museum of Natural History. Solid work, to be sure. Perhaps not revolutionary, but competent. But before that, the man had had a job with showman P. T. Barnum. Collecting live alligators to display to paying crowds, that sort of thing.

He was also an Arcane Taxonomist, Third Rank. While he was with Barnum, he would cause a Fiji mermaid to swim around in a tank of water, making it seem alive. To be fair, that was years ago, and since then he'd done the work to establish himself as a serious naturalist and Arcanist. Like so many of them, he was looking for an expedition, something to cement his reputation. He'd then write a book, launch himself on the lecture circuit, and advance his ranking. The man occupied an uncomfortable space between science and sensationalism and seemed unaware of the ambiguity.

It could be argued that Anton occupied the same space, selling postcards of himself standing with his rifle next to the hide of the polar bear he had shot. But Bran kept him honest.

Ashford was a tall man, quick and energetic, with light-brown hair and an engaging smile that crinkled his eyes. He'd hold back the flap of a carnival tent and lure you inside with promises of marvels. Here and now, he turned up a card on the table: a reproduction of an Audubon painting of two awkward black-and-white birds paddling on a shoreline.

"I'm sure one of you can identify this bird? Mr. Torrance, perhaps?"

"Not my forte, I'm afraid, Mr. Ashford," Anton replied.

Bran came up beside him, arms crossed. "*Pinguinus impennis*. The great auk. They've been extinct for thirty years."

The great auks were flightless, useless vestigial wings hanging at their sides. Hunting them to their doom had been a simple thing.

"We *think*," Ashford said grandly. "We think they are extinct."

"I beg your pardon," Bran stated incredulously.

Ashford launched into his show. "My greatest hope lies in how much we don't know of this great territory at the South Pole. In fact, I believe the region might reveal great treasure: species of creatures that we believe are extinct may yet live on in some undiscovered habitat. Many animals are migratory and capable of traveling great distances. Why not consider, then, that some of them could have fled to sanctuary? I believe a lost colony of *Pinguinus impennis* may yet be discovered in the South, along with other untold wonders! And of course, the Arcane power that accompanies such discoveries."

"The great auk was flightless," Bran announced, attracting stares. "How would it cross the entire length of the Atlantic Ocean to reach this oasis?"

"It would swim, of course," Ashford replied, without hesitation.

Bran was considered one of the country's foremost authorities on North Atlantic seabirds. Ashford was planting a flag on that territory with this. And planting a flag on Anton's next intended target. He gazed at Anton and Bran with a narrow, calculating expression suggesting he would have thrown a glove at their feet if he'd had one.

Bran had gone still, his gaze turned thoughtful. Surely he wasn't taking Ashford seriously.

Anton wanted to ask Ashford what experience he'd had in cold climates. Would the ship he hired have a reinforced hull? Ice-breaking capabilities? What was his schedule? If he was smart, he'd travel in early summer, when seabird breeding colonies were most active. He might be assuming there'd be no sea ice at that time, but he would be wrong, and sea ice was at its most dangerous when it was unexpected. What cold-weather gear was he bringing? What would he be using for a launch, to make landfall? So many questions. Anton asked only one. "Ashford, correct me if I'm wrong, but you've never traveled farther north than Newfoundland, have you?"

"Are you questioning my qualifications? I think I have the knowledge and . . . *talent* to be a success." He meant his Arcanism. The man was planning to rely on magic. Members of the Naturalist Society didn't like the word *magic*. They were supposed to be scientists. Linnaeus's *Systema Naturae* was supposed to be methodical, precise. If it were really so, they ought to be able to teach it better. It would be consistent from one Arcanist to the next. In truth, most Arcanists couldn't explain exactly what it was they did, however indisputable the results were. So Anton called it magic, if only to himself.

"Do you have the skills?" Anton asked. "You need them all."

Bran was more direct. "There aren't any great auks left. I'll put money on it."

"You'll need all your money for your own expedition, won't you? No need for bets," Ashford said.

"How would you break out a ship frozen in pack ice?" Bran asked. And here it was. Anton relished the duel, even if it was just with words. He knew how it would end.

Ashford chuckled, as if the question were simple. "Melt the ice, of course."

Bran shook his head. "No, that takes too much energy. It'll freeze again before your ship makes any headway."

Bran's opponent raised a brow. "Oh? Then how would you—"

"How I *did* it was by shattering the ice. Break it to pieces, and the ship cuts right through. It's how Hooker did it. If you bothered to read his accounts." Bran didn't even look smug. Just matter of fact, like he was delivering a lecture to his students.

Ashford didn't seem to appreciate the lesson. He pitched his voice lower, as if they were alone and not before an audience. "You can't promise the same old adventure, tromping around in the snow in picturesque clothing, and expect to capture people's attention. This isn't meant as criticism, mind you. Both of your accomplishments are admirable. I'm just promising a bit . . . more."

Ashford twitched a hand and spoke a bit of Latin under his breath. His gaze got a vague, inward-turning look to it. Anton wouldn't have recognized it if he hadn't spent so much time with Bran. But being where they were, a lot of the men recognized what Ashford was about to do, and many of them shuffled back, out of the way.

He flicked his hand, and the flash of a firecracker, accompanied by the pop of burning gunpowder, sparked through the air straight toward Bran. Fairy stories would have called it elf-shot.

Bran calmly caught the projectile, squeezed, and opened his hand to let a scattering of ash fall harmlessly away. His expression never changed. Anton felt such a surge of admiration, his breath caught. Such performances made him want to *ravish* the man.

"Gentlemen, please," Andrews said sternly.

Ironically, the demonstration of Arcane Taxonomy within the halls of the Naturalist Society was discouraged for exactly this reason. Such competitive shows of power were frowned on. Ashford seemed unrepentant.

"My apologies," Bran said to Andrews, smiling thinly. "Mr. Torrance, I think we're late for our lunch appointment."

"Yes, I think you're right. Gentlemen." Anton nodded.

Ashford wasn't finished. "I'm sorry, I probably shouldn't say this. But without Harry Stanley and his connections, will you be able to raise what you need?" He seemed not to notice how very thin the ice had become.

Bran stiffened, his gaze hardened. "Of all the mercenary—"

Anton interrupted. "Kind of you to express your sympathies at Mr. Stanley's passing."

Ashford couldn't leave it alone. "The Arcanist who can reach the poles will win the world. That's my prediction. This goes beyond science."

Silence followed this, Ashford's words settling. And this was where the worlds came together, the idea—the hope, even—that the blackboard with all those firsts meant more than setting records. It meant power.

If Ashford gave the impression that he knew more than he was telling, that he'd learned some secret—well, that was part of his showmanship. Uncertainty had come over the gathering; the pursuit of knowledge should not have been a race, but it was. Ashford was going to make it a race, to get his funding.

Anton gave a nod. "Good luck to you, Mr. Ashford. You'll need it."

He put his hand firmly under Bran's elbow, and thankfully, Bran let himself be steered, frustration coming out in the way his steps pounded on the carpet. Coats and hats retrieved from the porter, they finally made it outside to the street and open air. They decided to walk rather than hail a cab. The day was clear and cool, perfect for walking.

"Would you forgive me if I decide to punch him some day?"

"I'd rather you didn't," Anton said. But yes, he would forgive Bran.

"All right. I won't, then."

"I forbid you from ever speaking to that man again," Anton said. "Nothing good ever comes of it."

"We can't seem to avoid it. Should we move to San Francisco?"

"He'd hunt us down. We would be invited to a lecture, and it would turn out to be his."

"I can't believe he's planning an Antarctic expedition. That's our territory!"

"It belongs to whoever gets there first," Anton said. "That's the point. But is he actually planning an expedition or just raising the money for one?"

"Meanwhile, he's hitting up *our* supporters." Turning thoughtful, Bran said, "If I spent a couple of years working for one of those mining companies in Alaska, that might get us the money we need."

"If you sold out, you mean. Would that satisfy you?"

"No, not at all."

"Well then. We'll make do."

They walked another block; Bran continued stewing. "They're putting a knife in Harry's work when he's barely in the ground. His work is alive and well, if we could just . . ." He hesitated, scratching his chin. Balancing on a thought. Bran might lose it entirely if he were prodded, but it was frustrating waiting for the man to sort himself out.

"Mrs. Stanley would never agree to it," Bran said finally.

"We should leave her alone. She made clear it's none of our business." Anton felt a bit of desperation, hoping to talk Bran out of whatever he was thinking. This was a project they didn't need to take on. Mrs. Stanley was better off without them. She had her world, they had theirs.

"I'll just write her a letter. That won't do any harm, will it?"

"Because a letter worked so well the last time."

"I have a better idea of the terrain this time."

"If you say so."

They walked under the shade of trees, watching the sky for clouds.

"If I ever throw a punch at Ashford, you'll stop me, won't you?" Bran said.

Anton was about the only person in the world who could. "We'll see. I may just let you."

Bran let out a curt laugh.

Alexander Wilson was one of the first great American Arcanists. Until his death in 1813, he traveled throughout the United States collecting, describing, and painting birds, publishing his results in his great work, *American Ornithology*. Birds followed him, he spoke to them, and they willingly posed so that he could sketch them.

President Thomas Jefferson himself corresponded with Wilson, at first only about the identification of bird species but later to ask him to use his abilities on behalf of the nation: to assist in the exploration of the West, to serve the military, to hobble British shipping routes, to evoke clairvoyance. Such requests, recorded in multiple letters back and forth between the president, his secretaries, generals, and various scholars, made clear that Wilson was talented and powerful. But Wilson would not accept a naval commission, and while he was an admirer of explorers like Meriwether Lewis, he never took part in a western expedition himself. Wilson had only one mission, one goal: to complete his catalog of American birds. The irony is that his obsession—the precision of his observations, the thoroughness of his studies, and the fineness of his art—gave him the Arcanist abilities that made him so sought after by men of power.

More species of birds are named in honor of Alexander Wilson than any other American naturalist.

SEVEN

Pandion haliaetus

Dear Mrs. Stanley,

First, may I offer my sincere condolences on the passing of your husband. This is a great loss to the grand pursuit of scientific endeavor, but that must feel as nothing to your personal loss.

Second, I regretfully must decline the opportunity to print Mr. Stanley's last remaining essays, however close they were to completion upon his death. Since he is, clearly, unable to verify and validate the information contained in them, we cannot rightly consider them complete, however many assurances you give us.

Your understanding in this matter is most appreciated. Again, deep sympathies.

Sincerely,

Mr. Stuart Endicott, Editor, *The Pinfeather*

Having had a taste of a career as a naturalist, Beth found she didn't want to give that up. But the obstacles might prove insurmountable.

She crumpled the letter and threw it in the waste bin by the potting table. She had estimated she could present three, maybe four, more articles under Harry's name, claiming they had been finished at the time of his death. He had been pursuing so many ideas, and in honor of his legacy, those last essays ought to see print. Then, just maybe, she might present three or four more articles, ones that had *almost* been finished and required just a little extra writing. To these, she could add her name. Harry Stanley's dutiful widow ensuring every last scrap of his studies was saved.

Once Harry's colleagues got used to seeing her name next to his, she could take the next step: She would tell a story about how inspired she was, reviewing and arranging Harry's writing, how much she learned just by being in proximity to the man and his notes—a Harvard degree by osmosis. Clearly, she must continue on her own, under her own name. Elizabeth Stanley, woman naturalist. It would seem perfectly logical.

A bigger lie than even the one she'd been telling about Harry and his work, but she would still have the work.

Now it seemed she could not even accomplish the first step, and Harry's career—her career—would fade into obscurity. She should have known it was impossible when Mr. West and Mr. Torrance expressed such shock over the true authorship of Harry's work. Oh, they believed well enough that she had done the work. But they could not accept it.

Never mind her work as an Arcane Taxonomist.

When Beth was a little girl, her family's housekeeper had talked to mice. Well, not exactly. But she did *something*—whispered over a bit of mint that she scattered in the larder, drew chalk lines on the thresholds of doorways—and mice stayed away. Milk in her kitchen never spoiled. Cut flowers seemed to last twice as long as they should. One might call it folklore, but never Arcane Taxonomy.

By the time Beth was older and had begun lighting candles and waterproofing her coats with Arcane Taxonomy, the old housekeeper had died, and Beth never had a chance to ask her exactly what she did and how she learned what she knew.

What Beth did know: that Arcane practices were more common than the university naturalists would ever admit. And Harry had been right all along—her secret stayed secret because the men of the Naturalist Society would simply never listen to her. Mr. Endicott's letter proved that.

She had brought the morning's letters to the garden to go through them over a cup of tea. Half of them were addressed to Harry, and she resigned herself to the knowledge that she'd be getting letters addressed to Harry for the rest of her life.

They included thanks for his articles, questions raised by his observation notes, requests for more details about those observations, invitations to lecture, requests to write a column for a new nature journal. Harry's reputation was growing, the opportunities expanding. It was all so exciting—or should have been. She could do all this work herself if anyone let her.

She would have to write to every single one of these correspondents and tell them Harry was dead. Or not write, and let the news of his death spread through his professional circles, with no effort on her part. His colleagues would feel a twinge of remorse, and then they would move on. His obituaries in the various magazines and journals should be coming out in the next month or so.

She put these letters in a stack, to be put in the box with the rest that she hadn't decided what to do with.

At last she came to the letters addressed to her and found one marked from Florida, from Alice Wallace, the wife of one of her father's business partners and a fellow member of several ladies' bird and nature organizations Beth belonged to. A wonderful, perfect distraction from the annoyances of the last few days and her own tears.

The ospreys are back, Alice wrote, and listed observations with dates and circumstances. Right on schedule, after vanishing from the north. For three years they'd exchanged letters, telling each other what they saw and when, tracking patterns, and marveling at how the birds knew when it was time to fly to warmer climates, and then how they knew to return to the same areas, every year. New information, new pins for her map, showing a road that had nothing to do with human construction: the paths the birds flew, season to season, north to south to north again, following the sun. It wasn't random; she'd been tracking these observations long enough to know the patterns didn't change. The fascinating mystery was how.

Beth had a whole network of correspondents who sent her their observations, from Florida to Texas and even Mexico. She tracked migration patterns of two dozen species. No travel required: she simply wrote letters and cultivated friendships with anyone who liked watching birds. She would not stop. Even if she never published another article, she would still keep on, for the joy of sticking another pin in the map.

She found one more letter at the bottom of the stack, from Mr. Brandon West. She checked the name again, sure it must have been meant for Harry and waylaid. But no, Mr. West had written directly to her, only yesterday. What about, she couldn't guess. She had expected to never hear from him again after that awful meeting.

"Ma'am?" Ann stuck her head out to the garden.

"Yes? Who's come to bother me now?" She set Mr. West's letter aside.

The maid winced. "Mrs. Clarke and Mrs. Stanley. The other Mrs. Stanley."

"Both of them together?" Dread filled her.

"Yes, ma'am. I couldn't put them off this time. They said they would wait."

She had given up on keeping people out of the house—they would begin to think her ill, or mad. So she'd thrown out the lilies and let it go. Mr. West was the only one who'd noticed the Arcane *practica* she'd used.

She supposed she ought to get this over with all at once, but her eyes had begun stinging, and for God's sake, when would she ever stop crying? She was sick of crying.

"I'm sorry. I'll think of some new excuses for next time."

"I suppose we couldn't put them off forever."

Ann shrugged a little. "I wouldn't mind trying."

That got a smile out of Beth. "Bring plenty of tea. And anything resembling cake we might have on hand."

"Joan baked a lemon cake this morning that will do nicely," Ann said. As if Joan, the cook, had expected they would need a nice cake to serve with tea this afternoon. Thank God someone was able to think of these things.

"How is it everyone but me seems to know what to do?"

"You're in mourning, ma'am. You're not really meant to know anything right now."

Beth sighed. "You are really extraordinarily too kind to me, Ann."

Ann dipped a curtsy and fled to the kitchen, leaving Beth to face the gauntlet of the parlor alone.

She was not wearing gloves. Should she be wearing gloves? A veil? Surely not in her own home. Suddenly, she couldn't remember when she had last left the house. Since Harry's funeral? She must have been out since then, but she couldn't remember.

She delved into the secrets of life but couldn't manage a few social niceties.

Her dress and hair were neat. That would have to be enough. Not that turning herself out perfectly would stave off criticism. They would find *something* to bother her about. Smoothing out her skirt one more time, she thought of tall, straight pine trees, the fierceness of barracuda, and presented herself at the doorway.

"Oh, Beth, love, how are you getting along?" Mrs. May Clarke swept from one of the sofas toward her, very much how some charging lion must look. Beth prepared to be valiant, to hold her ground and accept whatever embrace was offered. But she was entirely startled by her mother's hat: broad brimmed, pinned at a jaunty angle on her coiled pile of hair, a creamy beige, fixed with a taxidermy white dove, some variety of the genus *Columba*. Not just feathers, the actual whole bird, preserved with its wings outstretched, neck yearning, as if it were coming to land amid a pile of green and violet silk flowers. Tiny black beads glistened in place of eyes.

"Mother, what's that on your head?" she blurted.

"Oh, do you like it? Isn't it elegant?"

It was ghoulish. One thing to collect specimens in the pursuit of science, but this, using birds as decoration, seemed a waste.

"It's a bit much," Beth said instead of anything else she was thinking.

"I believe doves are meant to convey peace, especially in times of grieving. At least that's what the milliner said, and I thought you could use all the help you could get."

Symbolism only. No actual Arcanist power was conveyed, but some people liked to think they could partake, with dead birds and the odd symbolic flower. Beth was suddenly exhausted. Something in her expression must have seemed particularly dismayed, and of course Mrs. Clarke misinterpreted the meaning.

"Oh, there, there, dear." Her mother finally got her arms around her, held off somewhat by the volume of their skirts. Mrs. Clarke gripped her arms tightly, as if she thought she was holding Beth upright, no matter that Beth was doing that on her own. Beth patted her mother's arms back and tried to smile.

A glance past her mother's shoulder showed her Mrs. Stanley sitting at the edge of an armchair, lips pressed tight with impatience. Beth tried to remember the last time she and her mother-in-law had been in the same room, and once again that bit of knowledge was simply gone. Ann was right: she apparently couldn't be expected to know anything right now. The funeral—surely she had seen Mrs. Stanley more recently than the funeral.

Maybe not.

Mrs. Stanley was the elder of the two mothers by about ten years, her hair a perfect blend of dark and gray, mostly hidden under a hat with a froth of netting around the edges. No dead birds, thank goodness. She sat erect, buttoned up and serene in a walking dress—the black of mourning, of course. Harry had gotten his refined features from her, but what his good humor had made bright and welcoming, her sense of authority made intimidating. Hard not to cower around her, and the other Mrs. Stanley liked it that way.

Mrs. Clarke . . . Beth wished she could be more like her mother, outgoing and pretty and at home in every situation. She made friends instantly and always knew just what to say. Beth had been raised by this woman. How could she be so different?

"Oh, I can't imagine. I *can't*." Mr. Benjamin Clarke was still alive, and they had been married for thirty years. Beth and Harry had three. It was nice of Mrs. Clarke to admit she had no idea what Beth was experiencing.

"Ann will have tea out in a minute. Are you well? Father? Will and his family?"

"Very well, very well, don't worry about us. In fact, Will would like to invite you over for dinner if you're ready, and I specifically told him I'd try to convince you—"

And her mother was off. Beth barely heard the rest of it. She would say yes, she must say yes to these invitations at some point, and her brother, Will, would at least provide a familiar setting.

Ann arrived with the tea cart and lemon cake, luscious enough to smell, and they were kept busy for the next few moments, arranging themselves around the low table. This was familiar, this was fine, simply tea in the parlor and nothing more. Beth ate a bite and chewed slowly.

The pair of mothers spoke of nothing.

"How are your other sons getting on, then?" Mrs. Clarke asked.

Mrs. Stanley tsked. "They have their studies to occupy them. Martin has said he intends to go into law, and Stephen might follow him, they've always been so competitive with one another. They should distract themselves, is what I told them."

Yes, Beth was trying to distract herself, she wanted only to distract herself, but the clock was silent, and the square of sunlight moved across the room as time passed. And where could she go?

The warblers would be gone soon. She would very much like to take a walk through Central Park before the weather turned, to see the last of the summer birds before they left. Maybe she could make a picnic of it, which sounded lovely, but she probably ought to find someone to go with her. What would it look like, a woman in mourning black sitting all alone on a blanket on the grass, scribbling in her notebook? Did she really care what people might think? She should be allowed some eccentricity right now.

"It's still all so unsettled. Beth, what's the news about the estate? Is it settled yet? Do you need Will or Father to have a word with poor Harry's lawyer?" Mrs. Clarke paused. "Beth?"

The call brought her back, but the parlor seemed strange, just for a moment. She took a long drink of cooling tea. "Yes, Mother?"

Her mother sat back in the chair and frowned, and Beth knew that look. No, she almost said, before her mother could ask. No, she had not been paying attention, and she was not even sorry.

On the other hand, Mrs. Stanley set her cup aside and leaned forward with great interest. "My dear, are you feeling entirely well?" She raised an eyebrow to indicate that the question meant more than the words implied.

"Yes," Beth answered. "Entirely."

Mrs. Stanley apparently didn't believe that Beth understood the question. "If there's some change in your condition, I'd dearly love to help you . . . should there be a need." She raised her brow.

Mrs. Clarke caught the thread and grabbed hold. "Any change in appetite? Any odd sicknesses? Any odd feeling at all?"

They thought she was stupid. They thought she was such a naive child that she didn't know what they were hinting at.

"No, I am not pregnant," she said, staring into her cup. They hoped to hear that Harry had left behind some legacy, would continue his bloodline.

They might have gasped a little.

Agnes Stanley oozed frustration. "You can't know that, not for certain. You might still be early."

"I'm not," Beth said firmly.

"But—"

She glared at them both, meeting each of their gazes in turn, and said as clearly as she could, "I know I'm not, and that's that."

Let them ask, if they dared. Let them be even more direct than they already had been. Let them demand that she tell how she knew that she could not possibly be pregnant.

And then let them try to figure out whose fault that was.

They needed a moment to work through the implications of what she had said, but understanding alighted at the same moment for both, and simultaneously their gazes dropped. How terrible the silence was, then.

"The cake is lovely," Mrs. Clarke said finally, raising a delicate bite on her fork.

"Thank you. I'll pass compliments along to Joan," Beth said.

Worse than Harry's death was the fact that Harry had not left any children behind, not in three years of marriage, and it must somehow be Beth's fault. Nothing she could ever say would change that assumption. There was rage in that thought, which Beth had to quickly turn away from or it would fill and devour her. She'd wanted children, she'd loved Harry, and he . . . she hadn't understood him, not really.

"I know! You must come to the Carnation Society charity luncheon," Mrs. Clarke said. "It's a perfect outing if you don't feel up to a full dinner. You've been cooped up here so long, your friends would so much like to see you."

They were Mrs. Clarke's friends, and Beth rather liked being cooped up here. She liked not having to speak to anyone. She liked not having to bear the speculation, the pity. She loved her garden, and sitting in a comfortable chair where she didn't have to worry if her back was straight or if she needed to smile.

"Is it entirely proper for a lady in full mourning to attend a social function?" said Mrs. Stanley.

"It's *fine*. It's at my home, and she'll be among friends."

"Beth, dear, I do hope you plan on a full year of mourning."

Beth hadn't thought that much about it. A year seemed like a vast canyon of time; she could not see to the end of it.

"Beth will be very proper," Mrs. Clarke said, a bit testily. "Beth, please come."

Mrs. Stanley glanced at her, frowning. "If you're ready for company, you'll have to come have dinner with us as well. I know Harry would want me to look after you, and you'll always be part of our family."

The two matrons exchanged a glance, full of politeness and subtext, a couple of hens scratching out territory.

"Thank you. That's very kind," Beth said. Ominously, her future filled with luncheons and dinner parties, and she only now realized how much of a shield Harry had been for her at these events. She had used him as an excuse to decline invitations. At unavoidable social functions, she could stand quietly and let him speak. He would hold her arm and be effusive on her behalf. She had forgotten what it was like, not having an arm to cling to. And now she must learn again.

She took a very long, slow sip of tea to give herself a moment to close her eyes. He'd died and taken their whole life together with him.

"Beth?" Mrs. Clarke's tone turned serious, the cheerfulness of her society chatter falling off.

Beth wondered how much more conversation she had missed. "I'm just a little tired."

That turned out to be enough of a hint, and the mothers put aside their cups and plates and made noises about getting on with their days, and how nice it was to see Beth, and when would they see her again, and if she needed anything, anything at all, and on and on. The fact of their leaving renewed her strength, and she showed them to the door and even kissed their cheeks as Ann handled the coats. Blessedly, finally, the door closed and silence fell again.

Ann lurked a moment, as if she wanted to ask a question—the usual question, most likely: *How are you? Are you well? How badly do you feel today?* But she merely said, "I'll clean up the tea things, ma'am."

Beth followed her to the parlor and went to the grandfather clock. She opened the case and found the chains to set the weights, then gently set the pendulum swinging. Holding her breath, she waited—the clock had broken, the mechanism had stiffened, it would not work. But then it ticked, its rhythm steady, and relief pulled at her. She had no idea what time it was; she supposed she would have to find out. Joan must have a pocket watch. She could fix the time later, but for now, the clock was alive again, the ticking sharp and steady, the pendulum working, back and forth. And this was better. This was right.

She next went to the study to find her basket with her pencils, journal, and opera glasses. Another part of her abandoned for the last months, another bit of her life she hadn't touched. Well, now it was time.

Ann found her in the foyer, shrugging on her coat. "Ma'am?"

"I'm going out," Beth said. "Just for a little while."

EIGHT

Geothlypis trichas

Four days a week, Anton walked. Marched, really. Six blocks over and up Fifth Avenue to the park, then all the way around. He wore a pack with bricks in it to build strength. Took off down the pavement, waving now and then at familiar faces who smiled back, but he never paused. His reputation was established enough that he was considered a feature of the neighborhood. *Look*, folk would say to visitors, *there's the famous explorer Mr. Torrance preparing for his next expedition.* The walk was never enough to exhaust him but enough to make him feel that he had accomplished something useful. The exercise was especially good when he had an excess of frustration. Montgomery Ashford had scheduled a lecture and fundraising tour at every museum, hall, and club between Philadelphia and Boston over the next two months. Anton and Bran were lagging, facing the prospect of asking the same audiences to donate to a cause they had already supported.

Anton had just come around the easternmost tip of the lake when he pulled up short, so suddenly the bricks knocked into his back.

Mrs. Stanley was sitting on a blanket on the grass. He doubted it was her at first, but she was all in black, with that sparrow-brown hair tucked under a simple hat, the netting of a half veil pushed back. She was staring through a set of opera glasses, studying a nearby grove of trees. He wondered what show was playing.

He ought to continue walking, but his curiosity got the better of him. "Mrs. Stanley?" he called, still several paces away.

She turned from the glasses, blinking at him in confusion before her expression settled into serene politeness. A mask, he thought, and wished he'd kept walking rather than disturb her.

"Mr. Torrance?" She fluttered a bit, looking around as if searching for a cup of tea to offer him. She only had the opera glasses in hand, a pencil on a book lying open on her lap, and a basket.

"I only wanted to wish you a good day. I'll leave you alone."

"You startled me, is all. It's lovely to see you." He couldn't tell if she meant the sentiment or was just being polite. In fact, she wasn't looking at him at all. That clump of vegetation had all her attention.

"Might I ask what you're looking at?"

"Well, nothing at the moment," she said, pressing her lips in a quick thin smile. That was *not* a mask, and the expression made her seem lighter. "There's a yellowthroat calling in the rushes over there. I'm hoping he'll come out and let me look at him." He cocked his head to listen, and a bright witchity melody came from the branch where she'd nodded. She raised the glasses to look.

The piercing, distinctive song came again. He held his breath to listen. "Yellowthroat? Are you sure?" He tried to remember if he'd ever seen a yellowthroat in Central Park and couldn't say he had. Not that he'd paid attention, to be honest.

She gave him a scathing sidelong glance but spoke politely. "Yes, I'm sure."

"Ah." He stood awkwardly, uncertain what to say next, which hardly ever happened.

"There you are," she murmured, peering through the glasses. He squinted to see what she was seeing and spotted a flutter of movement at the end of a branch. A slight dip, a shimmering among the leaves.

He couldn't quite make the creature out; he only recognized that there was, in fact, a bird there.

She reminded him a little of Bran, just then. Bran could find worlds in the smallest detail. A flash of color or hint of movement would occupy his whole attention. It was one of the things that made him a good scientist.

"Are those actually useful?" They were a simple set of opera glasses, the kind that fit in a lady's clutch, ivory with bronze trim. Pretty, shining, a piece of jewelry more than an eyepiece. He wouldn't have thought them good for much of anything, even at the opera.

"Would you like to try?" She shifted aside to make room for him on the blanket.

Well, why not? He dropped his pack and settled on the edge of the cloth.

"Goodness, it sounds like you've got bricks in there."

"Um. I do."

"So you practice like you're hauling a hundred pounds of gear on your back?"

"Just so."

"Hmm." The sound was neutral. She handed him the glasses and pointed to the rushes with a gloved hand. "He's right at the end of that third stalk from the left."

The glasses felt tiny in his hands, and ridiculous when held to his face. He carried telescopes on his trips, nothing so delicate as this. If Bran could see him now, he would laugh. He let his vision settle through the lenses, focused the dial, and tried to see what she was pointing at.

"I don't see it." Leaves jostled, and he followed the movement. "Wait."

And there it was, emerging long enough for him to get a look. The view wasn't totally clear, but the bird was unmistakable, the tiny distant thing brought into enough clarity to identify it: overall olive, bright yellow on breast and throat, and a black bandit's stripe across its eyes.

The little fellow opened its bill and sang a loud series of notes. It shifted its stance, tilted its head, and then was gone, flown off.

"Well, isn't that lovely." He handed the glasses back. "You do this often?"

"I try, when weather allows. Especially in the spring and fall, to see what comes through on migration."

"And you keep a list." He eyed the notebook, which did indeed have a list with hatch marks and notes.

She granted him another one of those scathing sidelong glances, which he was beginning to interpret as a sign that he'd said something stupid. "The list, the individual sightings—they feel like a prize. Hunting without the noise and blood. But what's important are the observations over time. The patterns. What happens year after year. I've been coming here for three years, ever since Harry and I moved into the brownstone."

"He came here with you?" He was asking too many questions, getting too personal. He ought to say farewell and leave.

"Not often. He didn't really like sitting still for so long. I—" She hesitated, glancing away, then recovering. There was only a small hitch in her voice. "This is the first time I've come here since he left."

How extremely disorienting it was to look into this part of Harry's life that none of them had known anything about and find such clear portraits of Harry there. Didn't people think her odd? They must. But she also seemed so at ease here, far more than in her own parlor. The yellowthroat had moved on, but its song still came through from beyond the rushes, and she smiled fondly at the undergrowth where it was hiding. This was her peace.

"Harry would shoot it because that's what his naturalist friends do," she said. "The collecting. But I like letting them alone. Listening to them sing."

Impulsively, he said, "Mrs. Stanley, Mr. West and I are giving a lecture at Columbia on Friday. Would you like to come?"

Her eyes brightened briefly, but the moment passed and the sad mask returned. "I'm not sure that's a good idea."

"It's a society event," he quickly explained. "All are welcome. It's part of the regular lecture series Bran—Mr. West—organizes there. I seem to recall you and Harry attended a few of them."

"Oh yes, he loved them. I did too." Ah, there it was, the fleeting smile. He was satisfied.

"Then you should come. Bring friends." Friends with money . . . "By the way, I think West might have written you a letter. He said he might."

Her gaze went vague for a moment, and then that scathing look seemed to turn inward, as if she was reprimanding herself. "I'm afraid I haven't looked at it yet. Slipped my mind. So much seems to slip my mind these days."

"The fog," Anton said. "I lost a sister when I was young. It was the same. Missed whole days."

"Yes, exactly. Do you know . . ." She shook her head. "Yes. Thank you so much for the invitation. And please give my apologies to Mr. West. I'll look at his letter soon. I take it you see Mr. West regularly?"

One could say that. "Ah, yes. We're planning our next expedition."

"Harry would have loved hearing about it all."

She was an observer. A naturalist, clearly. At some point, would she notice that Bran and Anton lived at the same address? Would she wonder about that? They'd have to be careful around her. That raised a question: How much had she known about Harry? Anton was suddenly uneasy thinking of it. He ought to flee before he got any more into the weeds. "Well, I'll leave you to it, then. I'll hope to see you on Friday."

Before she could argue out of some sense of politeness, Anton got to his feet and hauled the pack to his shoulders. Tipping his hat, he wished her a good day and was gone while she was still stammering that she wished him likewise.

NINE

Buteo jamaicensis

Beth should have declined the invitation. The last time she'd come here, Harry had been with her. She couldn't stop thinking about him and had to remind herself to breathe.

The hall was packed, with many familiar faces in the crowd dressed for an afternoon out. This was an event people attended to be seen, not because they had a particular interest in the topic. She'd forgotten what it was like . . . Why had she forgotten? And so many women wearing plumes in their hats, egret feathers, entire wings of colorful songbirds. She hadn't been so bothered before. But this much ostentatious death was . . . draining.

In full mourning she didn't have to think about what to wear, which was convenient, but the black gown marked her. The netting on her hat was a barrier between her and the world. She entered the lecture hall, cavernous, voices echoing, and the crowd parted. Glances passed over her, studying her, then quickly looked away. Murmuring followed in her wake. *Harold Stanley's widow.*

She found a spot by a wood-paneled wall that she could put her back to. The lecture hall belonged to the natural history department and was decorated with specimens—taxidermy heads on the wall, deer and elk, even a bison. A pheasant was mounted and displayed above a door; above another, a golden eagle. A glass case held the fossil skull of some giant prehistoric creature; more common fossils filled another: trilobites and ammonites, jagged and textured, neatly labeled with little cards, all so orderly. She knew all the names. She cocooned herself with knowledge.

The place smelled of stone, dust, bodies, breath. Footsteps knocked on the floor, skirts and jackets rustled.

This morning, she'd finally gotten around to reading Mr. West's letter and been startled all over again. She couldn't think of a reason for him to write unless it was to plead with her again about handing over the specimens and the rest of Harry's things, which had never really been Harry's at all. But if she was going to see West at the lecture, she knew she must refer to the letter.

> Dear Mrs. Stanley,
> I hope this finds you well, or as well as can be under the circumstances. Thank you again for meeting with myself and Mr. Torrance the other day. I very much appreciated the chance to speak with you about Harry, and to learn of your deep involvement in ornithological studies. I apologize for my shock at the revelation. It must have been insulting to you, and I would never wish you any such pain. I confess, though, that I have had to reassess much about what I thought I knew of one of my oldest friends. Harry was a good man, I will stand by that claim, and I will always mourn him. But in death, he continues to be as occasionally exasperating as he was in life, and I find that frustrating.

Beth had paused here and laughed into her hand, because this was a perfect description and precisely matched her experience of Harry.

I have been thinking about your situation. That you have, in effect, lost the blind from which you have been making your observations. Or maybe lost your decoy is a better metaphor. You worked unseen while Harry drew the attention. I think there must be some solution, to allow you to continue the good work that you have done. To bring worthy attention to the work, if not to yourself, though I think you underestimate the scientific community's willingness to accept you. If you will allow me, I would like to assist in this endeavor, and if you are willing, find a way for you to continue your work thereafter.

I hope to hear from you. Either encouragement to move forward, or a gentle refusal.

Your Servant, and Companion in Mourning,

Mr. Brandon West

Wrong, so terribly wrong, all of it. Did he think she hadn't thought of such a thing herself? That she hadn't already tried? The scientific community would *not* accept; it had already proved it. He didn't know what he was talking about.

That she would have to explain this to him in person made her feel ill all over again.

She shouldn't have come.

"Is that Beth Clarke I see?"

Beth's mind had been wandering, and she flinched a little, brought back to herself. An older woman, stooped and walking with a cane, approached slowly but steadily. She squinted through a pair of wire-framed spectacles and lit up with a smile when she came close enough to confirm her guess.

"Mrs. Harrogate." Beth's own smile answered when she finally recognized and remembered her, a frequent guest at her mother's ladies' luncheons. "I'm Mrs. Stanley now. Or at least I was."

"Oh yes, I remember. I was so sorry to hear of it. What a blow, what a blow, everything upended." Mrs. Harrogate had lost her husband ten years ago. She'd become one of those wealthy widows that gathered in New York, attending all manner of luncheons and lectures and clubs. "Your mother spoke of it last week when I saw her. At length." She shook her head, tsking. "She's quite worried about you."

"I'm well aware," Beth said, a bit of acid in her tone.

Mrs. Harrogate endeared herself to Beth by chuckling at this and patting Beth's arm. "Stay strong, dear. I know it seems dark now, but you'll get through."

How? she wanted to ask. How was she supposed to get through? She had to build a new life, but she felt she had nothing left to build with. Everything reminded her of Harry. "It's so strange," she confessed. "You're the only one who's come to speak with me."

"As if widowhood is contagious, yes? I sometimes looked on it as a blessing when I wore mourning. Like a wall I could stand behind."

"Yes, I can see that."

A man in a gray suit with a mustache too large for his face went up to the stage and announced that they should take their seats. The lecture would begin soon.

"May I sit with you, Mrs. Harrogate?"

"Of course, dear."

Chairs lined up before a raised platform, something like a stage, at the far end of the hall. A podium stood to one side. On the other side, a table with a cloth draped over it, hiding what lay underneath, wondrous artifacts from the men's journeys. In previous lectures Beth had attended with Harry, Mr. Torrance had displayed spears and knives made from bone and walrus tusk by the northern natives, and Mr. West had shown skulls, feathers, taxidermy specimens of puffins and petrels. Their lectures on natural history always seemed to leave her with a million questions that she never asked. The crowd that would press toward them at the end was so daunting, she held back, and Harry never thought to ask about the specimens. She expected the same would happen today, though she should try to talk to Mr. Torrance so he would know that she'd been here.

This lecture wasn't like the last one she and Harry had attended. Part of the arrangement included a framework at the back of the stage, holding up what seemed to be a roll of canvas. Like a theater backdrop that could be pulled down at a dramatic moment. There was a good deal of anticipation, wondering what would be displayed on the backdrop.

A printed program announced the lecture's title: "Polar Exploration: What Is Left to Discover?" A whole other world, she would have thought.

The man with the large mustache, who Beth gathered was director of zoological sciences at the university, made a grand introduction, some words about Torrance and West and their accomplishments, which were extensive, but also about Columbia's natural history department and all the great work it did, and on and on. Beth started getting impatient, as did the whole gathering. No one was here to see him. Finally, he stepped aside.

Mr. Torrance and Mr. West emerged from a doorway at the back of the stage to much applause. They paused a moment to regard one another—a gesture of long acquaintance and assurance—before turning to acknowledge their audience, nodding smartly. Hard to imagine them bundled in furs and skiing across a frozen landscape; they seemed so comfortable here, on display.

Torrance was the one who claimed the podium and spoke in a voice that carried. "Ladies and gentlemen, you have my deepest gratitude for your presence here today . . ."

He told the story of the famous Greenland expedition. Beth already knew much of it—she had read Mr. Torrance's memoir of the trip, which was harrowing and full of poetic descriptions that made Beth want to make an expedition of her own.

Meanwhile, West drew back the cloth over the table with a flourish and revealed snowshoes, a reindeer-skin parka, boots, several skulls, furs, spears, and a rifle—the famous rifle that had shot the polar bear in the photo cards they sold. They brought it out at every lecture, as if it had its own fame. All concrete evidence of the adventures they'd had, making them seem more real.

She shivered, imagining ice in the air and the expanse of a frozen world. With so many people pressed in close, the hall had become stifling, but a decided chill now fell over them. Around her, some were even hugging themselves, rubbing their arms for warmth. Mrs. Harrogate wrapped her shawl more tightly around her shoulders. Beth swore her breath fogged and imagined a needlelike stab of an icy wind on her face.

Onstage, Mr. West's head was bowed slightly. Was he murmuring silently? Maybe. He'd worked some Arcane *practicum* to make the hall feel like winter, she was sure of it. Between Torrance's words and this spell of cold, the audience was made to feel they journeyed to the Arctic.

When Torrance spoke of the aurora borealis, the sheets of light that adorned the sky in Arctic winters, lights appeared above the stage, a rippling burst of green fading to yellow, like ribbons in a breeze—more of Mr. West's work. Showing off his skills as an Arcane Taxonomist was part of his allure. The audience was smitten, gasping and clapping at the performance.

Beth wondered if she could do something like it. If she would ever have the courage to ask Mr. West how he did it. She didn't think she would. She would have to learn the *practicum* herself. She would start with the names of some of the bioluminescent creatures that populated ocean waves. Learn more about Lampyridae, the firefly family, to recreate the gift nature had given them. She pulled a notebook and pencil from her clutch to make notes.

Torrance continued. "Exploring the last frontiers of the globe, at the North and South Poles, requires a certain fortitude, and no episode in this trip illustrates that more than our encounter with the great bear of the North. We came face to face with one of the largest specimens ever recorded. Now, I can say that, and I see you all nodding in agreement, but I'm not sure you quite realize the danger. I fear you might think of the bears you've seen at the zoo, lolling in their den, or one at the circus, trained and docile. This, an Arctic bear at the height of its fury, is something else altogether. Mr. West, perhaps we could show them?"

The moment arrived: West took hold of the end of the curtain and drew it down to reveal a painting of the bear in question—life size, nine feet from nose to tail, hulking. It dwarfed West, who paced along the canvas. The bear would only have to open its jaws to devour his face. The man was so clearly inconsequential beside it.

Gasps rose up. Beth's own heart skipped a beat. West didn't need any Arcane *practica* to sway the audience this time.

"Now imagine this great beast as close to us as you there in the first row, charging as fast as a racing horse, bearing down on us. It will not need its teeth and claws. It will shatter you merely by crashing into you, and not even notice that anything stood in its way."

West stepped up. "To this day, I'm grateful for Mr. Torrance's skill with the rifle. Instead of reading my obituary, you can visit that very bear as a specimen at the Museum of Natural History."

Easy to believe West was a man who had looked death in the face not just once but often, and it didn't cause him any more trouble than getting caught in the rain without an umbrella. Very impressive. The pair of them were. Standing on either side of the canvas backdrop, they regarded one another across the stage.

"As for the rest of the bear, we didn't waste a bit of it, did we?" Torrance said. "Tell me, Mr. West, do you think it made good eating?"

"No, Mr. Torrance, I do not. The poor beast's meat had the consistency of leather from all that hard Arctic living, but it did fill the stomach well enough when there was nothing else at hand."

The audience laughed appreciatively.

"I suppose you might think an expedition to the Antarctic would be safer, because there are no polar bears in the south. However, there are other predators to contend with."

West unrolled a second canvas in front of the first, a painting of a creature even larger and more impressive: a leopard seal, bigger than the polar bear, twelve feet nose to tail. Mr. Torrance produced a skull, solid and blockish, with a gaping mouth full of pointed teeth. Even more astonished gasps greeted this horror.

"And how does one keep safe from this?" Torrance asked.

"Stay out of the water," West answered.

The laughter that followed was maybe more nervous than amused.

"Mr. West and I hope to see these magnificent creatures for ourselves. To learn all about them. To use that knowledge."

Mr. Torrance went on to describe what was known about the far southern reaches of the globe, but more importantly what wasn't known, and how they hoped to accomplish the next voyage of discovery to bring the light of knowledge to those dark spaces. The odds were no one in this room would ever see a leopard seal—except for the great explorers, who risked their lives on behalf of the general public. They invited the audience to travel vicariously.

Beth drank it all in. Imagined the searing light that required those odd slotted goggles, wondered how it would feel to wear a parka. Penguins: she wanted to know about penguins.

Harry had wanted to go with them on this trip. She wondered now if she would have been able to let him. If he would have so easily left her behind. Of course he would have. To stay home with her, or to sail off with these two on one of their adventures? Wasn't even a question. She knew what she'd have done if she were Harry.

Enough of that. Useless thinking there.

At the close of the lecture, the men received a standing ovation—a good sign for their fundraising. To her surprise, Beth was glad she had come to see this after all.

After the lecture came the grimmest part of the evening: working the crowd. It wasn't begging for money, Anton constantly reassured Bran. It was seeking support from a like-minded audience who longed for the opportunity to feel included. He and Bran were simply offering that opportunity. A neat bit of semantics there.

As they left the stage, Bran found himself searching for the tall, dark shadow that was Mrs. Stanley. He'd peeked out at the audience before the lecture and spotted her, striking in black. An astronomical body affecting the orbits of those around her. She'd taken a seat in the middle of the room with what seemed like a whole gaggle of other society ladies. He should at least say hello to her before the end of the event, but that meant swimming through the crowd, a whole mass pressing toward them with congratulations or questions or even, they could hope, money. He lost sight of her. She had probably fled, and he'd lost his chance.

A wall of studious-looking men flocked to Bran and Anton, determined to shake hands and ask tedious questions. What models of rifles did they use, what did they hope to shoot with them, how cold would it be before the rifles stopped working, how did they clean their rifles in the cold. A certain demographic had an obsession with the weaponry they carried on expeditions. These men, generally older, watched them down their noses, no doubt imagining how they could have gone on such expeditions in their younger days. Every man who had ever fired a bird gun in his youth believed he could hunt bear, if he'd only had the opportunity. A certain line of thought said that if you wanted to raise money, you must pander to such men, assure them that yes, they were suited to wilderness, they could go themselves into the unknown and do great things, if only they didn't have their businesses, their trade, their responsibilities keeping them at home. Encourage them to see themselves as partners, and their contributions were financial—the money that they had spent their lives earning was intended for this noble purpose. Such men could be flattered into generosity, and you most certainly never implied they'd be dead within days when confronted with true hardship.

Bran didn't hold to this. This might have been because he wasn't any good at flattery and was even worse at hiding expressions of contempt. As he saw it, the purpose of these lectures, the reason most of the audience was here, was for them to make themselves an exhibition. He and Anton must set themselves apart. To insist that by study, preparation, and their very natures, they were special, uniquely suited to thriving in the wild places of the earth. Men like them were willing to put themselves in harm's way for the sake of science and discovery. A noble and specialized calling. A rare breed, exotic, and wasn't it a privilege to know that such men walked in the world? To meet real, hardened explorers should seem a wonder and a privilege, as was witnessing what a great practitioner of Arcane Taxonomy could accomplish. A mystery none of them could understand but might get close to, could claim association with, by contributing.

In any case, he must be polite to their potential benefactors.

A man pushed himself to join the gathered admirers. Bran drew back, startled: Montgomery Ashford. He kept turning up, like mice in the food stores or wet socks. Bran nearly snarled at him. Thankfully, Anton intervened before Ashford could get in the first word.

"Ah, Mr. Ashford, how good of you to come," Anton said, hand outstretched.

Anton was much better at this than Bran was, so Bran left him to it while he kept searching for Mrs. Stanley. Suddenly, there she was, and he caught her gaze. She smiled.

Oh, she looked like a different person when she smiled. A bit of flush in her cheek, everything brighter. He could take this to mean she enjoyed the lecture, which made him puff up a bit.

"Mrs. Stanley, it's good to see you," he said.

"I'm happy I could be here."

She seemed to genuinely mean it, and he felt a little ridiculous, shoving his hands in his pockets and asking, almost bashfully, "Did you like the lecture?"

"I did, very much." She held herself so formally, Bran wondered if she was only being polite. "Though I think it's all compelling enough on its own, I'm not sure you need the Arcane effects." Her smile turned wry, and she spoke low, conspiratorially. "The burst of cold—that was effective. I want to run home and build up the fire after that."

"Caught that, did you? It's supposed to be subtle."

"Not like the aurora?"

"Sensationalist, I know. But it seems to work."

"Maybe next time you could try making the bear growl."

"That's not a bad idea."

"And maybe . . ." She blushed, ducking her gaze. He would have given anything to set her at ease again.

"Yes?"

"The aurora. Maybe you could tell me how you did it. If you're inclined to share your secrets."

She had no one to talk to, he realized. She'd had Harry, and now she had no one. He would tell her anything. "Oh, nothing I do is secret. Not really."

Nearby, he felt Anton stiffen, as if bracing for some attack, and that drew his attention, listening to the conversation in progress.

Ashford was declaiming. ". . . while of course the esteemed Mr. Torrance and Mr. West must be celebrated for their past achievements accomplished, well, many years ago now—"

"Three," Bran said, crossing his arms. "It's been *three* years."

Ashford waved him off, unconcerned, as if saying that three might as well be an eon. "I intend my own expedition to make use of the most modern advances in instruments, weaponry, tools, everything. It will be the most modern cold-weather expedition ever launched."

"The Inuit people have survived in Arctic climates for a thousand years with the most primitive equipment and have done well," Anton said evenly. "Sometimes, simple is best."

Ashford shrugged expansively. "I suppose you would know more about primitive habits and methods, wouldn't you?" Looking him up and down, Ashford raised a skeptical brow. "I would have thought someone of your race would be more suited to traveling in tropical lands. Don't you find the cold and ice goes against your nature?"

"You absolute jackass—" Bran clenched his hands into fists and took a step forward, but Anton touched his elbow, stilling him.

This wasn't the first time some idiot had asked Anton about *his race*, and the idiots never seemed satisfied with the answer. Bran asked Anton once why he never just up and laid one of these clowns out. Anton had said softly, "I don't dare. I must always be amiable."

Those around Bran had drawn back, staring with some alarm. Punching a rival might be pushing his reputation for wildness a bit far. Bran forced himself to settle down.

Smiling indulgently, Anton regarded Ashford's smug expression. "I find suitability for Arctic—and Antarctic—travel has more to do with one's will and training than any fundamental racial nature. The cold tests everyone who dares her climate." He turned from Ashford, dismissing him entirely, to address Mrs. Stanley. "Mrs. Stanley! I'm so glad you could come."

"So am I. Your lecture was enthralling." She'd seemed to regard the confrontation with mild interest, a raised brow just visible behind her hat's netting. Bran was suddenly glad he hadn't punched Ashford in front of her.

"Not Mrs. Harry Stanley?" Ashford asked. And why hadn't he walked away yet? He'd been about to.

Her hooded, wary posture returned. Like that of a hawk about to fly off. "Yes," she said. "And you—"

"Montgomery Ashford. Poor Stanley might have mentioned me once or twice."

She opened her mouth, then shut it quickly, as if holding back words. So yes, Harry had spoken to her about him.

"My sympathies on your loss," Ashford went on. "Poor, poor Harry."

"Thank you," she murmured. "Oh—Mr. West, Mr. Torrance, I'd like to introduce you to my friend—" She turned back and drew out of the crowd an older woman in a frothy dress, soft wrinkled face peering up at them, and she seemed delighted. The dress said wealth, so Bran prepared to be polite again. "Mrs. Harrogate, these are friends of Harry, Mr. Torrance and Mr. West."

"Very pleased to meet you," she said. "I did have a question—"

Bran prepared himself for the worst. Probably something about how he could stand the cold or how many times he'd nearly died. "Of course, ma'am."

"I wondered if I might ask . . . What do polar bears smell like? Or does the cold affect your sense of smell?"

This . . . was actually a good question. A question by someone who was interested in the world. "Do you know, no one has ever asked me that. Mr. Torrance?"

"Me neither. I suppose you'd expect them to smell like the bears in the zoo, but they don't, do they?"

Bran explained, "The cold does affect smell, often simply because we go around with our faces covered, so all we smell is the wool and fur of our wraps. But I think polar bears smell much cleaner than you'd expect, probably from all the time they spend in the water. In fact, they smell a little like wearing a fur coat on a windy day by the sea."

She smiled at this. "Well, that's a lovely image, isn't it? I wish you gentlemen the very best of luck on your expedition and hope to read all about it very soon."

"Madam," Ashford said, inserting himself in the conversation. "If you'll pardon me, my name is Ashford, and I'm also planning an expedition to the Antarctic—"

"Then why don't you all combine your efforts and make the expedition together?" Mrs. Harrogate said.

Well, that was incredibly logical. "Philosophical differences," Bran said curtly.

"Oh, hmm."

Ashford offered a sugary smile. "Yes, involving very complicated logistical details. We wouldn't want to bore you."

Mrs. Stanley maintained some of the closed-in hawk's attitude, the one that suggested you shouldn't get too close. Chin tipped up, she glared, eyes glittering. About to pounce. "I only caught a small part of your conversation earlier, just before we barged into it, and the complicated details seem mostly related to your discounting these gentlemen's years of experience for a bit of flash, whether it's useful or not." She looked at Mrs. Harrogate. "Or perhaps they simply can't decide who should be in charge?"

"Oh, indeed," the old woman agreed. "Men and their ranks, hmm?"

"Mr. Torrance," Mrs. Stanley said. "I saw copies of your book for sale on the table out front, and I do believe I'll buy one. I hope you will sign it for me. And I'd like to pledge a little something to the expedition. For Harry. Maybe you can name a seabird after him."

"Mr. Torrance has a book?" Mrs. Harrogate asked. "I think I'd like one too."

Mrs. Stanley might have given him a wry wink at that. The flicker of expression passed so quickly he wouldn't have put money on it. The pair moved away slowly at the pace Mrs. Harrogate set. The men watched them go.

"What just happened?" Ashford said.

"I think I finally understand what Harry saw in her," Bran murmured.

"Gentlemen, if you'll pardon me, I think I should go autograph some books." Anton tipped an imaginary hat at them and walked off, grinning like a cat.

Bran discovered later that Mrs. Harrogate had made a rather large donation to the expedition, on Elizabeth Stanley's encouragement. Never mind naming a bird for Harry; they'd have to name one for his wife.

James Clark Ross commanded the HMS *Terror* and HMS *Erebus* on a scientific expedition to Antarctica in 1839-43, noteworthy for mapping much of the coastline and determining the position of the magnetic South Pole. The success of the expedition made his reputation—he was knighted soon after. British botanist and Arcane Taxonomist Joseph Dalton Hooker was a surgeon on the expedition, and Ross gave much credit to Hooker's abilities for ensuring their success—protecting the ships in the fierce weather, breaking them free when they became icebound, providing light in the darkness.

However much Ross insisted on the necessity of including Arcanists on expeditions, not all explorers with the British Admiralty approved of their use. In 1845, Sir John Franklin took command of the *Terror* and *Erebus* to launch an Arctic expedition to navigate the Northwest Passage. He specifically excluded Arcane Taxonomists from his crews, believing their abilities too unreliable compared to modern techniques and technology. In private he was overheard declaring that he considered the use of Arcanists to be "a cheat, unbecoming of true officers of the Royal Navy." There is no record of Ross's response to this statement.

After becoming bound in the sea ice, the two ships vanished, all the officers and crew presumed lost. In 1848, Ross commanded an expedition to search for the *Terror* and *Erebus* but was unsuccessful.

The debate on the necessity of including Arcane Taxonomists on expeditions of high risk continues.

TEN

Ectopistes migratorius

Beth received another letter from Brandon West and realized she had never responded to the first. Then Mr. Torrance wrote, thanking her for, well, for lots of things. He invited her to their next lecture—and hinted that she should continue gently persuading society matrons to give money. He wrote with a light touch, friendly, encouraging. He might have been joking; he might not have been.

She did something daring, then: she invited them both to tea. Beth wanted more stories, and talk that involved something other than how sorry everyone was about Harry.

As soon as the letters were sent, she regretted it.

And then didn't regret it. And then she sat in the garden and cried for a minute or two, because Harry would say she should absolutely invite them over for tea. He would want them to be friends.

The hour arrived, and she fussed.

"Is there enough tea? Is it the right kind of tea? I'm sure Mr. Torrance has very specific opinions about tea. Is three cakes enough?"

"Joan's got it taken care of, ma'am. Please don't worry."

Abruptly Beth sat at the edge of a chair. "I used to be better at this."

"Before," Ann said.

"Yes. Before. Ann, why do you put up with me? Surely you could get a better position than this."

"Oh, I like it here. It's quiet. Better than a factory."

Beth tilted her head. "Was that a possibility? You working in a factory?"

"My sisters do, sewing shirts."

Beth realized how little she really knew of Ann. Maybe that should change. The bell at the door rang, and Beth froze.

"I'll just go get that," Ann said mildly, and whatever would Beth do without her?

She was standing calmly, if stiffly, in the middle of the parlor when Ann announced the two gentleman, who, after removing hats and coats, approached tentatively, as if this was not their native habitat.

"Good morning! Ann, will you get the tea things?"

"Yes, ma'am." Ann fled, leaving her alone with them.

"It isn't really necessary. We aren't expecting to be—" Mr. West said.

Mr. Torrance shifted, and West suddenly left off. Torrance had nudged him and now smiled blandly. "How thoughtful. Tea would be lovely."

Ann rolled in the cart, and Beth set about arranging cups and pouring, which gave her something to do besides just stand there. They gathered on the chairs and sofa around the small table in front of the fireplace.

Beth didn't know how to begin. She had invited them; she ought to begin. She sipped her tea and stared at the cup. The two men had good manners but gave the impression that they weren't entirely tame. A bit feral, even. Their gazes darted to windows and doors, looking for escape.

"Mr. West," she said suddenly, "have you seen the yellowthroat in the park? By the south end of the lake. It's probably migrated by now, but it might still be there, if you wanted to have a look."

"Ah . . . no, I haven't. I'm afraid I don't get to the park as much as I'd like."

"Oh, I go all the time. It's . . ." He wouldn't be interested in hearing her confession, that the park was an escape, her refuge, that she relied on it. "It's so close."

"You did mention—I meant that on our last visit, you mentioned that you record all your sightings." He set his cup aside, leaning forward as if he was actually interested.

"I've kept journals since we moved up here. After a couple of years, the patterns really start to come out. This is the latest I've ever seen a yellowthroat."

"May I see? If you're willing to show them."

Same as Harry had asked, years ago. And she'd shown him, he'd proposed, and her whole life had changed. Now, she shouldn't feel as if she stood on the edge of a cliff. That was the grief, welling up. She thought she could trust Mr. West not to impulsively propose marriage to her. He probably wouldn't mock her.

She went to the study to get this year's logs, with dates and lists and tallies. Came back in a rush before she lost her nerve. Set the books on the table in front of Mr. West, then sat back down, hands clasped, fidgeting like some awkward student. He picked up the first and started reading. The pages scraped against one another as they turned. She had started to apologize for her handwriting when Torrance spoke.

"I must tell you again how grateful we are. If you ever feel you have a calling for soliciting donations, we'll gladly give you the opportunity." His smile was kind.

"I'll introduce you to my mother and her society ladies. It's their help you want."

"I may take you up on that. Harry—" Torrance hesitated, as if reconsidering. *Please,* Beth thought. *Please tell me about Harry; tell me what I didn't know about him.* "Harry was so good at navigating these social circles. It's mercenary to say it, but we'll miss that."

"Oh, but it's true," she said. "He always loved going out and meeting people." She brushed the fabric of her skirt, staring into her lap. At least she didn't instantly start crying.

West spoke up before the silence got awkward. "These are good. But you already know that, don't you?"

Beth was entirely self-taught. She'd had no chance at a degree, no hope of recognition. She made all these records because she wanted to. They brought her satisfaction. "Thank you. I want them to be good."

"All these observations right here, not a mile away. I ought to make my students do field studies in the park for practice."

"They'd be less likely to injure themselves, certainly," Torrance said.

"Oh, don't bet on that."

"People can get hurt anywhere," she said abruptly. "There's always a chance. It's just not heroic if it happens at home, is it?" She quickly leaned in to pour more tea. The noise of it seemed loud in the pause.

"You mean Harry," Mr. Torrance asked gently. "If it's not too forward, may I ask what happened?"

She didn't want to talk about it. She could barely think of it. "I'm sorry, but I'd rather not say more."

"My apologies," Torrance said, and the silence grew very fraught.

West cleared his throat. "Have you considered continuing your work? I think you should be able to publish an essay or two under Harry's name posthumously. Then, once you've gotten people used to the idea of you handling his legacy, publish another several with yourself as collaborator, finishing work that he started, and then—"

She listened patiently until she couldn't anymore. "I tried that already. I sent an article to the *Pinfeather*. Mr. Endicott said that because Harry couldn't verify the information, he couldn't publish it."

"That's nonsense," West said.

Did he not believe her? Or was he talking about what Endicott said? She wasn't sure. She was being irrational. "I'm afraid I threw the letter away, or I'd show it to you. I was just . . . angry."

"The coward," Torrance said. "He doesn't know how to deal with widows, I think."

"Few people seem to," she murmured.

"You didn't throw away the essay, did you?" West asked.

The essay was waiting on the writing desk; fetching it only took a moment. Why stop throwing herself at them now? She deposited the pages on the table. The title written at the top glared, brazen: "Observations of Declining Avian Populations." The byline still read Harold Stanley.

Bran leaned back in the chair and read. This was the first time he'd read her work knowing it was hers and not Harry's. Her hands were shaking; she pressed them into her lap.

Mr. Torrance was so precise and polite, cup and saucer perfectly at home in his hands, a picture of Englishness at odds with his reputation as a rugged adventurer. "Harry traveled for fieldwork. You must have accompanied him?"

Gratefully, she answered. "Oh yes. He enjoyed the trips. Not so much the work, but he tried." She smiled fondly. In a cottage at night, they would hear an owl calling outside, and he would ask what species it was. She always knew, and he always seemed pleased that she knew, and this pleased her in turn. "We went to the lakes, the sea, upstate, and as long as I was with Harry, no one thought anything of it." But if she tried to go alone, she'd hear about it from her mother, if nothing else. "We were planning a trip to Florida. I know it isn't as exciting as Antarctica—"

"Florida sounds like a fine trip."

West turned to Torrance. "When was the last time you saw a passenger pigeon? *Ectopistes migratorius*?"

"I hardly pay the sort of attention that you do," he said noncommittally.

West pressed on. "The old accounts of flocks of millions of birds blotting out the sun—have you ever seen a flock of them like that?"

He thought about it and evidently couldn't. She knew he couldn't.

"No one has, not for twenty years," she said. "I've got the dates written down, starting with the journals I kept as a girl. The numbers go down every year, until I stopped seeing them at all. The wilderness Mr. Audubon studied is not the same wilderness we study, and we must stop pretending that it is. I fear the passenger pigeon faces the same fate as the great auk. Is it natural selection when these species are hunted to oblivion?" She paused; she hadn't meant to get so passionate. "There are implications for Arcane Taxonomy—fewer species to catalog means less power to draw upon, and what abilities we have become . . . truncated. At least . . . it could be a possibility. I'm not sure how one would test it."

"Mrs. Stanley," West said. She waited for him to tell her she was being foolish, that any connection between extinction and the reduction of Arcane abilities was impossible. He stared at her and not the pages. "This is good. You're a good naturalist, and it isn't fair that Endicott put you off."

Ah, now the tears threatened. This time, she'd remembered to bring her own handkerchief and dried her eyes. "I know you really believed Harry was the good naturalist. I'm sorry he lied to you."

"He was daft," West said. "He was a dear friend, but he was daft. What was he up to, hiding you from us all this time?"

She'd hidden herself. "It's not considered polite for women to have any aptitude in Arcane Taxonomy." No one had ever paid attention to her family's housekeeper, who had performed her *practica* when no one was looking. But Beth had noticed.

West turned thoughtful, his gaze vague. "All of a sudden . . ." He shook his head.

"What is it?" Torrance prompted.

"I'm suddenly thinking of Mrs. Agassiz. Professor Agassiz's wife."

"Oh—I read the book about their expedition to Brazil," Beth said. "Really fascinating."

"That's just it. She went on all his expeditions, wrote about everything he did . . . and we hardly noticed her. And now. Well, I'm just wondering."

Professor Louis Agassiz, Harvard's famous naturalist—Harry had known him. But he'd never spoken about Mrs. Agassiz. She wrote memoirs, wrote about education and how to recognize young people who might have an aptitude for Arcane Taxonomy . . . she had never just referred to boys. Professor Agassiz had passed away some years before, but if Beth remembered right, Mrs. Agassiz still wrote, still worked, and was starting a college for girls near Harvard.

Might she possibly be an Arcane Taxonomist herself? If Beth wrote her a letter, would she answer?

"Hiding in plain sight," Beth murmured.

"Just so." West held up the pages of her essay. Earnestly, he said, "I'll speak to Mr. Endicott myself."

"That isn't necessary," she argued. "I don't think I really expected—"

"I'll tell him I know that Harry finished this before he died. I'll insist he look at it."

On the one hand, she hoped he succeeded and that the obstacle was this easy to overcome. On the other hand—was her own word worth so little? She reached for her tea so she would have something to look at that wouldn't stare back at her.

"Now, tell me about fossils in Antarctica. I just read an article that said if there are fossils, it proves the climate there used to be very different . . ."

ELEVEN

Zonotrichia leucophrys

Brandon West was born on January 27, 1851, the exact day of John James Audubon's death. It was fate, an omen, a sacred trust to take up the work, to fill his life with the natural world as his predecessor had done. To claim abilities that made him more than ordinary. He could change the world if he simply learned enough about it. But as Beth observed, it was already a changed world from Mr. Audubon's.

In Bran's era, a generation after Darwin, simply describing the natural world wasn't enough. One must hypothesize how it got that way, what it might become, and why. By some accounts, Darwin had undermined the entire field of Arcane Taxonomy. How could one ever hope to know a world that was constantly, inexorably changing? The knowledge of it slipped through one's fingers like air, insubstantial. Bran relished the challenge.

Audubon hadn't been a scientist—*scientist* was barely even a word in his day. He was a man who had talent with a rifle, paintbrush, and a bit of taxonomy. That was enough, back then. He conveyed information, accomplishing an astonishing feat of description and observation. His images were still the standard. His painting of the great auk was nearly all that was left of the bird. Men like Wilson and Audubon had been largely self-taught or worked by sponsorship and apprenticeship. The whole system was so much more organized now, regulated. There had not been so many universities in Audubon's day. Bran could not simply paint pictures and expect to make a name for himself. Mainly because he was a terrible artist. One had to be endorsed. Recognized. Make connections, join an institution, earn a rank.

That had been a struggle. He was a good naturalist and a better Arcane Taxonomist, but his family didn't have connections. None of them had ever gone to university; they knew no one in business or politics or society. Bran had studied with borrowed books and scraped together pennies to follow a destiny somewhere else. When he'd learned that every living thing had a name and the Latin started rolling off his tongue . . . then, the world finally made sense. But then he had to prove that he belonged. The other men at Harvard hadn't grown up side by side with the birds in the fields and orchards of his home—he had the advantage there. But they looked askance at his old hand-me-down suits, until Harry got him to a tailor for something better. In the end, they couldn't argue with his scholarship.

Then what of Beth Stanley, who he had to admit was also a good naturalist and Arcanist, and who also did not fit in the current structure of taxonomic classification? Harry should have said something. He should have told Bran about Beth—Bran would have understood. He would have *helped*. Harry had never said a word about Beth, because he wanted the glory for himself, and for that, Bran was so angry at Harry he was trying to remember what he ever found attractive about the man.

Charm. The man used charm like some kind of weapon, like a snake hypnotizing its prey, and before you knew it, he had his coils around you. There must have been some sort of Arcane talent behind the ability.

Bran had met Harry at Harvard, which was a common enough story as to be unremarkable. In fact, later, Bran couldn't rightly recall the first time he met Harry. They must have encountered one another at a lecture, a club, or some meeting. They must have seen one another across the room multiple times before finally meeting in a way that mattered: names exchanged and remembered, a conversation of substance that entered the memory instead of melting away at the end of the night.

"You seem like the kind of man who has a favorite bird," Harry had said in the aftermath of a lecture, during which a man who had known John James Audubon personally had spoken about the necessity of precise fieldwork. Bran had been riveted, and Harry had noticed.

Bran had laughed. "The osprey. It's so suited to its habitat and purpose. So elegant. And a much better fisherman than myself."

"This is what I love about ornithologists: you don't just say your favorite bird, you immediately have to say why, as if you have to justify yourselves. It's endearing."

"You speak like a man who doesn't have a favorite bird."

"Well, you see, I'm not a very good ornithologist. Harry Stanley." He'd held out his hand for shaking.

"Brandon West."

"Do you drink, Mr. West?"

"I do."

"Then let's go get something. I'm parched."

Bran had paused, taking a moment to regard the man. To study him as a naturalist would. The impeccable grooming, the fine tailored suit. His utter ease. The casual glint in his eye. This man was in his natural habitat.

Bran said, "Not afraid to be seen with the country boy with his patched-up coat and faded tie?"

Harry had smiled. "On the contrary. The suit makes you different. Different is interesting." Bran had blushed at that.

They had drunk a lot during their years at university. And talked, and traveled, and gone to every meeting of the Harvard Natural History Society, every lecture delivered by every explorer and naturalist and geologist and anyone else who had an interest in learning how the natural world worked. When Bran emerged as his class's most promising

Arcane Taxonomist and was taken in hand by Professor Gray himself, Harry had been the only one of their cohort not furious with envy. Harry had been thrilled for him. "Power through proximity, my friend," he said. He'd seemed content with watching the work unfold rather than having a hand in it himself.

One evening, Harry claimed not to understand a word of *On the Origin of Species*, which prompted half a dozen fellow aspiring scientists around him to leap in to explain it to him. That was when Bran realized that Harry didn't go to all these meetings and lectures for the knowledge. He went to watch the audiences. He had an interest in the topics, yes; he never seemed bored. But he'd gather a group of men around him, get them talking, arguing with animation and broad gestures and rising tones of voice, and Harry would look them over with a satisfied, possessive air. He understood Darwin just fine. He just wanted the men to talk at him about it.

Noticing this the first time, Bran felt a sudden overpowering need to get Harry alone, to himself. To see that appreciative gaze turned on him alone.

After a late night and a lot of drinks, Bran leaned close to Harry. Tried to whisper, though that was a bit beyond his control at that point, and said, "Harry, you're useless as an ornithologist, but you might have aptitude as an anthropologist."

"Anthropology," Harry said, looking at him. "The study of man."

"Yes. Exactly."

"Bran, love, I think you're right."

Bran had courted a couple of girls. Been to a couple of concerts and dances around campus and felt terribly out of place. The girls were pretty, and most of them were kind, but he never seemed to say the right things around them. They'd look him up and down and could tell he didn't have much money. It was yet another hurdle to overcome. If he had found one who liked to talk about birds, he'd have chased her down.

If he had found one who looked at him the way Harry was looking at him, with a kind of adoring hunger . . .

It had taken two more nights before Bran got up the nerve to invite Harry back to his room on the pretense of . . . something. Loaning him a book, or showing him a picture, or something. He couldn't remember exactly what; he just remembered flushing as he closed and locked the door and Harry strolled around the cramped space, studying the mess, the books and journals, fishing rods and plant presses, pins and paper everywhere. Harry drew the curtains tightly closed while Bran stammered and sorted through his desk, looking for whatever it was he thought he was supposed to show Harry that he couldn't remember. He'd forgotten that he'd invited Harry at all—hadn't Harry invited himself? That would be just like him. But no, Bran had only himself to blame. He should have done it weeks ago.

"Surely you've got some etchings around here somewhere?" Harry had asked finally.

"What?" Bran looked over his shoulder, rather stupidly.

Harry had taken off his jacket and was loosening his tie, which he drew away from his neck and deposited with his jacket. "Etchings. You know." He raised a brow.

Bran's heart beat faster, and his breath became shallow. An interesting physiological response. "Oh. Oh yes. I get it."

"Good," Harry had murmured. "Do you know why I like the Natural History Society so much?"

"You . . . are drawn to the wilderness. You're looking for answers to why . . . how . . . the world is the way it is . . ."

"Oh no. I joined because it's full of such very good-looking men."

That had set Bran on fire, and Harry knew it.

"Sit down," Harry said.

Bran immediately obeyed, sinking onto the slim wooden chair by the desk.

Harry straddled him, climbing right up to his hips, pressing heavily there with nothing but the fabric of their trousers between them while he looked right in his eyes. "Would you like to commit sodomy with me, Mr. West?"

Bran had very nearly come apart under him right there, but he managed to put his arms around Harry while they kissed.

And that was Harry, and he was lovely, and with him Bran had learned this quiet confidence in his own body, his own physicality, moving through the world with the idea that this was what bodies were for. He didn't even mind hiding so much because he turned it into cherished secrecy, a treasure too precious to be revealed. Imagine, looking at married couples out in the world and knowing that they were all fucking. While two men could be friends and no one ever suspected, because most people's imaginations couldn't comprehend. At least that was what he told himself.

He missed Harry. Harry had been so . . . warm, delightful, funny. A fool and a wise old man at once. The intimate moments they had spent together had felt chaotic and unreal; they had made him dizzy and happy. Full of shame, and learning to not care about the shame took some courage, and Bran believed with all his heart that the courage he learned from Harry had taken him into the Arctic. Let him do impossible things that he wouldn't have imagined otherwise. Good things.

Most of all he was grateful for Harry because when Bran met Anton, he'd recognized that feeling rising up, recognized the look in Anton's eyes, and been able to leap instead of hesitating. And he knew to always lock the doors and draw the curtains tight. To make sure to never stand too close to Anton in public, and certainly never touch him beyond a slap on the shoulder. In the wilderness, none of that mattered.

When Harry had announced his marriage, Bran had been . . . confused. Harry had never spoken of interest in women, much less marriage. He was like Anton, settled in the world of men and seemingly happy there. Unlike them, Bran was often torn. He thought *everyone* was beautiful. Men, women, everyone. They were all part of the world, and the world was beautiful. He'd loved Harry; he loved Anton. And sometimes, a slender neck and froth of silky hair caught his eye. It was a failing, he was sure. In places like the Naturalist Society, he knew just where he stood. In society . . . not so much. And what of Beth Stanley, who seemed to exist between the two worlds?

He had never spoken to Harry of any of this and wished now that he had.

As a boy, Anton Torrance had loved reading about exploration. He had books full of accounts of the great English explorers, from Sir Francis Drake and Captain Cook on up to Sir James Ross and Sir John Franklin. He was English like them, through his father, and yearned to be part of that tradition.

On the edge of adulthood, he realized he didn't just want to be one of them—he wanted to be *with* them. He would study the engraved portraits at the front of the books, admiring them, the farseeing looks in their eyes, the steel in their backs. He wasn't just in love with exploration. He was in love with *explorers*. As soon as he could, he raced to join them.

He quickly learned that portraits were idealized, images designed to evoke admiration. Reality was rarely so polished. On his first couple of expeditions, he met brave men and cowards; studious men and brazen; brilliant men and dull. He'd faced bullying and kindness from them. He'd loved two or three of them, but best of all he'd learned to master the cold with them. The reality was better than the static paintings.

Bran had caught his eye because he wasn't as polished as those formal portraits. He was rough and honest. Anton was in love with exploration, but Bran provided the why of it: discovery and knowledge.

Anton and Bran returned from the '76–'77 Greenland expedition with stories of their own to share at the Manhattan Naturalist Society. They might not have broken new ground or set records, but their work was still impressive, their survival even more so, given the unexpected storms and difficulties on that trip. It had been good practice—every day spent in the Arctic meant learning more about that environment, which made the next expedition a little easier. They returned to the chambers of the Naturalist Society to acclaim, endless toasts, and demands to tell all. Anton did so, and Bran bore the attention well enough. Get him talking about the differences between tern species and he could be positively animated. But he'd never feel at home in places like this.

Bran's reputation as an Arcane Taxonomist had been made on the expedition, when he broke the *Indominable* out of pack ice before they got locked in for the winter, literally shaking the ice to pieces, creating passages of open water the ship could traverse and saving them from becoming the next *Terror* and *Erebus*. He'd been granted his First Rank for it. "Our own Ross and Hooker," the men praised him and Anton, naming the great explorer James Clark Ross and his Arcanist, Joseph Dalton Hooker. The label was prophecy, Anton hoped.

In the halls of the Naturalist Society, Anton enjoyed standing at Bran's shoulder and soaking up the praise.

Shortly after their return, a particular gentleman cut through the crowd right for them, and Bran's expression lit like a lighthouse beam. The stranger was average height and build, unimposing. Paler than members of the Naturalist Society usually ran—so many of them spent most of the year out in the sun and weather. This man spent more time indoors. He was well turned out, at ease, amiable. He had a friendly, teasing light in his eyes, and he focused wholly on Bran after sparing an appreciative glance for Anton.

"The conquering hero returns!" the newcomer said and clapped him on the shoulders. Bran laughed and clapped him right back, and their gazes lingered on one another.

Ah . . . , Anton thought, *I was not his first.* He'd known that; Bran had been far too comfortable to have been new. Good at knowing what he wanted and what his partner might like in turn. Anton drew his mind back to the moment at hand.

Bran turned then to Anton and went stricken, eyes widening in a sort of suppressed panic, looking back and forth between them. The next moment in the social script should have been his, to make introductions. Anton could step in and rescue him by introducing himself, but he was rather enjoying Bran's confused moment. The gentleman's lips pressed together, stifling laughter—he had made the same calculations Anton had and had come to the same decision to let Bran swing a little.

"Um," Bran said. *Good start, lad,* Anton almost told him. "Um. Anton. This is Harry Stanley, an old friend. My good friend." Bran was now blushing *delightfully,* a pink shade under the stubble along his jaw. "Harry. This is Anton Torrance. Well known, and all that."

"Your partner in the grand adventures," Harry Stanley teased. Bran blushed harder.

"*Good* friend, eh? Pleasure to meet you, Mr. Stanley." They shook hands on it, making far too much of Bran's discomfort in introducing his former and current lovers to one another. Poor Bran.

"The pleasure is mine," Harry purred. "A real honor."

"Gentlemen. Please," Bran got out around a clenched jaw.

"Steady there," Anton said, patting his shoulder, and that broke things up.

"In all seriousness," Harry said to Anton, "I'd like to thank you for keeping him safe. For making sure he comes back to us."

This touched Anton. Pleased that someone else recognized Bran's worth, perhaps. Pleased to have all the elements of their partnership recognized. "You're quite welcome, sir."

"I . . . have a bit of news of my own." He ducked away, shuffled his feet a little. Even after a few moment's acquaintance, Anton knew Harry wasn't a man who normally had difficulty with words. But he was awkward now. "I ought to tell you before you read about it in the society pages. I'm getting married."

"To a woman?" Bran said, louder and with more astonishment than he should have.

"That's generally how it's done, yes."

Bran seemed poleaxed. *"Who?"*

Harry shrugged. "No one you know. Her name's Elizabeth. And she's . . . special." He wore a fond smile when he said this.

"God, Harry, I go away for a couple of years, and see what you get yourself into."

Harry smiled shyly.

At the time, Anton hadn't known Harry well enough to understand that this was shocking, that Harry had never shown an interest in women, much less marriage. If it were anyone else, Anton would have said Harry really loved this girl and was ready to leave behind his wild bachelor ways. But Bran was behaving as if a chickadee had just brought down a hawk. A man he should have been able to read had become illegible.

In a fit of politeness, Anton stuck out his hand. "May I offer my hearty congratulations?"

Harry brightened and shook on it. "You may. Thank you. And now I want to hear all about the expedition. Tell me—what was the very worst day, and what was the very best day?"

Anton immediately thought of getting caught in the blizzard, the fear that they would never find the ship again, Bran's brush with frostbite, and what followed, the needy kisses, the desire for more, though they'd succumbed to exhaustion, and how they'd managed to never be apart for more than a few days since then.

"I think they were the same day," Anton said, even though he'd never be able to explain. Bran met his gaze; the warm look there said he felt the same.

Over the next several years, Harry launched his career as a naturalist in earnest with a series of surveys and essays with pointed observations and intriguing speculation. He had finally settled down, people said. With a wife to manage him, he had become productive. Some rumors said he'd even begun to develop signs of Arcane abilities.

In hindsight, all became clear.

When the Young Ladies' Art Society made a trip to see an exhibition of Audubon's paintings in a gallery in Midtown, Beth was sure to attend. She wouldn't miss it. The girls brought their drawing books and pencils and were meant to make a sketch or two to practice their technique, and Beth dutifully carried hers tucked under her arm. She might sketch, but first she wanted to be sure she saw every single painting, memorized the names of every single bird, noted which ones she had seen herself and which she had yet to see, and learned their markings. These were still some of the most detailed paintings ever made of many of these species, and the colors were brighter and clearer than in preserved specimens she had seen.

She had managed to detach herself from the group, making her way into the next room of the exhibition. Other people were here, but she paid them little attention, intrigued by the painting of a great blue heron, its neck twisted oddly to fit on the page. She had seen herons with their necks held low and twisted like that, when they stalked the shallows for prey, but this particular image seemed unnatural to her.

"It's crass to say it, but it looks dead, doesn't it? With its head hanging down like that?" A trim man standing at the next painting over had said this. The next painting was a collection of warblers, wings spread, calling to each other on the branches of a flowering tree.

She looked at him sharply. He might not have been aware that he'd spoken out loud—he was gazing at the painting of the heron, not her. She should have moved off, ignored him, anything. But she couldn't resist.

"That's because they are," she said. "Most of the birds he painted were dead. He shot them, then posed and painted them. He wanted them to look alive. I think some of his attempts are more successful than others."

"Oh? I'd heard he used Arcane *practica*. Put them to sleep in order to capture them peacefully, that sort of thing."

"It was Alexander Wilson who did that. In all Audubon's portraits he's holding his gun, have you noticed? I'm sure he shot them. But he could make his paintings move. He would give lectures and use his paintings to demonstrate behaviors, like woodpeckers knocking on trees or robins feeding their young." With Audubon on hand, the painted heron could stretch its neck, stalk the wetland step by lanky step, and stab a fish in the shadows. She could almost picture it herself.

"It must have been quite a thing to see."

"But when an Arcanist dies, their *practica* go with them. I don't think these will ever move again." She might try one day, to recreate Audubon's work . . .

He looked back at her wonderingly, as if she herself were some new species that had never been observed before. His gaze narrowed. "Can you, ah . . . do that thing with the candle? Light the wick just by touching it?"

Stunned, she tried to stammer denials, but her mouth had gone dry. She glanced around to see if anyone had heard him. She should flee from this strange, forward man.

"I beg your pardon," he said quickly. "I don't mean to presume. It's just that the way you talk about this, the way you look—it reminds me of someone I know. An ornithologist. A talented Arcanist. I made an assumption." He was handsome, dark hair combed back from a clean-shaven, bright-eyed face, with an aristocratic look about him, like someone out of an old painting, but the fit of his fashionable suit might have contributed to that. He had a daring bit of blue in his necktie and an easy way of standing, as if he was happy to be wherever he found himself.

She was flattered that she reminded him of an actual real ornithologist.

"Yes," she'd murmured.

"Yes . . . what?"

"Yes, I can do the thing with the candle." She'd smiled slyly.

"Mr. Harold Stanley," he'd said, offering his hand. "But I'd be pleased if you called me Harry." He'd winked.

He was so forward she was shocked into liking him immediately. She shook his hand, which felt daring. "Beth Clarke."

Beth usually enjoyed art exhibits because she wasn't expected to talk to anyone. But the wink had stirred something deep in her gut. She knew nothing about him, his family, his profession or whether he even had one, but she wanted to know more.

"So," he said, and turned in place, surveying all the paintings. The older couple who had been in the room left; they were alone now. Very nearly scandalous. "Which is your favorite?"

"The white-crowned sparrow," she'd said without hesitation, pointing to the painting on the opposite wall. "They're so jaunty, they look like they're wearing little caps."

"Excellent. I like them too."

Reviewing the memory in later years, she decided that this was when Harry became interested in her. He'd gotten a thoughtful look about him, studying her like she was one of the paintings. He liked talking to people—could talk to anyone in nearly any situation; it was a real talent. But that moment, when he made her go around the room and name all the species while he covered up the labels, as if it were some kind of game, and she was laughing impolitely by the end of it while he became more and more thoughtful—that was when he'd decided to pursue her. They'd agreed to meet again at the exhibit, and then he'd asked to call on her.

She'd thought he was the easiest man in the world to talk to, and that was more than enough reason to let him pursue her. Thank goodness his family turned out to be respectable and well to do, full of lawyers and investors, very acceptable to her family of lawyers and investors. The pursuit was encouraged. By the time they married, she had stopped feeling as if he pursued her and more that they were running a race together.

Beth wondered now whether she had fallen in love with Harry or whether she had fallen in love with the life he offered. Meeting Harry had been a stroke of cosmic luck that would never happen again. Their shared career had felt like an adventure. He would be an equal among the friends he admired. She would be able to do whatever she liked. When he'd died so unexpectedly, she couldn't decide if she was still racing and had left him behind or if he had left her stuck in place, with no feet. Where had her feet gone?

TWELVE

Sterna paradisaea

Bran gathered in a corner of the second of the Society's halls with O'Connell, Heinz—both Second Rank—and Wentworth—Fourth Rank—and a few others. He was trying not to stare at Endicott, who was in an armchair by the fire, reading Mrs. Stanley's essay. Wouldn't do any good to loom over the man, so he'd left him alone.

They were clustered together, murmuring like starlings. One could usually spot the Arcanists at the Society like this—they all seemed to have these hooded, distractable expressions, as if their minds constantly turned elsewhere, to some lush wilderness or to the skies with the *Columba livia* outside. They obsessed over details: the identity of a bit of feather in the brim of a cap, the patterns of the clouds overhead. It was all patterns, and it all meant something—mastery. They could unlock cosmic secrets if they only found the right name, the right words. A hundred and fifty years since Linnaeus, and they still hadn't gotten to the bottom. It was bound to make anyone distracted.

"How long do you think you could hold your breath, then?" Wentworth asked Heinz, who'd been experimenting.

"I'm up to ten minutes."

"And then what do you do with it?"

"Survive drowning. Underwater salvage."

Bran hadn't given the topic much thought, but now he did. He tapped his finger against his chin—rough with stubble, he'd forgotten to shave again, dammit. "You want class Mammalia, not Osteichthyes—if you want to hold your breath and not breathe underwater, which I'm not sure is even possible—"

"—without the proper anatomy," O'Connell put in.

"Exactly, all the Arcanism in the world won't help you then."

"I'm not trying to turn into a fish," Heinz said, exasperated. "Just *not drown.*"

"*Physeter macrocephalus.* Some whaler logs say they can go ninety minutes without coming up for air." Now Bran wanted to try it, if he could get his hands on a sperm whale to catalog. Maybe if he went along on a whaling trip . . .

Arcanists tended to go around hunched in and distractable—except for Montgomery Ashford, who carried this smug grin like he planned on lighting a firecracker under your foot. The others continued on about whales and seals and how else they might use Arcane Taxonomy to escape drowning, but Bran—distractable indeed—watched Ashford glad-handing every Society board member between here and the door. Finally, Ashford came up to lean on the back of Heinz's chair, forcing Heinz to shift around in order to see him.

"Ah. Ashford," Heinz said. "The topic is surviving underwater. Might be useful on an Antarctic expedition."

"Might," Ashford said. "You'd need aquatic mammals, I think?"

Bran stewed—that was his idea.

Heinz nodded. "That's what West says. What's down there, anyway? Sea lions?"

"It's seals," Bran said. "Weddell, Ross, leopard, a couple of others."

O'Connell drained his tumbler of whiskey and set it on the table. "The problem with Antarctica is there isn't enough life down there to fill a bathtub. Arcane *practica* will be useless."

"Hooker wasn't useless," Heinz said.

"It's a bad assumption that there's not any life down there," Bran said. "It's just different than here, or even the Arctic. Cataloging the place will be like starting from scratch, and that scares you."

O'Connell glared. "*Scares* is an awfully strong word, West."

"It is," he said. "But if that continent doesn't scare you, then you're not paying attention."

Ashford tsked sadly. "He's making it sound terrible so he looks all the better for wanting to go. It just needs the right man for the job." He gestured, indicating he was clearly that man.

Bran congratulated himself on keeping his mouth shut.

"There's plenty of expeditions to go around. Wentworth's heading to Patagonia in the summer," Heinz said.

Wentworth was the youngest of the bunch, just out of Princeton. He'd frozen part of the East River in the middle of summer to celebrate, and that had put him on the map. Not the whole river, and not enough to actually walk on, but it was a good start. An expedition would get him his next couple of ranks, and then he could start making a name for himself. He shrugged modestly. "Just a collecting trip."

"Can't wait to read the catalog," Bran said. The young man flashed a smile.

"I still say the future is in commercial work. Prospecting, security." O'Connell tilted his glass.

Some scoffing answered this. "Security? That's not any better than joining the army!"

Bran turned thoughtful. "He's right. Business is where the money is. The problem is the *practica*. If you can't share what you learn because someone else owns it, where does the power go then?"

Standard Oil made its prospecting Arcanists sign agreements— the *practica* they developed while employed there could never be used for work outside the company. They couldn't publish. They were well paid but isolated. The Naturalist Society and other organizations had protested: such restrictions were monopolistic and threatened to stifle innovation. But so far no one had had the courage or resources to sue.

"Does it matter?" O'Connell shot back.

Heinz narrowed his gaze. "What've you got cooking, O'Connell? You've got a job you haven't told us about?"

The man gave a thin smile. "I can't tell you."

More scoffing. Bran got a sinking feeling. Over the coming years, how many Arcanists were they going to lose to mining companies and steel mills? Was he just being nostalgic for the days of Humboldt and Audubon?

Endicott was still reading.

"It's not like a single company can claim a monopoly on nature itself," Wentworth said. "Can they?"

Ashford tapped his chin thoughtfully. "Has anyone tried hitting up a private company for funding? Sell Standard Oil the idea of vast reserves in the Antarctic?"

"There's no profit at the poles," O'Connell said. "Just the glory of being first."

"Isn't that enough?" Heinz countered.

The North and South Poles were possibly the most tantalizing blank spaces on the blackboard that Anton yearned after. It must be possible to reach them—but no one had yet figured out how. Bran believed that the one man who had the best chance of accomplishing the feat was Anton Torrance, and he wasn't an Arcanist. He wanted it for the sake of it. To be the name in that spot on the board. Bran didn't care so much about the spot on the board; he wanted to go because he would see things no one else had. One couldn't be an Arcanist without having a sense of wonder, he believed.

But Ashford wore a hungry, challenging look, and he caught Bran's gaze with it. "If it were simple, someone would have done it already. West?"

"It's not simple at all, and it's a mistake thinking there's some trick to it," Bran said. "You've got the magnetic poles, the true poles, the space between them, the evidence that they change over time—"

"Evolve," Heinz said wryly, and Bran nodded.

"First thing you do is pick your target, right? All due respect to your experiments, Heinz, but I'm less worried about drowning than I am about navigation. Compasses stop working. The sun goes strange. We spend a lot of time just trying to figure out where we are. That's a problem I want to solve."

Ashford added, "That's a problem Standard Oil would love to solve."

"I don't care about Standard Oil." He was getting an idea. Birds didn't need compasses. How could he tap into whatever native instinct they used? Compasses lined up with the magnetic field, but what if there was some way to . . . shelter the instrument? When the lines of the magnetic field converged on the pole, what if the compass could still, somehow, point true? "Does anyone have a compass? Wentworth, go get me the magnetite out of the mineral cabinet in the next room."

"Wonderful, West is thinking out loud again." O'Connell wasn't a fan of public experimentation, which probably explained why he didn't see a problem with corporate ownership.

Bran was too caught up in the thought to worry about anyone stealing his ideas. It might not work, and even if it did, another Arcanist wouldn't have the same connection. This wasn't engineering.

Sterna paradisaea, he thought. He'd try that.

Heinz handed him a compass, a simple instrument in a brass case. Bran held it flat in his hand, turning one way and another, watching the needle, its direction stable toward north—magnetic north. Just like it ought to be.

Wentworth eagerly trotted up with a chunk of rock in his hand. An audience had gathered, the handful of Arcanists and another dozen members besides, clustered at the edges of the room. Bran was wholly engrossed in the compass and the piece of magnetite.

"Bring it up, Wentworth. Right next to the compass."

This had turned into a demonstration, and Bran used the magnetite, the lodestone, to show the effects of magnetism on the compass. Instead of following north, the needle followed the stone. He raised the compass over the stone—and the needle wavered, struggling to point straight down. A child's experiment. The field generated by the stone sent the equally magnetized needle spinning.

But what if it didn't? If Bran could insulate them from each other . . . make the compass like the arctic tern, unerring in its direction, not influenced by outside forces. Voices around him faded; the room grew quiet. With that quiet, the compass needle steadied. Ignored the pressure from the lodestone and settled on the greater influence of magnetic north.

Wentworth gasped, and the other Arcanists crowded in to look.

Heinz crossed his arms. "And that, gentlemen, is why Mr. West is a First Rank Arcanist."

And Bran lost his hold. The needle swung away, confused again by the lodestone. Suddenly tired, he ran his hand through his hair and sighed. He needed to get his hands on some paper to write this down. He wasn't sure where he could take this *practicum*, but he wanted to work on it.

Ashford was staring. "Did you just nullify a magnetic field?"

"What? No, not at all. It's more like trying to separate the influences of the two—"

"But if you *told* people you were controlling the magnetic field . . . the *planet's* magnetic field . . . imagine—you could shut down navigation all over the world!"

"But that isn't . . . I don't think . . ."

"You're a mercenary, Ashford," Heinz said.

"We'll see, we'll see," he said thoughtfully. "Gentlemen." He offered half a bow and walked off.

Ashford didn't have a plan. Couldn't. He wanted them to think he did, and he wanted Bran to ask. Bran stayed quiet.

"The poles are far too cold for me," O'Connell said, pretending to shiver. "Give me the Amazon."

"You can have it," Bran said.

"Mr. West?" Endicott waved the pages of the essay from the armchair.

"Excuse me." He tried not to rush over.

Endicott gestured, and Bran took the chair across from him. Just two men, colleagues, seated by the fire. Nothing to be nervous about.

"You're well acquainted with Mr. Stanley's work?" Endicott asked.

Mr. Stanley didn't do any work, he thought, but tried to appear earnest. "I'd say so. We were at Harvard together. Worked together ever since."

"Ah, of course. This is very good," he said, tapping the pages. "More, it's important. Of course we'll put it in the *Pinfeather.* We'd be remiss not to."

When Mrs. Stanley sent the essay, Endicott probably hadn't even read it. The ass. Bran indulged in a second of smoldering rage and considered setting the man's chair on fire. But he didn't.

"That's just what I thought."

"Did Stanley leave behind other nearly finished work?" Endicott asked. "Would you be willing to take on putting it together? It would be such a good thing for Stanley's legacy."

"I'd be happy to," he said, very flat, clenching his fists. Should he remind him that he'd dismissed Mrs. Stanley out of hand? And have him withdraw this offer in a fit of pique? No. Say nothing.

"Excellent. I'll find space for this in the very next issue. Maybe you could write up a memorial tribute to go with it."

Bran could hardly breathe from trying not to shout. "I should be able to."

Just think of it: *Harold Stanley, the lying charlatan, hiding behind his wife's skirts, that charming bastard, my first love . . .*

"Such a shame," Endicott said, and the way he said it, the tone of voice, the pitying shake of his head, grated on Bran even more. They all said it in just the same way, abstract and meaningless. "I understand it was a sudden illness but didn't hear any details. It's a bit ghoulish to ask, but I'm curious—did you hear anything?"

The naturalists wanted to put a name to everything and pin it to a board.

"I'm afraid not," he said curtly.

Bran salvaged his politeness, thanked Endicott for his time, and made his escape. The goal was won. Best he didn't ruin it over trivialities.

Anton was at the desk, writing letters, when Bran stomped in and went straight for the sideboard and poured himself a drink, without saying hello, barely looking at Anton. He'd spent part of the day at the Naturalist Society and had likely had a drink or two there as well, so he was definitely drowning something.

Either his quest to get Mrs. Stanley's essay a fair reading had gone awry or he'd had a run-in with Ashford. Perhaps both. Anton set down his pen, leaned back in his chair, and waited for the explanation.

"Well?" he prompted. Bran leaned up against the back of the sofa, glaring at the floor. He was looking particularly rugged today—his tie was gone, yet again, if he'd even bothered to put it on in the first place, and he'd been pulling at his collar. His hair needed a trim. His gaze was alight, and Anton could almost see thoughts burning behind his eyes. He was wild, alive, everything Anton longed for in the world. He enjoyed letting Bran spool out his thoughts aloud.

"How would you do it?" Bran asked. "Get to the pole. How would you plan it?"

"Which one?"

"Either. North, start there."

Anton had spent years working out the shape of the plan. Every trip north he'd made had been to practice the skills for such a plan. "We'd go up in the fall and winter over. Get a ship that can handle being frozen in the pack ice. Make the push for the pole in early spring, when there's sunlight but the sea ice is still frozen. That's the trick: we need that solid stretch of ice to get there and back. Two or three teams of sleds and dogs, one to break the trail and the others to carry gear."

"If I could learn to freeze the pack ice, keep it frozen, we could start later—"

They had discussed this. It was a sticking point. "And if you couldn't?"

"Light and heat," he said, persisting. "Those wouldn't be a problem."

"We'd still need to pack fuel. You can only do so much."

Bran held the tumbler but hadn't drunk anything yet. Anton wanted to sit him down and ask what was really wrong.

"What about south?"

"South . . . I don't know. We *can't* know, yet. We literally need the lay of the land and to learn how far the pole is from shore before we can plan."

"So it's a navigation problem. What if I could fix compasses? So they work at the poles? So they always point where we need them to?"

"That might help, but it wouldn't be a deciding factor."

"Ashford's up to something. He made . . . noises. Using outrageous claims to sell his expedition. But if he really could . . . well, who knows what he could do?"

That clarified what at the Society had gotten Bran riled up. "He's blustering. Trying to aggravate you, and I daresay it worked."

"What if he's found a way? Some . . . taxonomic *practicum*—"

"Do you think such a thing exists?"

"Well, no. But that's the point, isn't it? I don't know. I don't know everything. I'll never know everything. None of us ever will; we're all just muddling along. We don't know what's possible."

"Which is why we're planning this trip, isn't it? To get closer to learning what's possible. Stop thinking about Ashford."

Finally, Bran looked up, looked right at him. "Would you even need me on the trip? You never seem to make plans that include Arcanism, much less *rely* on it—"

Ah. That was the problem. The thing was, Bran was right—Anton would never make a plan that would fail without having an Arcanist along. He always made redundancies. If Bran knew he wasn't as enthusiastic about the use of Arcanism on expeditions as Ross was, it would break his heart.

"Both plans, north or south, rely on hunting seals for food, and you are the best man I have ever known for that, outside of the Inuit peoples. You always have light on hand, and I wouldn't trade that for anything in a polar winter. Who knows what else you might discover? I always look forward to that. Besides, you have all the skills you need without Arcanism. Assuming you can keep your socks dry."

"So. We can do this, you think?"

"God, Bran, I know we can. We need the both of us together for this, and Ashford doesn't have that."

Bran set his still undrunk glass aside and strode across the room to throw himself into Anton's lap. Anton gladly swept him up and held him close.

That night, Anton dreamed of ice.

The frozen world was quiet. Muffled, rather, because it certainly wasn't silent, but the sounds one heard were otherworldly, nothing to do with ordinary human experience. The groan of a calving glacier, the thick slosh of near-freezing water knocking up against the ship's hull. A crystalline quality to the air that seemed piercing, but only to the imagination.

This was the sound of his dream, where he moved through cold air thick with anticipation and foreboding. He stood on a rocky waste. It must have been summer: the sun was low, unmoving, and would not dip below the horizon. Some thirty meters off was a cairn marking one of the *Indomitable*'s supply caches. A pile of stone four feet high, pyramidal, with an iron stake driven in at the top to which a packet of oiled leather containing logs and letters was secured. Anton needed the supplies—he had not eaten in days. Confidently, he moved toward the cache. It receded. He tripped on a stone, and the rocky plain transformed into a maze, and though he never lost sight of the cairn, he couldn't get any closer. The cairn moved, the land shifted, his boots failed him, his legs froze, he could not move, and then he rolled away, as if gravity itself had betrayed him.

He called to Bran for help, but Bran wasn't there. Never was, in these dreams. Anton was quite alone.

Realizing this was a dream only added to his frustration, because he ought to be able to control his own dream, he ought to be able to simply wish himself beside the cairn and make it happen; this was his own mind betraying him. That frustration stayed with him as he became slowly aware of his bed, the pillow under his head, the darkness, and the clock ticking in the next room.

Bran lay next to him, breathing hollowly, right on the edge of snoring but not quite. Naked, wrapped up in the sheets, legs flung out, hugging a pillow, looking ridiculous and alluring at once. They'd ended up in the same bed tonight. They didn't always—they had two bedrooms, on the chance that they'd need to prove that they had two bedrooms, two beds, and therefore no reason for anyone to be suspicious. Sometimes they even slept in the two beds, usually when Bran was up late, reading, copying notes, working on some problem. Or when Anton got too restless and drove Bran to find rest elsewhere.

But tonight, and most nights, they were together.

Anton rested his forehead against Bran's shoulder and tried to go back to sleep.

"Hmm?" Bran questioned, not fully awake. His eyes didn't open.

"Having trouble sleeping."

Bran made a sound, spoke no words. Full of understanding, he took hold of Anton's hand and pulled it around his middle. Went straight back to sleep, and as long as he lived, Anton would never understand how Bran did that. Anton still would not be able to sleep, but here he could remind himself that he wasn't alone.

Spiritualists and occultists believed one could find meaning in dreams. The meaning here seemed to be annoyance. Obstacles. No dread, just . . . not being able to get to where he was meant to be. He wanted to go back to the ice.

"You know what you need?" Bran asked suddenly. So he wasn't asleep after all.

"What?"

"You need to get out of the city. Someplace where you won't hear another human voice. Just for a few days. That usually makes you feel better. Maybe the lakes?"

Anton thought about the cool glacial lakes northwest of the city, deep and still, surrounded by forests, blanketed in quiet. At once, the knots in his shoulders unclenched. He was able to ease himself more firmly onto the mattress instead of holding himself rigidly against it.

"That'll do. Yes."

"Then we'll go. As soon as we can. I'll telegram ahead and see if the little inn at Seneca Lake can put us up. We'll bring our fishing tackle."

"That sounds . . . marvelous." A few days would hold his need to travel at bay for a little while. He was a fiend for it, like it was opium.

"Get some sleep now, right?"

Anton held on to Bran and did just that.

THIRTEEN

Gallus gallus

Beth's mother came over for tea, again. Letting her do so was easier than arguing. If Beth refused to let her in, Mrs. Clarke would send doctors, and that must be avoided. They would tell her that Harry's things, what they would assume were Harry's things—the specimens in the study, all the books and journals, the map with its pins—were affecting her nerves and she ought to get rid of them, and she would have to argue with them. They would say she was hysterical, and that might lead to more revelations. If they discovered her Arcanism, either they wouldn't believe it at all or they'd see it as a symptom rather than a talent.

Best to avoid this.

The mail arrived in the middle of the visit, and Beth took the stack of letters to the desk while her mother talked and sliced cake. Beth hoped that eating would slow her down some, but she managed to eat, talk, and still be elegant. Barely dropped a crumb.

"This is lovely, isn't it? I'm so glad Joan has stayed with you. Not all cooks would, in your situation."

With only one person to cook for. Without a whole household. Beth almost asked what her mother really meant by this, but she already knew—Beth needed a new husband.

"It is, yes. Ann has been wonderful as well."

"Your girl? I suppose, but she's a bit forward, isn't she?"

Ann, still at the doorway after bringing the tea service, glanced over, brow raised. Beth sighed deeply and didn't answer.

"Any interesting letters?" Mrs. Clarke asked.

"I'm still looking." A couple of letters were from her observers in the south. A couple were for Harry, of course. And . . . one from Brandon West. This one, she opened right away.

Mrs. Clarke went on. "What's this I hear about you being at a lecture at some college or other? That you went alone? Beth?"

"I'm sorry?" The question was startling, and she stumbled over both the denials and shame-filled explanations that were so reflexive. Why must they always question her, and why must she always feel like apologizing?

"A lecture. At the university. *Alone.* Mrs. Harrogate said she saw you, and I couldn't imagine why you would be there."

Bran's letter was in her hand, unfolded but unread.

Beth stared at her mother. "Are you spying on me?"

"Of course not, dear. We were simply talking, and the topic came up."

It wasn't Mrs. Harrogate's fault. *She* hadn't seen anything wrong with going to a lecture by herself. Why should any of them care what she did? It made her want to go to lectures alone every night for the next month.

"Friends of Harry's invited me. Do you remember Mr. West and Mr. Torrance, the famous explorers? They were at the funeral."

"Oh, well. Perhaps next time you might invite myself or your brother or *someone* to come along, so you don't have to go alone."

Beth was a grown woman who didn't need to be chaperoned. The whole point of being married was so that she would no longer need chaperones.

She turned back to the letter.

Dear Mrs. Stanley:

I'm not sure if this is good news or not, but Mr.
Endicott has agreed that "Observations of Declining
Avian Populations" should be published and will
appear in the next edition of the *Pinfeather*. That the
same essay when submitted by me was acceptable and
when submitted by you was not—well, it rankles.
You tried to warn me, I didn't listen, and for that I
apologize.

We have another piece of data in the ongoing
experiment, at any rate. Congratulations. The essay
really does deserve to see print. If I may be of further
service, you have only to ask.

Regards,

Mr. Brandon West

She understood his sentiment exactly: She was thrilled that the
essay would appear in the *Pinfeather*. She was incensed that Endicott
would not deal with her directly. Maybe Mr. West had the right way
of looking at it: this was a piece of data, a single observation. Record it
and move on to the next. See what happened. She could do that. She
must write to him and thank him.

"What do you think, Beth? Will you come?"

She was startled all over again. "What? Yes? Yes, I think?"

"Oh, good. It's just a small gathering, friends and close family. Will
so wants to see you. It will be good for you to get out. Trust me, you'll
feel better."

What on earth had Beth just agreed to? She wasn't sure she dared
ask. Will, her brother—dinner. They'd been conspiring to get her to
dinner, and she must have just agreed to it.

Well. How bad could it be?

Beth began to consider Ann's advice to faint if the dinner grew too difficult, and she hadn't even arrived yet. She could faint right now. Horse's
hooves clopping, the carriage turned onto a tree-lined street, nearing
Will's neighborhood. This would all be over soon . . .

"Beth. You know you're still quite young."

"Mother." She said this as a warning.

"Your reputation—"

What *was* her reputation? Beth had no idea. A pool of darkness in
widow's black, moving silently through the world.

"—you really should think of marrying again."

No. A thousand times, no. It had been mere weeks; grief still had
hold of her.

She could do a hundred things to get out of this. She felt in her
bones that she could. *Charadrius vociferus* would drag a wing alongside,
pretending it was broken as it led predators from its nest. A decoy, a
distraction. What distraction could she implement? Break the wheels
off, fill the carriage with smoke. Cause a crack in the road itself, an
Arcane earthquake to divert their path, like the root of a tree coming up
through the pavement. Wouldn't her mother be so surprised? Surprised
enough to call the doctors.

Beth did nothing but whisper a few words to induce calm in herself.
A gliding swan, a soaring hawk. *Cygnus olor.*

"I went through all that once already. I don't see why I have to do
it again." She had money. Harry had provided for her. She had a home
and time to try to find some meaning for herself, and she meant to do it.
Reputation as a philosophical concept had become vague to her. Who
was reputation meant to serve? Herself, or everyone else?

"Just think about it. That's all I'm asking."

Beth was thinking entirely too much already, but she offered a con-
ciliatory smile. Postponing the debate rather than settling anything. She
shut her eyes for a moment and took a deep breath because yes, tears
threatened. She would not cry here.

If she behaved pitiably, then maybe people would pity her, and if people pitied her, maybe they wouldn't try so hard to talk to her. Then again, to be treated so *strangely*, like some infected creature, was untenable. She wanted to feel normal, and never would again.

Mrs. Clarke held Beth's arm as they went up the walk from the carriage to the door. "Now, this is all family and friends. You needn't worry about a thing; just let us all take care of you. I hope you'll let us take care of you. You haven't asked for a thing since the funeral."

Yes, she had asked to be left alone, but no one listened to her.

"I don't know what to ask for," she said. She wanted solitude. Peace. A trip to the coast to walk in the sand and study shorebirds, and she wasn't sure how she was supposed to manage that sort of thing now without Harry. Especially when going alone to a lecture across town had scandalized her mother. How was she ever to go anywhere? Well, Mr. West and Mr. Torrance wouldn't be scandalized. Briefly, fleetingly, she thought of asking to go along on one of their expeditions.

Beth dreamed of eccentricity. To let her hair loose and dress in wild rags, just so everyone would leave her alone. But they wouldn't leave her alone; that was the trouble. If she tried to go wild, she would be taken away to a hospital and tied to a bed.

If she told her mother she needed the sea air for her health, maybe she could make the trip. Once there, she could figure out how to get away. A small plan was better than no plan. She would think on this. The tears went away.

The door opened, a butler waited to collect their coats, and voices echoed in the foyer.

"Mother! Beth! How are you?"

Her older brother, Will, was tall and dashing, perfect in every way, or so she had thought when she was a little girl. He could climb the highest trees, shoot anything with a rifle, and run faster than anyone, and he was smart and won all the arguments. Whenever she tried to follow him, he laughed. At first, this made her want to try harder, until she realized he hardly noticed her trailing behind him. So she stopped trying at all. She was a chicken trying to soar with an eagle.

She had thought he would make a marvelous naturalist, that he could be like the Arcanists in the dime novels with the striking covers. But he wasn't interested. He shot birds without ever really looking at them.

They'd grown apart since he went away to school, then university, then a law practice, then a marriage. They had almost become friends when she married. As two married adults they'd had more in common than they'd ever had as children and had finally had something to talk about. Harry had seemed to like Will, who never realized what a compliment that was. Now, Will treated her like a very fragile vase that ought to be kept in packing.

He came and put his hands on her shoulders and gently kissed her cheek. Looked deeply into her eyes, but she doubted he actually saw her. "Oh, Beth, you're so pale. We need to get you outside. Come to the parlor. Sal's been looking forward to this, and you can meet the rest of the party."

"I've been outside. I've been to the park," she said, but he didn't hear her.

They shuffled into the parlor like a herd of cattle.

His wife, Sally, was next, coming forward, grasping her hands, tsking over her until Beth felt smaller and smaller. She smiled wanly and was grateful that no one seemed to expect her to say anything except *Thank you* and *You're very kind*. She said these phrases over and over again.

And then Will said, "I hope you don't mind, but I've invited a couple of friends I'd like to introduce to you."

Damn her arrogant brother for this.

He steered her to the first of these friends, who had risen from the sofa.

"May I introduce Mr. Ronald Benson. He's just come down from Boston to join the firm. We expect great things of him. Benson, my sister, Beth Stanley."

He was average height, with a trimmed beard and searching dark eyes. A good suit, pride and dignity, all the markers of a well-to-do gentleman of business. He held out his hand, and long-ingrained habit made her take it, and her heart thrummed when she thought he was going to raise it to his lips. *For God's sake do not let him kiss my hand.* But he merely squeezed and dropped it again.

"So pleased to meet you, Mrs. Stanley. I hope you'll accept my condolences on your loss."

"Thank you. You're very kind." Her tongue was sticking, and she would do anything for a glass of water right now, but she had to suffer without.

Will steered her to the next bachelor on offer. "And this is Mr. Montgomery Ashford, a client. I believe he was friends with Harry, over at the Naturalist Society? He's an Arcanist, you know."

Polished and poised, Ashford smiled blandly, stepping forward to greet her. Once again, habit made her arm reach out to his offered hand.

And what was she to do with this?

"We've met," Beth said, salvaging calm out of her anger.

Will seemed shocked that she spoke at all. "Oh?"

She smiled thinly. "As you said, a friend of Harry's."

"How lovely to see you again, Mrs. Stanley," Ashford said politely.

If she was going to faint, now would be the time to do it, but she did not.

Small talk followed, and jostling, both eligible bachelors offering their seats to her while she chose an entirely different one. Every choice she made this evening would mean something to them; it was intolerable. Finally, the housekeeper announced that dinner was served, and Will and Sally led them all to the dining room. Beth clung to her mother's arm rather than accept an escort from either of the gentlemen.

She prayed for the strength of eagles.

Ronald Benson was seated directly across from her. Montgomery Ashford to her left. Her mother was at one end of the table, Will at the other. Sally was near enough that maybe Beth could talk to her instead of the two men. Or she could play wan and pitiable and not speak at all.

Benson studied her the entire meal, smiling every time she chanced to look at him and asking far too many questions in an attempt to start conversation. She answered with only one or two words and at one moment saw her mother looking back at her with such an expression of anticipation. Or was it pity? Hardly mattered; Beth only felt some relief that someone noticed that she wasn't doing well. Beth caught her gaze and silently pleaded with her, *End this; get me out of here.*

But the conversation moved on, and they were only on the fish course, and if she tried to beg illness to flee, they would all think she was pregnant, and she refused to give them that satisfaction, so she sipped wine and waited. It really was too warm in here.

The fact that Ashford didn't impose himself on her almost endeared him to her. He studied her as much as Benson did, but at least he was quiet.

Will was explaining what a good position the firm was in, especially with the addition of Mr. Benson. "We all know Benson will go on to do great things."

"You flatter me, Will."

"Well, yes, but only because you deserve it. A man should know his own worth."

"Leavened with some humility, I hope," Mr. Benson said, glancing at Beth, as if looking for her agreement. She stared at her plate. "I'm looking forward to getting to know the city better. New York has a personality all its own. Mrs. Stanley, if I might ask, do you have a favorite spot? A favorite pastime? Where would you recommend I go to see the city's best?"

"Central Park," she said instantly.

"Oh?" he said, sounding surprised, and that surprise doomed him. "Do you ride, then? Or are you one of the ladies who enjoys a promenade?"

She met his gaze. "I watch the birds there. A hundred and forty-two different species of birds have been recorded in the park, and I mean to see them all. I've seen seventy-six so far."

An awkward silence followed this, until Ashford leaned in. "That's more than I've counted there, and I have a professional interest in the matter. I'm impressed."

"Thank you," she said softly.

"I suppose a naturalist of any stature must have an interest in such things, but I have to admit it seems a little obscure to me," Benson said.

She couldn't stay quiet. "I think that one of the beautiful things about birds is they aren't at all obscure. Everywhere you go, every continent, in the middle of a city or the farthest wilderness, we find birds. They are so . . . reliable."

"Mr. Stanley was a great naturalist," Ashford said. "It's admirable that you take such an interest in his work."

It was the other way around, she thought.

"You should try the theater, Mr. Benson," Sal jumped in, to spare further floundering, and the conversation shifted as one course was removed and the next brought in, and more wine was poured, and the evening dragged.

Finally, the meal ended, and they retired to the parlor. Beth took an armchair so no one would sit with her and yet wasn't at all surprised when Ashford managed to sit nearby, claiming a chair and shifting it close. Better him than Benson, she supposed.

"I get the feeling you'd much rather be in the park right now. Looking for owls, maybe?" He spoke low, just for her.

She studied her hands. "I do like owls."

"I regret not knowing Harry better than I did. I suppose his will left his collection and work to Harvard or some archive."

And there they came to it, what they all assumed.

"I'm keeping it. Harry left his work to me."

"Oh? Then you must be quite familiar with his research."

Why was this such a surprise? "What exactly do you want to know, Mr. Ashford?"

His smile was indulgent. "I'd heard that he was helping Mr. West in his Arctic work. I just wondered if you knew of any insights he might have had about polar exploration. About magnetism and navigation, maybe?"

"There's speculation that the magnetic field influences the migration of birds."

He raised his brows suggestively. "If you allow me to look at his notes, I might find some useful information there."

She had made lists, and Harry had passed them on to Mr. West. Various *practica* she had been working on, observations that had inspired them. Harry could be circumspect; he was merely offering West suggestions. Her work became useful, by this route. Was that what Mr. Ashford sought? Did he have any idea what he was asking for?

"I'm not really sure I can help you."

"Harry must have relied on you a great deal."

Startled, she met his gaze. She shouldn't have reacted at all, but she couldn't hide her surprise.

"We relied on one another," she said.

"Oh, of course. I just . . . I hope you'll consider ways you might continue your husband's work. I would like to help. If you'll have me."

It very nearly sounded like a proposal; maybe she was being oversensitive. "Mr. Ashford, we've only just met."

"And yet we have so much in common."

"You being here this evening—was it your idea or my brother's?" She suddenly wondered how recently Ashford had become a client of Will's firm. Very, she suspected.

He only smiled.

She couldn't help it. Well, she could—she was entirely in control of herself—but her patience had come to an end, and her fear of any consequences quite vanished. *Dryocopus pileatus* could murder trees with its bill, driving into wood until it was shredded. All she did was put a little notch in one leg of Ashford's chair.

The next time he shifted, it cracked all the way through.

The chair collapsed under him, and he let out half a shout, tumbling over once before ending up sprawled out, spilling sherry everywhere. "Good lord!"

Beth took the opportunity to leap up and away from him, hand to her breast in feigned shock.

From the floor, Ashford looked right at her, caught her gaze, and his eyes were round, wondering. He was an Arcanist himself; he recognized exactly what she'd done.

Will and Sal swooped in with apologies, picked up Ashford and put him back on his feet, and called a maid to clean up the mess. Beth went to her mother and whispered that she'd had enough. Her mother whispered to Will, and excuses were made.

Before she could make her escape, Mr. Benson rushed to take her hand one more time, and Beth only bore it knowing she would be gone soon.

"Mrs. Stanley. This has been an absolute pleasure. I do hope you'll allow me to call on you at some future date."

"No," she said, her voice breathy and horrified. She tried again, reaching for politeness. "That is, I'm still very much in mourning, Mr. Benson. I'm simply not in a state to be good company. I'm very sorry."

"I quite understand." But the chilled look on his face said that he did not.

From across the room, Ashford studied her with that expression of calculating wonder. Like he was sizing her up and speculating about her taxonomic designation. She quickly looked away.

"I'll see you out," Will said, ushering Beth and their mother to the foyer, where they retrieved coats and waited for the carriage.

Beth couldn't leave without a word. "Will, I know you mean well, but please never do anything like that to me again."

"Do what?" he answered blithely, chuckling as if she had made a joke.

"Throw men in my path. I'm barely ready to see people I like, much less strangers with designs on me. How dare you!"

"Beth, really, you're being dramatic—"

She stormed out.

After some long minutes, her mother followed. They must have had some conversation. Beth might hope her mother had told Will that Beth was not anywhere near even thinking of marrying again. A more terrible possibility existed: that Mrs. Clarke had known all along and even encouraged Will to invite eligible men to dinner. The longer Beth thought about this, the more it seemed likely.

"Did you know?" Beth asked when they were in the carriage.

Her mother put on a look of false innocence, same as Will. "Know what?"

Disgusted, Beth looked away.

"It's just that we're all worried about you, cooped up all by yourself. You'll have to get out again sometime. At some point you really will need to consider marrying again."

Beth said nothing. What was there to say? Especially when no one listened to her.

Her mother went on, and on. "I wish you'd had children. I think this would be easier if you had a child to occupy you."

Easier, raising a child without a father and having to endure all that extra pity besides? What madness.

"You might think of coming back home to live with your father and me until you're feeling better."

Absolutely not. No. Never. She would not move backward; she would not leave behind her garden, her study, her books. She wouldn't leave *herself* to go backward.

"I'm very tired and would rather not speak about this anymore." Beth turned to the window. The carriage rolled on.

The next day, a package arrived, its label declaring the gift to be, with compliments, from Mr. Ronald Benson, and Beth's heart fell. This was so deeply inappropriate. He hardly knew her. Did he think to bribe her to his side? It was like he saw a chance and pounced.

When she opened the box, she felt a terrible, explosive rage: packed inside was a hat decorated with feathers. An entire bird's wing, preserved and mounted, white and gray, streamlined, sweeping in a graceful arc along the pale-gray brim. Belonging to some variety of gull, she thought. No way to tell which species, without the rest of the bird. It was obscene. A card inside read *For your enjoyment of birds, with respect, Mr. Ronald Benson.*

Alive. She wanted them *alive.*

The package included a note from the milliner informing her that in Arcanist lore, gulls meant peace and grace. As if any Arcanist power could be conveyed by this monstrosity. Most people wouldn't know any better.

Gulls were scavengers. They took what they could, and they knew how to weather storms.

Ann found her in the parlor, crying, and not just over the hat and the bird that had been killed for vanity, but for all of it. For not being seen, not being listened to. For being alone.

"Ma'am?" Ann knelt by her chair, her worry plain.

"What am I supposed to do with this?" Beth shoved the box at her. "I can't wear it. I won't. God, he will expect me to wear it. I can't ever see him again, that's all. I've never been so . . . so furious! I'll send it back to him. It's inappropriate for a strange man to be sending me gifts in any case. He ought to know better—they all ought to know better."

"I'll pack it right back up, then."

"Thank you." The parlor had a small desk in the corner, more decoration than of practical use, for a lady to look pretty while she wrote letters. It had paper and pen, at least, and she immediately wrote the note.

Dear Mr. Benson,

I must return this gift. However thoughtfully it was meant, I don't believe it is appropriate for me to be receiving such tokens at this time. Also, you might have missed the nuance that my preference is for birds that are *not dead*.

    Respectfully,

    Mrs. Harold Stanley

Mr. Ashford had merely sent a note telling her how nice it had been to speak with her and how illuminating the evening had been. Very decorous.

Ann lingered. "I'm not sure I should leave you alone just now. You're unwell."

"I am, aren't I?"

"Oh, ma'am. Shall I fix a bath up for you?"

"Will it make me feel better?"

"Not sure, but it's a nice distraction."

Distraction, yes. There were not enough distractions in the world.

Normally at bedtime, in the normal from before, Harry would be talking. Their room would be filled with his voice. Telling what he'd done that day, passing along conversations he'd heard, silly things someone or other had said, with the hope that she would laugh—she usually did. Asking what she'd done and answering himself because he already knew. Sometimes she would stop paying attention. Not maliciously, but the words sometimes were less important than the sound, the rushing stream of good-natured commentary Harry seemed to need to make on his whole life. If she hadn't been there, he would probably talk to himself. She would already be in her dressing gown, having emerged from her room, where Ann had unbuttoned and unlaced her. She would sit quietly and brush her hair, watching and listening while he prepared, clothes off, nightshirt on, coverlet on the bed turned back.

She would join him there at last, and they would kiss. Usually, especially as time went on, she would kiss him first. She liked kissing him. They made love, and she liked that, too, though it seemed an effort for Harry. What of the lust of men she had heard so much about, the ravishing that filled so many scandalous novels? Beth would like to be ravished, she thought. But that wasn't Harry, and as time went on they came together less and less. He would kiss her, hold her hand, and fall asleep, and she would stare up at the dark ceiling, hurting, with no idea what to do about it.

There must be something wrong with her, she had concluded.

"Could I have done better, Harry?" Her voice fell hard in the still room, making the air shiver, rattling her ears. Maybe she could get a canary, some finch that would sing and fill these hard silences. She rubbed her thighs, imagined his kiss, and the flush she felt was bittersweet. She lay back and stared up at the ceiling, still hurting.

In the morning, she wrote to Mr. West to tell him about the encounter with Ashford and ask if she should be worried.

Inevitably, the practice of Arcane Taxonomy came to be utilized in warfare. While Benjamin Franklin's plans to recruit Arcanists to the cause of the American Revolution never came to fruition, Napoleon Bonaparte's ambitions in Europe made full use of these resources, mainly in the person of Georges Cuvier, who was appointed an imperial councillor. Cuvier, France's great Arcane Taxonomist, expanded the Arcanists' field of study to prehistoric creatures as well as the living, earning him a designation as the father of paleontology. From the material evidence of a vast and different world that had once existed—the possibility of transformation—Cuvier drew a relentlessness and a profound sense of awe that served Napoleon's empire politically and militarily.

Cuvier advocated the idea of catastrophism—that profound changes revealed by the geological record came about not through gradual processes taking millions of years but through abrupt, catastrophic events that molded the surface of the planet and caused periodic mass extinctions—to explain the vast fossil record. He found ways to bring catastrophism to the battlefields of Europe.

But catastrophism was a flawed hypothesis that could not explain all the features of Earth's geology or of the incredible diversity of its life. A widely accepted theory explaining the process of speciation—evolution by natural selection—would come later. Meanwhile, Napoleon's army fell victim to the risk that all

Arcanists faced: to name a thing was to know a thing, but not sufficiently knowing the thing one wished to draw power from risked failure at the very least. In an attempt to turn a catastrophe upon one's enemies, one risked bringing that same catastrophe on oneself. Napoleon believed Cuvier was the most accomplished Arcanist in Europe and that all the French Arcanists who had been trained by him must also be the best. However, German naturalist Alexander von Humboldt's Arcanist abilities rivaled Cuvier's, and he had been secretly training a cadre of Arcanists in Russia. They caused food stores to rot, broke up roads with crevices, and burned fields before battles could take place on them. They were a force that Napoleon's army simply couldn't overcome.

Cuvier's scientific reputation was strong enough to survive Napoleon's defeat, but his uses of Arcane *practica* in warfare served as a warning to later naturalists, many of whom resisted recruitment into military endeavors. The problem, many believed, was killing. Arcanists drew their power from knowledge of the living world. Turning that knowledge to the practice of death increasingly struck many as an irreconcilable contradiction.

One notable exception was the career of Dr. Amos Alexander Evans, who served as surgeon aboard the USS *Constitution* during its most famous battles in the War of 1812. His skills contributed to the ship's victories against the superior British navy: he controlled the weather gauge in battle and could change the course of cannonballs. This was in addition to his ordinary skills as a surgeon. Evans went on to earn a medical degree from Harvard and was named the American navy's first surgeon of the fleet. He worked toward the application of Arcane Taxonomy in the realm of medicine and healing. Since then, most Arcanists in the American military have been surgeons.

FOURTEEN

Dryobates pubescens

"You did *what?*" Bran stared at her with frank admiration. "Oh, I'd have paid good money to see that." Anton laughed outright.

"It was very childish of me. But satisfying. At any rate he was asking questions about Harry's work, and now he knows about me."

Bran was offended more than seemed reasonable at the idea of Ashford courting Mrs. Stanley.

They had arranged to meet at the park, at the footpath entrance on the east side, near the Met. She'd been waiting; the men apologized for being late, and she insisted she was early. Finally they got past the awkwardness to take their walk down toward the lake.

This late in the season, the outing required coats. Well, Bran required a coat. Anton never seemed to feel the cold. Or rather, he relished it, striding along with his face to the sun as if it were a lovely summer day. But the leaves had turned, and the air had a chill.

Mrs. Stanley's coat was full mourning black, like the rest of her wardrobe. Even the fur trim around her neck was black, along with her hat and elegant gloves. She was a shadow moving through the world.

"Must you do anything?" Anton asked. "He knows, but does it change anything?"

"I wouldn't worry for myself, but he hinted that there was some information that he expected to find in Harry's work that would give his expedition an advantage. He talked like a spy. If he knows that I did the work, if he thinks he can use me against you . . . well, I won't stand for it."

"He thinks there might be some Arcanist power in magnetic fields." Bran pursed his lips and considered. "Harry and I had been speculating—but that means you and he had been speculating, doesn't it? Is there anything to it?"

"The planet's magnetic field might play a part in bird migration." Her gaze went vague—her face scrunched up and seemed even younger when she was thinking. "There's power there, certainly, but whether an Arcanist could access it—I think you'd need to talk to a physicist. But physicists aren't Arcanists. I think it would be more useful learning how birds' ability to navigate during migration might give one access to the poles rather than obsessing over the poles themselves. The magnetic poles are not the same as the true poles, after all, and the true poles are what matter to explorers."

Again, Bran had this blazing-clear vision of why Harry had married her. When given free rein, when she felt safe, well, she just spilled over, didn't she? She drew her ubiquitous notepad out of her bag and started writing. Anton smiled wryly over her bent head.

After a few more steps, Anton asked, "By any chance do you have any interest in Ashford? Socially?"

Bran almost yelled at him about asking such a rude question, because of course Mrs. Stanley wasn't interested in him. And why did he care so much what she did, anyway?

Mrs. Stanley shook her head. "I can't say that I'm socially interested in anyone right now."

Bran was relieved—and also, oddly, disappointed.

None of them walked at the same pace. Anton marched. Anton was always traveling straight on toward some destination at the horizon. Every now and then he realized he'd gotten too far ahead to hear their conversation and slowed down. But he could never walk slowly for more than six or seven paces before his natural tendency toward speed came to the fore again.

Mrs. Stanley had the casual stroll of a society lady, graceful and elegant—and necessary, with the long skirt. Bran had never really paid attention to how women managed their clothing: the stiff posture necessitated by the bodice, the sweep of the long skirt, folds of fabric draped to the ground. He would have thought such clothing impractical for the outdoors, but she seemed at ease, lifting the hem over grass, pushing the drape of skirt with a hand when she turned this way or that. It must have been easy for her; she'd been doing it her whole life, hadn't she?

Bran walked at a pace between them both, eager to keep up with Anton but also lingering to look at a plant or a bug, an interesting slope of branch, or the way light reflected off the lake. He found himself ricocheting between the two of them, hurrying to keep up with Anton while hanging back to talk to Mrs. Stanley, who also stopped frequently to look at a bird or a branch. Several times, she made a mark in her book.

"That's twelve," she said, apparently at random.

Bran was confused. "Pardon me?"

"Feathers from twelve different species of birds on ladies' hats."

Bran glanced over his shoulder to look again at a middle-aged society matron with an impressive wide-brimmed hat pinned to her carefully styled hair. A cascade of long gray tail feathers drifted off the back. *Ardea herodias*, great blue heron feathers, he wagered.

He'd honestly never thought of it before, the sheer number of dead birds displayed on women's heads.

"It's the fashion, I suppose," he said, a bit lamely.

"There's no power to it. It's vanity."

They went on. Bran listened for birdsong. Ahead, Anton shaded his eyes to look across the lake. Bran had started toward him, to ask what he'd seen, when Beth suddenly marched a few steps off the trail. Fumbling at her bag, she drew out a set of opera glasses. Anton had told him about her opera glasses, and he hadn't quite believed it, but here she was, staring through them at a patch of foliage.

He squinted at where she'd focused her attention. Not even a flash of movement. Annoying, to think she had better eyes than he did. He practiced patience, letting his vision go soft.

"I don't know what it is." She sounded amazed, as if she ought to have known. No one knew the birds of the park better than she did—he'd seen her journals. He, famous Arcanist Brandon West, could admit that.

Then Bran saw it, a warbler-size fluff of yellowish feathers. It flitted to the end of a branch, visible for a moment before retreating back to the shadows.

Glasses still at her eyes, Mrs. Stanley waited, unmoving, for it to reemerge. A couple of passersby on the path turned their heads to stare at her. It *was* odd, a primly dressed woman intent on a patch of shrubbery as if it were a stage. She didn't even notice. Bran was as intrigued by her as by the bird.

And there it was again. If Bran had his gun, he could shoot the thing and examine it thoroughly to determine the species.

"Hold this," she said, handing him the glasses and going back to her purse for her paper and pencil.

If he was going to hold them anyway, he might as well try it, though the men at the Naturalist Society would laugh at him if they saw this. He looked through to where the mystery bird had reappeared against a backdrop of brown leaves. He was astonished to see details brought into clarity. Not perfectly, not like a good nautical spyglass would have done. But he saw the bird's round black eye and details of plumage on its head and wings.

Predominantly yellow, black at its eye, gray blue along wing and tail. "It's a blue-winged warbler," he said, but he couldn't keep the doubt out of his voice.

"Not with that much black on its throat," she answered. She was scribbling notes and making a sketch.

"Lawrence's, then."

"Not enough black on its throat." On such details were taxonomic feuds built. "What's the pattern on its wing?"

"Bars, I think. Yellow?" Should have been white, if it was a blue-winged. It didn't make a sound, so they couldn't identify it by its calls. If he could shoot the bird and get it in his hand . . .

It flew off, gone.

"I've never seen that species before," she said with something like triumph. She made a few more notes. "I'll check the cabinet when I get home."

"I can look at the collection at Columbia as well."

"Oh, that would be lovely," she said, smiling happily. He'd never seen her so happy.

He offered her the glasses back, venturing a question. "Did Harry give you these?"

"Oh no," she said. "I had these before we were married. He did give me a pair for my birthday one year. Mother-of-pearl, absolutely beautiful. Too nice to bring to the park."

In fact, the simple brass pair in her hands looked beat up, as if she'd been bringing them to the park for a long time.

Ahead, Anton had stopped to wait.

"I'm afraid we're holding up Mr. Torrance," Bran said, throwing Anton a smile. Anton smiled back.

Mrs. Stanley frowned. "Oh, I'm so sorry—"

"Not at all," Anton said, backtracking to rejoin them. "It's a pleasure watching good naturalists at work. You're enjoying the expedition, then?"

"Oh yes," Mrs. Stanley said. "An expedition to the far-off wilds of Central Park."

"It's all in the mindset," Anton said. "Anything can be an adventure. Any day outdoors is a good one."

"He would rather be someplace colder, I think," Bran said.

"This is all the expedition I'm likely to embark on for the foreseeable future." Serenely, sadly, she gazed over the water of the lake.

"Surely not," Anton said. "Look, Mr. West and I are going to Seneca Lake next week, before winter sets in. The summer crowds will be gone; the leaves are turning. It's a perfect time. Do some observing, a bit of collecting, some fishing. Do you fish?"

Bran froze. The lake was supposed to be an escape, just him and Anton. The conversation raced on without him before he could figure out how to politely argue. He tried to catch Anton's gaze, but the man was refusing to look at him.

"And it would get you out of town and away from Ashford and any other unwanted suitors," Anton added.

Bran couldn't argue after that.

"Harry and I used to go there in the spring. There's a wonderful little inn in a village right on the southern end."

"The Morgans'? I'm the one who told Harry about that inn," Anton said.

Bran found his tongue. "Would it be appropriate, a widow traveling alone?" With two unrelated men—

"Hang propriety. She wouldn't have to tell anyone, would she?" Anton chuckled like a man who'd been hanging propriety all his life.

Bran raised a questioning brow, trying to convey all his arguments in the expression. Anton merely raised an eyebrow back, like a dare. There he was, marching forward, relentless.

Mrs. Stanley got a flush back in her cheek. "The Morgans know me. I could bring my sketchbook. Do a little writing. It sounds . . . yes." Her following sigh was filled with longing.

"It's settled, then," Anton said. "We'll collect you on the way to the station."

She looked so happy after that, Bran felt like a heel for wanting to argue.

They finished their tour and took the path back out to Fifth, and then Anton insisted on walking her home. At least she didn't invite them in for tea. They were able to make an escape. The afternoon light was fading. They'd spent *hours* walking with her.

"We should visit the park more often," Anton said on the way home. "That was delightful."

"You could have asked me first before inviting her." He sounded harder than he meant to. This was getting under his skin more than it should.

Anton glanced at him. "What's the matter? You've gone all surly."

"I'd rather not have to look after her on what's supposed to be *our* trip."

"I think Mrs. Stanley could look after herself if anyone ever gave her the chance. That poor wounded creature needs rescuing, can't you see it?"

He could, that was the trouble. "That doesn't mean we're the ones who need to do the rescuing."

"Who else will? Ashford?" he said.

"What's he up to, do you think?"

"Trying to get his hands on Harry's work. Like the rest of us." He had the gall to wink.

FIFTEEN

Gavia immer

Beth did not flatter herself to think the strange warbler—here far past the season, all by itself—was a whole new species. One simply didn't find new species in Central Park, ground that had been thoroughly gone over by naturalists for over a hundred years. One had to go to the Amazon or Antarctica to discover new species these days. To bestow a name and all the power that went with it. She had never dreamed of such a thing for herself, but her fingers itched, thinking of it.

Still, she could find a bit of power here by identifying it, naming it true.

Looking over her notes again, she considered that it might have been a blue-winged, as Mr. West had suggested, but there were a couple of other species with similar markings. This one didn't match any of them entirely. The coloring of the wing wasn't quite right; the pattern on the face didn't quite match. It might have been molting, and this was part of the challenge, wasn't it? Where was the line between variation within a species and a whole new species? Linnaeus himself had grappled with the question. What happened when those lines blurred?

Meanwhile, she had an expedition to prepare for. Could Beth be so grandiose as to call this an expedition? Not with Anton and Bran along.

This was merely an outing for them. A jaunt. Hardly worth mentioning. But to herself, she called it an expedition.

Ann put up an entirely proper argument about the trip. Beth didn't care.

"Should you go alone, ma'am?"

"I won't be alone."

"You know what I mean."

"Am I to spend my life cooped up, then?"

"Of course not, ma'am." Ann was helping her pack, and Beth kept telling her to put things away—she wasn't going to need dinner clothes or good hats or anything but a couple of walking dresses. The maid regarded her skeptically. "Do you think . . ."

"Think what?"

"That you'll marry again?" Ann winced, as if she could guess Beth's answer.

No other thought made her so tired just now. She should want to marry again, shouldn't she? Shouldn't she want to avoid the prospect of spending her life alone? On the contrary, solitude had seemed like a fine idea lately. To be alone meant not having to explain herself to anyone.

"The chances of finding a husband who will put up with a wife who spends so much time with birds are very small, I think."

"Mr. West or Mr. Torrance would put up with it, I think."

They would, wouldn't they? But neither of them had shown any interest in her in that regard. Her work, yes, but her? Maybe Ann was right. The prospect of traveling with the two gentlemen seemed suddenly daunting. Maybe she ought to shift her thinking: She wouldn't be *with* them. She was simply journeying at the same time and in the same direction.

"Well." She left it at that.

Beth didn't even leave letters for her family. Ann argued about this, too, but Beth was feeling reckless.

She brought only a valise and small trunk packed with a sturdy skirt, along with blouses and jackets, leaving corset behind so she would be able to dress herself. Positively wild. A good straw hat to keep the sun off, and a thick coat against the morning chill. The valise with her work—papers, ink, books, and a copy of a natural guide to the region—was heavier than her clothing. She imagined West and Torrance traveling with nothing more than satchels slung over their shoulders, like old mountain men in the wilderness.

In fact, they had trunks for their clothes, a case for their collecting materials, another for their guns, and yet another for fishing gear. Harry had never been so dedicated as this. Beth was brave enough to make a joke about assumptions over who would have the most luggage. They were polite enough to laugh.

They spent the train ride as companionable friends sharing a compartment. Mr. Torrance asked if she'd grown up in New York. Telling about her childhood meant asking about theirs, and that took care of conversation for the entire ride.

She told them of her girlhood in Westchester, running in the woods, following her older brother, who shot squirrels while she collected frogs and caterpillars and owl pellets, which she dissected to get out the tiny skulls of mice and voles. Then her brother had gone away to school. She didn't remember the war, only that her father had gone away for a bit, then come home. Mr. West had a similar memory, and then he was the one who went away to school, then to Harvard. She had gone to secondary school, read every book in the library, then finishing school, where she learned passable piano and became quite good at sketching.

Mr. Torrance's upbringing was positively exotic by comparison. He had grown up in Nassau, in the Bahamas. His father was a high-ranking bureaucrat, knighted for his trouble and now retired. His mother was the daughter of a local merchant, of mixed race. His father had wanted him to go to school in England and become a lawyer, the usual. Instead, he got himself a place on a steamer headed to Greenland and never looked back. Joining the crews of several survey missions and scientific expeditions followed, and he made a reputation as a man who didn't just survive on the ice but thrived on it, and enabled the survival of his crews. He spoke a couple of Inuit dialects, could handle a team of sled dogs, and had survived for weeks on the sea ice.

"I wanted to see what cold was like," he said flippantly of the Arctic. "It turns out I like the quiet most of all. There's little time to argue when you're bent on survival." He and West exchanged a glance, the knowing smiles of shared experience, and Beth suddenly felt shut out. The little sister, tagging along, merely tolerated.

It was still better than Will's dinner parties.

She stepped off the train at the small village station, and right there on the platform, across the road, the forest spread out, reds and golds in a chaotic mash, a carpet reaching to water just visible through a break in the trees. It wasn't the city. It was freedom.

On the platform, she turned to remind Harry to take charge of the luggage as it came off the train. Pure habit, from the dozen trips they had taken together. She gaped for a moment as his loss struck her all over again, and she thought her heart would stop.

Then Mr. West counted the luggage for her, collecting their bags together and summoning a porter while Mr. Torrance went to order a carriage. The moment passed, and the two men never noticed her distress.

She caught her breath. Moved on.

The Morgans' inn was in a building said to be a hundred years old, begun as a modest cottage, then expanded and expanded again, growing into what was very nearly a manor, with two stories and a dozen rooms at the back of an expanse of lawn and garden, with a path running down to the lake. Light blue, with white shutters and a cupola at the highest part of the roof.

On stepping out of the carriage and touching earth, she felt a weight leave her, as if carried on a wind. Her shoulders had been aching, and she hadn't realized it. At the edge of the water stood a heron, tilting its head at something under the surface.

She grabbed for her handkerchief and wiped away tears before the men noticed.

While the others handled transferring the luggage to the inn, she wandered from the drive to a gravel path that led past a small flower garden—a few dried heads of blooms on a patch of mums still lingered—then to the edge of the trees, and then to the lake. The vast stretch of it lay before her. She took a deep breath and smelled, well, a thousand scents that had nothing to do with the city. Wet stone where the water lapped against the shore. Trees, drying out as their leaves died, more wood than sap now. A chill rose from the water, tasting of ice on the back of the tongue. A touch of rot, as the life under the surface lived and ate and died and settled. A pair of ducks flapped by and away, too fast and too silhouetted by the afternoon sun for her to identify them.

From the porch, the inn's matron, Mrs. Morgan, called to her.

Beth's black jacket, skirt, hat, and half veil explained her better than words could when Mrs. Morgan started to ask about Mr. Stanley, then closed her mouth. She fussed over Beth the way everyone did these days. This time, the attention was comforting, as it was meant to be. Mrs. Morgan didn't make her feel as if she owed her anything. She was given a room on the second floor, in the corner, looking over the lake.

Later, she overheard Mrs. Morgan ask Mr. Torrance what had happened to Harry. Torrance said illness. The simple answer, so easy to believe and dismiss.

She took supper in her room, assuring Mr. West and Mr. Torrance that she was too tired to be good company. From there, she watched the sun set over the quicksilver water, and the serenity of it felt like a gift.

SIXTEEN
Haliaeetus leucocephalus

Anton and Bran were up before dawn to trek a couple of miles up the shore of the lake, fishing poles over their shoulders. Anton assured Bran, who worried about Mrs. Stanley feeling abandoned, that the woman could fend for herself, and besides, society ladies never got up before ten. She had barely spoken a word since they arrived but had looked over the water with such a profound sense of tranquility, as if she might melt into light and air. Anton had been right. The poor thing had needed to get out of the city as much as he had.

Meanwhile, Anton needed silence, dirt under his feet, and nothing artificial around him but his own clothing and tools. To imagine that civilization had vanished. That ever-present impulse to seek out some primordial land, to try to find out what the world was like before trains and coal fires and steel, before people had built on top of what nature had made.

Impossible. The land changed the moment man set foot on it. Go to the shore of a lake like this and the ducks would swim away, unless one trained them with food to seek one out. One's presence changed what one was looking at.

When he was younger, he thought this impulse for travel was for solitude, to escape expectation. Judgment. Eventually, he had met like-minded men, and their company could be a comfort. Bran was good company because he understood the need for quiet. He walked a few paces behind, barely making a sound. Companionship without obligation. Someday, Anton might decide to flee society for good. An eagle flapped overhead, and something large splashed near the shore. Fish, or some predator jumping in after it.

He saw the wilderness as a way to prove himself. To make a mark by accomplishing the impossible. There weren't many others who could do what he did, and he would do *more* before he was through.

He picked their first spot, and they settled in. Bran unpacked a flask of coffee and sausage rolls for breakfast, left out for them by Mrs. Morgan, a saint. They fished and had no luck at all, which was just fine since they weren't depending on the catch to survive. The quiet went on; the sun rose higher and turned the lake bronze.

Bran set aside his pole and took a long look around—no one here: they were alone. Anton knew what came next, as Bran sidled up to the rock he was perched on, draping his arm along Anton's leg. An invitation, and a request. Bran made suggestions or requests; he rarely demanded. Mostly because Anton was happy to oblige without much persuading. So he set aside his own fishing pole, touched his lover's chin, and kissed him.

Later, he managed to catch one unimpressive trout and still counted the morning a success.

When they arrived back at the inn, Beth Stanley was sitting on a chair on the small dock at the inn's shore, opera glasses in hand, notebook in her lap, writing. A cup of tea sat on a small table beside her. She made a charming picture, and Anton wished he knew anything about art or photography to try to capture the moment.

"Should we ask how she's doing?" Bran whispered near his shoulder. "Or should we leave her alone?"

"Leave her alone, I think," Anton said, amused at Bran's uncertainty. He wasn't usually so bewildered.

"It would be rude to just walk by without saying anything, wouldn't it?"

"Are you always this dense around women, or just this one in particular?" He hadn't often observed Bran around women, now that he thought of it. Unlike some of the men he'd been with in his younger days, he didn't think Bran would ever decide he'd had enough and run off to get married and have a proper life. Bran was just as drawn to the wild as he was. "You aren't getting any ideas about her, are you?"

"Of course not," he said curtly. "You have all my attention. You know that."

She glanced over then, lowering her glasses and smiling at them.

"Ah. Now we can't just walk by," Bran said. "Can we?"

Enough. Anton walked forward, straight to the edge of the dock. "See anything good?" he asked, which was better than asking how she was, which he expected she'd been asked enough these last few months.

"Loons," she said triumphantly and held up a sketch of two black-and-white streamlined birds, dagger bills tipped up. "They called all morning. Did you hear them?"

They had: the haunting, wailing calls echoing across the water, ghostlike and thrilling.

She continued. "Also some grebes, and a glimpse of a green heron before it flew off. The warblers are all gone for the season. I haven't heard one."

"There was frost on the grass this morning," Anton agreed.

"I know they'll come back in spring, but I'm still sad to see them go. Did you catch anything?"

"One sad little trout," Anton said. "It'll do for a bite for each of us, so we'll have to eat whatever they're serving at the inn."

"More trout, I think. You can hide yours with the rest and no one will ever know that you didn't bring back a bounty," she said, and he laughed.

Bran said then, "Can we bring you some coffee or tea? Do you need anything?"

"Thank you, I'm fine. I'll probably go up to the house in a few minutes anyway." She brought the glasses to her face again. Anton looked out and saw her target: the pair of loons, black spots gliding on the water.

Anton took hold of Bran's arm and steered him toward the house. "You see? She's perfectly satisfied."

"Would Harry be angry with us for bringing her here without him?"

"Harry is dead," Anton said. "He doesn't get a say in what happens anymore."

Beth allowed herself to study the two men in their natural habitats, as it were, rather than cooped up in captivity. They were different here—neckties gone, collars undone, trousers rumpled, wearing walking boots instead of polished shoes. They moved through the wild with relish, so much more comfortable than they'd ever been in her parlor.

That afternoon, they fished on the dock while she sat on the porch with her sketchbook, ostensibly making drawings but mostly watching, taking in as much of the scene as she could, since she didn't know when she would be able to come back. She brought that cloud on herself, worrying about an undetermined future. She could come back whenever she liked. She must believe that.

For now, she watched West and Torrance. Imagined field notes on two varieties of *Homo sapiens*, adult males. *Homo sapiens torransus* was the taller of the two, more muscular, as was clear when he removed his jacket and rolled up his sleeves. The flexing of his shoulders became apparent. His skin was a warm brown color between tan and teak, depending on where he stood in the light. His dark eyes held a glint, the hint of a laugh, and had a farseeing quality to them—surely no detail escaped him. He studied the shore as if watching for predators.

These points were not very objective or scientific. He was *this* tall. The plumage on his head and chin was short, dark. He had powerful limbs and a purposeful way of moving. There, that was better.

Homo sapiens westus had a more studious air. His gaze sometimes turned inward, so he could not be said to be looking at anything. Someone would call to him, and he'd shake himself to awareness. He moved quickly when he put bait on a hook or fetched the net to bring in a catch. He didn't seem to use his Arcanism to help him catch fish—luring them with lights, hauling them to the surface in pockets of air. Somehow, this made her think well of him, as if he didn't consider himself above mundane pursuits. He smiled a lot, laughed softly. His hair was a disheveled brown mess. He never seemed to touch it or smooth it back, letting it do what it would.

The pair had such an easy way of working together, no doubt because of the expeditions they had been on. There must be a particular connection between people who had risked their lives together.

This, right here, traveling alone with two men on an outing by a familiar lake, was the most daring, risky thing she had ever done in her life. That seemed . . . sad. She imagined a next moment of daring: she might fling off her jacket and shoes and plunge into the lake, swimming as far as she could, then floating on the surface to look up at the sky and watch the stars come out. She had known how to swim when she was a little girl, splashing about during lakeside holidays with Will and whatever other children were around, but she hadn't tried it in years. She might not remember how, and her heavy clothes would soak through and pull her under, drowning her. Well, surely Mr. Torrance and Mr. West could be relied on to rescue her if she failed at swimming. What a scene that would be. Might be worth trying, just to see what would happen.

"And what are you smiling about, dear?" Mrs. Morgan asked.

"Just enjoying the view."

The older woman gazed down the lawn to the dock, to the two men in shirtsleeves there, and gave a suggestive hum that made Beth blush.

Bran liked her. *Liked* her.

This realization settled over him warmly, deeply, in the pit of his gut. He stared as she walked through the garden, as she sat on the porch with a cup of tea. He couldn't help staring. The line of her arm leading to a delicate shoulder, down the slope of her straight back; her body contained in the stiff black dress and jacket. So much grace held in the bare length of her neck. Her frown was scholarly as she studied the notebook in her lap, focused on it in a way that Harry never had on his.

Harry had been with her, had possessed her, and that made Bran like her more. This woman had belonged to Harry, who had enjoyed her. That put in his mind an image of the pair of them together. He had known Harry's body, and now he was imagining hers, with him, the pair of them tangled together, and it was too much.

There was another possibility. In the spirit of scientific inquiry, one had to consider all the evidence, additional scenarios that explained the observations: in three years, they'd had no children.

What if Harry had not made love to his wife at all? He had never known Harry to be interested in women until Beth came along. It was not Bran's concern; he should not even be wondering. This was prying into Mrs. Stanley's most delicate affairs. Mrs. Stanley, Elizabeth Stanley. Beth. He could ask. He could simply ask. He didn't dare.

He decided to march along the lakeshore looking for . . . for whatever he could find. Anton followed and had to yell at him that it was time to turn around if they wanted to get back to the inn for supper. The sun was setting. Reluctantly, Bran turned and went back, where he would have to see her and spend the rest of the evening suppressing these tangled thoughts.

The pair walked up the path, and from her seat on the porch, Mrs. Stanley—Beth—looked up. Stared right back at him, and he feared he was burning up.

"Mrs. Stanley," Anton said blithely. "How was your afternoon?"

"Quiet, and I enjoyed it very much."

Blast it, Anton stopped at the porch to keep talking to her. "Any good sightings?"

"Pileated woodpecker."

"Oh, very nice!"

Then they simply went inside as if nothing were wrong. Up to their rooms to wash up for supper. The whole world must have seen him blushing, but no one said anything.

Here, for propriety's sake, they had separate rooms. Bran did not go to his own room, though, but kept on at Anton's back, straight into his. He closed and locked the door.

"I need to drag you to bed now." Bran had wound himself up into a state, and he needed Anton, needed him *now*.

"Right now?" Anton seemed skeptical, but nevertheless he got that familiar smug look and pressed forward until he touched Bran, then kept pressing until Bran stumbled back against the wall.

"You can be quiet, can't you?" Bran breathed.

"Hmm, of course." A slow wry grin. "If you insist."

"I do."

Bran kissed him hard, Anton's hands clenched on his shirt, and finally Bran's heart settled, and he was home again, and all was well.

The next morning, Bran went out to the end of the dock to see the loons and anything else that might happen by. He'd done formal surveys of the region, so his odds of seeing something new weren't good, but he found value in observing the familiar. He rarely got such a good look at the common loon, and these were lingering close to the inn. The two sleek birds glided soundlessly on the water. One dove, then the other, and both reappeared on the surface a few yards away, shaking water from their smooth heads, splashing tiny droplets that lit up in the morning sun. Like a spark in midair, two opposing elements of fire and water combined.

He tried it himself, murmuring a tribute to his inspiration, *Gavia immer*, as he scooped up a handful of water, letting it spill over, reflecting the light as it shone, sparking. Caught it in his other hand, until he held *light*. Pure golden light, a glowing bit of sun on the water. He scooped more water, dripped more sparks, until the collection grew so bright he had to squint, a warm glow rather than burning fire, and with this he could make light anywhere, no wick or fuel required. Simply pour water from a flask and be able to see in the middle of the night, in the middle of an Arctic winter. He must try this with snow, with ice—imagine, using a piece of broken ice like a lamp—

"How did you do that?"

The sunlight and water in his hands scattered, fell back into the lake and went out, dim and normal once more, and he felt like he'd been caught out at something secret. He flinched back.

Mrs. Stanley was watching him from the other end of the dock. He had no way to escape her except by jumping in the water. That would be even more embarrassing, though he was tempted.

"Ah . . . sorry. You startled me. How . . . so. How long were you watching that?"

She looked away, kneading her hands. Maybe they were both embarrassed. "The whole time?"

"I'm not sure I could teach you."

"It's the loons, isn't it? The light on the water. I saw it too."

She'd astonished him so much, he ought to be used to it by now.

"Come here, let's give it a go." He made room for her at the end of the dock. She pulled up her skirts and sat right down without hesitation. Her expression had turned positively hungry.

At first, Bran wasn't sure he could replicate the experiment, so he cupped his hand in the water, keeping the scene in mind, the light, the flash of elements—

The water in his hand lit up. The glow reflected back in her face, her smile, her eyes.

"Oh, it's beautiful," she murmured. She put her hand down and stirred her fingers in the water.

He was pleased. "Do whatever you do to make fire, but bring the loons into it—"

"*Gavia immer . . .*"

"The element of water. That fire in their red eyes."

Her attention turned to the water streaming out of her hand. The first time she tried, the sparks came from reflected sunlight, but the second and third times she lifted out a handful of water, the droplets sparked their own glow, flashes like the signals of fireflies, blinking in and out. Her light had more of a reddish shade, and he suspected that whatever source she used for fire was red and bold. She carried that power with her.

She laughed a little. "You'd never need a candle again."

"Not sure how long I can keep it going. I'll have to work on it."

She let a handful of red sparks fall and fade, then dangled her fingers in the chill water as if she could lure something to her. "It's so calming. I've been tempted to jump in for a swim."

"You swim?"

"I used to when I was younger. Lots of things I used to do when I was younger," she added softly.

"Here's something." He flattened his hand a foot or so above the surface and pressed down, as if pushing a column of air.

The water seemed to part, a curved lens dimpling inward, revealing a clear view beneath the surface. He thought of it as a bubble, a pocket of air pressure breaking surface tension. Interrupting the deformation of light that happened between the air and water.

Beth lay flat on her stomach, head over the edge, to get a closer look. Here, the lake bottom was only a couple of feet down. Bits of green-brown algae covered the scattered rocks and mud, and a dozen or so minnows schooled past, taking advantage of the shelter by the dock posts.

"You can do the same thing with a piece of glass in a box, but this is more impressive. Professor Gray at Harvard taught me this."

"Professor Asa Gray, the botanist?" she asked, and seemed awestruck. He couldn't help but preen a little.

"Yes."

She nodded. "What are those little ones, juveniles of some kind?"

"*Oncorhynchus mykiss*, I think. Rainbow trout fry."

"Ah," she breathed. Taking it in. Taking it all in. The fry disappeared into shadow, and she glanced at him. "When did you know? When did you realize you could do more than just look?"

He'd read Linnaeus when he was fourteen, and the possibilities—that the natural world held more wonder and knowledge than could be seen—seemed immense. He'd started experimenting with the master's own *Linnaea borealis*, bringing up the inherent power of life in a scrap of foliage. He'd tried to show his father—and his father had been frightened. Such knowledge was meant for educated men, men of consequence, not a farmer's son. It all could have ended there, except once Bran had felt the possibilities, he couldn't turn away.

"When I was a boy," he said. "Young. Most of the Arcanists I know now didn't start until they got to university. But I . . . my father, my siblings, they just saw birds. They just heard noise. I saw . . . felt . . . so much more. And you?"

"Very much the same. I was sixteen when I lit a candle the first time."

"What do you use?"

"*Piranga olivacea*."

"Ah." He recalled the bright red of the scarlet tanager, flashing like a burst of flame in the foliage. Easy enough to talk to her when they spoke of what they both loved. This encouraged him to ask other, more difficult questions. "Harry's work, his essays, when I thought they were his—part of why they were so good, so useful, is he seemed to have an

Arcanist's eye. He wasn't just interested in classification and description but what it meant, how species fit into the larger world. The connections. I'd ask him questions, and he always had answers, but in hindsight he only repeated what his writing—your writing—said."

"We would practice," she said. "Conversations, lectures. So he could hold his own at the Naturalist Society during the arguments you all get into."

"I'm a poor observer. The signs were there, and I couldn't see them."

"You weren't expecting them. That's the weakness, isn't it? We often don't see what we don't expect to find."

"How much can you do? Have you ever tried to really push yourself?"

She touched the water again, and a lacework of frost curled out from her fingers. The frost thickened, deepened, popping and cracking as the water froze, pressure and volume changing. A sheet of ice ten yards wide crawled out from the dock, maybe an inch or so thick—he could still see the brown of the moss beneath. A chill rose up.

Next, she flattened her hand on the ice and sent out heat. Water formed, pooling, then ran out in rivulets, turning into mist, and the whole sheet broke apart and returned to liquid as quickly as she'd formed it.

Wentworth at the Society had his pick of jobs with that trick. And here she was, unknown, completely camouflaged by her plumage.

"I practice. I do what I can," she said. "I dream of learning to fly."

"Don't we all."

"Did you ever hear the story about Mary Anning saving Reverend Buckland from a landslide? She willed the cliff to stop falling, and it did." They all knew that story. It had the tenor of a legend. Most thought it exaggerated, a tall tale. "I've thought about that story a lot, and what it would take to hold back the earth itself. Whether it was her familiarity with the land, her affinity with what was buried there, that gave her that power. Whether someone who hadn't spent their lives naming fossils would ever be able to accomplish anything like it. People have been trying for a hundred and fifty years to discover how all this works and what it means, and no one's done it. It's different for every one of us, and however much they wish to bottle it up and teach it like it was tennis or piano, they can't."

"You've thought more about this than half the Arcanists at the Society," he said. "They think in terms of careers. For most of them it's a tool. But since you have no expectation of any of that, your interest is for the thing itself. And . . . I think that gives you power."

"I couldn't save Harry." Her voice cracked.

"I don't think it was your responsibility to do so."

Familiar tears collected at the corners of her eyes. She cried so quietly. He wanted to help her, if only—

God help him, he was hatching a plan.

He looked back up the lawn to the inn's porch. Mrs. Morgan was there with a tea tray, along with Anton.

He said, with forced brightness, "I don't know about you, but I haven't had breakfast yet, and I'm betting Mrs. Morgan has baked something wonderful to go with tea. Shall we, Mrs. Stanley?" He got to his feet, brushed himself off, and offered his hand. She accepted, letting him draw her to her feet, and this pleased him irrationally.

"Call me Beth. I think we're friends enough by now."

"Then call me Bran."

"All right."

He wondered if he should offer his arm for the walk back, but she went on ahead, saving him from the dilemma.

The last night, the three of them dined together in the inn's front room. They were the only guests; Mrs. Morgan made a roast chicken, and it was all very comfortable. Anton felt the trip had been a success because he was actually looking forward to getting back to the city and diving into their next round of lectures. Every bit of work got him closer to the goal.

As with any long trek, the closer he got to the destination, the more anxious he felt. His spine itched with nerves. He wanted to run.

"I have an idea," Bran said when the meal was almost finished. Their plates had been taken away, and Mrs. Morgan was bringing around coffee. "An experiment."

"Oh?" Anton asked. He'd been talking about their next lectures, who else they needed to talk to about possible sources of funding, and how to get a meeting with the Signal Corps about sponsorship. Bran had seemed distracted and hadn't answered much except for *yes, of course*, and *that's fine*.

Mrs. Stanley had been quiet, mostly, but that was usual for her. She looked up now, politely interested.

"Beth, I think we should take you to the Naturalist Society. Show you off a little."

Anton noted that he used her given name, the first time he'd done so.

"Women are barred from the Society," she said gently.

"And every mountain has been declared unclimbable at one point. Until someone actually climbs it," Bran countered.

Anton warmed to the challenge; he'd faced such obstacles before, often. "There are those who insist I shouldn't be allowed in the Society, either, because of my race. The trick is to bowl them over with accomplishment until they can't argue."

Bran was almost giddy. "The next issue of the *Pinfeather*—the one with your essay in it—will be out soon. That'll be our excuse. It's a tribute to Harry; we should invite his widow to accept the praise that should have been his. It's perfectly reasonable. No one can argue."

"A sleight of hand," Anton said.

"I'm not sure." Beth clutched her cup with both hands, like it was a shield. The fragile wounded creature returning.

"I for one am quite used to marching into places where other people think I don't belong." Anton would relish the looks on the faces of the old codgers.

"Well. If you don't think it'll cause too much scandal."

"So what if it does?" Bran said blithely. "Who cares about scandal?"

They did, Anton wanted to remind him. They cared every time they locked the door and drew the curtains of their own apartment. Every time Bran reminded him to be quiet because they didn't know how thin the walls were wherever they were staying.

She seemed to be making the same calculations. "My family cares very much about scandal."

"We'll be with you," Anton assured her. "If they want to get angry at you, they'll have to get angry at us first."

She granted him a thin smile. "That's very chivalrous. Thank you, Mr. Torrance."

"Call me Anton."

In Arcanist circles, Mary Anning is most famous for rescuing the Reverend William Buckland, the renowned geologist and paleontologist, from a terrible landslide. The seashore around Lyme Regis—where Anning worked her whole life, collecting from the area's extraordinary fossil beds—was known to be unstable and dangerous. The same traits that made the area such a rich ground for fossil hunting—the geologic makeup of the ground, the constant excavation by waves and weather that continually revealed new specimens—also made it treacherous. Buckland spent a great deal of time in the area, working with Anning. On this outing, he'd spotted a potential find and gotten up on some rocks for a better look. The ground under him, soaked through after a recent storm, gave way, and the mud over it collapsed, threatening to topple him and bury him alive. Anning was able to stop it by freezing the rock and mud in place until he could retreat to safety.

Buckland would say it was the greatest feat of Arcane Taxonomy he'd ever witnessed in his life, and as a member of the Royal Society, he would have been acquainted with all the great British Arcanists of the day. He advocated for her throughout his life. On the other hand, his colleagues felt that his brush with death had biased his opinion on the matter. Other naturalists and Arcane Taxonomists suggested tests of Anning's skill. She refused to participate.

A friend of Anning's wrote about her: "She says she stands still, and the world flows by her in a stream, that she likes observing it and discovering the different characters which compose it." Poor and self-taught, Mary Anning discovered and preserved some of the most noteworthy fossil specimens from the region, such as the first complete ichthyosaur and plesiosaur skeletons.

She was never offered membership in the Royal Society because of her sex.

SEVENTEEN

Archilochus colubris

Harry had loved the Naturalist Society and its meetings. On those evenings, he'd come home late, after Beth had gone to bed—he insisted that she not wait up for him, so she didn't. In the morning they'd have breakfast together, and he'd tell her everything he learned from whatever lecture or presentation had been offered, about the hunting habits of lions or the variations in blossoms of flowers found in different valleys in the Alps. Beth drank it all in.

Entering the halls of the Naturalist Society herself was like traveling to a country she'd only heard tales of.

Beth changed to half mourning, probably far too early. Instead of the relentless black, she wore a dark-gray walking dress and jacket with black trim, without anything in the way of flounces or ruffles, along with a simple gray hat. Still somber but letting some light into the room. She should wait half a year, at least. A full year, according to some, including Harry's mother. But the black had begun pulling at her like a weight.

Ann saw her off in the foyer. "You look much better, ma'am." She was always prim and professional, but her sly smiles often betrayed her feelings.

"That's good to hear." She'd felt that she might never claw her way out of whatever hole had captured her. The gray, Ann's smile, the opportunity before her now—all were sunlight, and she reached for it. Like the sparks at the lake, holding light in her hands. She could do anything.

"Will you be all right?"

"Still worried about unaccompanied expeditions with strange men?"

Ann shrugged a little. "If you aren't worried, why should anyone else be? But . . ."

"But people will gossip, yes. I've decided I don't care." *People* were not her, and they did not know her.

As promised, Mr. West and Mr. Torrance—Bran and Anton— arrived at the brownstone in a cab to collect her.

"You look well!" Torrance greeted her. "That color suits you."

This was encouraging.

The three of them stuffed in the carriage made the ride a bit crowded, but Beth reassured herself that they were friends. They were her native guides.

The cab stopped at a lurking building in Midtown, the kind that housed offices and clubs, with lots of brass fixtures and classical statuary. Anton leaped out of the carriage first and helped her down, and she craned her neck back to look. She was rarely in this part of town, full of lawyers, banks, and men's clubs. If this was an expedition, she ought to take notes: to classify and identify the men walking to and fro on the sidewalks according to the color of their suits, fashion of their beards, and briskness of their walks. These traits identified the investors, while these others marked the politicians, and the men of industry . . .

Putting her between them, an honorable escort, the pair guided her inside, through large double doors into a marble foyer, and from there to the Naturalist Society's lair. The motto above the doorway seemed to glow in gold: *Ex Natura Veritas*. Ironic, given the lies she and Harry had built up to gain access. From nature . . . whatever stories one could get away with telling.

Past the Naturalist Society doors, the vestibule—a plain, sedate room full of dark paneling and carpets and gas lamps that hurt the eyes—was full of men. She knew it would be, but it was still a shock, somehow. What was it rabbits did, huddling in perfect stillness to avoid the eyes of predators?

Bran was at her side. "May I take your coat?" Gently, he helped her slide the coat off her shoulders. She might have gotten tangled up otherwise.

The porter by the desk at the back of the vestibule gaped at her, as astonished as if West and Torrance had brought in a horse.

"Sirs?" he questioned, tone pitching up into panic.

Anton jumped in. "Yes, Teddy, this is Mrs. Harold Stanley."

She tried to be pleasant. "Good afternoon."

"That new essay of Harry's is just published, and we'd like her to see how much he meant to us all. I'm sure an exception can be made." Anton didn't give him much room to argue.

The porter remained nonplussed. "I'm very sorry . . . I'll need to check with Mr. Andrews or Mr. Endicott."

The room had fallen silent, all the men staring.

"You can let us in to wait, I'm sure," Bran said. "So that Mrs. Stanley can have a seat."

"There's a seat right over here, uh, Mrs. Stanley. If you'd like."

She remained standing. They were at an impasse, the two parties staring at each other.

"I'll just go see Mr. Andrews, then," the porter said, backing toward the second set of doors.

"You do that," West answered stiffly.

The porter fled through the doors behind him, and Beth caught an intriguing glimpse of a vast library beyond. She wondered if she'd never get to see it.

"This was a mistake," she murmured.

"It's too early to give up," West murmured back, glaring at the rest of the room with a confident smile.

They waited for what seemed like ages before the far doors swung open again, the porter returning with two distinguished men whom Beth *did* recognize from photos in newspapers and Harry's descriptions. Mr. Hubert Andrews and Mr. Stuart Endicott, two of the senior men on the board of the Naturalist Society. She was flattered she merited such high-ranking attention.

"Mr. Torrance, what's this? You know we absolutely cannot allow—"

Anton was undeterred. "Ah, Andrews, good man, I know you can clear this up. May I introduce Mrs. Elizabeth Stanley. Harry's widow." He stabbed the word like a weapon.

This stopped them. They might as well have hit a wall. The silence drew on.

Be brave, she thought. *Be a hawk, be a swan.* Falco peregrinus. Cygnus columbianus. *Nature, grant me courage.* Her back straightened, her shoulders squaring. When she met their gazes, hers was serene.

Mr. West glanced at her. He'd felt her use of the *practicum*, then. The two dignified gentlemen were staring. Had they sensed it?

"Mr. Andrews," she said earnestly. "Thank you so much for this opportunity. It means so much to know that dear Harry's work is still appreciated, and since this might very well be his last publication, I wanted to witness the moment on his behalf, since he can't be here himself. Harry thought so very much of you and the Society."

There, let them argue with that.

Andrews seemed to deflate. "Mrs. Stanley, my deepest condolences on your loss."

The words had become formulaic, meaningless. She was able to return a smile. "Thank you. And if I may, your article on raptor eggs that appeared in last summer's issue of the *Pinfeather* was so informative, I—that is, Harry enjoyed it very much and told me of it." In fact, she wasn't sure Harry had read it at all, however much he said he ought to ingratiate himself to the Society's board members.

"That's quite flattering," said Mr. Andrews, though his bafflement seemed to increase. "I suppose, just this once . . ."

On the other hand, Endicott seemed horrified. "Are you sure?" he hissed at Andrews.

"What do you want me to do?" Andrews hissed back.

"Gentleman," Torrance said in his aristocratic lilt, "what would it cost to have a bit of sympathy?"

At that, the two men fell quiet and stepped aside. The porter opened the doors.

And here she was, at last, doing a thing that was not supposed to be possible. She walked into the halls of the Naturalist Society. Stopping to stare, she gawked, as if this were a snowcapped peak or crashing ocean. Something to inspire awe.

The longer she studied it, the better she understood it. This was a space for *men*.

Studies, clubs, and libraries were masculine, designed with the sensibilities of men, as opposed to feminine parlors and conservatories. The latter contained soft chairs and plush carpets, flowers and figurines, a place for a tea cart, circles gathered for conversation. The former, the bastions of study and business, were all leather and pipe smoke, rows of serious books—no novels—and expansive desks spread out with acres of work. There might be a deer head on the wall or a stuffed pheasant on the mantel.

This club was a masculine space, amplified. Aggressively masculine, if that wasn't redundant, saturated with the smell of tobacco and whiskey. There wasn't so much as a painting of a flower. Three great animal heads were mounted on the wall: the expected deer; an elk, if she wasn't mistaken; and a wildebeest, gray and bearded. The room had the sense of a tower, with its high ceilings, and bookshelves that went all the way up on three walls, with ladders on rollers to assist. Rifles and sabers hung in a display above a fireplace. The chairs and sofas were leather.

This was a shrine to accomplishment. Between a set of shelves a blackboard stretched from floor to ceiling, marked with a grid, a list of places and names. Peaks, rivers, islands. Latitudes, north and south. Elevations. The boundaries of the world—and the names of men who had conquered them. Anton glanced here first—and she guessed that he was looking for any new names that had been added since his last visit. He narrowed his gaze, as if searching a distant horizon.

Her attention turned to another wall: a display of portraits, great Arcanists from Linnaeus on up to Professor Gray. She recognized them all, and their gazes seemed suddenly judgmental. What did she mean, coming here? Did she really think she could be one of them?

No portrait of Mary Anning hung among them, and Beth thought there should have been one.

She had a sense that there had been conversation when she'd entered the hall. Now, all was silent. The men before her stared, continually. One would think they'd never seen a woman before. She wondered if a woman had ever crossed this threshold before now. At least a woman who wasn't here to clean. Beth didn't spot any dust, not even on the bookshelves. They had maids, their own Anns and Joans, to care for them, unacknowledged.

So yes, there *had* been women in these halls before. Just never one dressed as she was.

She could be daunted or move through it as a gull in a storm. Serene, be serene. She imagined Harry here, taking her arm. Charming anyone who would argue. There; that was better.

The silence stretched and stretched until it broke, and a dozen male heads bent together. Several men rushed to confront Andrews and Endicott. Whispers traveled out, like ripples in a pond, as she was identified and the information passed on: Harry Stanley's widow.

No one came to talk to her. A space remained around her, Bran, and Anton. They might as well have been plague ridden.

"This is going well," Bran said sourly.

"You'd think this lot would be more interested in a rare creature," Anton murmured back.

"On the contrary, they come here to escape from creatures like me," Beth said, and that earned a sharp look from both of them.

Bran called out. "O'Connell. Tell me, what's new at Princeton?"

She knew the name: an Arcanist, an academic. Had traveled in the tropics. She wondered if he would talk to her.

O'Connell glanced at her, then Anton, then back to Bran. The man raised a questioning brow and said cautiously, "Absolutely nothing, I'm happy to say. The battle over the museum directorship is over. Mitchell's got it, and he'll do fine." He bowed at her a little and walked away.

Well, that answered that.

Anton bent his head to her. "Would you like something to drink?"

She said that she would like sherry, hoping it would settle her. Anton raised a hand to a waiter. At least there was no argument about bringing her a drink now that she was here.

She spotted Montgomery Ashford in the next room over. She should have expected him to be here as well. He wasn't looking this way, gave no indication that he saw her. She turned away before she could catch his gaze by mistake.

Mr. Andrews marched to the back of the room, near the immense fireplace where a wide desk stood. On it were stacks of pamphlets, an engraving decorating the front cover. The latest issue of the *Pinfeather*. The whole excuse for being here. Beth's hands itched to get hold of it.

Andrews tapped a brass letter opener to a glass, calling for attention. "Gentleman, might I ask you to extend a gracious welcome to Mrs. Harold Stanley, here to help us memorialize her late, much-mourned husband. Our condolences to you, Mrs. Stanley."

Murmurs, bowed heads, and obvious discomfort followed. She smiled wanly in response. But a bit of the tension faded. Some of the looks were not quite as hostile. It might not have been a universally accepted reason for her presence here, but at least it was a reason. The members were assured that this anomaly wouldn't happen again.

Anton found a seat for her, a straight-backed chair that she could perch on the edge of, that wouldn't swallow her up. She studied the garnet-colored surface of her drink, the cut pattern in the glass.

Andrews continued in what was obviously the speech he expected to deliver this afternoon about the current state of ornithological research among the city's naturalists. He offered an amusing anecdote about his own recent trip to Long Island to collect shorebird specimens—he'd lost a shoe in the mud—and made a meandering series of comments about the articles in this new issue, petting the stack of pamphlets beside him.

She could picture Harry here, maybe sitting in that overstuffed chair, his ankle propped up on the opposite knee, glass of bourbon in one hand. His head tipped back to gaze up at those gathered around him, listening to him go on about his opinions. During the lectures, he wouldn't be looking toward the lecturer; he'd be watching the rest of the audience, noting who was paying attention and who wasn't, whose expressions were screwing up with disagreement. It was the idea of all this he loved, not the deep studies into the foraging habits of antelope. He came here for the company.

He'd had a whole life without her. She'd known this, but she hadn't had any idea what that looked like until now. This was the difference between academic study and field observation. She wasn't supposed to care.

Suddenly Andrews stopped talking, and men gathered around him, claiming their copies of the journal, going through them like children with new toys. Bran West brought back three, offering her one like a treasure. The cover illustration was of a hummingbird sitting on a nest, a dainty molded cup just big enough for the bird to fit into, its head and tail jutting over each edge. The drawing gave no hint of the scale—this bird and its nest would fit entirely in her hand.

Rather too quickly to be polite, she set aside the sherry and opened the journal, flipping pages until she found the right one. Harry usually got hold of these before she did. For the first time, she'd be the one to see her words in print before he did.

And there it was.

Observations of Declining Avian Populations

By Mr. Harold Stanley

The work of the incomparable John James Audubon continues to loom large in our studies. I have especially been grateful for his precise images of birds that have vanished from the earth, such as the great auk (Pinguinus impennis), while mourning the fact that I will never have the opportunity to view a living specimen of that bird myself. I grow thoughtful, considering that Audubon's work is not a comprehensive and final survey of the birds of America but rather a moment in time, one might even say a photograph of a particular era. As much as we revere and rely on them, we perhaps should not always trust earlier accounts of bird populations and behaviors to provide good information for the current status of a species, given the clear evidence that the status can drastically change over time.

We emphasize collection and disregard the power that is in living birds. We ignore the consequences of losing an entire species, their names taken from our arsenal, and the subsequent reduction in our strength achieved through Arcane Taxonomy.

The members of the Society read, and she waited for their reactions.

Meanwhile, now that her presence here had been defined and delineated, a few men approached and offered condolences, and she gave them the usual polite thanks. She'd had a lot of practice at that by now. Mr. West introduced them, and she recognized some of their names from articles they'd written, from Harry talking about them. A few she knew Harry liked and admired. She wanted to talk more with them. She wanted to feel easy enough here for deeper conversation. But she didn't.

She was quiet and unobtrusive enough that bits of conversation carried to her.

"It's ridiculous. In a hundred and fifty years, there's never been any evidence of extinction causing a reduction in Arcane power. The fossil record—"

"The dinosaurs weren't hunted to extinction by mankind," another answered.

"Convenient that he isn't around to argue about it," another said testily.

But I'm here, Beth thought. If they had questions and arguments, she would like to discuss them.

His companion chuckled. "Well, you can write a counteressay for the next issue."

"Would that be disrespecting the dead? Doesn't feel right. God, Harry, getting in the last word again."

"He's beyond caring, I'd think," someone muttered behind her.

If the men did not talk to her, they certainly didn't have a problem talking *about* her. And they didn't seem inclined to keep their voices lowered, as if they didn't believe she could hear them. She didn't want to listen, but they kept saying Harry's name, and every time they did, it was like a hook catching her ear.

"What killed him, anyway?"

"Illness, I heard."

"That's very vague. I can't remember, does he have children?"

"No, none."

They glanced sidelong at her, wondering how a man with such a young and pleasing wife didn't have children.

Beth met the wildebeest's glassy stare and sighed. She had a sudden curiosity about the freezing point of distilled liquors, and the distance at which she might be able to exert an influence on them. In the spirit—no pun intended—of experimentation, she thought of that sharp, stabbing quality of very cold air on a winter night, *Bubo scandiacus* fluffing up its feathers to survive while the temperature dropped and dropped. Much colder than ice, and colder still. Bran and Anton would know how to survive, but would these men?

A clunk followed as one of the men behind her dropped his tumbler. The glass hit carpet; they all jumped back. "Goddamn it!"

"What happened?"

"Which one of you did that? Someone here's pulling pranks—who is it? West? O'Connell?"

"Wasn't me!"

A steward rushed over to clean up the mess—the bourbon hadn't spilled, because it was frozen and fell out of the glass in one piece. Anton glanced at her sidelong, lips caught in some confused curl between a frown and smirk.

This was all she'd ever managed, pulling pranks in sitting rooms.

"If you want to know how Stanley collected his information, I think Mrs. Stanley knows." And suddenly Bran was beside her, with Mr. Andrews in tow.

"Oh?" Andrews frowned skeptically.

"Just ask, she doesn't bite."

Beth blushed. So did Mr. Andrews.

"I . . . ah . . . yes. Well. I wondered about all those numbers in his essay," Andrews said. "I know Harry traveled some, but not that much. Those surveys aren't direct observation."

"I—" she started, and stumbled. "He . . . we . . . he gathered much of his information from correspondences, asking friends and colleagues to send surveys from all over the country." Her friends, colleagues from women's clubs and societies, and Mr. Andrews would never know. "Darwin also relied on correspondence for his information," she said. "I'm not sure it's possible for one person to be so thorough. Collaboration is essential."

"You were a secretary for him?" Andrews asked, raising a brow.

"Something like that."

"Then you've actually read Mr. Stanley's work?" Andrews seemed incredulous.

She was starting to get flustered. "Every word." *Chin up,* she reminded herself.

"Extraordinary," he murmured. "And what do you know of Darwin?"

"I've read him as well," she said.

"So you see," Mr. West hurriedly said, "I do trust Mrs. Stanley's opinion in reviewing her late husband's work. She's very familiar with it. He left other essays that I think could be made ready for publication."

"Well, you'll have to discuss it with Endicott, of course."

The prickly editor would never agree to it. This peak was unclimbable.

One of the others came up to them in a bit of a panic. Graydon, one of their cohort from Harvard. He studied fossils. He'd been at the funeral. He didn't even look at Beth.

"Torrance, there's a man from the Signal Corps here. You've got to get to him before Ashford does." He nodded across the room, where a gentleman in an army uniform stood speaking to a couple of others with the rugged beards of frontier explorers—or worn by people who wanted to look like frontier explorers.

"Oh, bloody hell," Anton muttered and stalked off.

"What's that about?" Beth asked Bran.

"The United States Signal Corps is a potentially rich source of funding for exotic expeditions," he said. "If they can be convinced of the value."

"And they won't likely give funding to two Antarctic expeditions."

"Or worse, Ashford will say something ridiculous and spoil them on the whole idea. Will you be all right here for a moment?"

No, she would not. She would be adrift and at the mercy of . . . she didn't even know what. "Of course I'll be fine. I'll go read labels on jars to occupy myself."

He drew back like he couldn't tell if she was joking. Then he gave a nod and chased after Torrance.

To think she had expected this to be a solemn, enlightened gathering dedicated to the pursuit of pure knowledge and scientific achievement. It had more in common with her mother's charity luncheons than she'd have thought, with all the gossip and scurrying for status. Maybe she should write an essay on the comparative territorial behaviors of male and female tribes.

Turned out, the labels on the jars were quite interesting, a whole collection of specimens she'd only ever seen at the American Museum and a few she hadn't, including a human brain with a name attached—a rather personal donation, she thought.

When she turned to the next set of shelves, Mr. Ashford was standing there, smiling in a way that might have been pleasant if Beth hadn't felt so much foreboding.

"Mrs. Stanley, what a surprise to see you here."

"Mr. Ashford."

"So, what do you think of it all?" He glanced around, taking in the jars, the displays, the crowd of men, the haze of pipe smoke.

"It's a bit overwhelming."

"Not exactly friendly, I suppose," he said.

"No," she admitted.

"Harry never really fit in here, either, if I'm being honest." At her sharp look he quickly added, "Oh, he was well liked. No one begrudged his membership. But he . . . well, lacked a certain drive. But you . . ."

She forced herself to smile. "I'm very unremarkable."

"We both know that isn't true."

An Arctic wind, right against the back of her neck. She stared at him, stricken. Ashford remained easy; anyone who looked over would think he spoke of the weather. "You flatter me," she said softly.

"I suspect you deserve to be flattered more than you are. Mr. Stanley knew your worth, didn't he?"

She rolled up her copy of the *Pinfeather* and squeezed. "Harry and I were very happy together." They were mostly happy together. Satisfied, they were satisfied together, but that wasn't any of Ashford's business.

"What you and Mr. Stanley had—do you hope to find that again? Because West and Torrance can't give it to you." His smirk curled, vaguely insulting, but to whom?

And what did that mean? "I'm not entirely sure what they have to do with anything." The protest sounded lame.

"You could never have entered these halls without your connection to Harry, and I simply wondered if you had . . . ambitions. Because I admire ambition. And I hate to see talent wasted."

Would she be satisfied, embarking on the same partnership with another? She didn't know. Bran and Anton were still occupied with the army man across the room. She wondered how she might signal for help without screaming.

Ashford went on. "Have you given any more thought to what we discussed the other night?"

She had, but she didn't want to say so. She didn't want to encourage that mercenary gleam in his eyes.

"What's the greatest difficulty with any journey to the poles?" he asked.

"The cold. The hostile climate. Carrying supplies over the distances—"

"Exactly. The travel," he said, like a magician whisking away a screen to reveal wonders. "What if . . . well. I've been thinking about compasses. Navigation. The migration of birds—they make it look so easy, don't they? There must be a way to use that."

She became interested in spite of herself. Arcanists could sometimes see through the eyes of their subjects, vicariously replicating flight or journeys underwater. Such feats were spoken of in whispers. They were dreams, impossible. The power of flight required more than simply wishing for it. But what if . . . she met his gaze, questioning. Had he discovered something? Or was he just fishing?

"You're talking about flight," she said. "Have you tried?"

"How would you go about it?"

She was surprised into answering. "Albatross. They glide on winds for hundreds of miles without beating their wings more than once or twice. It's not necessarily the birds themselves but how they use the elements, so we should find some *practicum* that uses that ability. Learn how they might use the magnetic field to migrate—"

"Aah," Ashford breathed, smiling with satisfaction.

He'd been fishing, then. He didn't have a clue.

She had ideas, yes, but were they *good* ideas? Achievable? To find some *practicum* that used these invisible currents of power . . . a hundred years ago, no Arcanist had ever frozen a river. The telegraph hadn't been invented. Who knew what was possible?

"Just think on it. Your brother knows how to reach me." He bowed slightly and walked away.

Suddenly, she felt as if all eyes turned to her, and she was exposed, caught in a storm with no shelter. Some of these men would tell their wives that Beth had been here, and their wives would tell her mother, who would be appalled. Her mother and Will would both demand to know what Beth thought she was doing, exposing herself to . . . to . . . she didn't even know what. How much more would they discover? She should never have come here.

She had ruined her copy of the *Pinfeather* from squeezing it so tightly. *Be careful.* That thought suddenly filled her, words spoken in Harry's voice. *Just . . . be careful.* Her eyes filled, that sudden unexpected onslaught of grief that should be familiar by now. If she wiped her eyes, people would know she was crying. If she didn't, tears would fall: the same outcome. She needed to go.

She walked out of the great suffocating chambers of the Manhattan Naturalist Society. The porter seemed relieved to hand over her coat and offered to call a cab for her, but she insisted she could find her own. She knew how cabs worked, had coins in her purse, and could damn well get herself home. She didn't need the Naturalist Society. She didn't need Mr. West and Mr. Torrance, however kind their intentions. They had more important work to do than look after her. She would not bother them again.

She didn't even need Harry, in the end.

EIGHTEEN

Aptenodytes forsteri

Lieutenant Beaumond, the Signal Corps officer, was sharp, and Anton was determined to win him over. He was able to engage the man in conversation by asking about his service, his various tours, how he liked the city, and what sort of expeditions he thought would occupy the government's attention over the next few years. Detailed mapping of the western coastline was on the list. Some officials were still interested in finding better ways of sailing around Cape Horn, even though the completion of the transcontinental railroad a decade before made that journey almost obsolete. A canal through the Isthmus of Panama was under discussion, perhaps just for the grand feat of engineering it would represent. Anton steered him so that Beaumond himself brought up the polar south.

"It's turning into a race," the officer confided. "The French and Russians are making noise about expeditions, recruiting all the usual suspects. You've heard about this German push for what they're calling an International Polar Year? No one wants to let anyone else get all the glory."

"Indeed." Torrance could play this. He had the experience; he already had the plan, the crew lined up, the scientists. He had only to get someone in charge to *listen*. Someone with deep pockets.

Beaumond's conspiratorial tone continued. "I have to ask, some of us are expecting you to throw in with a British expedition. No one's really sure where your national loyalty lies."

That was rather by design. Anton would throw in with whoever could get him what he needed. "While I have a great deal of fondness for my father's country, Britain's record in polar exploration hasn't been particularly impressive of late."

Beaumond chuckled. "You'd take an Arcanist with you?"

"Brandon West. I think he's the best Arcanist doing fieldwork. And he's got polar experience." Beaumond nodded thoughtfully, and Anton was sure he had the man hooked. Reel him in gently, gently. Bran was already heading over; Anton caught his gaze to hurry him along. He made introductions.

Shaking his hand heartily, Beaumond said, "I'm aware of your work, Mr. West. I heard about your trick with the compass. Impressive."

"Thank you."

Anton had also heard about the trick with the compass. Bran had demonstrated for him, talking to himself and making notes in that squirrely academic way he got when he was deep in his work. The effect itself had been eerie, the compass needle unaffected by the magnet alongside it. The practical use at the poles was obvious. "I assume you'll be planning experiments along those lines at the poles."

Say yes, Anton urged him. *Say yes now.* This was exactly the sort of wedge they needed.

"I'm planning a lot of experiments, sir," Bran said.

"You need to come to Washington, talk to the people who actually make decisions. Tell the polar bear story. Torrance, did you really shoot a charging polar bear?"

"I did, with a Winchester repeater, in two shots," Anton answered.

"That must have been something to see." He drew out a card, with a name and address. "Send me a note. I'll put you in touch with the department."

This was exactly what he and Bran needed. "Thank you. You'll hear from us soon, I think."

"If you'll excuse me, gentlemen."

They did, then spent a moment beaming at one another. "That was encouraging," Bran said.

Except . . . Beaumond was now talking to Ashford, who seemed to have intercepted him. Now Ashford was getting him a drink . . . Anton must ignore them. He must pretend that Ashford was nothing to him. As he kept telling Bran, Ashford had no chance, no experience. Everything about Anton's proposal was superior.

Still, Ashford might put the right word in the right ear and win it all. If there was a race on, if this became a matter of national pride, the Signal Corps would practically throw money, but only at one of them. The men with the power to hand over money, ships, credibility—always the chance they'd take one look at Anton's skin and pass him over.

He couldn't give them that chance. That was all there was to it.

Suddenly Bran asked, "Where's Beth?"

Even in her shadowed gray clothing, Beth should have been easy to spot, but she wasn't here. Had someone driven her out? Perhaps she'd just gone out for some air.

Bran was working himself into a panic, racing to the next room and back, searching, until Anton put a hand on his shoulder. "We'll ask."

In the foyer, Teddy informed them that Mrs. Stanley had indeed collected her coat and left without a word.

Anton was a little put out. "Did you at least get her a cab?"

"She said she could find a cab, sir. She insisted."

Of course she did.

Anton had known it wouldn't be easy, bringing her here. He'd been sure she could manage. But he of all people should have known how difficult it could be, entering a space where one was not welcome.

He went back in to report to Bran, who growled. "I thought if they could get used to seeing her here, they might accept her work too."

"I adore your optimism."

"We should go after her. Find out what happened."

"I think we can guess. She wasn't exactly made welcome here, and then we walked off and left her." She wouldn't likely want to talk to them after they'd abandoned her.

"Did you see who spoke to her last? Who might have, I don't know, said something off-putting? God, the worst I thought anyone would do was ignore her."

Dear sweet Bran. Anton was so very fond of him and also exasperated at him. "We can send her a note—"

"That's always your solution, so very polite."

"Bran—" Across the room, Lieutenant Beaumond shook hands with Ashford and seemed entirely too pleasant about the whole encounter. What he wouldn't give to know what they'd said. He wondered if Bran had some trick that would play him back the last ten minutes of someone else's conversation.

Of course Ashford approached, to gloat or antagonize them, and Anton had to consciously square his shoulders and don a disinterested smile.

"How do you do, Torrance? Quite the day, isn't it?"

As if they were in the park on a sunny afternoon. "Quite."

Ashford glanced around, brow lifted. "Your, ah, pet seemed to have left the building. Just as well; she didn't seem to be enjoying herself."

"What did you say to her?" Bran demanded.

"Her name is Mrs. Stanley, and I don't believe she's anyone's pet," Anton said. "She may come and go as she pleases."

"Ah. Just so. I hope you'll remember that. Good afternoon." Ashford even winked before walking off.

"Now what does that mean?" Bran said, dubious.

Anton had no idea.

NINETEEN

Haemorhous mexicanus

The next afternoon, Beth sat on the floor of the study, skirt tucked under her, books piled around her. She tried to imagine great stretches of land she had only ever seen on a map. And then, how did one imagine traveling across a space that didn't even have a map? That was what Bran and Anton would be doing in Antarctica.

The suggestion that one might use Arcanism to simply *leap* across distances to one's destination, bypassing all the danger and uncertainty . . . Beth pondered. Maybe float above the land as in a hot-air balloon, to see all the obstacles in advance and be able to plan for them. Attain some kind of clairvoyance.

Could one really learn to fly?

More than trying to replicate the flight of her beloved birds, she would need a specific kind of flight: that of the cold-weather, long-distance birds like skuas and petrels, able to withstand storms. Did birds even reach all the way to the South Pole? Ross's expedition had brought back emperor penguins, *Aptenodytes forsteri*, and they were said to be able to withstand brutal cold, but no one knew the extent of their range. She had seen a stuffed one at the American

Museum and had marveled at its height, its striking coloration. But penguins didn't fly.

The glass cabinet in the study had a lodestone—magnetite. She pulled it out and sat with it a while, found some pins to hold against it. The metal wavered, tugged, stuck. It was a curiosity, but it wasn't Arcane. All its power was its own. A magnetic field in miniature, but it gave her no more insight into the planetary field than she'd had before.

So much they didn't know: that was the whole point of an Antarctic expedition. How did one answer the questions one needed to conduct a successful expedition without the information collected by that very expedition? One simply had to plunge into the unknown.

To name a thing was to know a thing, but there was more to it than that, wasn't there? She had a copy of Hooker's *Flora Antarctica*, with its brilliant color plates of kelp and lichens and other specimens that were alien to her. Kelp grew to magnificent lengths, very quickly—was there some essence of travel she could learn from it to unlock that power? But she had never seen a specimen herself, and she couldn't imagine the cold that it grew in. She made notes anyway. An Arcanist, Hooker had cataloged the species, accessed them, used their power. He had saved men from drowning by parting the water around them. He had split rocks, as the roots of trees do over decades, to get at the minerals within. He and Darwin had spoken to one another across hundreds of miles, using conch shells.

In some sense, the earth's magnetic field bound the planet together. How might one use that?

On the wall above her, the map with its pins showing migration patterns beckoned. These birds traveled such great distances every year, marked their calendars by it as a matter of course. The striking thing wasn't the distances but the *ordinariness* of the journeys. Make it ordinary and it wouldn't be so terrifying.

Sterna paradisaea, the arctic tern, was said to migrate from the Arctic to the Antarctic and back again, every year. The terns were certainly found in both regions, but the idea that it was the same individuals traversing such a distance—she would not say it was impossible. Not in a world that had produced both hummingbirds and ostriches from a common ancestor.

If you could catch a tern in one place, release it, then catch the same tern on the other side of the world—would that give you mastery over the distance? Except no one knew how the birds knew where to go.

This was the central mystery of migration. If someone could discover how birds navigated hundreds, sometimes thousands, of miles without map or compass . . . that knowledge possibly held a great deal of power. It would be of significant benefit to explorers like Bran and Anton.

She was sure that Ashford hadn't found the secret. Rather, he was prompting her, nudging her so that she might discover the secret for him. Almost flattering, that he thought she had so much ability. The one man at the Society who'd listened to her, and it had to be him.

Setting down her pencil, she leaned against the desk and sighed. Too many questions, too many problems. Movement, travel . . . five open books held possibilities but not answers. She reached, thought of a breeze, the air from a tern's wing—she had only ever seen a few terns, chance sightings on the coast. They held so much power in their delicate wings. She curled her finger.

A page turned without her touching it. The book sat three feet away, and she had moved it. Could she move more, at greater distances? A whole ship in calm waters if its engine was broken? A sled across the ice?

Steadying her breathing, she tried again, reaching—the whole book this time, close the cover, slam it shut. Nothing happened, and she decided that she was tired, cross, and unhappy.

A knock came. "Ma'am? Letters just arrived," Ann said from the other side of the door.

Beth called her in, and Ann handed the day's mail down to her. Ann was used to her sprawling out on the floor like this and didn't even blink. Beth quickly sorted through the letters. Two were from Bran and Anton. Well, how did she like that? She'd left them at the Society without saying goodbye, which was very rude. What both men must think of her. Her curled-up copy of the *Pinfeather* sat on the desk where she'd dropped it, leaving it untouched when she should have flattened it and put it on the shelf.

She should read the letters. She would have to write back, to apologize, but found she didn't have the heart for it. Her eyes were starting to blur, so she picked herself up, brushed her hands, and straightened out her skirt. Ann was still waiting, with that hovering sense of worry that was on the way to becoming permanent.

"Could I have tea in the garden, please?"

"It's quite late; Joan's already gotten supper—"

"I know. It's just for a bit."

Ann had a tray ready in moments. She and Joan always seemed to have a tray ready, and Beth was grateful.

Outside, she settled into the chair and felt herself growing heavier, though this was surely her imagination. She was melting into the ground like a puddle of tar. The sun was setting earlier and earlier these days, and the air was cold. She hugged her shawl, watched the patterns steam made, curling up from the cup.

The house finches stayed through the winter. They called from the climbing roses on the far brick wall. One ventured out to the tray of seed. Seemed to glance at her, turning its pink head, shivering the streaky feathers of its breast.

She had so many plans, so many ideas, so many questions. She wanted to take her maps of migration patterns and compare those maps to surveys of average temperatures throughout the year. These records were available from naturalists but also military expeditions and meteorological observations, and if she could compile *those*, she could see if changes in temperatures over the course of seasons correlated with migration patterns. Was it changing temperature that told birds to leave the summer homes for warmer climates? Or maybe it was the changing position of the sun. She could learn to use a sextant, to measure the sun's position, then compare those measurements to the migration schedules. Maybe if she talked to astronomers or military navigation experts—

None of them would ever talk to her. They'd certainly not listen. Her brief, rare time at the Naturalist Society proved it.

Maybe she could write under another name. She might not be able to use Harry's name anymore, but maybe a whole new name, a whole new invented figure to hide behind. Send reports from a different address, disguise her handwriting. Or maybe she could ask Bran to play proxy for her, using his name as she'd used Harry's . . . until he set off on his next expedition, leaving her alone for years and unable to use his name for anything. Besides, he had his own work; why should he care for hers?

And then Ashford had essentially asked for her help. What did she make of that? Should she give her work to him instead?

If all she ever did was sit here in her refuge and feed house finches, would that be enough? No, it wouldn't. Back at the table, she covered her face and cried, just a bit, three or four sobs, soaking half her handkerchief. The finches never stopped calling, rustling the branches as they flew back and forth. The sound calmed her when nothing else could.

She got up and scooped some seed from the can on the potting table to refill the tray. The finches scattered but returned before she moved off. They were mere feet from her. They had grown used to her.

She held some seed in her outstretched hand. Stood very, very still. Try, she could only try, wasn't it worth trying—

A finch landed on her hand. Its tiny claws dug into the tips of her fingers, a thrilling pinch of warmth, a bit of fluttering life. It hardly weighed anything at all, and its wings brushed air across her hand. It pecked at her palm, snatching at seed, looking up between every bite, tilting its head to show off shining eyes. This close, she could see the shading of pink across its head and chest, the way the rose color streaked into the brown like a smeared bit of ink. The brown, which seemed so plain from a distance, had a dozen different shades to it, every feather holding its own pattern, much more vibrant than the corpses of its brethren in her study. Every barb of every feather shivered with life. And then it was gone, shoving off from her fingers. She still felt the pinch of its feet after.

Saw herself in its eyes, like a mirror.

Then *through* its eyes, looking down on her garden from a height. The bird flew to the top of the wall, flitting back and forth among the rose's highest branches, and she saw *herself*, looking back at it, and then the whole view swooped and tilted dizzyingly, like she was falling from a chair—but falling *up* instead of down—

And the vision was gone, finished. Gasping for breath, she put her hand to the wall, her head swimming.

A bit of seed still clung to her hand, and her skin still tingled with the fluttering touch of the finch's claws. She could have held a thousand bird skins in her hand and not been able to do what she just did. But a single living bird in hand—

Maybe she really could fly. But maybe she could only do it here, where the birds knew her, where she felt safe, with no one else looking on and judging her.

She wouldn't tell a soul about what she'd just done. No one would ever believe her.

Drawing a fresh breath, she wiped her face and went inside to Harry's—no, to her study, and sat at the desk. She lined up her pens, which needed to be cleaned, put them next to the bottle of ink, stacked the notes and journals and pushed them aside, and found the fresh package of paper she had just opened. The blank pages glared.

She had an idea for a different path.

She took the lid off the ink and chose a pen. She did not have to solve the mysteries of nature and the universe. The old path was closed; her life with Harry was done.

But she could still write. She would write of delight.

Resistance to the idea of evolution arose not just from religious quarters but from Arcane Taxonomists. It shattered the notion that Arcane Taxonomy was fixed and could be delineated by fundamental laws. Naturalists and Arcanists could not accept evolution without an explanation as to why and how it happened. When that explanation arrived, it blasted apart assumptions about the entire natural world, and by extension, Arcane Taxonomy.

A name that meant something to Linnaeus meant something different to Darwin and would mean something else again to naturalists who came after. Nature, geology, climate, the world, *changed*. Linnaeus himself acknowledged this, by the end of his life. Many Arcane Taxonomists, fearing for their power, could not. By contrast, those who embraced evolution grew more accomplished, more powerful. They could use that change.

Charles Darwin might be the greatest Arcanist who ever lived. It was said that he could make plants grow, that he lured birds to his hand, that with the proper specimens in hand—a shell from the genus *Strombus*, for example, or a homing pigeon—he could communicate with people on the other side of the world. The dilemma was he never wanted to be a great Arcanist.

Like Linnaeus, Darwin made only one great expedition. On his voyage aboard the HMS *Beagle*, he circumnavigated the globe, spending almost five years collecting, surveying, investigating, and writing. The journey launched his career as a naturalist, and his research led to the development of his theory of evolution by natural selection. It has been said that this revolutionized the natural sciences even more than did Linnaeus's system of classification. Darwin sought to answer not just how many and what kind of species populated the natural world but why so many species existed and how such variety came about. His investigations drove toward fundamental questions of life itself. This made him powerful. His skills and advice were in demand throughout the later part of his life.

If Darwin had used his abilities in service to the British Empire, he might have solidified its power for a thousand years. Generals, government ministers, titans of business, and philosophers tried to entice him to exert himself in business, politics, and territory, but Darwin was a recluse and couldn't be swayed. He was independently wealthy and couldn't be bribed. He seemed only moderately interested in patriotism, mostly by assisting and promoting other British scientists and Arcanists. He sank himself into studies of the minutiae of the natural world: the differences between species of barnacles, the motion of plants as they grow.

He was, almost everyone agreed, an enigma.

A contemporary and colleague of Darwin's, Alfred Russel Wallace independently developed his own theory of evolution by natural selection. He might have supplanted Darwin as his era's great master of Arcane Taxonomy, except for a matter of timing, and perhaps class. Self-taught, Wallace came from a working-class family and therefore had to make his living as a professional collector, traveling the world to gather specimens for other scientists. Still, he wrote extensively on what he discovered and corresponded with the great scientists of his day, including Darwin and Hooker. Much like Darwin, he couldn't seem to be persuaded to use his Arcanist abilities to advance any great national or military cause. He eventually turned his studies and Arcanist abilities inward, to the question of Arcane Taxonomy itself and the source of Arcane power. Was the primary component of such power physical or spiritual, and what did that say about religion, God, and the life beyond? His questions were considered dangerous by some; he did not seem to care. He felt that study of the natural sciences could not entirely explain Arcane Taxonomy, which blurred the line between science and miracles.

This is the great paradox that becomes clear again and again: that the greatest Arcane Taxonomists simply don't care about power. They care about knowledge gained through close observation. They spend their time chasing after beetles, studying feathers, and watching the leaves of plants unfurl. They are brilliant, obsessed, and odd.

At the time, much was made of fellow Arcanists Joseph Dalton Hooker and Alfred Russel Wallace serving as pallbearers at Darwin's funeral. Was some astonishing Arcane *practicum* planned? Some great feat that would extend Darwin's power after death? In truth, it was only this: they did so because they were his friends.

TWENTY

Vermivora cyanoptera / Vermivora chrysoptera

Bran had classes to teach, while trying not to think about Beth Stanley. They'd sent notes; she hadn't replied. He ought to visit her. Invite her to go for a walk in the park to see if their warbler was still there. *Their* warbler? God, what was he thinking?

He didn't do any of these. He was a coward.

"Mr. West?"

The disaster at the Naturalist Society was a sign that trying to keep up Harry's work—*her* work; it was hers; she was talented and ought to be encouraged, supported—was a lost cause. If she wanted to speak to him, she would, and if she didn't, he ought to leave her alone. Anton told him he ought to leave her alone. They had disrupted her life enough.

"Mr. West!"

He sat up, startled. He was leaning on the desk at the front of a small lecture hall, sunlight coming in through windows that needed washing, wooden crates full of specimens stacked on shelves along the walls. The chalkboard behind him had a list of questions written on it—the letters were blocky and careful, otherwise his writing would be illegible. The chalk was still in his hands. His students, a dozen bright-eyed boys, looked back at him from their seats expectantly. Someone had asked a question, and he'd been too distracted to hear it.

"Yes," he said, stopping himself from wiping chalk dust all over his trousers just in time. "You have a question?"

"Yes, sir. I don't understand how the animals know to stay in their own territory." Frakes was a willowy blond boy in the second row. He took lots of notes, always raised his hand, and never answered a question correctly. God knew what he was doing here.

Bran practiced being patient. "You've got it backward. We define the territory by where we find them. That's the whole point of field observation."

The boy furrowed his brow for a moment, let out a huff that made him sound just as confused as before, and wrote something down.

Bran was trying to teach them how to conduct a regional zoological survey. Choosing a location with lush habitat, returning to the same location at different times of day, then different times of year, collecting specimens, counting species. Simple. But it was an impossible task, because they were seventeen- and eighteen-year-old boys being asked to *sit still* for two hours. If only he could put the information in them with a pump. Bran had surely never been this . . . *obtuse*.

Not a particle of Arcane talent in the lot of them, alas.

He encouraged them to go to the park for an hour or so—without guns—and simply observe the birds, squirrels, rodents, and other fauna. He thought of Beth and her opera glasses, following birdsong.

At last the hour was finished. He packed up his work, checked for messages in the mail room—none—and walked home. The city was the same blur of traffic and noise that it always was. Central Park offered some respite. He counted a dozen different birdsongs, including that of a hermit thrush. He should tell Beth about it.

He shouldn't be thinking about Beth at all.

A week later, Bran couldn't stand it anymore and brought his bird gun to the park in the hopes that damned unidentifiable warbler was still lingering. If he could get the bird in hand, take measurements, make comparisons with his own collection, he'd classify it once and for all and present the findings to Beth. A strange gift—a stuffed bird skin and a Latin name. This wasn't how one generally endeared oneself to women. Flowers and chocolates were considered more acceptable.

But he reminded himself: he wasn't trying to endear himself to anyone. This was about the warbler. The unknown, a new name, the power that came with it. He could use a bit of power just now.

He found the row of viburnum, which had started dropping its leaves for winter, and stalked patiently. Some blue jays were carrying on at the other side of the lake. He watched for movement, saw the trembling of a branch, searched for the tiny creature that had caused it. His hopes rose, but when he got a look at the bird, it was a junco, not the mysterious warbler. He moved on, doubled back. His breath fogged from the cold, and he rubbed his hands together to warm them.

A spot of yellow against the drab backdrop caught him. He held his breath. A branch shook, a flutter of movement followed—and there it was, the tiny creature with the baffling set of markings that made it neither one thing nor the other.

He stopped time. His hunting trick—freeze his target for a moment, like a hovering kestrel, *Falco sparverius*, suspended. The warbler stood in plain view, unmoving, so unnatural. He could walk right up to it and get a look. Carefully, carefully, he raised his gun, took aim—

She will not thank you for killing it.

He blinked, his vision blurring. The spell let go; the bird shivered, free, flittering to a new perch. It still offered a good, clear view. Now, he should take the shot now.

Bran lowered the gun. It was clearly a warbler, no debate about that, with the narrow bill and low posture, small body swept to a sleek tail. Entirely out of season, but sometimes if a bird found enough food, it might not migrate. Its coloration should have made it one thing, but the markings on face and wing made it another. If it sang, that would be another clue, but it was the wrong time of year. No wonder Beth was so intrigued. Her good instincts and knowledge were telling her two different things—

The bird was two different things. A hybrid. Bran should have known from the first. The name was ambiguous, and so its taxonomic power scattered from his senses.

To name a thing was to know it, and he could name the parts and pieces, but that didn't give him the knowledge he sought. The naming took more work, and there was a lesson to be had there. *Patience, be patient . . .*

He tucked the gun under his arm and walked out of the park, straight to the Stanleys' brownstone.

After a couple of hours tromping around the park, he was disheveled, slumped in his travel coat, a little sunburned. Anton would tell him his hair was a mess, but he couldn't do anything about that. He rang the Stanleys' bell anyway, without so much as a card to announce himself, which seemed dangerous. Really, he'd rather be stuck in a blizzard in Greenland than navigate these Manhattan social circles. He fully expected to be turned away. That bright young maid would tell him the lady of the house was indisposed and he could leave a message.

He must have looked a little crazed and desperate. The maid—Ann was her name—disappeared inside for some minutes and returned to say the lady would receive him in the study. After handing over his hat and coat, Bran gently set the gun in the corner. Ann eyed it warily but said nothing. She escorted him down the now familiar passage that led to the study. The curtains were pulled back, the room filled with early afternoon sun, and Beth was seated at the desk, writing. Ann said his name; she set down the pen, looked up, smiled. "Good morning! Would you like to sit? Ann, can you bring some tea?"

Whatever had given him the idea she was angry with him?

He went straight to the cabinet where the specimens were stored, opening drawers until he found the warblers, the bright little gems of color all laid out. Ah, yes, there they were, and seeing the two likely parents resting side by side made him even more sure.

"Bran?" Beth asked.

He drew out the pair, the golden-winged, the blue-winged, and a set of the females besides, the whole family, and their mystery warbler displaying traits from each. He laid them on the desk in front of her like a cat delivering a catch.

"Found your warbler," he said.

She regarded the specimens, and her confusion vanished. "A hybrid." They beamed at each other stupidly for a moment.

She sorted through some pages and found her sketches of the warbler, set them next to the specimens, took up her pen, presumably to make notes . . . and hesitated.

"I suppose you should be the one to write up the sighting, if you think it's worth writing about," she said. "Then there's a chance of it getting published."

"Oh, Beth," he said softly, an apology.

"It's not as if we can give it a new name. Funny, isn't it? We spend so much time putting these things in boxes and adding the right labels, but there's always something that gets away from us. Is there taxonomic power in naming a hybrid?"

He settled into a chair by the wall. "I believe there is taxonomic power in everything, if we only know how to find it. But that's the problem, isn't it? There's so much we don't know." His voice faded, the truth of the statement overwhelming him.

Ann arrived with the tea cart and frowned at him while setting out cups on the desk, pouring, asking about cream and sugar. Bran took his black. They remained silent until Ann left. The door stayed open.

He downed half the cup and let it burn his tongue. "I'm sorry. For leaving you alone at the Society. For . . . for everything. I had hoped for better."

"You don't need to apologize. You were busy; you were there to work. And I can take care of myself. Really."

He should believe her. Why didn't he?

Books lay piled on the floor, along with a couple of rolled-up maps and an open notebook filled with writing. So she hadn't been entirely discouraged. She was still writing. Good. "What're you working on?"

She hummed a little. "It's a surprise."

He desperately wanted to get down on the floor and read the pages spread out there. Could he distract her? Make something fall over in another part of the house, so she'd be forced to run out to look?

Could he freeze time for a moment? He'd never tried the *practicum* on a person.

She glared at him over her teacup. "Don't even try it."

"Try what?" He blinked, hoping to look innocent, failing.

"I don't know, but you've got that look. You're about to do something Arcane. I won't have it."

"Ah. You know me well."

He couldn't interpret her expression, then. He didn't know her at all.

"There's a puzzle I'm trying to work out," she explained, clinging to her teacup. "If I figure it out, I'll tell you, but I'm probably wrong, so it doesn't matter."

"If you need help—"

"I don't *want* help. Regardless of if I need it or not." She caught his gaze suddenly. "May I ask a favor?"

"Of course, anything." He was far too eager.

"Don't shoot the hybrid warbler. I know it would make a good addition to your collection, and you must desperately want to have it in hand, but if there's only one, it should be left alone."

He tipped his head back and chuckled. Maybe he did know her. "What?"

"I came straight from the park, and my bird gun is sitting in your foyer right now. I did intend to shoot it. And then . . ." He shrugged a little. "I didn't. You're right. It should be left alone." And so should she, if that was what she wanted. He started to get up, to set aside the teacup and excuse himself.

Then she said, "Can I show you something?"

"Of course."

She led him into the hallway. Instead of taking the turn to the foyer, she led him through a second door that he hadn't noticed before. Not that it was hidden, just that it hadn't been relevant. It led to the private part of the house, and so he had dismissed it.

They went through it to a sort of dining nook off the kitchen. A window here let in light, and another door led out to a garden. She brought him here with a solemn air, as if they entered a church. The space wasn't big, maybe fifteen feet on a side. It was big enough to get some sun, and the brick walls were shrouded with growth. Dozens of shrubs, vines, and a bit of lawn with overgrown grasses gone to seed. In summer, it would be bursting with flowers. An instant quiet enveloped him. In the middle of the city, the peace of the forest closed in. The smells of earth and growth, the perfume of roses, even this late in the season.

At the far end, feeders hung from iron stands: trays of seed, a cage of suet. A low basin of water on a pedestal nearby. Birds flitted from it and took refuge among nearby foliage.

"Be quiet," she whispered, pressing him into the chair by a table.

He identified the calls of three different species straight away. Finch, chickadee, sparrow. As he listened, the calls grew, proliferated, and he realized there were more birds here than he ever would have guessed at first glance.

Gardening tools, along with spare pots and planters and a bin for compost, occupied the corner by the door. A cupboard contained sacks, cans, and jars. She pulled out a handful of seed from a can and went to the brambles along the northern wall. He caught movement there, among the leaves.

He waited quietly. This he knew how to do, sitting in a blind while his quarry drew close.

She held out her hand and stood still, a lovely statue. The calls didn't stop; the birds didn't flee. The fluttering drew closer, closer. Suddenly, a burst of feathers and motion hovered over her hand, and a house finch, *Haemorhous mexicanus*, perched, its claws curling at the end of her index finger. It dipped its head to the seed in her hand. Its streaked plumage blushed with pink on its head and breast, a bit of color against the drab. It perched there, calm, for ten, twenty, thirty seconds, eating all the while.

A connection between them rose up—he could feel it on the back of his neck, like he'd shoved his hand into a wellspring of power, the valve of a gaslight flaring. Beth took it in, making it part of herself.

The finch flew off, back to the brambles. Beth dropped the remaining seed on the ground and brushed her hand off on her skirt.

"I never bring anyone here. Even Harry rarely came here. This is my refuge from everything. I know you must think this is very silly."

"Not at all," Bran murmured. "I . . . I think the world of you." He would not look away. If he were very still, very patient, perhaps she would come eat out of his hand.

She approached him, her steps cautious.

Leaning, she touched his chin. Daring and frightened, both at once. He had seen such a look in men on sea ice that was cracking underneath them, who must leap to get to safety. Leaps of faith and necessity.

She kissed him. Very lightly, no more than the flutter of a wing at the corner of his mouth. He stayed very still indeed, and once again felt that bright connection between her, the finch, this place . . . and him. He didn't think of what he would use such power for. He simply sat with it, and that was enough.

She turned away, back to the house. Her touch on his skin still stung. He took a moment to catch his breath, then leaped to follow her. She wasn't in the dining alcove, or in the hall beyond, and in the foyer he found Ann waiting with his coat and hat in hand.

"Mrs. Stanley sends her apologies; she's tired and has gone to rest." Butter wouldn't melt in her mouth.

He could yell at the maid if he liked, if he wanted his tumble of feelings to go somewhere. He could storm to Beth's rooms and demand to know what she meant by that kiss—and he was sensible enough to recognize that would make him a monster.

What else could he do but take his hat and coat, pick up his gun, and leave?

TWENTY-ONE

Spinus pinus

Anton wrote to Beaumond about arranging a meeting with the Signal Corps and waited for a response. And waited. Tried to focus on the work, arranging new lectures. They had received some invitations, which was encouraging. They would require travel to Philadelphia, Baltimore, other cities. They had to follow every lead.

He began to think about appealing to companies for sponsorship. This . . . was not ideal. A sponsoring company—Standard Oil, for example—would claim a proprietary interest in an expedition's research and discoveries. Carnegie of Carnegie Steel was rumored to be interested in sponsoring scientific expeditions, but the man put his own name on everything. It would be these companies' flags planted on the territory, not any nation's. Their names would go up on the chalkboard at the Naturalist Society.

Anton had to think about how much he was willing to compromise.

The arrival of mail at the flat became fraught, both he and Bran jumping at the stack of letters and getting surly when they didn't find what they wanted. Bran had gone particularly quiet in the last couple of weeks, burying himself in books and writing.

"Are you feeling well?" Anton made the mistake of asking once, after a long evening of silence.

Bran scowled. "Why wouldn't I be?"

"God, how should I know?"

"Fine. I'm fine." Which was what Bran always said, unless he was starving or suffering from frostbite.

They were tired, that was all. The autumn weather was wearing on them.

He'd been waiting for word from the Signal Corps for a month when they both ended up at the postboxes in the building's foyer. Bran claimed the contents, and Anton almost snatched the letters out of his hands, he was taking so long to sort through them.

"Here's one." Bran handed over an envelope. "Looks personal. Not business."

Anton recognized the writing: his father's secretary's. Nothing for it but to open it and see what it was about. He read it during the lift ride up to their floor.

"What is it?" Bran asked, concerned, when Anton didn't say anything. "You're biting your lip. You only do that when you're upset."

Anton gave him a look. The lift stopped, and the operator clanged open the door and let them out. He didn't speak until they were in the flat and he wouldn't have to worry about being polite.

"It's from my father," Anton finally said. "He's in Boston. Arrived yesterday."

"Did you know he was coming?"

"No. I think he wanted to sneak up on me so I couldn't scurry off on some expedition and avoid him."

"You need an excuse not to see him? We can make an excuse. I desperately need to go count pine siskins in the Dakotas. My academic career depends on it, and you have to come with me to make sure I don't fall into quicksand."

Anton laughed in spite of himself. "I appreciate the offer, but I think I should go see him. If nothing else, it will prevent him coming here to look for me." He refolded the letter and slumped onto the sofa.

Bran did likewise, wrapping his arms around him, trapping him. Now that felt good. A nice distraction.

"Is he that terrible?" Bran asked.

"Oh, not at all. He's a good man. But . . . we always seem to have the same conversation."

Bran chuckled. "The one about settling down. A sensible profession. Marriage."

"That's it."

"When will you go?"

"Let me write to him. We'll see. Maybe I can chase down some leads while I'm there."

"Maybe you can ask him for money for the expedition?"

Anton had never asked his father for money directly. He might consider it.

Anton arrived at the Parker House Hotel, where Sir Archibald had taken a suite for his visit. Combining diplomacy and business, he would meet with his firm's investment partners as well as make trade inquiries on behalf of the Home Office. Sir Archibald could do it all.

At the entrance, the doorman blocked his way. "Workman's entrance is around back."

That nearly did him in. He wanted to grab the man's collar, shake him, and spit out the words *Do you know who I am?*

Instead, he chuckled bitterly. "Do I look like a workman?" His suit and overcoat were fine wool, tailored. His bowler hat and polished shoes came from London. He looked every inch his father's son. Except for the color of his skin, which was all the doorman saw.

"Well . . . I mean . . ."

"Sir Archibald Torrance is expecting me. If you won't let me in, you must go explain to him why not."

The doorman yielded.

Inside, the valet was more cordial. He showed Anton to the door of the suite and rapped twice. "Mr. Anton Torrance to see you, sir."

The valet let him into a small but elegant parlor, everything clean and neat, polished furniture arranged on plush carpets, lovely paintings on the wall, a fire in the grate, and dark velvet drapes pulled back from a window overlooking the street.

Anton's father rose from a desk with writing materials scattered over it, and the valet bowed himself out. Sir Archibald wore a fine suit, his beard and hair impeccably trimmed. More gray than Anton remembered. Almost all gray now, in fact. Made his face seem even paler than usual. He'd lost his tan from his years in Nassau.

Sir Archibald smiled broadly, coming at Anton with his hand extended. "Greetings, Mr. Torrance," he said brightly, indulging in the joke. He'd been calling Anton *Mr. Torrance* since he was five years old and begging to see the office where his father worked.

"Sir Archibald," Anton answered right back, shaking his hand. "Father."

Their skin and hair might not match, but Anton got his height and build from his father. They stood eye to eye, both broad shouldered, athletic—Sir Archibald had played cricket at Cambridge. Their handshake was hearty, arm rattling. His father clasped Anton's hand in both of his own.

"Come, I've just had tea sent up." Sir Archibald led him over to the chairs and sofa by the fire. He poured two cups and let Anton add his own cream and sugar, which he'd also been doing since Anton was five. They exchanged the usual questions about travel, how things were back home, and so on.

Sir Archibald then said, "Now tell me, what have you been up to?"

Anton had practiced what he would tell his father, a quick summary of the lectures he'd been giving, the travel, the plans for the Antarctic expedition, sounding as confident as possible, everything assured.

He stopped himself from mentioning Bran and how much he relied on him. If he started speaking of Bran, he wasn't sure he'd be able to stop and how much he might reveal. There were things his father didn't need to know.

"I'm proud of you, son. You do us proud." When Sir Archibald said *us*, Anton wasn't always sure if he meant himself, the family, or the entire nation of England. Perhaps he meant all at once.

He ducked his gaze, hiding a smile. "Thank you, sir."

"And then after this expedition, will you be ready to come home?"

This was the argument Anton knew was coming. "Honestly, I haven't thought about what comes next. I plan to write a book or two about the trip, of course. After that, we'll see." The Himalayas. The poles. Another trip to Antarctica—exploring the place would take more than one expedition.

Sir Archibald set down his cup and sat back, gaze narrowed and appraising. "I confess, I worry about you. All this adventuring. It's one thing when you're young, but you won't be young forever—"

"I'm thirty-four, hardly ancient!"

"Oh, of course, of course. But . . . I suppose it wouldn't do any good to ask when I might expect news of the possibility of an heir?"

This was also a familiar conversation, but once again Anton noted the overall gray of Sir Archibald's hair. The lines on his face; a softness he'd never noticed before. His father was getting old. This might not be about Anton at all.

He'd always had his expeditions as an excuse—it would be irresponsible to leave behind a young wife and child when he continually put himself in danger. He was ready with all his usual denials. But this time, oddly, he thought of Beth Stanley. She would be at home in this parlor. Both his father and mother would like her. He could imagine himself . . . comfortable with her, at least. Harry had done it, despite his prior inclinations. For whatever reasons Harry had married her.

No, it wouldn't be fair to Beth. It wouldn't be honest.

His father noticed the hesitation and raised a brow.

"Several things would have to happen first," Anton said cautiously.

"You know, it's become rather fashionable for fine young men to come over and find sweet American girls to marry."

"Sweet, *rich* American girls?"

"Well, that too." They shared a smile.

"Their fathers tend not to like the color of my skin."

Frowning, Sir Archibald drew himself up. He'd been an abolitionist, back in the day. "If you came home—" *Home* meant England. It also meant Nassau, but this time, clearly Sir Archibald meant England. "No one would give you trouble."

Anton chuckled. "They'd give me a different kind of trouble." They might not snub him to his face the way the doorman had. But there were always those who would subtly turn their backs when he entered a room. Those who would avoid looking at him, speaking to him, acknowledging him at all. Mostly, they'd behave this way when Sir Archibald wasn't around.

"My name protects you."

And that was the problem. "Father. In England I will always only be your son. Here . . . at least I have a chance of being my own man. Surely you understand." Sir Archibald had had the same argument with his own father about going to the Caribbean. Anton had gotten the stories from his mother, Margaret.

"Then you could make a career in Nassau."

"Oh no, far too hot." He had an excuse for everything, didn't he?

"You've always been contrary, haven't you?" Sir Archibald said fondly.

"I suppose I have." One thing at a time. Antarctica, then . . . then they'd have to have another version of this conversation. "Let me plant a few more flags first. Then we'll see."

"All right. Now, let's talk about where we might have supper . . ."

222

TWENTY-TWO

Sturnus vulgaris

Beth hadn't told her mother that she had changed to half mourning, so when she arrived at the Clarke house for the Carnation Society's charity luncheon, Mrs. Clarke greeted her with an expression of horror. She actually stood there open mouthed, as if she had witnessed a terrible carriage accident in the street.

As if Beth wearing half mourning only a few months after her husband's death was the worst thing her mother had ever seen. It probably was. Harry's death was the worst thing Beth had ever seen. The two were no more comparable than a duck and a vulture.

"Beth, really, I didn't expect you to wear black for a full year, but don't you think this is too early? What will Mrs. Stanley say? The other Mrs. Stanley, I mean."

"I'm sure I don't know," Beth said. "If it's proper for me to come to your luncheon, then I'm going to be dressed in half mourning, and that's all there is to it." Kissing Bran had made her brave.

Mrs. Clarke briefly clutched her chest, then had little choice but to let the maid take Beth's coat and welcome her inside.

The parlor and dining room were already full of the society ladies of Mrs. Clarke's set. Beth's father had fled to his study, and she popped in to say hello and kiss his cheek. He was reading a newspaper and blinked up at her absently before focusing.

"You're looking better, Bethy," he announced with a bit of confusion.

This pleased her. "I'm feeling better."

"Good, good." He chuckled and returned to the paper, and she swept back to the luncheon, where it turned out her mother didn't expect her to do anything but sit and drink tea and accept the now habitual rounds of condolences and commentary. Beth hoped that being here would mollify her mother enough that she would wait a month or so before asking her to another one of these gatherings. Or maybe a week or so, at least. She could try to be optimistic.

Chatter went on around the spacious parlor, clusters of conversation continuing, breaking up, forming again in different configurations. There must be some natural law to it, as with the combining of chemicals or the flocking of starlings. The group would not achieve stasis—the bustle was the stasis.

Beth was thinking about the park, the hybrid warbler, the navigational talents of migratory birds, and the power of lodestones. She sipped tea and watched guests arrive, cataloging behaviors, who seemed most effusive, who seemed annoyed. Who bent their heads in gossip and who stood in a daze. A group arrived that Beth recognized: a mother with two daughters just come into society, second cousins of some sort on Beth's mother's side, all the height of fashion. Mrs. Clarke was bringing them up, introducing them around. Beth was almost sure they had been at her and Harry's wedding.

The elder daughter was wearing an enormous and extremely fashionable hat decorated with egret feathers draped artfully off the back of the brim, fluttering down her neck. Beth was no longer indifferent.

Estelle Humphries, wearer of the hat, was in that first flush of being out in society, excited by it all but not yet feeling the desperation of needing to marry and settle down before she missed her chance. Beth remembered that air of competition, when all her friends and cousins of that age could name every single male of their acquaintance under the age of forty, their professions, pastimes, and relations, as if they were labeling horses in a race and placing their bets, with marriage as the finish line.

Beth set her cup aside and started across the parlor, but her mother hooked her arm and brought her up short.

"Beth, do not say anything to Estelle Humphries about her hat, I'm begging you."

"I'm only going to talk—"

"You charging at her across the room will only frighten her. Maybe you could write her a note later."

"You're always saying I should get involved in charitable causes. *This* is my cause."

"A *cause* means raising money for orphans or educating immigrants or park beautification. Why *birds*?"

"Because I *like* them."

"I forbid you from speaking to Estelle Humphries about her hat. Now, come help me with the cakes."

Helping with the cakes meant directing the maids on how best to arrange them on the sideboard. "Bring out the lemon next. No, not the ginger lemon, the plain lemon!"

Beth's help wasn't needed at all. Mrs. Clarke set her against the wall with an admonishing look, silently telling her to stay put as if she were a child.

While Mrs. Clarke's attention was in the kitchen, Beth escaped. From the dining room into the parlor, she hunted for Estelle Humphries and found her by tracking down the fluttering white plumes. She stood near the tea table with her mother and sister.

Beth pounced. "Estelle, how lovely to see you," she murmured, sidling up to her and taking her arm.

"Beth! Oh . . . oh, Beth, I'm so, so sorry!" Estelle's eyes began to well up, so Beth acted quickly, drawing her into a bit of a walk around the room.

"Thank you. I'm getting on as best I can."

"I can't even imagine!"

Beth hoped she'd never have to. "I wondered if I could talk to you about your hat."

"Oh, do you like it?" The tears vanished instantly. Smiling, she petted the brim, a gesture so precise she might have practiced before a mirror.

"Well, honestly, it makes me think of the birds who died to provide those feathers."

The tears started up again. "What? But . . . they're so beautiful!"

"Yes, and they're even more beautiful when the birds are wearing them."

Estelle clutched Beth's hand. "But you see, egret feathers mean good fortune."

Beth stared, nonplussed. "I'm sorry?"

She leaned in conspiratorially. "If you wish to attract good fortune, you must wear egret feathers. Gilly Cooper wore egret feathers for a month and an English baron proposed to her! You wear dove feathers if you are facing a confrontation. Robins are supposed to bring joy, and you wear the feathers of a bluebird if you are taking a long journey—"

Beth scowled. "Is that what the Arcanists say?"

"Oh, yes! They say it's good luck if you know the names of all the birds. I'm practicing." She beamed.

"That isn't how it works, Estelle. That is a . . . a terrible misunderstanding of Arcane Taxonomy."

"Don't be silly. I've got a whole book on it. Besides, don't they simply pluck the feathers and let the poor things go? I thought they grew them on a farm, like minks!"

Beth summoned the patience of a sparrow on her nest, incubating her eggs. "They kill the minks, too, Estelle." She produced a handkerchief from her sleeve and offered it to the girl. "The real problem is, so many of the birds are being killed that they're becoming rare. They're dying out."

"But how is that possible? There are just so many of them."

Mrs. Clarke appeared to take the girl's place next to Beth. "Oh, Beth, there you are. I can really use your help in the dining room. Will you excuse us?" She offered Estelle a stiff smile and dainty laugh. Beth let herself be led away.

"Please tell me you did not harass that girl about her hat," Mrs. Clarke said when they were alone in a corner.

"I thought she should know where all those feathers come from."

"It's ghoulish."

"Yes, it is. That's why I told her."

Mrs. Clarke didn't leave her side for the rest of the luncheon. It couldn't possibly be because three more ladies had entered wearing hats with feathers, made all the more excruciating as Beth could identify the birds whose feathers had been plucked. Flamingo. Heron. Cormorant.

She imagined a scenario: The egrets with the limpest, dullest feathers would escape the hunt for the milliners' trade. Flamingos with pale, uninteresting colors would not be sought after. These birds would then go on to breed, producing some offspring with equally dull feathers. According to Darwin, in a number of generations, egrets would no longer be fluttering white beauties but drab and tattered. Flamingos, herons, even parrots might all then become plain as sparrows. Natural selection, steered by fashion. Women's hats could change the course of nature.

Sweet revenge.

Beth was not adapted to the environment of the Naturalist Society, and while she also clearly wasn't adapted to her mother's habitat, she thought there ought to be some middle road between them.

Not too many temperate days remained in the year, so when the sun came out one morning, she put on her coat, collected her opera glasses and notebook, and went to the park, especially the section near the lake where she'd seen the warbler. She saw no sign of it and hoped that meant it had finally traveled south for the season.

Plenty of other birds remained. She walked up the path, intending to stop at a bench that had a view over the water to count ducks, when a gentleman in a coat and bowler hat approached. She recognized Montgomery Ashford and stopped cold. He saw her, smiled, and didn't seem surprised.

"Ah, Mrs. Stanley," he said. "I was hoping to see you. I wondered if you've given any more thought to the subjects we discussed."

"Mr. Ashford," she said cautiously at the coincidence of him being *right here*, so specifically wanting to talk to her. How lucky indeed. "May I ask first—are you spying on me?"

He laughed a little but didn't deny it. "I might have decided to walk in the park more often than usual the last few days, hoping to run into you. I'll confess that much."

At least he was honest, to a point. But he had a whiff of the Arcane about him, a thread of lingering power. She thought of the alarm calls blue jays made when a raptor was near. He could set an alarm on her front door, to alert him when she walked out. That was how she would do it, at any rate.

"*Sterna paradisaea*," she said.

He leaned in, eager. "Have you by chance—"

"I'm not sure what you want to do is possible. Playing with a compass is one thing. Our access to the planet's magnetic field is . . . it's indirect. Maybe the arctic tern can sense magnetism; maybe it uses it somehow. We can learn from the creatures we study, but we can't *become* them. The tern's journey belongs to itself, and since we still don't understand how it navigates or even how it manages such a feat of endurance—"

"I don't really care about the details. I just want to be able to use that power."

But didn't he see it? The details *were* the power. To some, Arcane Taxonomy was merely a profession, a set of tools. But it was so much more, the ineffable quality that made the natural world beautiful. It was . . . divinity. Arcanism occupied a space between knowledge and wonder.

She had seen through the eyes of a finch. In Antarctica, one might see through the eyes of a tern, and that would be a good way to scout beyond the coastline. But there was still the question of range, and whether there were any species that traveled all the way to the pole. Even with Arcanism there'd be no shortcuts, not like Ashford wanted.

"What do you know about magnetite?" she asked.

He narrowed his gaze. "Every schoolboy plays games with lodestones, sticking nails to them, that sort of thing. What's that got to do with anything?"

"Isn't it interesting," she said, "that boys use nails to play with lodestones and girls use pins? I'd never noticed that before."

"How far did you get?"

"You speculated about exerting some power over the earth's magnetic field. Try it with a lodestone first, and see where you get."

"That's all I'm going to get from you, isn't it?"

"I'm pursuing other topics of inquiry these days, Mr. Ashford. I'm sorry."

He smiled. "You were wasted on Harry Stanley."

She flushed, an almost familiar fury rising up. What did he know about Harry? What did any of them know? And how dangerous were the assumptions people made. "I must be going. Good day."

She turned and walked off.

Anton had only been gone a few days, but Bran was going mad. He hadn't realized how much of a steadying influence Anton had become for him these last couple of years. He relied on that brief touch on his shoulder whenever he was at the Naturalist Society and wanted to yell at someone being daft. Then Anton sent a letter saying he'd be gone another week—he'd lined up meetings and lectures in Boston and was having good luck soliciting the universities and naturalist groups there for funds. Made some noise about introducing his father around and that having an Englishman of his status along was helping. As much a novelty as the polar bear, he joked. Anton might not ever ask his father for money, but he seemed perfectly fine using him as a prop. Bran approved.

To avoid being alone in their flat, Bran spent more time than usual at Columbia. He avoided walking in the park because he didn't want to accidentally run into Beth. Rather, he *did* want to accidentally run into Beth. So he avoided the park.

But he missed talking to her. She hadn't so much as written him a note since she kissed him. And he . . . he didn't know what to feel.

The city had had rain, which stopped, leaving the streets wet and the skies clear. He almost wanted the rain to start up again so he could be even more miserable. If he could complain about being cold and wet, he wouldn't complain about everything else.

"Mr. West!"

Bran was three steps past the doorman when he stopped at the call, backed up, and summoned a smile. Or at least the strained politeness he was reduced to this afternoon.

"Package for you." The man handed it over. It was the size of a magazine, wrapped in brown paper.

He took it, confused. No address on it, just his name in familiar handwriting: Beth's. "Why not leave it in the mailbox?"

"Mrs. Stanley dropped it off herself."

"Oh? Thanks."

At home, he locked the door out of habit but opened a curtain to let in some cold light. Took off his coat and shoes and poured himself a drink before sitting on the sofa to confront the package. It was just some token. Something of Harry's she thought Bran should have.

He pulled away the wrapper to reveal a magazine, the *Ladies' Home Helper*.

Why in God's name was she sending him this?
A card sticking out of the top marked a spot.

Bran:
I have found my way forward.
—Beth

He flattened the magazine to an article: "On the Attraction and Enjoyment of Birds in the Garden," by Mrs. Elizabeth Stanley. It was illustrated with a simple, sentimental drawing of an unlikely assortment of songbirds gathered on an ornate platter that would have been more at home in a well-appointed dining room than in the outdoor backdrop pictured.

Bran stared and must have read the title five times before gathering up any sort of reaction. She, Beth, had been writing new essays without telling him, and he was . . . surprised? Unhappy. He was unhappy.

Despite misgivings, he read on.

> If you cannot go into the woods to visit our
> sweet singing friends, then think of bringing them
> to you. You can make your garden attractive to
> them, and so make your own little Eden.

She went on to list varieties of seed, sunflowers, and thistles, even peanuts and oranges, and how best to arrange them, provide space, clean up after them; she then described the different birds that could be expected to partake of the feast. He pictured her garden as he read, her refuge, arranged just how she liked. This essay was all her and what she had learned there.

There was nothing of the natural sciences in this.

> If you are very patient and calm, you can draw
> the little creatures to you. Put some seed in your

palm and hold out your hand. Now, the first time
you do this, no bird will come near. It is too strange;
they're not accustomed to you and don't know yet
what to do. But as I said, be patient. Try this at
the same time every day, for a number of days in
a row. They will grow used to you and see you as
just another flower in your garden. They will flutter
closer and closer. When they are used to you, they
will perch on your fingers and eat from your hand.
Such grateful, delicate creatures will lift your heart.

It was . . . fanciful. Imprecise, sentimental . . .

He hated it.

The rest of the magazine was filled with recipes, articles on fashion, illustrations of hats, discussion of etiquette and the latest trends
in charity luncheons. Bringing new life to old linens with embroidery,
for God's sake.

Maybe it was the glass of bourbon that did it. It was late afternoon,
and long shadows cast by buildings already stretched across the city. Far
past the decent hour to call on anyone, much less a young widow. He
knew that much about society. But he couldn't wait until tomorrow.
He'd never be able to sleep, gnashing his teeth over this.

He put his shoes back on, grabbed up his coat, and left.

Throughout the 1860s and '70s, members of the US Cavalry reported encounters with the Plains Indians that suggested some natives displayed Arcanist abilities. These reports were discounted almost universally by military leadership and Arcane Taxonomists of the major universities, since these cultures lacked the education and training normally associated with Arcane practices. They could not possibly know the Latin of binomial nomenclature that was considered a requirement to practice Arcane Taxonomy.

Nevertheless, the cavalry's overwhelming defeat at the Battle of the Little Bighorn in 1876 made even the greatest skeptics reconsider. In particular, stories about the Lakota leader Sitting Bull gave some credence to earlier reports. That year, during a Sun Dance ceremony, Sitting Bull had a vision that predicted a great victory against their enemies. The battle ensued mere weeks later. Commentators on both sides of the conflict raised a possibility: that Sitting Bull's vision had been not a prediction but a working of Arcane skill that ensured Lakota success. Even if these were just stories, they made Sitting Bull famous and marked him as a threat to American authority. He was eventually confined to a reservation in the Dakotas, but rumors of his power persisted.

Many native communities throughout the continent tell stories of their medicine and spiritual leaders who are able to speak to trees, summon bison on command, control the weather, and wield many other powers. Some scholars suggested that these communities developed their own *lingua arcana* independently. They advocated sending scientists to study the phenomena, but military conflicts continued and made such studies difficult, if not impossible.

Besides that, the native peoples rarely share what they know, except to a chosen few, who are keeping their secrets. White scholars, they say, have proved untrustworthy and lack the connection to the world around them that fuels their knowledge.

TWENTY-THREE
Catharus guttatus

Beth was writing in the study when voices sounded from down the hall.

"Mr. West, please," Ann pleaded as heavy male footsteps thumped on the floor.

Beth set down the pen and was ready when Bran West came through the door. His glare was more than a little crazed. His collar was open; he wore no tie.

Ann fluttered behind him. "Mrs. Stanley, I'm so sorry. He wouldn't stay at the door."

"Ann, don't apologize. You can hardly help it when a man decides to be a brute."

Bran had the sense to look sheepish at this.

With a chance to catch her breath, the maid composed herself. "Shall I bring tea?"

"Not right now," Beth said. "We shouldn't reward such behavior."

Bran had stopped just inside the study and seemed frozen now that he was here. He clutched a rolled-up magazine in his hand, and she began to suspect the source of his temper.

"You got my package."

She waited for him to speak. And waited, while he grew even more flustered. Finally, he smacked the magazine against his opposite hand. "You're better than this."

"Ann, it's all right, you can go." Ann glanced sidelong at Bran, who didn't seem at all civilized just now.

"Ring if you need me," Ann said, glaring at Bran.

"And don't wait outside the door eavesdropping," Beth added.

"I'll just go check if Joan needs help with supper, then, should I?" She slipped out and closed the door behind her, leaving them in silence.

Beth turned back to Bran. "Well? I thought you'd be happy to see I haven't given up on publishing my work."

"This isn't what I meant!"

"What exactly is it you think *this* is?"

"Telling silly girls that they can make pets of wild birds? This is frivolous. A waste of your intelligence."

"*Silly. Frivolous.*" She looked away, wearing a smile that felt cruel. "You're being demeaning."

He seemed taken aback at this. "I am?"

"Yes."

"But I thought you wanted an academic career. I thought you wanted to be recognized as a naturalist, an Arcanist—"

"Ah, but as we have seen, natural history has no interest in recognizing me. Can you blame me for going where I'm wanted instead? If I can instill a love of nature in some young girl somewhere, convince just one woman that she doesn't need egret feathers in her hat, isn't that something?"

"What would Harry think?"

"Harry isn't here."

He drew back from this, donning a blank, inward look, as if he had never considered such a thing. As if he'd been trying to keep Harry alive through her.

Was that all this was?

She suspected Bran had created an image of her that had no resemblance to her reality and that he did not care to learn the difference.

"Did you even love him?" Bran said.

How dare you, she almost said, but held back because the words were so rote, so predictable. Her anger felt so . . . *plain.* So she held the words back.

"I did," she said. "I'm not certain he loved me. He *liked* me well enough. But I'm not sure he would have missed me if I'd died first."

Bran set down the magazine and pulled over another chair, so they were looking at each other across the desk. She noticed then that she had torn a piece of paper into shreds out of nervousness.

"He did love you," Bran said. "How can you think he didn't? I can't imagine him marrying anyone else but you."

This was a thing she did not want to talk about. She looked every place but at Bran, and everything in the room reminded her of Harry, his smile, the delight he took in running his fingers over the curve of an ammonite, the way he would stand over a tray of bird skins and beam happily even if he couldn't identify a single bleeding one of them. He liked the colors, the shapes, the wide variety. The idea of them. He liked having them. He liked having her, part of his collection.

Bran knew Harry better than she ever had. If she could give him information, as a scientist, perhaps he could help her understand.

"I am trying to think of the most delicate way of saying this. Some things between Harry and myself were not what they should have been. No matter how much I tried, how much I wanted—" She swallowed, wet her lips, and could think of no gentler way to explain. "He did not want me as a husband wants his wife."

"What do you mean?"

"Intimately," she bit out, blushing. "I am sure something must be wrong with me."

Bran leaned back, smiling a little. He wasn't shocked. He didn't even seem startled.

"There's nothing wrong with you." He said this so confidently, but he didn't know; he couldn't possibly know.

"It's kind of you to say so."

"No, Beth. I mean—now it's my turn to try to be delicate. It was Harry's fault, if there was any fault at all, and not just . . . awkward circumstances. Harry. Well. Did you never guess that Harry preferred other company?"

"I think I would have known if he'd had a mistress."

Bran laughed harshly. "All women say that, and most of them are wrong, but no, I can assure you he didn't have a mistress. Do you want to know why we were all so shocked when Harry married you? And it isn't because there's something wrong with you. Not at all. Not even a little." His voice grew fierce enough to make this even more awkward. "I don't know how to say this. I need other words . . ." He closed his eyes a moment, and his voice turned rhythmic. "'And it seems to me if I could know those men, I should become attached to them . . . O I know we should be brethren and lovers, I know I should be happy with them.'" He fell into the words—the poetry.

She had to think but then recognized them. "That's Whitman." Ah, Bran's smile lit up at that.

This was not what she had expected. This was not what she expected *at all*.

Every word felt awkward. "So when you say he preferred other company . . ."

"Male company."

She had heard of such a thing, in distant whispers and innuendo. The sort of thing that happened in places where people like her did not go. Like hearing about dolphins in the Amazon River. Two men, in bed together, embracing . . .

She blushed very hard then. She had to think about it rationally, scientifically. Hold what Bran had told her at arm's length and consider. And . . . she found it did not surprise her. In fact, it explained a great deal.

"But how do you know this?"

He tilted his head and raised a brow in such a pointed, suggestive manner that she gasped. The two men in her imagination gained faces. Bran and Harry.

"Oh. I see."

"Hmm. Yes."

A new round of mortification followed. They were both blushing. The temperature in the room must be rising, they were producing so much heat between the two of them.

"So you see, my dear, you are not in the least bit broken," Bran said. "Far from it. You are . . . you are . . ."

Harry had never, not once, looked at her as Bran was now looking at her. No, Harry had looked at *Bran* that way. And now Bran—

Beth had never *wanted* the way she did right now. She studied the feeling from this angle and that. Approached it rationally, or attempted to.

"Do you only like men?" she asked, trying to sound detached and scientific. Failing.

He didn't answer, which was itself an answer. The core of science was repeating an experiment to see if the outcome was the same. She had a sudden, brilliant thought and could find no reason not to proceed. Just try. Just see what he would do.

She went to the door. Turned the key to lock it, then set the key on the desk. Next, she turned on the lamp, to give them a little light, and went to the window to draw the curtains. Privacy. She pressed the edges of them together and turned to look at Bran over her shoulder, to see if he caught her meaning, if he understood what she was asking. Prayed that he did or she might never be able to speak to him again. If he wished to flee, she had left him a path to the door; he saw right where the key was.

His lips parted, and he strode toward her—then stopped. He raised his hand, reaching, then hesitating. His gaze held such longing, and the lines in his brow held such anguish.

She looked away. "I'm sorry, I've overstepped," she murmured, and started toward the door to unlock it.

He grabbed her arm and kissed her. Laced his fingers in her hair, held her cheek firmly, and kissed, insistent and determined. She held tight to his arms, then his shoulders, trying to pull herself closer, though they were already standing pressed body to body. This was what she had wanted: an enthusiastic, delightful ravishing. How to make this go on, how to encourage him to continue.

"Bran. Will you come to bed with me?" she asked, her breath catching. The worst that could happen, he would say no and leave her and never see her again. She'd be right back where she'd started. But then— he might come to bed with her.

He nodded, a lock of his hair falling into hers, his breath against her lips. "Yes. I think I will." He hummed a laugh against her. "I have to tell you, I really don't have much experience—"

"Neither do I."

"Practice, then?"

"Oh yes."

They spent a gently delirious night together, whispering reassurances and encouragements, occasionally laughing at the awkwardness and the tenderness. He was gone by morning. He kissed her before he left and promised to call again soon. She believed him.

She was alone when Ann brought tea. "Mr. West is very handsome," Ann said evenly, setting down the tray and opening the curtains to let in light.

There must have been signs of what had happened. It must have been obvious. What point would there be in trying to hide it? This was Beth's house; she could do as she pleased.

"He is."

"Hmm."

"Indeed."

Ann swept out wearing a cheeky smile and didn't say another word.

They came together three more times over the next week. The whole time, Bran waited for Anton to come home and rescue him.

He also did not entirely want to be rescued.

When he was with her, he felt such peace, such warmth, he was overcome. When he was not with her, he missed Anton and felt sick with betrayal. He found himself comparing their kisses. Beth's were soft, curious, with no beard scratching against his cheeks. Anton's were confident, rough, tactile; he always held on tight, fingers curled in Bran's shirt or gripping his arms. If Bran had to choose which he preferred . . . he couldn't. When Anton returned home, the contradictions would disappear, he would stop seeing Beth, he would plunge headlong into their work, and all would be as it was.

He did not know if he wanted all to be as it was.

TWENTY-FOUR

Fulmarus glacialis

In dreams, Anton swam in freezing waters, graceful as a seal. Soared over iced-in seas like a fulmar. How beautiful and simple to be a bird, a whale, a creature born to this world, and not a man who had to force his way into it.

Bran spoke sometimes about what it was like, sinking into the being of other creatures, of making them part of himself, so attuned to them that he felt as if he swam through the water or soared through the air. Anton said it sounded like dreams, but Bran shook his head. No, because it was so much effort to maintain, Latin phrases swarming, having to pin the right words like insects to a board. It was no more natural than a man swimming in icy waters.

Dreams were easier. Dreams you just fell into.

Anton longed to fall into this next journey.

Finally, exhausted beyond reason, he returned to New York. He'd allowed his father to bring him along on his many social engagements—to show him off. Anton had shamelessly taken advantage of the situation to pitch his expedition, to solicit support. And it had worked. He'd collected an impressive number of pledges, signed books, made himself charismatic, a figure out of a story. It all made up for the few times he'd entered a salon and had the room go quiet as gazes turned on him with disdain.

He said farewell to his father and caught the train back to New York. Didn't bother sending word ahead to Bran—he'd beat anything but a telegram home.

Anton hired a cab at the train station to bring him home in record time. Many travelers spoke of how lovely it was returning home after a long trip, and Anton could understand that in the abstract. He was certainly looking forward to seeing Bran.

Bran was home, more than any place was. He was eager to share news of his successes in Boston.

"Help with your bags, sir?" the doorman asked from the curb as the driver handed down his valise.

"Hullo, James! I think I've got it, but thank you."

"Oh, there's a telegram just arrived for you." He drew the folded paper from a big pocket in his coat.

"Let's see it, then." Might be anything, and he was a little annoyed at the delay in getting back to the flat.

Then he read the message, which was from the Signal Corps, informing him that a panel would be meeting at the end of the month to hear proposals for an Antarctic expedition. Far too long to wait, yet almost not long enough to prepare. Except he'd been preparing for this for years. This was it; the chance was here.

Anton almost hugged the doorman. "Has Mr. West seen this? Is he at home?"

"No, sir. He isn't in at the moment."

"Oh? Do you know where he is?"

"Been calling on Mrs. Stanley, I think."

Anton paused, feeling a particular blaze of insight that came from relying so much on his instincts and observing closely the world around him. That little nudge that told him a polar bear was lurking on the other side of a ridge. The way he could tell if groaning ice was about to break under him or merely shift.

He spoke carefully, testing, tapping, to see how thick the ice really was. "He's been helping her with Mr. Stanley's things."

"Yes, he's there often."

The ice was thin, cracking.

"Thank you, James."

James held open the door, and Anton carried his bag inside, determined as ever.

In truth, if he was honest with himself, Anton should have known this day would come, though he had avoided thinking of the details of exactly what that would look like. He couldn't imagine the conversation that must happen, the changes that must necessarily come to this life they had built together if—when—Bran remembered women. When he decided to embrace the conventional life, marriage, and all the rest. Beth was such a good match for him, Anton could hardly begrudge him.

But he did, and would for a while.

When he entered their flat, it seemed abandoned. Too quiet, as if it had not been slept in in days. The grate was cold. Anton left his valise sitting in the middle of the floor. He couldn't imagine the conversation that must happen between them, and perhaps that was because the conversation should not happen. Perhaps a quick, clean break would be simplest for them all. Like a rifle shot. A path presented itself. A set of concrete actions that gave him a sense of purpose. Yes, this was what must be done; he could do this.

After all, he was already packed, his bag already sitting there.

He glanced around their shared parlor, which was full of things he wasn't sure he had a right to: books the two of them had shared, trophies, specimens, equipment gathered for the next expedition. That could be dealt with later, if at all. He should leave a note for Bran, he supposed.

He found pen and paper on Bran's desk, and then his wits failed him. He'd been told he had a poetic hand in describing his journeys; his memoirs had been well received. But this was beyond his skill.

He simply wrote, "I wish you well," and signed his name, as if he were autographing a book. A souvenir.

He took up his valise and went to find a hotel.

TWENTY-FIVE
Molothrus ater

The doorman stopped Bran on his way in. "Mr. West, Mr. Torrance was asking about you."

Bran felt a shiver. "Mr. Torrance? Is he back?"

"He came back yesterday and went right out again."

Yesterday? Anton had come home *yesterday* and not sent word? And then . . . he knew. Somehow he knew. Bran's breath hitched in a moment of panic. He must see Anton as soon as possible. Immediately. And he dreaded seeing Anton.

He raced to the flat and sensed an alteration. Anton had been here, though couldn't say how he knew. Something in the air had shifted. The smell of Anton's coat lingering, maybe. Anton should be here, there should be a fire in the grate, they should lock the door and draw the curtains and kiss, and then trade all the news—

He saw the note on the desk. So direct, so simple. A final stab that left him bleeding. The bear might as well have killed him after all.

Bran had made a terrible mistake. A whole raft of them.

He crumpled the note and sat. How could Anton have found out? How could he have suspected? Didn't matter. Came home expecting to find Bran here, and he was gone. Maybe he'd suspected all along. Bran should have gone with him, he should have stayed away from Beth, he should have—

He had to find Anton immediately. Anton had to come back for his books and things eventually. No, he didn't. He'd send for them. They'd have to talk eventually about the expedition. The expedition was bigger than both of them; it would have to go on.

The prospect of spending years on an expedition with Anton as a professional colleague and not his partner in all things . . . it was unthinkable. He couldn't *think*.

He smoothed out the note he had crumpled, studied the lines. Went to the shelves and found a guide to the city with a map in it. Arcane Taxonomy usually wasn't much good for divination, such as speculating on investments or predicting outcomes of events. The future wasn't fixed any more than species were. But this had some logic to it: Anton was in the city somewhere; it was just a matter of narrowing down the possibilities. He set a pin on the page to point the way, considered the great navigation skill of homing pigeons, and—

Nothing. He didn't feel anything. No shift in the natural order around him, no power gathering to him. Anton was his heart. How could he not find him? How could he not know instantly?

He stepped back from the desk and paced a moment. Swept back his hair, which was feeling particularly tangled. He usually relied on Anton to straighten it out for him.

He got out a candle. Cleared the desk of everything else, all possible distractions. Remembered those early lessons, those first heady weeks at Harvard when the Arcane world opened up. To name a thing was to know a thing, and to know it was to use it—

He touched the wick.

Nothing happened.

Something broke inside him. He stared at the dull unlit wick for . . . for he wasn't sure how long, but the sun had nearly set when he got himself moving again. He had to move. He had to do something. He had to see Beth; she could help him—

No, Anton first.

Anton would tell him *This is a task that could be done without Arcane Taxonomy. So do it.*

He grabbed his hat and went back out. Stopped again to speak to the doorman. "When Mr. Torrance left last, did he say where he was going?"

"He didn't stop to talk, sir," the man said. "He had his bag with him."

He'd fled entirely, then. And what if he didn't want to be found?

They had some favorite watering holes. Bran went to them all, hiking along sidewalks on some kind of forced march. A bar, a bookstore, a club. Anton wasn't at any of those places. Bran was sweating, pure nervous anxiety. He would overheat. His socks were getting wet. Wet feet ran the risk of frostbite . . . not in New York City, not this time of year. He was being idiotic.

Around midnight, he admitted defeat—just for the day—and stumbled home to try to sleep in a too-quiet apartment that didn't have Anton's coat and hat hanging up, and so the whole world was spinning wrong.

He got up at dawn and tried again. Spent two days staking out Anton's usual path in Central Park. No Anton. Maybe the man had fallen into a ditch somewhere. Jumped off a bridge? No, not likely.

At the end of the second day, he went to where he probably should have gone first: the Naturalist Society. He realized he hadn't gone there first because he couldn't imagine Anton there without him. They almost always went together. And now Bran walked in alone.

After working hours, the foyer only had a few hangers-on; Bran didn't even notice who they were or if they said anything to him. He leaned on the porter's stand. "Teddy. Has Torrance been by?" He hoped he sounded casually curious and not desperate.

"Yes, sir."

"Any idea where he's staying?"

The man furrowed a skeptical brow. "I'd have thought if anyone knew, it'd be you."

Bran kept his expression frozen at frustrated rather than despondent. "Well, we seem to have gotten our wires crossed. He's been out of town."

Teddy seemed reluctant to tell him. Maybe wondering what kind of gossip he could dig out of this situation. Bran would have to strangle the information out of him.

Finally he said, "He asked me to forward his mail to the Monaco, sir."

A hotel uptown, not far from the park. "Thanks."

"Have a good afternoon, sir."

Not bloody likely.

He stationed himself in the lobby of the Monaco Hotel, on a plush chair beside a *Dypsis lutescens* growing in a wide glazed pot. The doorman was eyeing him warily, and Bran realized he was wearing the same clothes he'd had on yesterday and still hadn't brushed his hair. He'd crammed some bread and tea into his mouth that morning, but he hadn't had a decent meal since yesterday either. Like he was on an expedition.

As people walked to and fro, he straightened his back and at least tried to pretend to be respectable. But the longer he waited, the harder it was to stay composed. Anton had to walk by sooner or later.

And then, just like that, there he was. Bran blinked a few times, not sure it was him. He had a constant picture in his mind of Anton dressed in sealskins, beard overgrown, squinting into an Arctic sun. This Anton was perfectly turned out in a suit and tie, bowler cap pulled down just so. Dark alluring eyes that narrowed when he finally saw Bran, sitting there so pathetically. Anton's lips pressed in a line. Usually, he smiled when he set eyes on Bran.

Bran didn't even know where to start with him. He might fall at his feet, sobbing, but that wouldn't be very dignified. He could wait for Anton to say something, but Anton might just as easily walk right past him without acknowledging him.

He stood, hat in hand. "Mr. Torrance?"

Anton stopped, which meant there was no turning back. "Mr. West. How do you do?"

Oh, so that was how it was. "You didn't have to leave, you know."

"I thought it best."

"Best for whom? For what?" he responded, beseeching. "I should be the one to leave. I'm the one who made a mess of things."

Anton ducked his gaze, hiding a flicker of a smile. "Is there a mess?"

"Of course there's a mess, when you walk out—" He stopped; slumped. He really shouldn't be shouting about this in public. They shouldn't be discussing this at all. "I can't light candles, Anton. I can't do anything."

"Let's go walk," Anton said, and invited him to the door. Once outside, they walked side by side, which was so familiar and normal Bran wondered if he'd imagined the whole thing, the last few days of anguish. He was hungry and not thinking straight, and Anton probably knew that. At least now they wouldn't yell at each other in the middle of a hotel lobby.

They went silently for blocks, as if neither wanted to be the one to speak first. As if neither knew what to say.

Anton finally asked, "What do you mean, you can't light candles?"

"I can't focus, I can't think straight. Every word of Latin gone straight out of my head. I'm useless."

"Maybe you should have thought of that before you made the mess," Anton murmured.

They walked a few more steps, and Bran finally recognized Anton's muted tone as dangerous. Furious.

"How can I make it right? How do I . . . unmake the mess?"

Anton stopped, turning on him and grabbing the lapels of his jacket. Almost going so far as to shake him, fierce enough that a couple of passersby turned their heads to look. "Bran. You *betrayed* me."

Bran swallowed, trying to speak with a suddenly dry mouth. "You can go ahead and punch me. Might make us both feel better."

"God," Anton muttered, dropping his jacket and walking off again. Bran hurried to catch up. "I'm sorry."

"Are you, truly?"

And that was the rub, wasn't it? "I'm sorry," he said again, useless as it was.

"Being sorry doesn't make it right."

"How did you know?"

"An educated guess," Anton said. He sighed, and some of the anger seemed to dissipate with the breath. "When did it start?"

Bran felt miserable. "Not long. A week."

"She's a lovely woman. If you prefer a conventional life, you should take the chance."

Bran stopped and stared. Anton went on a few more steps before looking back, with apparent disdain.

"How can you say that?" Bran said. "Can you really just walk away?"

"Do I have a choice?" Anton said, so practical. "Seems you've already decided."

"It was a mistake. I'll never see her again." But that thought hurt as much as betraying Anton.

"Oh, don't do that. If you never see her again, then I could never see her again. And I like her. Do you know, my father asked me again when I plan on marrying, and I immediately thought of her? Do you think she'd accept if I asked?" Something manic and teasing lit his gaze.

"You wouldn't."

"Would you?"

Bran took hold of Anton's arms, right there on the street. "You and I have too much together. I won't let you go."

"If I decide to go, you can't stop me." He was the taller of the two, stronger. The one who shot bears, the one who could haul sleds the farthest. He could simply pick Bran up and set him aside. "Unless you plan on using one of your Arcanist tricks on me. Freeze me in place so I can't move."

"I told you, I can't!" Had Anton even been listening to him?

"What do you mean you can't?"

"My Arcanism is gone. I can't do anything."

Anton seemed amazed. "Well, you've got to get it back."

"Yes, of course, but how?"

"You're the Arcanist, you tell me!"

"Then . . . you still want me on the expedition?"

"Of course I do. Here." He drew out a piece of paper from his pocket, a telegram, and handed it over.

Bran read it, read it again: a summons from the Signal Corps. The meeting they'd wanted so badly. The chance to pitch the expedition. Anton ought to be smiling; they ought to be celebrating. They just stared at each other. "This . . . this is wonderful. Isn't it?"

"It should be."

It was the first glimmer of sunlight on the horizon after an endless Arctic winter. "Then I've got to fix this. How do I fix this?"

"Your Arcanism, or . . . us?" Anton started walking again, and they went on, close, their sleeves brushing. "I expected this, you know."

"You did not."

"That you'd find someone. That once you got back on shore, back around women, you'd want to settle down with one. The right one."

"I never intended it. I never looked for it."

"I can't . . ." He sighed, deeply. "I'm trying to decide if I could share you. Maybe I could, but I think I'd always be afraid that you just wouldn't come home one day. And—"

"It wouldn't be fair to Beth," Bran said. "Harry wasn't faithful to her. Those late-night sessions, when he'd go out to the clubs after lectures at the Society. He could usually find someone to go home with."

Anton hesitated before asking, "Did he ever go home with you?"

"No, never," he said earnestly. "I've been wondering if I should tell her."

"I don't think you should. At least not yet. Not while his grave is still fresh."

And then the question that Bran just couldn't answer. "And what about us?"

Anton glanced at him. "We need to get your Arcanism back."

The *we* was like a warm fire in a blizzard. "I should get out of town. Someplace fresh, clean."

"Someplace cold," Anton said. "And wild."

"Yes," Bran breathed. "Mr. Torrance. You do know how to seduce a man."

"Well, I know how to seduce *you*."

They'd go away, into the cold, where they could be closer to who they really were. Away from any confusion.

TWENTY-SIX

Junco hyemalis

My Dear Beth,
I'll be away for a time on business.
    With affection,
    Bran West

Bran had sent her the cryptic note and then vanished.

She expected another letter from him to follow, saying where he'd gone, maybe telling her what birds he saw there, but nothing arrived. What affection was there in silence?

Was she simply meant to wait quietly until he finished whatever it was he was doing? Did she get any opinion in the matter at all?

She went to the park; she wrote; she fed the finches. Flew with one partway across the neighborhood, gently steering it toward Bran's building, maybe hoping for just a peek into the window, but the flight was abrupt and dizzying and she quickly left off, back in her garden to sit gasping for breath.

This was edging close to spiritualism, putting a question out into the universe and hoping for an answer to fall into one's lap. Years ago the famous Fox sisters claimed to be able to speak to the dead through the power of Arcane Taxonomy, praying over bird skins and grinding up fossils, playing at being some sort of Arcane alchemists. Easy to dupe a public that didn't understand.

She wrote to Anton Torrance—surely he'd know where Bran had gone. It seemed brash, all this writing letters to unrelated men. Anton didn't reply. She assumed her letter, or the reply, had been misdirected and sent a telegram. Still no reply.

She decided to go in person and leave a card, approaching the doorman of the building with confidence. The uniformed man frowned, and she tried to sound reassuring.

"Good afternoon. I'd like to leave a card for Mr. Torrance."

The doorman set his frown. "Mr. Torrance left town, ma'am. Mr. West too."

"Both?"

"They travel often," he said. "North this time, I think. They do like the cold." He seemed to shiver at the thought.

"But why . . . never mind. Thank you."

She walked away, more briskly than was comfortable, all the way to Fifth Avenue and finally to the park, where she took a footpath at random. The truth was plain: Bran had fled. From her. And taken Anton with him.

She stopped and stared across the lawn. He had fled with Anton.

Oh good God, her powers of observation were *terrible*. And she pretended to call herself a naturalist. No—be fair. She had lacked context for the behavior she had observed in the two men. If you had never seen a jellyfish feed, you would not know what its tentacles were for. Bran preferred the company of men. He had said so himself. He and Harry, he and Anton, who had always been such a perfect gentleman . . .

She had been an aberration.

The grass was wet or she would have sat right there, feeling sorry for herself. Well, what did she have to complain about? She had been thinking they should leave her alone so they could concentrate on their more important work. But . . . she'd seen Bran almost every day this last week. He had become a habit.

He could have told her. He *should* have told her when he told her about Harry. He could have, and simply didn't. And now she was furious.

She threw herself into work, clinging to what she had, her small amount of power and influence. She had written more essays for ladies' magazines about identifying birds, listening to their songs. She wrote for young women like Estelle Humphries who might never have imagined themselves outside a parlor. Beth thought of herself opening a door for them: *Look, just look.*

The polar maps, books on magnetism, and monographs on arctic terns were still spread out on the floor. She spent time with them as well. Wished she had a specimen of *Sterna paradisaea* in the cabinet, something concrete to focus on. Maybe she could visit the one in the natural history museum.

One of the books lay open to a diagram of the earth's magnetic field, a sort of cage of lines looping from one pole to the other. She could make a three-dimensional sculpture of it with wire and a globe, and that might help her better visualize. A compass followed the lines, but that seemed a step removed from the power itself.

Like the terns. Their migration route followed the same lines, north to south and back again. As if they followed some internal compass of their own.

Then, how could that be used?

Sterna paradisaea. Unerring direction. To send herself on that same route, as she had with the finches. She didn't think she could make such a journey herself, but if she could send some kind of . . . signal, like a telegraph? And who would she send it to? Another Arcanist, someone who could help her test this, perfect it.

Bran. Tell me where you are.

Electricity, magnetism—she imagined the whole earth as a telegraph, auroras sparking across the atmosphere. What if they could be made to send messages? She thought of Bran's imitation aurora in the lecture hall. He never had told her how he did it.

Bran, talk to me.

The message flew out. She was sure it had. Her own force reached for him.

It was not instant any more than birds or sound or anything else traveled instantly. She leaned back against the desk, compass in hand, and waited.

Nothing answered her, and this was frustrating.

Before giving up for the evening, she wrote down her work, every detail of the *practicum*. The associations she made between *Sterna paradisaea* and the Arcane power inherent in that connection, a power that could connect the world. Filled up several sheets. Made a copy, just in case, and put the copy in her journal.

Still nothing from Bran. The logical assumption was the *practicum* didn't work. In which case she needed to talk to another Arcanist about what she could do to make it work. Again, Bran was the only one she knew who would even speak to her.

Well, Ashford would speak to her. But she didn't want this to be for him.

She could send Bran her treatise. Or . . . a daring thought intruded: she could bring it to him. Maybe even try the *practicum* to tell him she was coming. See if he was surprised. Assuming she could find him.

Strix nebulosa: no better hunter than the great gray owl in cold climates. This was the largest skin in the collection, taking up nearly a whole drawer on its own, the smaller species—screech owls and barn owls—nestled around it. Its feathers were impossibly soft, the shape of its wings allowing it to fly silently, to strike without warning. She seemed to remember that Bran had given Harry the specimen; a look at the tag confirmed it. He'd collected it in their Harvard days.

Another connection straight to Bran. She could use this. Use its senses, follow the trail. Hunting wasn't just eyesight, it was intuition. This wasn't clairvoyance, it was weaving together threads. The power of insight.

She focused on a spot on the shelves, issues of the *Pinfeather* from the last three years, all lined up. Her hand reached unerringly for one issue over all the others. Scanning its contents, she found it: "Annual Survey of Winter Birds in Windham, Maine," by Mr. Brandon West. He'd gone to the same spot for the survey the last two years. Were there even any birds to be found on such a trip? Yes, there were. Evening grosbeak. Pine siskin. White-crowned sparrow. A dozen others, even in the dead of winter. The list brought up a deep longing in her. No matter where, no matter when, no matter what else was happening or what the people around them were doing, there were birds. Bran included the name of an inn in his introduction, thanking the proprietors for their hospitality.

A simple letter. She would write to tell him what she was working on and that she would like his help—that the *practicum* might be of use to them on the Antarctic expedition. Yes. It wasn't for him, it was for the expedition. He'd want to know.

She had access to wonders. She had the power of her own determination. Why shouldn't she go? She would go to prove that she could. That was all.

Worried that the inn would be shut up for the season, Beth telegrammed ahead and was relieved to receive a reply within the hour: this time of year the inn took in guests for ice fishing and would be happy to welcome her. What a delightful adventure, going on holiday at exactly the wrong time of year. No wonder Bran and Anton enjoyed this.

"This time you really shouldn't go, ma'am," Ann said, but continued helping Beth pack anyway. Just a valise, no more than she could carry. Ann was too amenable; she couldn't not do what Beth asked.

"Oh, it's fine. It's not like I'm going to the Arctic. I don't think I'll ever be out of sight of a train station."

"But alone?"

Beth glared. They'd had this conversation before.

"And what am I supposed to tell Mrs. Clarke when she calls?"

At this, Beth paused. She could give Ann any blithe answer. Easy enough to do when Beth wouldn't be here to face her mother herself.

"I don't know." Beth sank into a chair to consider. She shouldn't leave; she would worry her family. She could tell them she was going, and where—and they would throw a fit. The thought of it exhausted her. Bran and Anton didn't worry about telling anyone they were going. She stood again, smoothing out her skirt. "I'll write a letter. If she calls, you can give it to her. But she may not even call."

Ann gave a fierce frown, an indication of how likely she thought this was.

"Don't look at me like that. You know I have to do this."

"Yes, ma'am. I know."

She had planned all the Arcane *practica* she might need to use to help ease her way—to make herself unseen, to turn the attention of others away, to open doors. The talents of drab sparrows and starlings that got in everywhere. As it was, she didn't need to use any of them. Her mourning garb worked all on its own. A woman dressed in mourning, even half mourning, traveling alone and with urgency in winter, must be on some desperate mission and so ought to be helped along her way as much as possible. Porters took charge of her valise, guided her to her seat, brought her tea, asked after her health, and gave her detailed directions on each leg. She took advantage of this impulse, going so far as letting tears fill her eyes at the tiny train station at Windham when she inquired about finding a carriage, or wagon, or anything at all that could carry her to the inn near Jordan Bay. A delightful black-lacquered sleigh on runners, pulled by mismatched draft horses, was summoned. She was tucked into it, a blanket over her lap, and off she went.

The afternoon sky was blue, the road covered in well-packed ice and snow, which the sleigh passed over with a soft hiss, punctuated by the thump of hooves. The sound would have lulled her to sleep if there hadn't been so much to look at. Pine trees, frosted with humps of glinting snow, more tracks weaving back and forth, the sparkle of sun on the frozen lake. The colors here were pristine. Snowfall in the city might stay fresh for a day, never more than that before traffic and refuse turned it to black mush. This might have been the first snow to ever fall in the world.

Redpolls. She bet she would see redpolls here. *Acanthis flammea.* She'd never seen one outside a specimen case.

The inn turned out to be an old saltbox house situated at the end of a drive, near a narrow inlet along the lake. Whitewashed, its roof covered with snow, it would have been invisible against the snowy land-scape if not for the bright-blue shutters by the windows. Half were closed, but half were open to let in the sun. The glass reflected the sky. Smoke rose from a brick chimney. The walk from the drive to the door was cleared, snow piled up alongside.

This was so exactly the opposite of where she had come from that she felt hope. A strange settling of peace, of possibility. Shelter in the middle of inhospitable territory. This was where she had needed to be for the last few months.

The driver deposited her and her bag at the door and rang a brass bell hanging there, as clear a signal for the break between where she had been and where she was now as she could wish.

Clearly, the inn was not used to hosting women in winter. The matron of the house, Mrs. McDell, went on about not having the nec-essary comforts appropriate to a woman of her standing. Beth replied that she didn't care: a warm room and porridge would do her very well. Oh no, Mrs. McDell assured her they could do better than that. If Mrs. Stanley was sure? She was. She would happily wrap herself in blankets and sit by a window for days.

She finally asked about Mr. West and Mr. Torrance. Why yes, of course, Mrs. McDell said. The great explorers. They visited almost every winter and stayed in a cabin about a mile up the lakeshore, though they came to the inn for a good cooked supper every few days. They were at the cabin now, in fact. Would she like to send them a message?

No, Beth said, hesitating. Not yet. She suddenly felt like an invader. She settled in to wait.

Bran had come back to Anton, and Anton was determined to enjoy him for however long the impulse lasted.

Arctic exploration was often a combination of desperation and boredom. A winter outing in Maine only partly recreated the experience, but partly was enough for now. It was cold. A wrong turn meant getting lost; the wrong clothes and boots meant risking frostbite and hypothermia. The landscape was beautifully stark and pristine, but it was hard to feel much desperation when just a mile through the woods sat a well-stocked inn that put up a good supper, especially around the holidays.

Without the desperation of survival, one had time to really examine the surroundings. To take in the experience, the chill in the lungs, the frost that formed on the tip of one's beard. To enjoy returning to the warmth of a roaring fire in a stone fireplace. Anton would always embrace the challenge of a death-defying Arctic trek, but currently he enjoyed not spending every waking moment on the problem of survival. How lovely, tromping around on snowshoes all day and then falling into a warm, comfortable bed at night. Especially if the bed had Bran in it.

And Bran fell into their bed with an unsettling mania, as if determined to prove that whatever he had with Beth Stanley was an anomaly, soon forgotten. Anton wasn't entirely convinced, but he didn't say so. This was a distraction, so let them both be distracted.

They needed each other. Their expeditions needed both of them, working together.

Bran's mania extended to collecting. His Arcanist talents were still hibernating. At least, they hoped the ability merely slept, temporarily. As a possible cure, Bran had gotten it into his head to make a survey of lake fish in winter, to collect and name and classify until Latin nomenclature filled his mouth enough for him to direct it somewhere. He cut a hole in the ice, dropped in hooks and lines, and brought strings of fish to the cabin. Ate a few and pickled the rest.

Several times a day he touched a candle, but the wick stayed cold and dark.

"You're still an excellent naturalist, no matter what." Anton tried to reassure him, but Bran wasn't reassured.

"If I can't do this, what am I?"

He'd never had to ask the question before. Not like Anton had.

You're Bran, Anton wanted to tell him. *And I love you.*

Bran went on, frantic. "If I can't get this back, what am I supposed to do? Take up farming? Arcanism—it's all I've ever had."

Anton was growing frustrated with him. "You've got me. And you've got a meeting at the Signal Corps."

Bran had scrubbed hands through his hair and settled down. "Right. You're right."

Anton didn't have the patience to sit there, continually breaking ice to keep the line free. He hiked, testing new snowshoes, making adjustments, trying out a set of skis to see if they functioned better. In the evenings they worked quietly, Bran preserving specimens in alcohol, making drawings and notes, Anton tying up the sinews on a set of shoes, the fire crackling in the background. As comfortable a situation as one could wish for, doing good work with good company.

One need not think of the future at all.

A few days in, Bran tromped back to the cabin carrying a string of fish, which he shook at Anton, who was sitting against the wall in a rickety chair, contemplating what it would take to make a pair of skis from deadwood. It was an impressive catch, gray and shining, frost tipping the fins as they began to freeze.

"I've got an extra couple of trout. I thought we might take them up to the inn and have Mrs. McDell cook them up for us."

"You don't like my cooking?" Anton exclaimed in false outrage. "I'm shocked, Bran, truly."

"Well, I didn't want to be the one to say it. Also Mrs. McDell has butter in her pantry and we don't."

Bran cleaned the fish. They washed up, got their lantern—Anton used a match to light it, since Bran refused to go near it—and headed out on the path stomped down along the shore to the inn.

Dusk had fallen. The ground floor windows shone with lantern light, as pleasant and inviting a picture as one could wish for. At the door they rang the bell, stomped to get the snow off and get blood moving again as Mrs. McDell welcomed them in, accepting the string of trout with apparent delight. They deposited their coats on the rack before retreating to the drawing room to warm themselves by the fire.

There, in an oversize chair, sat Beth Stanley.

TWENTY-SEVEN

Strix nebulosa

Beth had about given up on the pair ever coming up to the main inn when suddenly they did, tromping into the parlor around dusk. They caught sight of her on their way to the fireplace and stared. By their expressions, they might have stumbled on the scene of a murder. They were horrified to see her.

She closed her book and rose from the chair. "I've made a terrible mistake. I'll go."

Gracious, lovely, kind Anton recovered first. "Mrs. Stanley, please stay." He touched her arm; the feeling shocked her, like a spark of electricity. She thought of how few people had touched her since Harry died. Bran, mostly.

Bran was blushing and wouldn't look at her.

Anton gestured her back to the chair; obediently she sat.

"I hope your journey wasn't too difficult?" he asked, pulling over another chair, as if they were in her own parlor.

"Oh no," she said, forcing herself to brightness. "It was lovely. Such a novelty, traveling in winter. I think I like it."

Anton glanced over. "Mr. West, sit." Bran found his own chair and did so.

Finally, Bran looked at her. "How did you find us?"

Beth suppressed a moment of anger. *Why didn't you tell me where you were going?*

She caught his gaze and spoke low, haunting. A witch casting a spell. "*Strix nebulosa.* The hunter's skill and insight. At home in the north. You gave a specimen to Harry—it's got your touch all over it, and I just followed." Then she smiled. "Also, the Spring 1879 issue of the *Pinfeather.* Your annual winter-bird survey listed the address."

Anton laughed outright, and Bran scowled.

"If you'd just explained yourself, I wouldn't have come." She rubbed the back of her neck, hoping to soothe the sudden tension there. "I just wanted to tell you . . . I'm working on an experiment, and I need your help. Have you . . . how do I explain this. Had any random thoughts about *Sterna paradisaea* the last few days? Thoughts that aren't yours? Here; it might be more clear if you just read this." She'd brought her notes. "I think it might be useful for your Antarctic expedition."

She held the packet out; he regarded it as if it were venomous.

"It might be worthless," she said. "If you could look, I trust your opinion more than any other—"

"I can't," he said. "It's gone."

"What's gone?"

"My Arcanism. It's gone. I can't help you."

She lowered her hand, the pages resting in her lap. She had never heard of such a thing. "But . . . how? Why?"

"He's distracted," Anton said wryly. "We came here to try to . . . undistract him."

"Can I help? I'd like to help." She only wanted to be useful. Bran might decide whatever there was between them was a mistake, but surely he'd let her be *useful.*

Neither answered her. She nodded. "Then I really should go."

"No," Bran said. Then, softer. "No. You're here, and you're right. A winter holiday is lovely, and you should enjoy it. Don't worry about my problems."

But she wanted to worry about him. She couldn't just shut that off.

Mrs. McDell brought out a tea service while they waited for supper, and they had an awkward, superficial conversation about the weather and the number of pine siskins they'd seen this season. She could see it now, the way Bran and Anton glanced at each other, the easy way they sat shoulder to shoulder. However kind they were to her, she could never intrude between them. They regarded her as if she were some odd, unclassifiable creature bubbled up from the mud.

"I brought my sketchbook," she said. "My coat's good wool. I think I can walk for a little while at least. Make my own little survey, though it won't be anywhere as good as yours." She took a sip of tea; she had put too much sugar in it.

Anton leaned back, resting his cup on his leg. "Have you ever walked with snowshoes?"

"No, not at all."

"Would you like to?" he asked.

She had never considered that she could do such a thing. She might never get another chance. "Oh yes, please."

"I'll be here with extra shoes in the morning to show you how."

Bran looked sharply at him. She supposed he wasn't happy about this offer and decided she had no sympathy for him.

Supper that evening was fried trout. Bran had apparently caught them through a hole in the ice on the nearby lake, which seemed very in keeping with his character. Seeking out treasure in hostile environments, from frozen lakes to widows' parlors. Making the task as difficult as possible. The meal was pleasant enough, though Bran hardly spoke and Beth hardly dared look at him. He seemed so unhappy. She was the cause, and yet she could say nothing to make it right.

Her own feelings seemed to have become irrelevant.

The area right around the inn and this part of the lake was well trod, which meant the snowshoes didn't make that much of a difference, and tromping around in them was mostly a matter of setting one's feet in the right place and working very hard not to fall. Anton said that on real ice, he put nails on the bottoms to really dig in. She tried to imagine it, the kind of landscape he had traveled in. This was just a taste of it. A bit of down feather, not a wing in flight.

They moved off the packed trails around the lake, heading into the forest proper, where the snow lay in undisturbed drifts, thick and soft. Here, the snowshoes came into their own, stamping down the snow to make passage manageable. She would have sunk up to her knees, otherwise.

She even managed in her skirt, with a good thick set of wool knickers under to keep her warm. Anton had been forward, asking wryly if she was covered up. "Rather not see you get frostbitten anywhere sensitive."

She'd laughed. "Not as good as your sealskin trousers, but good enough, I think."

"This isn't anywhere near cold enough for sealskin trousers. You'd roast in them here."

It was cold enough that her eyes and nose stung; hard to imagine much colder. But the Arctic was frequently forty, fifty degrees or more below zero. A lake in Maine? Merely cold, not vicious. Anton went out with his head uncovered and collar open, like this was balmy. She remained humbly bundled up with hat, gloves, scarf, and a fur-lined coat.

She kept waiting for him to ask about Bran. About her and Bran together. He never did. He was far too polite. Part of her wished he would, just to get it out in the open. She couldn't figure out how to do it herself.

Bran never made an appearance.

"I could march all the way around the lake in these," she said. Wondered if she really could. Walking in the shoes took effort. She relished effort.

Torrance chuckled. "A jaunt to the cabin and back might be more reasonable."

"Oh, I don't think Mr. West will like it if I invade your domain," she said good naturedly. "I've already invaded far enough, I think."

He glanced away. "Yes, well."

They walked some ways among a grove of widely spaced birches, bare and spindly without leaves. She gamely pressed ahead, scudding through powdery snow; he followed to keep an eye on her. She was breathing hard with the effort and paused to admire the puffs of fog her breath made, the vapor that froze on the fibers of her scarf.

A pair of chickadees was rasping back and forth somewhere to her right; she couldn't spot them.

"He cares for you," Anton said. The words had a particular ringing quality in the chill.

She had many questions she'd like to ask Anton just now. She wasn't certain he would answer or that she wanted to know the answers even if he did. "I'm sure he does. But I'm not sure he wants to."

"He's confused."

"Oh, certainly." She was not, but that hardly mattered.

She wanted to know about those late nights after Naturalist Society meetings when Harry didn't come home and if Bran had been involved in those. She wanted to know how long Bran and Anton had been together, and if Anton had ever been with Harry, and if Harry would have ultimately been happier without the charade of being married to her. He had seemed happy with her, but now she wasn't sure she would have recognized it if he hadn't been. He put up such an amiable front, and they'd had the work between them.

If only Anton would ask her something, she might know what to say to him. She dared a look back at him; he was watching her closely—studying her, even—his lips in a sad frown. She certainly didn't want him feeling sorry for her. She wiped a bit of moisture from her eyes. It was just the cold.

She started up again. Big, exaggerated steps, delighting in the feel of snow compressing under her, miniature flurries flying up behind her. The chickadees made an appearance, flitting from one tree to another, one of them hanging upside down, pecking at something, flying off again. They never stayed still, never seemed to rest. So much energy in tiny little bodies.

She got herself turned around to head back to the inn.

"I think I might be cold and wet enough to have earned a dollop of brandy in my tea," she said. "Do you mind if I keep the shoes for a couple of days? I'm not sure I'll stay here much longer than that."

"You should stay for as long as you like," he said.

"Or as little. It's all right. I came, had a look around. That's enough, I think."

"Mrs. Stanley—"

"Beth. Please don't stop calling me Beth. No one does anymore. It's like I've lost myself." He seemed like he might argue—some proper British manners coming through—so she added, "I'm a widow, you know. I don't have to care about such things."

He gratified her with a smile, then shushed through the snow to follow her. "You should come up to the cabin. It'll make Bran uncomfortable, but it'll be good for him."

She laughed. "Oh really?"

"I suspect he has not been entirely honest with either of us."

That sounded true. "I would like to sketch the lake a bit. Maybe I will, then."

The path to the cabin was packed down, and she didn't need the snowshoes as long as she was careful to watch for icy patches. Walking in the cold and snow was still a novelty, so she took her time, pausing now and then to look across the icebound lake.

The cabin itself was solid and welcoming. She had imagined something bleak, a roof and shelter and no more, but this had a pair of windows looking over a small front porch, a sturdy chimney, and a generous woodpile on the side.

She kept her distance, however much she wanted to look in and see what state the two bachelors kept their living space. Against the wide expanse of the frozen lake and trees alongside, the cabin made a pretty picture, and so she sketched it, just because she could.

She set a blanket on the curve of a bare stone and settled herself on it. The cold meant she wouldn't be able to sit long; she would need to keep moving to warm herself. But she could stay for a little while, drawing with her notebook balanced on her lap, setting down the pencil now and then to rub her hands together. She wanted to stay long enough to capture shapes: the pine trees reaching straight up, the green needles shading to gray under the overcast sky. The crooked branches of deciduous trees, like bent fingers, naked without foliage and thus clearer. In the fork of a high branch sat a bulky, grassy nest that would have been invisible in summer, but the abandoned nursery was visible now, one small detail against the stunning backdrop, trees ringing the open expanse of lake, preternaturally flat in its frozen state. Snow had blown off the surface, revealing patterns in the ice underneath, fissures, places where bubbles had risen and then been trapped as the water froze. When she held her breath, she heard a soft, gentle groan. An unseen split in the ice, a lurching of some underwater current, suggestion of movement, a shift in the apparent stasis.

The men never appeared. So many trails led off through the snow, it was impossible to tell where they had marched to. Avoiding her, no doubt. Well, that was their right. Meanwhile, the day was hers, and she would enjoy it on her own terms.

An evening grosbeak, bright gold smudge over its eye contrasting with its dark back and the white flash of its wings, rewarded her, alighting on the end of a branch and staying long enough for her to make a quick sketch. That seemed like a triumph for the day, so she packed up her things to return to the inn and warm herself under blankets, with a cup of tea.

TWENTY-EIGHT

Coccothraustes vespertinus

For a couple of days, Bran had hardly thought about Beth, and that gave him hope. He didn't necessarily want to forget about Beth. But being in wilderness simplified his life immensely, and simplicity was a comfort, just now.

And then she appeared, so wholly unexpected. He was shocked that the first thing he wanted to do was kiss her.

Then, she spoke of tracking them with the great gray owl, of the *practica* she'd written about, reminding him of what he couldn't do anymore. He no longer had any ability in Arcane Taxonomy. He'd never heard of anyone losing their talent, not in a hundred and fifty years.

Her offering to help smacked of pity, and he didn't want pity from her. He wanted nothing from her. Well, that wasn't true, and that was the problem, wasn't it?

Then Anton, *encouraging* her. The man's heart was too soft. When Anton mentioned that she might come out to the cabin, Bran had panicked; then he had made excuses. "What if she gets lost? What if she hurts herself trying to hike all this way? We'll have to rescue her!"

Patiently, Anton had answered, "The path between here and there is clear, and she's sensible enough not to go out if the weather turns. Give her some credit."

Bran concocted a plan to hike upstream, surveying trees this time. The fish hadn't brought him any fresh power; maybe collecting pine cones for study would. Anton chided him—this was a child's project, carried out dozens of times by dozens of botanists. He wouldn't be accomplishing anything but repeating the work of others.

"Multiple surveys over time allow us to see differences, to mark changes. I'll make a chart. It'll be very enlightening." *Empowering*, he almost said. He marched out at dawn, and Anton gamely followed him. They returned to the cabin in the middle of the afternoon, with two bags full of carefully labeled pine cones—agonizingly tedious work, as Anton had said more than once. The Latin flowed from Bran's pencil, on his voice.

But it was just words.

If Beth had visited the cabin, she'd left no sign, no note at the door, no empty teacup or broken pencil. Maybe she hadn't come at all. He began to breathe a little easier.

"You can't avoid her forever," Anton said over their rather unsatisfying supper of fish and potatoes cooked over the fire.

"It's not forever, it's just until . . ."

"Until when?" Anton raised a brow.

Until his vast catalog of binomial nomenclature returned his power to him. Until he no longer thought of her naked. Until he no longer wanted to hold her, be close to her, listen to her speak, watch her hold birds in her hand.

"You, who have faced down polar bears, are frightened of a woman," Anton said.

Anton liked her too much, saw right through him, and wasn't any help at all. "It was only one polar bear, and to be fair I was frightened of it too."

"You've hurt her feelings." Anton stabbed at him again, and Bran felt it as if it had been an actual blade through his ribs.

"I'm a terrible person, Anton," he said.

"I don't think you are."

"That's very kind of you to say."

Anton's grin turned sly. "Yes, it is, isn't it?"

Bran managed a laugh.

The next morning, Bran overslept, and Anton had already left the cabin, probably embarking on one of those outrageous feats of strength or stamina in the freezing air that he loved so much. Bran lay for a moment, cocooned in blankets, and wondered what he should count and collect today. Juncos. Woodpeckers. After grabbing a bite of bread and drinking cold tea, he shrugged on his coat and went out.

She sat on a boulder that had been cleared of snow, a blanket spread over it, bundled in a dark wool coat and knit cap. Her skirt pooled around her. She looked surprisingly cozy. She was sketching, glancing up now and then. He wasn't sure if she was taking in the whole scene or some detail in particular. The sun was behind her, and in the morning light, her hair, peeking out from under her hat, shone and her gaze was bright.

Maybe he could sneak away before she saw him. But no, his next footstep crunched into the snow, and she turned. Her bright smile seemed genuine. Maybe she was glad to see him.

He wasn't supposed to be thinking of her at all.

"Good morning," she said, and went back to her drawing.

"Morning," he answered, neutrally he hoped. She seemed so much less affected by him than he was by her. Maybe she didn't care so much after all . . . and shouldn't that make this easier?

He wandered over. A simple task, easily accomplished. "I hope the walk over wasn't too difficult."

"Oh, no, you've got the path so well marked it was no trouble at all. The cold air . . . well, it's just the thing. My mother would faint if she knew I was here. Afraid I'll come down with some kind of hideous cold. When really, I think I feel better than I have in weeks."

She looked it. Smiling, open, engaged.

"Have you seen any common redpolls?" she asked. "I've never seen one. I thought I might get one here."

Acanthis flammea. He felt nothing in the words. "No, not this trip, I'm afraid. But I've seen them here before. Keep an eye on the birches."

"Would you like to sit?" She shifted over to give him a spot on her blanket. If he took it, he'd be sitting very close to her.

"No, no, I'm fine. I was just about to . . . go for a walk, I think. Maybe go recut my fishing holes."

She was adding shading to her drawing, rounding out a detail of . . . something. He couldn't quite see from this angle and couldn't resist shifting around to look. He turned to look at the spot she kept glancing at. A nest the size of two cupped hands was tucked in the branches, probably belonging to some sort of thrush. She was focused on the object, and her drawing was precise.

"You're good, you know," he said, nodding at the page, then felt ridiculous. She didn't need compliments from him.

"Thanks."

"Beth, what do you want from me?"

The smile fell; she drew back. "Nothing. Well, no, that's not true. A professional connection? You're my only one, you know. Friendship, maybe. I thought . . . I hoped we already had that." She turned back to her drawing, pressing the pencil to the page harder than necessary. The line came out too dark, and she smudged it with the tip of her glove to lighten it.

"What happened between us . . . what of that?" Why was he talking like this? He should leave her alone.

Her breaths clouded; he could count them. Two, three . . . "I . . . want it. All of it. But if you've decided it was a mistake, then there's nothing I can say except that I would like us to be friends in whatever capacity you deem appropriate."

"Well, that sounds bloody scientific."

"Evidently that's what I can manage." Her voice cracked, winding down to a whisper.

"You're being very . . . calm?"

"What would you have me do?"

"Cry?"

"Because that's what you expect women to do? Or because you want proof you affected me? Oh, Bran, really. You should know by now I don't cry if I can help it."

"It's not natural."

"It's practice."

"I don't know how to move forward without hurting either you or Anton, when I have no wish to hurt either of you."

"Or yourself."

"What?"

Beth still would not look at him, damn her. "You are also hurt," she said. "You have hurt yourself. You'd like to find a way out without feeling more hurt. I understand. But I'm afraid I don't have a solution. I also don't wish to hurt you, but anything I do will. I'm sorry; I never should have come." She slid off the rock and started packing her sketchbook and pencil into a basket. She didn't bother to fold the blanket, just wrapped it over her arm in a haphazard way that wasn't like her.

"Where are you going?" he asked.

"If we're all going to hurt each other, best do it quickly, all at once, rather than dragging it out. I'll go and you'll never see me again, and all will be well. Eventually."

"What kind of solution is that?" he said, growing flustered. This left all the hurt with her, when she had been so badly hurt already. God, he was mucking this up.

"This is like Harry's leg," she said abruptly.

"I beg your pardon?" What did Harry have to do with this?

"Harry hurt his leg. It was the stupidest thing, on one of our weekend trips to Long Island. He sliced his calf on a bit of rock while wading in a tide pool. It got infected. The doctor wanted to amputate right away, before the infection got worse. Harry . . . Harry refused. He was so sure he could fight it off, but also . . . also . . . he was sure I could fight it off for him. But I couldn't. How was I supposed to if I couldn't name the thing killing him? I tried, Bran, and I couldn't draw out the infection or heal the fever or anything. I begged him to let the doctor amputate; I didn't care if he was crippled. I didn't care—I wanted him alive." Despite all her control, she was crying now, a strangely silent thing, tears sheeting down her cheeks while her voice barely wavered. A crack, a tightening, nothing more. "They did, finally, when he was so delirious with fever he couldn't argue anymore, but it was too late."

Illness. The family had said it was illness, all the gossip said illness. An easy enough answer. But this . . . this wasn't illness, or not just illness. This was . . . he tried to picture it, doctors holding Harry down while sawing at him—or had they used chloroform, or . . . or . . . And had Beth been there the whole time?

He knew them both well enough he could just bloody see how the whole tragic episode must have played out, and he was furious with Harry all over again. Not just for dying slowly, in agony, but for making her watch.

"Beth, what are you saying?"

"It's my fault. I should have, if I really knew—"

"Stop it. It's not your fault. It's not. No one could have saved him."

"I bet you could have. You're so much more experienced—"

"And you think I know any more about germ theory than you do? I don't. Besides, I'm not that strong."

"You're one of the strongest men I know!"

"Well, that's very flattering, but I haven't been able to so much as light a candle in days. I can't think straight. My whole world turned into a mess. That's why. Nothing fits anymore. Because of you."

"Ah," she said flatly. "So that's my fault too."

"Beth, no—"

"It's all right. It's done and over. As I said, I learned that it's very best to cut off the wounded limb sooner rather than later. Goodbye, Mr. West. I wish you well."

She set off, back down the path. And wasn't this exactly what he wanted?

"Beth!"

She didn't turn around. He should chase after her . . . and then what? She never should have come here in the first place; she'd said it herself. Anger felt better than the way his heart was squeezing to pieces.

If she could march off in a huff, so could he.

Along the lakeshore, Anton hiked back, coming in and out of view among the trees, happily by all appearances. If Bran cut across the ice, he could meet him. Burn off some of that anger and see what was left.

He had been walking back and forth on the ice all week, and in hindsight that might have been the problem. It had seemed solid enough, and he varied his path so as not to put stress on any one part. He might not have varied it enough. The fishing holes he'd been cutting might have weakened the structure. A simple shift in the weather, in barometric pressure, might have changed the ice or the water under it. The whole dynamic system of nature was never entirely stable. He knew that very well.

But he wasn't thinking.

Halfway across: a groan, a crack. Some current, some anomaly in the water causing a flaw in the ice, which lurched under his foot. Oh, he knew that sound, that feeling. When the footing seemed stable and then suddenly wasn't.

If he'd been himself, if he'd had his power, he could have frozen it right over again. But he couldn't. Had to do this the hard way, as Anton liked to put it. He held his breath, braced his feet. Prepared to shift his weight backward, where he could be sure of himself.

Before he could move, the ice under him split, and he plunged into the cold water.

TWENTY-NINE

Corvus corax

Anton was passing behind a stand of young pines and didn't see what happened, but he heard the unmistakable crack of ice, the following splash, and knew exactly what it meant. He plunged past the trees to reach the shore, where he saw the froth of water heaving up at the jagged break—and then nothing. Stillness.

Across the way, Beth Stanley charged toward the break in the ice.

He held out his arm. "Stop! Don't move!"

She stopped, looking across the ice at him in shock and fear. Even this far away he could see desperation in her stance, and Anton guessed what he had missed: Bran, falling in. He waited for Bran to emerge, a flailing arm, a gasping face, anything. But he didn't appear, which meant he was caught, and half a minute had already passed. Another minute would be too late.

Keeping to the bank, he ran ahead, uncoiling a length of rope from his pack as he did, then ditching the pack. He tied one end around his waist and spared a moment to consider whether he trusted Beth with this. She had stayed right where he told her, clutching her skirt.

He didn't have a choice; he must trust her. He also thought that yes, she was up to this. She would persevere, and they could do this. They must.

Even with the cracks, the jagged gaps, he moved out to the ice, kneeling at the same time he tossed the other end of the rope to her.

"Hold on to this! Lie flat and avoid putting too much pressure on the ice! Don't you dare let go!"

The rope smacked against the ice; she quickly lowered herself, grabbing hold, then lay there, trembling.

Then she said, "The ice will hold you."

"It's already weakened."

"I will make the ice hold."

The temperature around him dropped ten degrees. Fifteen. He wasn't dressed for this and shivered. Beth—she hardly noticed. One of her gloved hands pressed flat on the ice, and she was murmuring. The ice groaned and took on an opaque shade, white, then almost blue, like icebergs. The world changed in a way he didn't understand that would have been impossible except for people like Beth and Bran.

Frost rimed the break in the ice, reaching over the black and trembling water. She was going to close the whole thing over if she wasn't careful. But the ice under him was now solid.

He slid forward to the broken edge. This was familiar: he knew what to do and had only to do it. Meanwhile, Beth tethered him. He reached the gaping break where the water had been exposed, dark as a bloody wound.

Still no Bran, but he fancied he saw a disturbance, as if someone just underneath struggled. The water was shadowed, only rough shapes visible. Anton filled his lungs and plunged his head and arms under, ignoring the body shock of the freezing cold.

A minute only had passed. Bran would be sinking, dragged by waterlogged clothing, disoriented and unable to find the opening.

The water was clouded, freezing, nothing but murk before him. His skin ached with the cold; he squinted against it and swept his arms methodically, starting on his right, working his way across.

His arms struck an object that flinched and flailed against him. Anton grabbed hold and hauled back, wriggling snakelike; the ice gave no purchase, he slipped without making progress. Bran's weight was an anchor drawing him under. Anton fought to keep hold, to get that weight over the edge of the ice and keep it there.

The rope around his waist went taut—Beth, pulling with him.

Anton broke the surface and gasped. Heaved back with another great effort, and Bran was out.

Water froze their hair and beards white, frosted their coats and gloves. But the ice under them held. Anton eased backward, sliding Bran with him, a little more, a little farther, and Bran was fully out of the water. The tension in the rope never slacked off.

Bran was lighter than Anton expected. Beth again, temporarily shifting some law of nature.

"Anton?" Beth called, her voice strained.

"A little more."

Together, they worked backward, easing away from the break. Bran still hadn't moved. Ice crinkled and snowed off Anton's sleeve.

Finally, they got to shore, shoving themselves up among tangled branches of half-frozen winter rushes. The chill in the air vanished, just like that. Beth lay back and closed her eyes—still breathing, just resting.

Anton sat up, pawing at Bran. His face was white; his lips were blue, his eyes closed. He cleared Bran's mouth, turned him to his side, and thumped his back. Bran coughed, then again, violently, choking out water, his whole body racked.

Clutching the rope to her chest in some kind of prayer, Beth let out a cry as Anton held Bran's face, trying to get him to open his eyes. He was alive, hissing thin and shallow breaths. His hands twitched, grabbing for nothing.

Anton pleaded with him. "Bran, Bran, love—"

Bran coughed again, and his eyes opened and seemed to focus, just for a moment. "Can't . . . can't . . ."

Anton told Beth, "Go inside, start a fire."

She scrambled up and ran off. He wondered for a moment if a society lady like her even knew how to start a fire. Then he remembered who she was—yes, of course she could start a fire. Anton loosened the rope around his middle but was having trouble using his freezing hands.

Bran's hair had gone white with ice. His skin was white. There was no fog to mark his breath.

Get inside, then worry.

He maneuvered Bran up and over his shoulders, then carefully went over the tamped-down snow to the cabin, fifty yards up the trail. He walked, however much his heart pounded. It would do no good to run, then slip and fall. Carefully, carefully. Bran felt unnaturally light, unreal. Anton's fear might have only made him seem so.

Beth had left the door standing open, bless her. A blazing fire roared in the fireplace, and she was shaking her hands as if she'd burned them. He recognized this, that she had used too much of her power too quickly. He'd seen Bran faint after such exertion. He hoped she wouldn't. He needed her.

Anton took Bran to the bed and pulled off his frozen clothes. His fingers were cold, clumsy. He tore off his own wet gloves, his ice-caked coat, and tried again. Removed Bran's coat, gloves, sweater, shirt, under-shirt . . . so many clothes, all properly layered for being outside in cold weather, damn him. Then he stripped off his own shirt because he was shivering, and he wouldn't get warm with wet flannel frozen to his skin.

Bran muttered. He seemed to be trying to wake up and couldn't. The top layers were all off, leaving Bran's chest naked, pale. Anton started on the bottom half. Boots, socks, trousers. At least the work warmed him up.

"How is he?" Beth asked. She went to close the door.

Bran had been soaked down to his knickers, so Anton took everything off, then got him under the covers. He was still cold, every bit of him icy to the touch, his lips still blue. He still wasn't shivering. He should have been shaking hard enough to rattle teeth.

Beth came up beside Anton and clutched his arm, shivering with either cold or nerves, needing comfort. Reflexively, he put his arm around her and held tight, kissed the top of her head. She clung to him. What else could they do but try to comfort each other?

"Can you help him?" Anton demanded. "Do you have some *practicum* to help him?"

She was shaking her head before he finished. "I . . . I don't dare, I don't know."

They had other ways of doing this. Anton studied her a moment. "Did you get wet?" She seemed not to hear him, and he repeated. "Beth. Are your clothes wet?"

"Only a little. My coat, I think—"

Frost, trails of freezing water, tracked over her coat. "Take them off."

"What?"

"You need to get your wet things off or you'll freeze. Bran needs warmth. Body heat. He can't warm himself, you've got to get under there with him. Body heat is best; fire will burn him. He needs warmth, *now*. Take off your clothes."

"I don't understand."

He had no patience for this. "Don't be so prim. I know very well I'm not asking you to do anything you haven't already done, which is to get in bed with him *now*. I can't do it—I'm half-frozen myself."

That seemed to convince her. Fingers shaking, she unfastened her coat and stripped down to her underthings, a lacy shirt and bloomers.

"Right up against him, if you want him to survive," he ordered her, holding up the blanket for her as she climbed in next to Bran.

"Oh lord, he's freezing," she murmured, unconsciously flinching back. She recovered and finally seemed to understand her mission: she draped herself entirely alongside him, twining her legs with his and embracing him. She started to shiver, but she didn't relent.

God, they looked so well suited together. He felt a stirring fondness even as his heart broke a little. A little more, rather.

Quickly, he covered them up. Then, finally, he was able to sit back and take stock.

The cabin had gone deathly still, except for the rustling fire and his own rasping, overstressed breathing. His hair grew wet as the frost that rimed it melted. Finally, he was able to put on a dry shirt. Checked on the fire, set some water heating, and then made himself go back to the bed.

Bran's hair had melted, leaving it wet and sticking to his skin. His lips were no longer blue, and some color seemed to be returning to his skin.

Beth rested her head on the pillow, gazing at him tenderly, holding him tightly. "I think he's just sleeping."

Sitting on the edge of the bed, Anton brushed Bran's hair from his face. He'd almost lost him. It was unfathomable.

"We fought," Beth said. "He walked away because we fought, and then . . . How could I ever stand it if he left us?"

"We agree on that." He smoothed back a strand of her hair that had fallen across her face. He did it without thinking, because she needed comfort as much as he did. When he saw his skin against hers, he almost flinched back. But she met his gaze. Smiled a little.

So he left his hand where it was, brushed another stroke along her head. She sighed and closed her eyes.

Anton left them and went to sit vigil in the chair by the fireplace.

Beth waited for Bran's body to feel less cold, less clammy. She waited for her own frayed nerves to settle, but her heart still hammered, recalling that slow sequence of events: the crack of ice, Bran's startled shout that had made her look over just in time to see him slip from view, falling straight into the water, swallowed up and vanishing with barely a splash.

Given how raw her throat felt, she must have screamed long and loud. Those few seconds had happened slowly; what followed came in a blur. Her power had blazed, a kind of clarity coming with panic. She had mastered nature—at least for a moment. That moment had been enough. She had understood. She had felt powerful. Then panic had overtaken her.

She hardly remembered anything else until the shock of Anton demanding that she strip. Part of her had been appalled, but then she saw the sense of it.

Anton seemed to be sleeping now, slumped in the chair by the fire. Her body was stiff and sore from bracing against disaster. From keeping tension in that rope, and from pouring herself into the world. She had tried to make herself a bird that could survive freezing water— *Fratercula arctica, Morus bassanus*—and then give that power to Bran. His body was still so limp, so unlike itself. Conversely, she was over-heated from exertion, from the close heat of the cabin and the blankets piled on her. She tried to fill Bran up with that heat.

Despite it all, she almost fell asleep herself—until Bran's sudden shivering woke her. All at once his body went rigid, his teeth chattering. She wrapped herself around him and murmured soothingly, nearly climbed on top of him so that her weight might steady him. Finally, finally, his skin grew warm, and his body held life, movement.

"Shh, you're all right." She put her hand on his face, stroking until he opened his eyes. Hazel eyes, looking right at her, and she could have cried.

"What are you doing here?" he murmured, his voice scratching. He ran his thumb across her cheek. His expression pursed, confused, as he saw her bare arm alongside his bare arm. Then came the realization that he was naked and she nearly so, plain in the lines on his brow. He closed his eyes, groaned softly.

"Do you remember what happened?"

"The ice."

"I'm curing you of hypothermia," she said, rather smugly, settling her arm on his bare chest with its dusting of hair. He traced her shoulder along the edge of her camisole.

As if he were still on the edge of drowning, he clung to her. "I'm warm now. Very tired."

"Then sleep."

He kissed her, a simple touch of lips. A gesture of comfort more than anything, but she felt it deep in her gut. Which meant she had to kiss back, and that encouraged him, and his hands traveled down her back, settling on her hips.

If they had been anywhere else but here . . . she glanced up—and met Anton's gaze looking back. He was slumped in the chair by the fireplace, his legs stretched out, arms crossed.

Flinching, she drew back from Bran, who was awake enough to look for what had caught her attention. The silence drew out; the crackling fire, the afternoon light coming in through the window. The close heat of the cabin made each breath thick.

"Well, here we all are," Bran murmured.

Each of them thought they should be the one to leave. Beth should find her clothes and flee, except that with all the buttons she couldn't do that as quickly as she wanted. Bran should get dressed and pretend that nothing had happened. Anton should take a walk, leave them alone to do what they so obviously wanted. But none of them moved.

Then Anton said, "Let me watch."

His tone was uncertain, almost a question. Her heart raced; under her hand, resting on Bran's chest, his heart raced too. Anton's hands were clenched. "If you continue, I would like to watch."

Beth and Bran took a moment of thought. Just a moment, watching the alluring blush on one another's cheeks, the need in their eyes. Neither so tired that they couldn't continue.

Bran threw back the blanket.

They kissed, gently and carefully, as his arms closed around her, and Anton watched closely, as if he observed some new behavior in a familiar wild creature. His arms uncrossed, and his fists pressed against his thighs.

Bran pulled her more firmly on top of him, tugging at her knickers while she shifted her leg over his hip. They had done this before. Not often, certainly, but enough to be comfortable. The gasps escaping her still revealed surprise, delight. Not taking anything for granted.

Bran suddenly stilled, clenching one hand on her hip to keep her in place and reaching the other toward the fire.

"Come here, Anton," he said.

In one graceful movement, Anton left the chair and came to kneel at the bedside. Bran held his neck, pulled him in, kissed him. Needful, desperate, and beautiful. When Anton's hand rubbed up her thigh, she pressed it there, their fingers twining.

They three came together, guided by instinct and longing.

When I heard the learn'd astronomer,
When the proofs, the figures, were ranged in
    columns before me,
When I was shown the charts and diagrams, to
    add, divide, and measure them,
When I sitting heard the astronomer where
    he lectured with much applause in the
    lecture-room,
How soon unaccountable I became tired and
    sick,
Till rising and gliding out I wander'd off by
    myself,
In the mystical moist night-air, and from time
    to time,
Look'd up in perfect silence at the stars.

Walt Whitman drew a connection between poetry and Arcane Taxonomy that had never before been considered. The possibility that Whitman himself might have had some Arcane ability was nearly heretical. Many considered his great work, *Leaves of Grass*, first published in 1855, to be obscene. Others found in it undeniable power.

Whitman wasn't a naturalist or a scientist of any flavor. He hadn't been trained at any university or under the tutelage of any of the great naturalists. As happened anytime a person without university training—Mary Anning, Sitting Bull, Harriet Tubman—displayed Arcane talents, experts declared such a thing impossible. But the documented facts stand.

Arcane Taxonomists invariably talk about feelings. Carl Linnaeus himself described his first Arcanist workings in terms of the emotions his situation evoked and how they transmuted into power, channeled by his knowledge of the natural world. The language of binomial nomenclature, Latin, has a natural cadence, a rhythm and meter that is akin to poetry or magical evocation.

Whitman's poetry is awash in emotion and sensuality, unconstrained by traditional poetic structure. He was a populist, celebrating working people, advocating connections between all walks of humanity and the world around them. The world held power that he longed to share. His audience fell under a kind of spell through his words; in his writing, he exerted a charisma that was almost supernatural.

Almost as a matter of course, Arcane Taxonomists must also be poets. The ones who acknowledge this possibility, and embrace it, have an advantage.

THIRTY
Archaeopteryx lithographica

A generation or so ago, naturalists believed that if they could describe everything, collect a specimen of every living thing on the planet and catalog it appropriately, name it exactly, then they would understand Nature. Nature, capitalized. God's opus, His masterwork. All of Nature would be spread out before them, ready to be interpreted, comprehended. Once that was accomplished, then God's plan would open like a book, a diagram. Information and the knowledge derived from it would become plain.

They found less than they hoped and more than they expected. The first Arcanists wondered if they had indeed reached into God's plan, God's power—it was blasphemy. This wasn't divine, most of them decided. This was more like discovering that lightning was electricity, tapping into power that existed by its own laws. Physics produced one set of laws, the life sciences another. That became the goal: to collect power.

To name it all would be to control the world.

And so they collected. Every bird, every barnacle, every kind of rock, every leaf from every plant, every seed, every fossil. Even when they realized the natural history of the earth reached back for millions of years, hundreds of millions, and life had grown, burgeoned, changed, died—evolved—across all of it, they continued to collect, thinking they could thereby contain it.

But there was no end to the collecting. Every animal caught and skinned, every mollusk put in a jar of alcohol, every fossil labeled in a box, every rock analyzed, every diatom identified under a microscope—a dozen more waited to be discovered. A hundred more. Nature, lowercase, was not static. It was ever changing. The work would never end; the book was not complete and never would be. It was constantly being added to. Edited. And that, it seemed, was God's plan. To make the plan uncontainable.

Never mind the hubris of believing that one could ever comprehend God's plan. What was the point of God if one could understand Him? And so science itself must be its own purpose. Exploration must be its own reward. Even as explorers mapped the last reaches of Earth, the farthest points on the globe, one had to have faith that there was always something new to be discovered.

Always was. Always would be.

Bran was the first to extricate himself. He stumbled away from the bed, found a candle on the table—and lit it with his fingers. Blew it out with one of those errant indoor breezes Arcanists were so fond of. Lit it again, blew it out again, and four more times, until he was openly crying. Anton and Beth gathered him up and held him tight.

The narrow bed didn't have room for all three of them, so they pulled the mattress off, piled every available blanket around them, and nested themselves before the fire. Bran lounging against Anton, Beth lounging against Bran, arms and legs draped where they would so that one of them stroked another and wasn't always sure who they touched, or who touched them back. Beth learned that Anton was missing two toes on his left foot, lost to frostbite on his first expedition. He did not seem to miss them. Anton made tea spiked with brandy; they shared the same cup.

"Favorite bird?" Anton asked. "You ornithologists all have a favorite bird."

"I'm not an ornithologist," Beth said.

"Yes, you are," Bran said, annoyed.

"It's kind of you—"

"Favorite bird, Beth."

"You know Harry asked me that, the day we met?"

Bran winced. "Oh God, what would Harry say about this? If he walked in right now, what would he say?"

"He'd ask to join us," Anton said.

"He wouldn't ask first," Beth stated. The bundle of mattress and blankets shifted with shared laughter.

Each of them had thoughts spinning out from that, speculation leading to memory, and for Beth at least, this was the first sign that grief was settling into something different. A nostalgic affection, maybe. Sadness lingered, but it held less ache than the stabbing loss. She turned the feeling over and wrapped it up so she could try to draw it out again at will. Recognize it when it came again.

"He'd be delighted," Beth finally said, and they agreed. "I told him the white-crowned sparrow."

"The drab little things with the jaunty hats?" Anton asked.

"Yes, exactly."

Bran laughed, then coughed, his lungs still tired, and the coughing grew worse, bending him double as he struggled to breathe, until Anton poured a finger of brandy and made him drink it down. That settled him.

"You're not getting sick, are you?" Beth asked with an edge of desperation. Oh no, she couldn't face that again, not now.

"No, no. Just tired. Injured, maybe. I'll heal." He settled back and sighed.

Beth caught Anton's gaze, and his expression was drawn with concern.

What could they do to keep him safe? What could they ever do?

The light outside was fading to a burnished afternoon.

"I have to go," she said suddenly, pushing back the blanket and searching for her clothes, gown and petticoat and knickers, too many pieces. "If I don't get back before dark, they'll send a search party."

They watched her, two sets of male eyes on her naked body, and it felt thrilling and scandalous and beautiful. She felt adored and didn't try to hide as she dressed but faced them full on. Let them look. The looking itself was another kind of pleasure.

"Will you come back tomorrow?" Bran asked. Earnest as a child. Anton's gaze amplified the question.

Desire ran through her all over again, a building heat, a shuddering sigh. "Of course I will."

After dusk fell, Bran still lounged with Anton by the fire. Anton was still fussing over him, making off-color jokes about overexerting himself. Bran intended to lie here with him all night.

"I thought I had to choose," Bran whispered.

"You are a lucky man, Mr. West," Anton whispered back, ruffling his hair.

Beth returned the next morning only an hour after sunrise, and they had breakfast waiting for her. They left off the ice fishing, snowshoeing, sketching, collecting, observing. Bran's annual winter survey might suffer, but he didn't mind. The birds would be there later. The trees, the fish, the fauna would not radically change in just a day or two. This thing right now felt fleeting and precious. An aurora ribboning across the sky that would change or vanish if he looked away even for a moment. So they stayed inside and clung to each other and it was good.

It might mean something different in a few days, in a different place. They surely could not go on like this when they returned to the city. He didn't want to think about that.

Now he could read what Beth had been working on and not flee in despair. He understood, and they bent their heads together, making lists of animals that made the migration north to south and back again, terns and plovers and humpback whales and probably dozens that hadn't yet been discovered, and the questions raised, the problems to be solved. Audubon had told a story of tying string on the legs of songbirds to see if the same birds returned to the same nests each spring, but the strings tended to fall off or get tangled. They had to find a way to track individuals without hurting them, which would defeat the purpose. Maybe if they put a spot of paint on the back of a tern. Do that in the spring before they left for Antarctica, then wish for the incredible luck of finding the same bird out of thousands when they went south, assuming the expedition even happened.

"But would it work?" Beth interrupted his thoughts. "Could you use Arcanism to scout, to chart the area before you got there."

"Some kind of reconnaissance," Anton observed thoughtfully. "Don't let the War Department find out about this."

"We won't tell the War Department," Bran insisted.

"I'm not sure what all the implications are," Beth said, writing notes in her ubiquitous journal, always writing. "But I'm sure there's power—not in the magnetic field itself, as Ashford insists, but in the way animals use it. When your compass fails, the birds won't."

A method of navigation that would not fail. "Well," Bran said. "We'll just have to go to the poles to test it, won't we?"

"When are you going back to the city?" Beth asked in what seemed like a small voice. No one answered at first; that future hung heavy on them.

"We're scheduled to deliver our proposal to the Signal Corps soon. We'll need some time to prepare. Another week, I think," Anton said finally. He played with a strand of her hair, running it between his thumb and finger, letting it lie on her shoulder, doing it over again. Hypnotic to watch, and her eyes were half-lidded, her smile vague and pleased.

"Why go back at all?" Bran murmured lazily.

"My brother will come after me if I don't," Beth said.

Bran tipped his head toward Anton. "We can handle one measly brother, can't we?"

"That's very sweet of you, but we should probably avoid doing something rash."

"See? You want to do something rash to him. That's right where your mind went when Anton and I might mean something completely different."

She raised an inquiring brow. "What's your definition of rash, then?"

"Pitch him into the lake?" Anton said.

"See, that's what I was thinking."

"Well, we're all in agreement, then," Bran said.

"We really shouldn't pitch him into the lake," Beth said with a sigh. "And . . . I should get back soon. I didn't tell anyone except Ann that I was leaving."

"When, then?" Bran said.

"Tomorrow. No—the day after. And please tell me the minute you get back to town. You should both come over for tea."

"Tea," Anton murmured, which inspired giggling.

The morning she left, they came and breakfasted with her at the inn, rode in the sleigh with her to the train station, and waited on the platform with her until the train steamed and rattled away, moving quickly out of sight around a curve and past a stand of trees.

THIRTY-ONE

Dryocopus pileatus

The dark of winter fell on the city, and Beth threw herself into work, organizing everything she and Bran had talked about into something resembling a formal essay, more theoretical treatise than practical application of their ideas about Arcanist methods of navigation. But they had to start somewhere. They might be able to test across greater distances before the men traveled to Antarctica. She could visit Mrs. Wallace in Florida, tracing that migration route. Not to mention see spoonbills and flamingos for herself. Perhaps on to Cuba. And why not farther— Brazil? Hawaii? If Beth started traveling, whole new lines of questions would present themselves. Naturalists had been surveying these places long enough, one could begin to track changes in populations. Did other regions have their own great auks? As a region became developed, as trains moved in, as commerce burgeoned, where did the birds go? Nature was not static; this had been proved. It changed. So, how did it change? Did migration routes change over time? If so, why?

The investigative procedure was simple enough, but the work involved would be tremendous: finding and compiling collection catalogs and survey reports, seeing how far back she could go and what patterns emerged. This would keep her busy for a lifetime.

Back in the study—*her* study—she paused with a hand on a book-shelf and thought suddenly of Anton's brown arm reaching around Bran's pale waist while she leaned her head against his shoulder, closing her eyes in bliss . . .

"You seem well, ma'am." Ann stood at the doorway, and Beth's cheeks burned. "I wondered if you might like some tea? You've been in here all morning."

"Oh yes. That would be lovely. Ann—" The maid turned back. "How would you like to travel? To Florida, maybe?"

"I hadn't ever thought of it."

"I was just thinking. What's to stop me from traveling? I wonder if I even ought to sell the house and simply . . . go on, for as long as I can. But then where would I put all the books?"

Ann drew back, seeming a bit stricken. No house meant no need for a maid or housekeeper, she was likely thinking.

"I would need a companion," Beth added. "There'd be so much to manage, and if I had an assistant to help with everyday things while I worked, it would all go more smoothly."

"I've never been outside the city, ma'am." Ann suddenly seemed young. Nineteen, Beth realized. She'd come to work for the Stanleys when she was seventeen.

"Then you *should* travel. It'll be good for you to see a bit of the country."

"I'm really not sure—"

"Well, I'm not going to decide anything right now. I won't be sell-ing the house tomorrow. It's my high spirits running away with me."

Ann's usual cheer returned. "Did you see your letters?"

"I've been avoiding them." A tray holding an impossible stack of correspondence rested on the desk, and Beth frowned at it.

"Your mother left a message every day you were gone."

"Surely she has better things to do. I don't need looking after."

The bell at the front door rang, and Beth got a sudden sinking feeling.

"I'll just go see to that." Ann dashed out.

Beth should have stayed in Maine. She could disguise herself as a man and accompany Bran and Anton on their expedition. God knows what she could *do* on such an expedition. But she wouldn't be *here*.

Ann returned a moment later. "It's your mother. I put her in the parlor."

"You couldn't have told her I wasn't here? Or I'm indisposed, or . . . or . . ."

"She saw you in the study window, ma'am." Ann winced in sympathy, or maybe apology for not coming up with a better excuse.

If Beth reassured her mother that she was alive and well, maybe she'd be *left alone*. "If you could bring that tea, at least we'll have something to do while we stare at one another. Wait—how do I look?" Beth quickly smoothed out her skirt and the front of her dress, checking to make sure all the buttons were in the right buttonhole. She hadn't done much with her hair; she hoped it wasn't flying every which way.

"You're fine." Ann ducked out to the kitchen, and Beth took a deep breath. Whatever her mother had to say, she could be mollified with concessions. A dinner at Will's, a luncheon for one of her charities.

In the drawing room, she found her mother pacing. From the fireplace to a window, glancing at a painting or two as she passed, back to the fireplace, wringing her hands all the while.

"Mother? How are you?" She kept her voice pleasant, determined to set Mrs. Clarke at ease. Beth probably should have given more of an explanation before she left.

Mrs. Clarke studied her, lips parted in apparent astonishment, some fear in her gaze. Beth felt a moment of panic. Had something terrible happened while she was gone? Her father was sick, or Will—

Her mother sagged. "Oh, thank goodness!"

"Mother, what's wrong? Is everyone well?"

"I was about to ask you that. Are you well, darling?"

"Of course I am. You looked so frightened just now. Father's well? Will is—"

"Beth, we were worried about *you*! What did you do?" Her voice increased in volume and pitch into something like outrage.

"What do you mean, what did I do?"

"You left! Nobody knew where you were or what you were doing—"

She was a grown woman with her own home. She didn't owe anyone an explanation, especially not when her mother was *yelling*. No one had ever fussed like this when she and Harry traveled together. "I went away for a few days, that's all."

"In the middle of winter?"

"Why not? People should go out in winter more often."

"But with strangers? With *strange men*?"

The ground lurched. Beth had a sudden awareness that whatever she said would be interpreted in ways she could not control. She had best speak very carefully, then. Specific, bounded answers that could not be misconstrued in any way. Scientifically precise descriptions. And she must hope her mother did not hear an undercurrent of guilt in everything she said.

"What *strange men*?" she asked. "What do you think happened?"

Mrs. Clarke began pacing again, a rushed racketing between sofa, wall, window, fireplace, like a caged cat. "Is it true that you actually went into a men's club? By yourself?"

"Are you talking about the Naturalist Society? It's not a men's club, it's a"—all right, yes, it was a men's club, but not in the way she meant—"scientific organization. And I wasn't by myself, I was with friends. With friends of Harry's, to see the journal where he'd been published."

"You should know that we've been hearing the oddest rumors about you."

"What rumors? From whom?"

"Will got word that you'd been spending an excessive amount of time with some of the men from the Naturalist Society. And then you *vanished*."

"Mother, you're overreacting."

"You vanished, and Mr. Ashford had it on good authority that you went away with Mr. West and Mr. Torrance. That you all three went together, to God knows where, for God knows what purpose." She made this a challenge.

Of course they'd heard it from Mr. Ashford. What would Mrs. Clarke say if Beth told her that those rumors were absolutely true?

This felt like when the ice broke under Bran, panic threatening to overcome sense. She rounded on her mother. "Why on *earth* would any of you listen to anything Mr. Ashford has to say? You know he's a rival to Mr. West and Mr. Torrance and wishes them ill."

"He's a respected naturalist—"

"You respect him more than me?"

"Beth. Please—where did you go? What were you *doing*?"

Would you like me to draw you a sketch? Beth did not say this. "It's my own business what I do with my time, or whose company I choose."

That brought her mother up short. "What? Then it's true? You did go with them . . . *alone*?"

The contradictory nature of that sentence didn't bear mentioning. "I went to an inn in Maine. A beautiful little spot where I could breathe some clean air and do some sketching. It helped. I feel *better*." As if her mother had ever cared how she felt; she only cared about the public face she presented. "They happened to be there as well. We certainly didn't go *together*. I'm not sure what else these rumors are saying, and I'm offended that you would listen to them."

Ann came in with the tea cart. Likely, she'd been waiting outside for a polite break in the argument. Blushing, Beth thanked Ann, who took longer than was necessary to arrange cups, pour, cut cakes, and set them out. At last, she glanced at Beth, asking silently, and Beth nodded back. Yes, she would be all right, eventually. Ann slipped out. Beth took her cup and sat on an armchair, all very normal, hoping her mother would do likewise.

"I wish you could have seen it," Beth said, trying to steer this encounter into something they wouldn't regret later. "The light on the frozen lake, the snow on the trees. I brought my watercolors, but no matter how much I tried, I couldn't capture the light. I learned to walk on snowshoes, and there's nothing like coming in to a warm fire after tromping around in the snow. You must have done so when you were a girl."

Mrs. Clarke wouldn't take up her cup of tea and wouldn't sit. "Snowshoes? What are you doing with *snowshoes*?"

Beth looked into her cup, at the steam rising from it.

"Beth. You'll never find anyone to marry you if you damage your reputation like this."

Damage it how? Beth wanted to ask. Make her say it out loud. Make her describe precisely whatever scandal she thought had happened.

"It's too soon to think of remarrying." She was beginning to think it would always be too soon and other possibilities had presented themselves.

"You wearing half mourning says otherwise. If you would find it in yourself to marry again, you would not get such wild ideas in your head."

She *liked* her wild ideas. She should have acted on them earlier.

Her mother went on, and on. "Beth. Darling. If you don't feel well, you would say so, wouldn't you? I know how hard things have been for you. If you need help—"

Oh, Harry had saved her from this, and she hadn't even realized it. "What kind of help do you think I need? I think I've been coping very well, considering."

"But you don't want to come to dinner, you don't want to see your family, you spend all your time locked up in that musty study, you keep dashing off on these absurd jaunts."

She could convince Bran and Anton to carry her to Antarctica, and then she could stay there. It would be cold, but it would also be quiet. And there were penguins. She would like to see penguins.

"You're right, Mother. Maybe I haven't been feeling well. Maybe I should go lie down." She wasn't even lying. A racking headache had started thrumming behind her eyes.

"I'll send for a doctor."

"Please, no. Just . . . let me rest."

"You might speak with one, just in case."

"I'm just tired. I'll come to dinner at Will's this week, I promise. Name a day."

Her mother didn't seem convinced, as if she expected Beth to disappear again, right before her eyes. But she finally sat and drank tea.

Beth only had to get through this encounter, then get through this week, then dinner, then the next one. It was like one of Bran and Anton's expeditions: you had to keep slogging if you wanted to survive. Just another step.

She agreed to dinner at Will's thinking she could set everyone at ease. Entirely normal, entirely respectable. How terrible could it be? But it was worse than terrible.

They gathered in the parlor before dinner, and everyone was congenial enough. No one brought up the Naturalist Society or odd trips in the middle of winter. It was all quite pleasant until Will's wife, Sally, left the room with a worried backward glance. Then her father left, nervously turning his pipe in his hands. He'd barely looked at her all evening, not even when she kissed his cheek hello. He was usually quiet and awkward, so she hadn't thought anything of it. Then her mother left and closed the door behind her, and the mood became menacing.

Will sat beside her on the sofa and took her hand, trapping her. Beth was put to mind of tales of animals who chewed off their own legs to escape traps.

"Beth, you must tell me what really happened when you left town last week."

She collected herself, letting her corset hold her straight, and regarded her brother calmly. "Why?"

He seemed taken aback. What had he expected, fevered denials? Tearful acquiescence? "If I'm to address this horrendous gossip, I have to know what really happened, to counter it with the truth."

What was worse, the gossip or the fact that her own family was so quick to believe it? "It's a wonder you're paying any attention to it at all." She laughed a little. "I don't even know what the gossip is. No one will tell me!"

Reveal no assumptions. Make them *tell her*, make them say out loud what they thought she had done.

"Surely you can guess."

She tilted her head, inquiring. "I don't believe I can."

He was growing flustered, and this pleased her. "You have exposed yourself to terrible scandal, and *someone* must counter it!"

"Why? If you are so sure it can't be true, why must it be countered?" she said. "I just want to be left alone."

"It isn't healthy! A young woman like you—"

She yanked her hand away from him; he was so startled, he let her. Intending to march out, she got up and went to the door. A month ago she never would have considered such a thing, but she'd had enough. She'd had a taste of being her own person, and she liked it.

The door was locked. She rattled the handle and, disbelieving, rattled it again. Didn't budge.

"Mother's locked the door," Will said. "You'll stay here until we hash this out."

Beth broke the door.

She hadn't known if she could. If she'd thought about it too much beforehand, she might have gotten tangled up in her own head and nothing would have happened, but she reacted by instinct. The driving rattle of *Dryocopus pileatus*, the relentless destruction of termites in a woodpile, filled her up, and she yanked on the door again and the wood around the lock and handle disintegrated, falling in a shower of sawdust to the floor. The brass handle followed with a thud.

Swearing, Will jumped back from the sofa and gaped at her—with fear. He was afraid of her, and wasn't that strange? Well, she'd gone and done it now.

"Did Harry Stanley teach you how to do that?" he breathed.

"Harry couldn't do anything like this."

"Ashford said you knew some Arcanist tricks. I didn't believe him. How long—"

"And why are you even listening to that man? He's only trying to ruin Bran and Anton."

"Who?"

"Will. I'm leaving. My reputation is my own concern. I don't want your help. I don't want any more of . . . of this!"

"Beth, be reasonable."

She thought she was being very reasonable, demanding her coat and hat from the butler and marching out of the house. This left her on the street alone, at night. She almost went back inside, shivering and gasping for breath. The streetlamps were lit, and carriages moved up and down. If she waited long enough, a cab was sure to come by. She could always walk home; it wasn't *that* far.

If only she could fly. But she couldn't.

She walked off before Will or her mother could come after her. In the end, she only had to go up to the corner to find a cab. She got herself home just fine, and there was a certain satisfying power in that.

Ann fussed over her, but she kept her coat on and went out to the garden. Even in winter, even at night, the garden was a refuge. A drift of unmelted snow lingered in a corner under a patch of evergreen holly. The color of rose hips glowed in the lamplight. So, so quiet, the world slept. Bundled in coat and hat and gloves, a blanket over her lap, sipping a glass of sherry she had poured for herself, Beth was calmed. She must not flail; she must not weep. She could observe, step outside herself and be reassured that beauty lived in the world. Wherever there were birds, trees, brambles, and wild water, a forest with soft earth, she could find refuge. No one would keep her from this.

Her mother wrote a note the next day, apologizing. The details of what she apologized for were a bit vague. For letting Will bully her, maybe. For being present for such an unpleasant situation. For not rushing out after Beth, leaving her alone. No mention of the gossip everyone was so worried about. No mention of being sorry for not trusting Beth to manage herself.

The letter ended with an invitation to another dinner. Beth wrote back a brief card to decline the invitation. The next invitation, Mrs. Clarke urged her to come to their own house rather than Will's, as if that would matter. Then she suggested they gather at Beth's for tea. And then what? Beth stopped answering. She might never leave the house again, except to go to the park. Except when Bran and Anton returned to the city. Then they'd see what kind of gossip they could work up.

A day later, Beth received an invitation to speak at a charity luncheon for the Ladies' Birdlife Preservation Society. *You are so eloquent on the topic, Mrs. Stanley, and such a well-known advocate for bird preservation.* How could Beth refuse?

When Mrs. Clarke wrote to say she was also attending the luncheon and would be happy to pick her up in the carriage on the way there, Beth agreed. It felt like a peace offering.

Meeting her in the foyer, Mrs. Clarke told her to get her hat and gloves, to make sure she was bundled up against the cold. Beth wanted to laugh, remembering the cold of Maine, the terrible stabbing cold when they pulled Bran out of the water. *That* was cold. This was merely uncomfortable.

They had been driving for half an hour when Beth asked, "Where are we going, Brooklyn?" They were leaving the city. Mrs. Clarke didn't answer. "Mother?"

"Just be patient, dear."

She should have known, right from the first. "There isn't a luncheon."

Mrs. Clarke took hold of her hand.

"Mother—"

Mrs. Clarke squeezed her hand harder. "Don't worry at all, Beth, dear."

Another half hour passed. They were in the country now. Fresh snow carpeted fallow farmland and scattered woods. There was some misunderstanding. This would all make sense soon. But the carriage passed through a set of tall gates, up the drive to a large manor house entirely surrounded by iron fencing. They passed a sign that Beth couldn't read from this angle.

"What have you done?" Beth asked as the carriage jerked to a stop.

What seemed like a whole crowd of white-uniformed men and women waited by the steps outside the front door. Standing among them, a man with gray-dusted muttonchop sideburns, wearing a prim suit, stared down his nose with an authoritative gaze.

Her brother, Will, was already here, speaking to the authoritative man. He glanced at the carriage, his smile thin and nervous.

Mr. Ashford stood beside him.

Her mother's grip on her hand wasn't comforting; it was restraining.

Someone opened the door to the carriage. One of the white-uniformed women reached for her, and Beth responded with the fury of a trapped animal, shoving her aside, racing out—where two men waited to intercept her.

She thought of the rage of geese when their territory was invaded. She imagined a battering ram to shove them aside. She thought of woodpeckers and broke the carriage. The splitting wood of the axle cracked like a gunshot, and the horses spooked and reared. Chaos and shouting ensued, and she ran—no matter that she had no place to run to; someone had shut the gate across the estate's drive. She ran out of simple instinct, to flee from danger.

And stopped, pressing into an invisible barrier, a wall of air and power, thrumming with Arcanism. She pounded her fist in front of her and might as well have been striking bricks. Air made solid. It was a good *practicum*. Ashford was there, his hand twisted in a gesture, Latin words on his lips. She could almost make out the names he summoned. *Casuarius casuarius*, violence and aggression. Or even the territory song of the American robin, a warning: stay back, keep back, keep away, submit, submit, submit—

The men in white approached, arms reaching.

Falco peregrinus was perhaps the most dramatic hunter among all the birds, diving faster almost than the eye could see, striking hard. Wind—the bird became almost like wind itself; think of the beats of a million wings . . .

A storm descended, fierce wind whipping across the drive, throwing up funnels of dust and gravel, pelting them. Beth put up her arm, ducking her face against the onslaught. Somebody screamed; men shouted. She couldn't see much beyond the rain of dust, but people were running. The dust grew thick enough to dim the sun.

Bran had asked her once if she'd ever tried to push herself, how far her power could reach. Ah, she wished he could see this. If only she could carry herself away on the wind.

She hitched up her skirt and ran. Surely there must be a break in the fence.

"Stop her!"

One of the white-coated men blocked her way. Beth pivoted, dashing sideways, then tried to turn the course of her storm likewise. The second of the men grabbed her arm, and then they were both on her, hauling her to the ground.

The words fled, she lost the storm, and the air suddenly fell still, quiet. The two men pinned her between them, immobilizing her. Her first thought—she was outraged that they dared to touch her. She reached for the storm again. Thunder rumbled, and the white-coated men worriedly looked up.

The man with the gray-dusted muttonchops—the physician in charge, she assumed—marched toward her, brushing grit off his coat. "Mrs. Stanley, I must ask you to desist, or we'll be forced to use more extreme methods of restraint."

They would dose her with laudanum. Chloroform. She didn't know any *practica* that would counter that.

The physician studied her. "I confess, when you said she was an Arcane Taxonomist, I didn't believe you."

"She's been practicing in secret," Ashford answered.

"Consorting with naturalists," Will added with disgust.

Mrs. Clarke's hat was half falling off, her hair tumbled loose from its pins, and a handkerchief fluttered in her hands. She'd left the carriage after it collapsed on its broken axle and now stood clinging to Will, who was covered in dust and glaring, murderous. Beth never should have spoken to them at all; she should have sent back all the letters; she should have stayed in Maine with her lovers.

The doctor turned to Will. "You said she's also suffering from female troubles? The usual?"

And what did that mean?

"She's recently widowed," Will said somberly. "No children."

"Ah." As if that explained anything at all. Her mother and Will bent their heads in conversation with the man. "Her use of Arcanism has deeply unbalanced her nerves, I fear. But we'll have her to rights soon enough."

This was a paradox. If Beth kept fighting, she would confirm their claims that she was ill and mad. If she went docilely, if she cooperated—how repugnant that seemed, when they were treating her like a child. They no doubt locked the doors in a place like this.

Beth told herself: *This is a storm, and I am a rock.*

"Mother," she said. "Will. I swear to you, if you leave me here, I will never speak to you again."

Will chuckled, shaking his head. Glancing at the doctor as if to say *You see how she is?* Mrs. Clarke fussed with her hair, trying to pin it back while her hat continued to wobble. It was comical. "Oh, darling. You'll feel better once you've had some peace and quiet to find yourself again."

"I am not mad, and I am not joking. I will never speak to you again if you leave me here." This probably sounded mad, to them. What woman would ever say such a thing to her own mother? Whatever she did in this moment they would interpret as a sign of madness. She could not win.

If only she had the power to fly. To be a bird and send herself away.

The doctor nodded at Mrs. Clarke reassuringly. "They all say that when they first arrive. Don't take it to heart."

"Oh really?" Beth said. "Is that what they all say?"

He flinched back a little. "They usually cry more."

Her eyes were dry as stone.

"We'll send for a new carriage for you, if you'd like to wait in our parlor," the doctor said. The pair of them went up the steps and didn't look back. "Thank you for your help, Mr. Ashford."

"I'm happy to do whatever I can for Mrs. Stanley's well-being." Ashford smiled so serenely, so pleasantly. He was only helping, the expression said. But his eyes were those of a vulture, calculating.

"Come, Mrs. Stanley. Let's get you comfortable." One of the men put a hand against her back and urged her forward.

"May I speak to her? Just for a moment." Ashford sidled up, so casual, so innocent. Only had her best interests at heart. Of course the doctor and nurses let him, and he leaned in, speaking softly, so no one else could hear. "Mrs. Stanley. Beth. Let me help you. I'll take care of you if you let me. Same arrangement you must have had with Harry. I want to know what you know. And I'll take care of you."

Very dark rumors said that some Arcanists had learned how to kill with a look. She hadn't wanted such power until now. But the basilisk was a mythical creature, alas. "You have no idea what Harry and I had together."

"Well, I know he couldn't truly . . . appreciate you. The way I could."

"Damn you."

"I can get you out of this place. Ask the doctor to send me a letter; that's all you need to do."

If she spat at him, she would confirm their assumptions. If she screamed, fought, wailed—she must be calm. She must think logically.

She stepped close to him, holding his gaze. Stared hard. His smug smile wavered; he leaned back.

"*Tinea pellionella*," she murmured.

"What? What is that? That isn't a bird—"

A hole appeared on the shoulder of his jacket. It widened as she watched, threads fraying. Another hole opened on one lapel, then on the opposite shoulder, right on the seam until the threads holding the sleeve gave way. Ashford grabbed the sleeve as it fell, realizing all at once that his jacket was falling apart.

"What have you done? What was that?"

"Clothes moth." She smiled.

Ashford shouted curses as his shirt was the next to break apart, then his trousers. By then the orderlies had led her away and into the house. She caught a glimpse of Will and her mother in a neat little sitting room. They stared after her, but she turned away, resolute.

Beth decided that she no longer had a family. This knowledge was somehow freeing. She had no one to worry about but herself now.

Attempts to use Arcane Taxonomy in warfare waned during the American Civil War. Several battles saw Arcane *practica* wielded directly against soldiers—destroying their weapons, altering the very ground under their feet, even crippling them. This was a violent and personal use of Arcanism that troubled most natural historians. Arcanists who participated in these battles often suffered mental collapses. But the Civil War marked the beginning of an era when machines could do more than Arcanists. In the end, gunpowder was usually more reliable than an Arcanist who might panic and forget what he was doing. Arcane Taxonomists gratefully left the battlefield.

However, this era saw an increase in the use of Arcane power in covert action, especially by abolitionists.

Abolitionists made great use of Arcane Taxonomy in the service of espionage, maintaining supply routes, and delivering prisoners to freedom. Many of the same skills and feats used by explorers in wilderness—surveying the land, predicting and controlling the weather, navigating through the knowledge of local characteristics—were also used by those on the Underground Railroad who guided enslaved peoples to freedom. Foremost among these agents was Harriet Tubman. Tubman was not a trained naturalist. She had received no formal education as a naturalist or Arcane Taxonomist, was not associated with any universities or societies that identified and trained Arcanists. And yet her Arcanist abilities are well documented. Her ability to find her way in all terrain, in all weather and circumstances, and to keep her charges safe was legendary. She could navigate overland in any condition, confuse her opponents, render her charges invisible, and cause bullets to fall from the air, as if she could adjust the force of gravity itself. It was said that in her years as a conductor, she never lost a person. During the Civil War, Tubman's actions as a reconnaissance agent and commander of Union troops were instrumental in the success of raids on plantations that liberated more than twelve hundred people.

THIRTY-TWO

Zenaida macroura

Anton and Bran returned to the city and sorted through their mail first thing, looking for a letter from Beth. Didn't find one.

"We'll call on her," Bran said. How fundamentally his attitude about visiting uptown brownstones had changed.

They arrived, rang the bell, and no one answered.

"Surely she arrived home safely," Bran said, worried.

She had gotten herself to Maine just fine. They'd thought nothing of sending her home on her own.

"There'd have been word in the papers if something had happened," Anton said.

Bran pressed a hand to the door and murmured some Arcanist *practicum.* It seemed to take a long time. Stepping back, he stared at the door as if it had stung him. "There's no one home. The house is empty."

Anton started to worry, then. His explanations sounded weak. "Then she's away. At the park, or her family's."

"The maid would be here. Why hasn't she written?"

Who could they ask about her? She had mentioned a brother. Did they even know her maiden name? How was it that they knew so little about her?

They avoided mentioning another possibility: that she regretted their time together. That she wanted nothing else to do with them. If she had decided to disavow them, how would they ever know? They would have to follow her lead and pretend that none of it had happened.

How bleak a prospect.

Because they must continue working, one way or another, they entered the halls of the Naturalist Society. It might have been Anton's imagination that today the stares of men in the foyer were not accompanied by awe. The whispers seemed subdued. Hostile, even. The skin on the back of his neck prickled, as it did when the pressure dropped in anticipation of a storm. The frowns were appraising, viewing a specimen that was judged wanting. Poorly preserved, perhaps. Rotten.

"Someone found a mistake in my kittiwake monograph," Bran murmured. "They're about to pounce."

Teddy took their coats and let them in with barely a word. In the chambers proper, the stares were undeniably hostile. Men who'd been staring quickly looked away. Some whom Anton had considered allies, whom he would have walked up to and asked what was wrong without hesitation, turned their backs.

"Enough of this," Anton said, and went to corner Andrews. Bran was hard on his heels. The man's eyes went wide, as if he knew he was being hunted.

"Who's been accused of plagiarism, then?" Anton asked.

"Oh heavens, nothing so lurid as that." Andrews wouldn't meet his gaze.

"You know how important it is to scout ahead. Do me a favor and let me know what I'm stepping into."

He gave a sigh of surrender. "Word's going around that you and West absconded with Stanley's widow to some wilderness."

After a first mortified flush, Anton was able to catch his breath and keep his composure. "I beg your pardon?"

"That's the story, that the three of you ran off together."

They hadn't run off together. Beth had chased them down, which was quite courageous of her, in hindsight.

Andrews added, "Ashford even went to her family about it."

"He—he did *what*?" Bran coughed, as if choking on the words.

Andrews had become fascinated by the lapels of his coat, smoothing them out, flicking off nonexistent dust. "Well, you know, he said something about you taking advantage of her, trying to get after Harry's work, and he was only trying to alert her family so they could protect her. I'm sure I couldn't say anything about any other insinuations."

Indeed.

Anton forced a chuckle. "Well, in a certain light that's almost flattering. But I might have to challenge him to a duel for this."

"That's primitive," Bran said. "These days you'll need to take him to court for slander."

Except it wasn't quite slander, was it? "I'm very disappointed that anyone would spread tales about Mrs. Stanley for any reason at all."

"Indeed, indeed," Andrews said quickly. "Really, Torrance, it's nothing, I'm sure. It'll all blow over soon."

A strange space remained between Anton and Bran and the rest of the group. Eventually, a few gave them a nod, a quick smile of greeting. Others offered knowing grins and arched eyebrows.

"Tell me, Mr. Torrance," Bran said in a low voice. "What're we supposed to do about rude gossip when it happens to be true?"

"Ignore them. Ride the ice floe and hope you reach land soon."

"You think word of this has reached her? Has she gone to ground, then?"

Perhaps. If that was so, perhaps they ought not to contact her at all.

That night, fever struck Bran and laid him out. His cough, which had grown worse since Maine, didn't let up.

Anton had never been so afraid in his life. That time when he drifted on an ice floe for weeks, he had not been afraid. He had not been afraid of the charging polar bear. In the deepest, darkest night of an Arctic winter, when he forgot what sun on his face felt like, he had not been afraid.

But watching Bran pale and sweating terrified him.

The doctor came and went and came again, seeming very somber and muttering about how he might think of summoning family if there was any to be summoned. Bran's family lived in Pennsylvania, and Anton felt no desire to bring them here.

He wrote to Beth and still got no reply. He sent a telegram, express. Nothing. A million things might keep her away, but not from this. Her silence was . . . unforgiveable. Inexcusable. He was furious with her . . . and then he was afraid.

If her family believed Ashford's gossip, what had they done to her?

Bran came to awareness long enough for Anton to try to speak to him. "Will you be all right if I go away for a couple of hours?"

"Of course," Bran murmured. "Unlikely to fall into a crevasse or . . . or . . . put my foot in a bear trap or some nonsense." He chuckled, then fell to coughing, a sound that had grown more and more rattling.

"I'm going to look for Beth. I won't be long."

"I would like to see Beth."

"So would I. I'll see if I can bring her."

"Good."

"Don't you *dare* leave me, Bran," Anton said. "You have to go to Antarctica and name a penguin for me."

"Of course I will." He patted Anton's hand. His skin burned, but Anton relished the touch. The touch meant he lived.

Anton watched the Stanley house and saw when the maid arrived—he knew there must be a maid looking after things. He gathered his most polite and decorous manners. He had always come to the Stanleys' house with Bran and wasn't sure how he would be taken on his own, so he must be perfect, unimpeachable. He rang the bell.

The maid answered, standing at the open door and staring, shocked to stillness. There was something rigid in her manner that he chose to ignore.

"Good afternoon." He bowed a little. "Is Mrs. Stanley at home? If she's not taking visitors, I hope very much that you'll see that she gets a note—"

The young woman started crying. She gasped a breath, and her eyes instantly turned red and shining with tears.

His tumbled thoughts struggled to remember—Ann; the girl's name was Ann. "Ann, whatever is the matter?" Oh God, if anything had happened to Beth . . . he would have heard, surely he would have heard somehow. "Is Beth all right?"

"I don't know!"

He pushed his way into the vestibule and shut the door so they wouldn't be doing this on the street. "For God's sake, what has happened?"

"She's gone, she's simply gone!"

That didn't make any sense, and Anton was on the edge of shouting. *Don't crowd the girl,* he told himself. He drew a handkerchief from his pocket and offered it to her. Ann quickly took it, wiped her eyes and nose, then crushed it in her hand.

"If you tell me what has happened," he said carefully, "perhaps I can help."

She nodded, collecting herself. Tears still fell but her breathing grew steadier. "Her mother—Mrs. Clarke—decided that Mrs. Stanley must be ill. With all that has happened . . ." She glanced up at Anton shyly, almost surreptitiously, and the gossip piled into his thoughts all over again. It was too much to hope that Beth had been spared. She had not.

"She came with a carriage to take Beth away on some outing, and . . . and . . ." She wiped her eyes with the handkerchief again.

"And . . ."

"Mrs. Clarke returned alone. Dismissed the cook and told me to shut up the house, that Mrs. Stanley wouldn't be coming home for a good long while. I'm kept on to look after the place, that's all. But I don't know where Beth is!"

Anton's heart grew colder, a sense of foreboding settling on him. He did not have to read to the end of this novel to guess what had happened.

"Ann, I'm so sorry. I fear this is my fault."

"Oh no. Sir, you've no idea how much better she was when you and Mr. West started visiting her. She was wasting away before, and you . . . you both saved her."

That was giving them too much credit, he thought. "I should have done something," he said. "I should have written sooner. I should have helped."

"I don't think there's anything you could have done, sir," she said, far more kindly than he deserved. "She was worried about scandal too."

He huffed. "Scandal would have blown over quick enough."

"It's different for women," Ann said.

What was to be done now? He had never felt so helpless.

"Thank you. I will . . . I will do what I can." He donned his hat and let himself out. On the walk home, he found himself doing something he rarely did: praying. That Beth was safe, wherever she had gone. That Bran would still be alive when he got home; that he would stay alive for many years to come.

And that he would find some gentle way to tell Bran what had happened that would not kill him.

THIRTY-THREE

Acanthis flammea

If Beth had volunteered for a stay at the Residence—they did not call it a hospital or sanatorium within the walls—she might have found it pleasant. Sunny rooms, attentive staff. Instructions to simply *rest*.

But she was not allowed to be herself here.

Her clothing was taken from her, replaced with a shapeless gray frock. Still in half mourning, which seemed unfair. Her hair was braided—they were not allowed pins to put their hair up. A dozen other women were patients here, and they were marched single file to meals held in what might have once been a ballroom, but the wallpaper had been torn down and the walls painted beige. Then they were marched back out again, either to individual rooms or to a sitting room with threadbare carpets and secondhand chairs.

Beth was sure they were putting some kind of medication in the food. Laudanum, maybe. To keep them calm. Because of this, she couldn't focus. The names of all the birds, every scrap of Latin she'd ever learned, were gone from her mind. She tried to get them back, and it was like trying to hold water. She couldn't feel a thing. She wanted to ask about the food, if they were being drugged. She suspected this would bring on punishments, so she refrained. If she stopped eating, there would also be repercussions.

That first evening, struggling not to scratch the rough fabric of the frock, Beth asked the attendant—some stern-looking woman was always nearby, watching—where the library was. If she could have a book to read.

"Reading's not allowed," the woman said with perfunctory calm.

Beth drew back, startled. "I beg your pardon?"

"You must rest your mind, Mrs. Stanley. That means no reading."

The shock of this froze her for a moment. "Then might I have a sketchbook and pencil? Surely a bit of drawing can't do any harm."

The attendant spoke at her like she was a child. "Your mind is disordered, and you must rest it. No reading, no drawing. Just sit and rest."

In the sitting room, she found a chair near a dusty window and sat. She hadn't been mad when she arrived here; she was sure of it. But she would go mad within days without a book or pencil or paper or anything. She squeezed her hands together until the joints of her fingers hurt.

It got worse. Her room—at least she had her own room—had a narrow bed and bars over the window. The door was locked; she checked as soon as it was closed. It might have been bearable if sound did not carry, but shouts echoed down the corridor. A woman banged on her door, begging to see her children: she promised to be good, promised she was well, she just wanted to see her boy and girl, please could she see them just once—

Beth put the pillow over her head and could not sleep.

The physician in charge—Dr. Cranstone, the authoritative man who'd spoken so confidently to her mother and brother—went on rounds before lunch, visiting and making pronouncements. Beth strived to be nothing but pleasant with him. Those who were not pleasant vanished for a time, and there were rumors of cold baths, restraints. Beatings.

"I was told you lost your husband some months ago. My deepest condolences," Dr. Cranstone said, as if reading from a script. She sat quietly.

"Thank you." Her hands rested lightly on her lap, her ankles crossed neatly under her skirt.

"Children can often be a comfort in such times, but I understand you were not so blessed."

Not throttling him in that moment was nearly the hardest thing she'd ever done in her life. She could almost hear Harry's voice whispering over her shoulder: *Do it, deck him, he deserves it, and it will be hilarious.*

Maybe she was going mad, but imagining Harry egging her on gave her comfort.

"No, it's been very difficult," she agreed calmly. She tried to remember the *practicum* she'd used to destroy Ashford's clothing and couldn't.

"Mrs. Stanley, it's quite unusual for a woman to involve herself in Arcane Taxonomy."

Beth suspected that it wasn't as unusual as men like this thought.

The doctor continued. "May I ask why you would turn to such a practice? Don't you think you'd be happier in more appropriate domestic pursuits? Like your mother's charities, for example?"

Beth closed her eyes against a racking headache. "The study of nature is appropriate for everyone, I think." She didn't like the way her voice shook.

"The study of nature is one thing. But I think you've taken it dangerously far, don't you?"

Not at all. She had not gone far enough.

"Well, I do hope you will come some way toward feeling more yourself during your stay here."

She was feeling more herself than she ever had in her life, but she gave him her most serene, trapped-in-company smile.

"You might consider remarrying. Mr. Ashford has expressed a great deal of care for you."

Ashford was mercenary. He wanted what she knew, her power. Cranstone would probably say that at least someone wanted her for something.

She didn't know what to say to this, so she said nothing, which she knew would be taken as a sign of madness as much as practicing Arcane Taxonomy and traveling alone. To him, she couldn't be herself and not be mad.

They were supposed to numb their minds with stillness. They were supposed to think of nothing at all. The food was bland, porridge and bread without so much as a pat of butter. Water, not even tea. Nothing to stimulate or excite.

Later, she asked to walk on the grounds, a narrow lawn with a few winter-bare lilacs along the edges, and was told she must earn that privilege.

"And how can I do that?" she pleaded and wasn't given an answer.

She slept. Her mind grew so vague, she could do little else, nodding off in chairs, even at meals. She was chided for sleeping so much, forcefully woken up, and made to shuffle around the room.

In the sitting room—she supposed she ought to call it a parlor, but it had none of the comforts of a parlor at home, no paintings on the walls, no soft chairs, no Ann to call for tea—she claimed the chair near the window. As close to a walk in the garden as she could get, so it would have to do. She thought she saw a redpoll on a high branch of the middle lilac. It was a busy thing, darting in and out on some foraging business. But with that pink on its breast, it might also have been a house finch, a more common bird. If she could get outside to get a closer look, or if she had her opera glasses, she could tell for sure. If she had paper, she could record the sighting. Take a regular survey of this little garden.

If, if, if . . .

In this mental fog, she couldn't trust that she was making a good identification. That almost made her cry when nothing else had.

A chair scratched on the floor. One of the other patients, a petite woman with a black braid, dragged her chair over, smiling pleasantly. "Do you mind a little company?"

Beth supposed she didn't, though it might have been polite for the woman to ask before sitting down rather than after. "Not at all," she said, mostly out of habit.

"I'm Mrs. Radford."

Beth might have preferred to learn her first name. "I'm Beth Stanley. Please, call me Beth."

Mrs. Radford, who apparently had no first name, ducked her gaze shyly. "You're new, yes? How are you getting on, then?"

A brief, unreasonable thought occurred to Beth: that this woman was a spy and would report any discontent to Cranstone. But if she lied and said all was well—that would be a sign of madness, too, wouldn't it? Considering how dour and unpleasant this place was. What should she say, then?

"It's still new. I'm still finding my way, I think." She smiled blandly. "How long have you been here, then?"

Mrs. Radford's eyes instantly filled with tears. Overfilled. She quickly wiped at them. Beth had thought it was an innocent question, but now she dreaded the answer.

"My husband brought me here and left. Just left me. I still don't know why, exactly. I cry a lot—doesn't everyone? But never where he could see. I tried to stop. He told me to stop, and I tried." Her cheeks were soaked now. If Beth had a handkerchief, she'd have passed it over. "I hadn't thought he could be so cruel."

Beth reached over and held her hand, squeezing. "I'm sorry."

"And you? Did your husband leave you here?"

"My husband is dead."

"Oh," she breathed. But there was a flash of hope in her eyes— maybe she wished her husband was dead. She shook it away, looked out the window. "I miss my children. That's all I want, to see my little ones again. Heaven knows how they're getting on."

Beth wondered if she was the woman who shouted at night. "Mrs. Radford, I'm sure you'll see your children again. You must be strong."

"But how?" she begged.

Beth . . . didn't know. She glanced out the window; the little pink bird had flown off. "You find a thing to care about. A passion that's all your own."

The tears subsided, but she sniffled, and her breathing remained ragged. "But you don't know what it's like. We'll see what passion you have after you've been here so long."

Beth didn't plan on being here that long at all.

THIRTY-FOUR
Pica hudsonia

He had fever dreams of tropical jungles growing on ice floes and polar bears climbing palm trees. He shimmied up the tree to escape, but the bear followed, and it had a human face that looked suspiciously like Montgomery Ashford's, and it was laughing at him. In the dream—he thought it was a dream; it must be a dream—he was sweating so much his hands were slipping, and the bear was right there, nimble as a monkey, which made no taxonomic sense, but here they were—

Finally, Bran opened his eyes. The scene before him was clear, and he was absolutely certain he was awake. He wished for nothing else but to lie still and feel the pattern of the quilt under his hand, see the rectangle of soft light cast through the window to the dark wallpaper. Midmorning, by the angle of the sun. That he could identify the time of day seemed like a great achievement, and he spent a moment congratulating himself.

He didn't have the strength for much more than that.

Finally, he looked to the bedroom door, which stood open, and felt a rising panic. Anton should be here. Anton *had* been here, he was sure. So where was he? Bran sighed and thought about falling asleep again rather than calling out.

Then Anton appeared.

He still had on his coat and hat, as if he had been out. His look was somber; if he had been wearing black instead of brown, Bran would have thought he had just come from a funeral. His frown was set, and his gaze held the expectation of dark tidings. A man walking into a room without hope.

Bran smiled and raised his hand, to try to reassure him. Anton choked out a garbled exclamation, threw down his hat, and stumbled to the bedside, grabbing Bran's hand, dropping it to touch his forehead, picking it up again, and squeezing just a bit too tightly.

Breathlessly, Anton finally said, "How do you feel?"

"Mangled," Bran said. "Alive."

Bending his face to Bran's shoulder, he murmured, "Thank God, thank God," over and over.

"It was a close thing, then."

Anton pursed his lips, that clouded look coming over him again. He shook it away and reached for Bran's pillow. "Let's get you sitting up. You must be starving. I'll get some broth."

"Wait a minute. Aren't we supposed to be in Washington? The meeting; we've got to get ready—no. Beth. I want to see Beth. Where is she?" He pushed back the covers, trying to swing around and out of bed. Anton pushed him back, very insistently, and rearranged the covers. Bran slumped, confused, his mind swimming in fog. Beth. The Signal Corps meeting. Antarctica. He didn't know which one he was supposed to be thinking about.

With another inexplicable clouded look, Anton pulled over a chair and settled in. Bran was too tired to be frightened, but the question of where Beth was should have supplied a direct answer, and nothing frightened Anton. This Bran couldn't interpret as anything but Anton being afraid.

"Right, what's happened?" Bran demanded in a soft invalid's voice.

"She's gone, Bran."

"What? What do you mean—" For a second, the fever seemed to return, flushing through him and spurring a cough.

"Here, settle down, it isn't like that." Anton retrieved a glass of water and made him drink. "She's vanished. Her blasted family sent her to an asylum. She seems to have escaped, but then she vanished."

"Where?"

Anton sighed. "Nobody knows. That is the definition of *vanished*."

"But . . . we have to find her. Don't we?"

"Yes. I think we do."

If Beth leaned too close to the window, pressing her forehead against it, trying to get closer to the hedges outside, an attendant came and chided her about posture and decorous behavior. If she didn't sit straight, quietly staring into her lap as if her brain were made of nothing, as if she had no thoughts at all, someone would make mild ominous threats about treating her affliction. What affliction? Her affliction was that she could not get *outside* to see the dusky little red-faced bird that might be a redpoll. She longed for her opera glasses.

She was sure they were putting laudanum in her food. Some mornings she felt she really could let her mind drift into nothingness and it would be a blessing. But the flickering movement in the hedges outside the window always drew her attention. If she sat long enough, the mysterious bird might draw closer.

She couldn't want it too much or it would never approach. The perversity of nature, unpredictable and contrary, and maybe that was why she loved birds; they never quite did what you wanted them to.

And there it was, right in the open, perched on a protruding branch against a clear sky, lit perfectly by the morning light. Audubon's subjects had never been so well posed as this. Dainty yellow bill with a spot of black on its chin. The streaks on its breast were broader, more sparse than the heavy streaking on the house finch. Rather than the finch's broad swathes of pink, this had a bold splash on its forehead, scarlet feathers puffed up in the cold. Common redpoll, *Acanthis flammea*. Beautiful.

Her senses sharpened. The light became clear, searingly clear. She could see the bird's individual feathers. Beyond the hedge to the estate's gates, and then to the snowbound road. On the floor above, footsteps, the heavy purposeful stride of one of the male attendants. The lighter stride of a nurse hurrying to meet him. Cranstone's voice in his office on the other side of the building, dictating a letter to his secretary, *Your daughter appears to be making progress; she has been quiet and has not attempted to leave since the first day . . .*

Beth could bring this place under her power.

Beth Stanley was a good naturalist, and over the next days, she observed. The Residence had a schedule, routines. Two brusque men served as something like guards, checking the locks on doors, walking the rounds. Their schedule was regular unless they were called away by disruptive patients. Beth thought of making a plan to persuade Mrs. Radford to cause a disruption, but she didn't want to bring any more trouble down on the woman than she already had. Instead, she found openings. Watching for the sea ice to melt, when a ship could finally get through, as Bran and Anton might say. She found leads that might release her to freedom.

The cook went outside every morning to collect eggs from the chicken coop and left the kitchen door open. The pair of housekeepers left a back door open when they went out to beat rugs and hang washing to dry. She learned where the housekeeper and groundskeeper hung up their keys at night. The housekeeper and attendants had rooms in the back of the house. One of them was always supposed to be awake; they were supposed to keep a lamp on in the hallway, for nighttime emergencies. Sometimes, the lamp went out and no one noticed, and it meant they were all asleep.

She might have encouraged this, thinking of bears hibernating, of squirrels in winter. *Sleep, sleep, conserve your energy . . .*

She ate as little as she could get away with to mitigate whatever drug they were putting in the food. She was hungry, and that was distracting, but she thought of Anton and Bran on the ice, living on rations. She could survive by their example.

By acting docile, by practicing extreme politeness, by agreeing with everything Cranstone said and doing what she was told, she encouraged the attendants to grow complacent. They even left her entirely alone sometimes, sitting by a window, gazing out while putting on a show of melancholy. She should have been an actress.

The patients' belongings were kept in boxes in a closet, labeled with their names. She found a workroom with boots and coats. She would need these things.

It snowed, then turned warm, so the snow melted into a muddy slush. One night turned very cold, and the slush froze into a crust. This was an opportunity.

If she was caught, she wouldn't get a chance to try again, so she worked carefully and moved quietly. She had a plan and gathered the strength to make it good. She thought of the ice on the lake, the trout that lived sluggishly in the cold under it, and froze the lock, made it hard like that ice. When the housekeeper came by to check that Beth was quiet in her bed, she went to lock the door—but the key did not move. The housekeeper shook the handle, which rattled slightly. A bit of light came through the gap between the door and frame, and Beth imagined the woman leaning in, holding the lantern close to try to see into its workings.

"Well, I suppose you're not one to give us trouble," the woman muttered. "Have to get Bill to look at it tomorrow . . ." And the light moved on.

Beth waited for hours until the house was quiet. She made her steps soft, like the down of an eider, the wingbeats of an owl. Stilled her own breathing, evoking calm. Creeping quietly, she picked her way down the stairs—she had tested them for creaking boards already. When she checked on the light in the hall, she must make a decision. If it was lit, did she risk drawing the attention of the night watch? Or wait but risk that she could not keep her door unlocked another night?

The lamp in the hall had gone out. The staff were all asleep. She continued, moving steadily and precisely rather than quickly.

She retrieved the box with her belongings and took them to the workroom, where she found a satchel for them. Found boots that did not fit well but were better than nothing. Good thick socks and a heavy coat. She winced at every little scrape and bump. Regarded herself for a moment: this was not ideal. She thought of Anton's sealskin trousers and fur-covered parka. He would tell her that such clothing was much too warm for an average New York winter night. She would manage.

She took the groundskeeper's keys for the main gate; carefully, so carefully, opened the workroom door, again with thoughts of owls' wings, of downy feathers, the quiet of a winter night; closed it behind her; and set off.

Her power surged. She might just tip the world off its axis if she put her mind to it. Change the seasons. If only she'd had this strength when Harry was sick.

In fresh snow, her tracks would be easy to follow. In mud, the same. But this broken slush, while hard to traverse, was too icy to leave a mark in. She slipped, stumbled. The slush broke under her, and the snapping sound reminded her of the crack when the ice broke under Bran.

She wondered if she would ever see him and Anton again.

The creak of the main gate echoed in the still night air. She hesitated, sure that *now* someone must discover her escape. But the manor grounds remained quiet. No extra lights appeared in the windows.

She slipped out, locked the gate behind her, and threw the keys as far as she could into the snow in the woods on the other side of the road. They'd be lost until spring, maybe forever.

The sky was clear, full of stars. No moon, so the world was silver and muted, still as a held breath. She had never been out so much in winter until the trip to Maine. She had never been out so much at night. She had missed so much. Well, no more.

She walked, assuring herself she didn't have to move quickly, but she must walk steadily, with determination. Her breath puffed in clouds, and her muscles ached with anxiety. If she was discovered, she would not be treated kindly.

This was not as cold as what Bran and Anton had survived. She repeated this to herself as she walked, in rhythm with her steps: *This is not cold; this is not cold.* Rather, it was cold, but not enough to kill her if she kept moving. She wouldn't even lose toes.

She remembered the route from the carriage trip and reached the village before dawn. The sky grew lighter. At the manor, they'd be discovering her absence soon. She didn't have much time.

The next part of the plan might have been the riskiest, the least likely to succeed: she had to present herself as a respectable lady in semimourning, after a nighttime trek through wilderness. She knew no Arcanist *practica* that would help her here. She had only her charm to rely on.

From the satchel of belongings, she pulled out her gray dress and smoothed it as best she could. Only Ann would be able to get all the wrinkles out, but maybe no one else would notice, especially with the coat over it. In a sheltered spot by an outbuilding, she changed, rushing. Cold air stung through the cotton of her chemise—again, she reminded herself this was just a sliver of what Bran and Anton had been through at the Arctic Circle. She had to leave off the corset, but the dress's bodice was stiff enough; only close examination would reveal she wasn't wearing it. She got on the dress, got the buttons up, got it all situated in a way that wasn't too awful. Her hair was hopeless; she retrieved her hat from the satchel and pinned the disheveled braid up under it. She had no mirror, had no idea how the whole ensemble looked. Horrifying, she was sure. But the goal here wasn't elegance, it was escape. She wondered, Were people here often on the lookout for crazed women fleeing from the manor house? She hoped not.

Suddenly, she thought of peacocks displaying their elegance, making such a pretty picture. This calmed her.

Among her belongings, her purse still had a few coins in it—she had thought she was going to a charity luncheon. She nursed an incandescent fury at her mother and Will for the lies. It might be enough to get her somewhere else. And from there, if she made it that far—well. She would need to decide.

She shoved the manor's plain gown in the satchel and took it with her, to be disposed of later. She couldn't afford to leave a trail behind her. The ticket office at the train station wasn't open yet, but she found a bench nearby and sank onto it. All her strength went out of her. She was exhausted, hungry, thirsty. Her vision seemed to vibrate, full of nerves, thrilled and frightened by what she was doing. Despite all this she managed to smile pleasantly and speak clearly when the ticket window opened.

"Good morning. I wondered if you could tell me how much for a ticket to Ithaca? I'm afraid there's a crisis in the family. I must get there quickly." She dabbed at her eyes, and the ticket agent was extremely helpful.

An hour's train ride was enough time to make plans.

She could not return to the city and home—her mother, her family, would find her there, and she'd be right back where she started. She fully intended on making good on her promise to never speak to Will and her mother again. She felt no grief or remorse at this, only a logical inevitability.

Her next thought: to send a telegram to Bran and Anton. But she couldn't wait for a reply, she realized. She couldn't wait for them to come find her until she got someplace truly safe. If only she knew where that was. The Residence had likely already sounded the alarm. She had to assume that people were already looking for her. She must keep moving; she could not stop. A telegram would travel faster than she could. She must keep pace.

Moreover, Bran and Anton didn't need to be saddled with her trouble. They had important work to do, and she wouldn't be a distraction to them. A brief woodland holiday was one thing, but if she in any way diverted them from the Antarctic expedition, she would never forgive herself.

But she longed to hold them. Have them close one more time, to tell them that they had saved her. She wished and then set the wish aside. At least she had been able to tell Bran about the *practica* on navigation she had started work on; she hoped the information would prove useful to him. Meanwhile, she would go where no one would think to find her. If she told no one, she couldn't be found. But she still needed help. She needed Harry's account and investment records. She needed to make herself back into a respectable widow so people wouldn't ask questions.

One person could help, one person she trusted.

Immediately on arriving at Ithaca, she sent a telegram to Ann, care of the brownstone, with a list of what she needed and instructions to send the package on the earliest train she could. Second, with the last of her cash, she checked in to a hotel and made herself presentable. Less noteworthy. A widow on business of her own, not an escaped madwoman. No, call it by its true name: she'd been a prisoner. She washed, got her hair combed out and pinned up, and felt more herself with every moment. Late afternoon, the package from Ann should arrive, and Beth could take the next steps.

When she returned to the train station, instead of the package, she found Ann waiting in the ladies' lounge. An unassuming young woman in a simple traveling gown, coat, and hat, with a stuffed valise on the floor next to her. Ann, who had never left the city, had undertaken this quest for her.

"Ma'am," Ann said carefully while Beth stared in shock.

"Ann, you shouldn't have come."

"What was I supposed to do, leave you alone?"

"Yes. I must go. I must travel very far away, and no one must know of it."

"But *why?*"

They had somehow taken hold of one another's hands. Beth wasn't wearing gloves.

"Because I can no longer be myself at home," she said simply.

"There's been an uproar. Mrs. Clarke came by this morning demanding to know if you were there."

Ah, then she had been discovered. The Residence had sent word. "You must not tell her. She mustn't know."

"I know that. I didn't say anything. How could I? I had no idea where you were! I'm afraid I cried at her."

"Serves her right. She needs to know the pain she's caused." No, Beth didn't feel grief over what had happened. She felt rage.

"But what happened?"

Beth told her, briefly. Her voice shook. Ann started crying. Beth wanted to give her a handkerchief, but she didn't have one. "It's all right, my dear. You see they couldn't keep me locked up. And, well, if there's something wrong with me, I don't think I care."

"Oh, Beth, I don't think there's anything wrong with you."

"Oh my dear, your opinion matters more than any of theirs. Thank you so very, very much."

"Mr. Torrance came by. Can I tell him? He's so worried."

Beth's heart felt pinched. She hesitated, all her thoughts in a rush, warmed at the thought of them both. Helpless because she decided, just then, that she couldn't have them. They had each other; they'd be fine . . . and, well. She'd always wanted to travel, so she'd be fine too. Somehow.

"You can tell him that I'm well," she said. "Give both him and Mr. West my regards. But I'm not going to tell you where I'm going."

"You don't trust me," Ann said tearfully.

"I trust you more than anyone in the world. But it's called plausible deniability, dear." Impulsively, Beth hugged her close. Another scandal to add to the list, such familiarity with the help. "You should stay at the house as caretaker. I'll make sure you're paid. Don't worry about me."

"I'll always worry, ma'am."

So would Beth, truth be told.

She took a quick look through the valise and found Harry's ledger, access to enough of his finances to get her started. Some toiletries, another change of clothes—a blue dress, not mourning garb. Beth approved.

And her most recent logbook. A list of birds, her last few trips to the park, her lists from the trip to Maine. Her power, all of it here. She could reach out and see through the eyes of an eagle, see the whole world laid out below.

She made Ann get on a train back to the city, and only then did she return to the ticket office and consider her own options.

She bought a ticket all the way to Denver.

THIRTY-FIVE
Corvus brachyrhynchos

Startling how easy it was for a woman of Beth Stanley's means and abilities to disappear when she wanted to.

Mortifying that Bran could do nothing, *nothing* about it. His body had failed him, and he was disgusted with himself. He was up now, walking, eating. He'd gone outside for an hour or so and slept half the day after. This minor expedition had exhausted him.

Easy to be angry with her for not telling anyone where she'd gone, not even those she most trusted. They might believe—at least they hoped—that she trusted them, and yet she had disappeared without sending word. She hadn't even told her maid, who only reported to Anton—and him alone—that she had seen Beth, who was well, but she had no idea where she'd gone next. Would it have been so hard to send a telegram? She had her reasons, certainly. Easy to believe she was wrong about those reasons.

Then Anton caught Pinkertons following them.

Outside the Naturalist Society building, a man in a suit stood with a newspaper open in front of his face, yet in ten minutes he never turned the page. The same man—different coat, different hat, but no doubt the same—stationed himself at the edge of the park as Anton was leaving after his walk, then followed, just for a block or two. Anton asked the doorman at their building if anyone had stopped by, and to keep an eye open. Later, the doorman reported seeing the same man standing at the end of the block three days in a row, watching. He also reported being asked several times if Mr. West and Mr. Torrance were at home. Each time, the doorman said he did not know. Anton tipped him well for the discretion.

Anton spoke calmly when he told Bran all this, but his whole manner was stiff with tension.

A crow—the same crow, Bran was sure of it; it had a tail feather with a broken shaft—sat on their windowsill four days running. Someone was watching them through its eyes. He sat at the window and watched back, using his own bit of *practicum*—a pigeon swooped in and dislodged the startled crow, which cried out and went flapping to a window at the opposite building.

Looking out of that window: O'Connell. One of the Naturalist Society Arcanists, on the Pinkerton payroll. There was that commercial job he wouldn't talk about. Bran thought about murdering the man. Cursing him, poisoning the air around him so that every bird he approached keeled over dead.

As an alternative, Bran wrote a stern letter to the Naturalist Society asking for a reprimand against any member who would use his abilities against another for commercial gain. As if that would matter where money was involved.

What it all meant: Beth had been right not to contact them. Anyone spying on them could find a way to get at their mail and messages. She had known the lengths her family would go to to control her, and Anton and Bran hadn't.

Maybe they simply had to wait. Pretend she had gone on some trip to some distant place with no telegraph service. She would return when she was done exploring and have such marvelous stories. Such an expedition might take years. They knew this. They must be patient.

Anton wanted to ignore the Pinkertons. Of course they targeted the two men implicated in the scandal that had driven Beth away. Everyone must assume they knew something. When the detectives didn't learn anything, they'd give up and move on to the next target. But he and Anton could not be themselves under this scrutiny, and that was irritating.

They took to leaving the building separately and arriving separately. They walked with space between them. They kept the curtains in the front room firmly closed. There had been enough scandal without them revealing even more of their relationship than they already had.

Bran wasn't so sanguine and felt the investigators' presence as an invasion. Bad enough that he missed Beth, their conversations about ornithological minutiae, the sound of her voice reading Whitman, the feel of her body pressed up against his flank.

Beth Stanley hadn't left, she'd been driven away, and someone was to blame for that.

Anton was irritated. Bran was furious.

He decided he was going to break the impasse.

"What?" Anton didn't take the news very well. Bran hadn't expected him to, which was why he hadn't said anything before he did it.

"I wrote to Mrs. Clarke. Beth's mother. I just asked her if she or her son are the ones who hired the detectives."

"Brandon West. *Really.*" Anton's tone landed somewhere between disgust and admiration. "So much for the rest of our reputations in society."

"She wrote back." Bran held up a folded note, the arrival of which had precipitated the whole conversation. Bran hadn't expected a reply at all. Anton considered it, nonplussed. "She's invited us to call on her so we might discuss the matter."

"And I suppose you intend to accept her invitation?"

"I was considering. Aren't you curious what she has to say for herself?"

At the very least, they might politely request that they no longer be an object of scrutiny. Their lives could be returned to them. So they buttoned themselves up in suits, and Bran even let Anton check his tie for him to make sure it was neat and straight. They arrived at the Clarke brownstone right on time. A servant let them in and guided them to a drawing room, where neither could bring themselves to sit.

It was a fine room, Bran was sure, but had little to distinguish it from a dozen others just like it in the neighborhood, which for some people was the point. The sedate landscape portraits and neatly arranged furniture said nothing about who lived here. The lack of dust or clutter said only that they could afford to hire someone to clean for them. Was this where Beth had grown up, or had the family moved here later? This didn't seem much like the Beth he knew, but he could also picture her here easily. It was what he'd thought when he first saw her, wondering how Harry had caught himself a society girl, prim and proper as all the others.

She was a chameleon, wearing her protective coloration well. This thought made him sad.

From across the room, where he'd left off studying some porcelain figurine of a girl in old-fashioned clothing, Anton met his gaze; his was also drawn and sad. Maybe thinking the same thing.

An imposing older woman swept into the room, swathed in gray silk and smelling of lilacs. She had Beth's tall stature and build, if rounder from the years. Her eyes were steel. A youngish man, well dressed and businesslike, followed her and seemed to struggle to hold himself upright in the woman's wake. This must have been Beth's brother. He donned a stern expression and tried to put himself forward, but the woman swept past him.

"Have you had any word from her, anything at all?" Mrs. Clarke demanded, stopping abruptly, her skirt swishing around her feet.

Bran gaped a moment, not sure how to respond. He wanted to march right up to her and accuse her of harming Beth, let out all the frustration of the last few days. But he'd learned enough about society to know you didn't do that in neat parlors.

Anton was better at this. He came to attention and bowed a little. "Mrs. Clarke. And Mr. Clarke?" The youngish man nodded, but his gaze darted to his mother. "I don't think we've been introduced. I'm Mr. Anton Torrance. This is Mr. Brandon West. We were good friends of Harold Stanley." There; that put them on better footing, their association with Mrs. Stanley—their right to associate with her—firmly established.

Mrs. Clarke looked him up and down in a way that was familiar, appraising him, with a furrow in her brow and a question curling her lips. Hand to her chest like a shield. Was she seeing the fine suit or the color of his skin? Could she acknowledge that the same man possessed both?

"A pleasure to meet you." Bran tried to be pleasant, even knowing that these two had caused Beth pain.

"Friends of Harry, hmm?" She walked a few feet, turned. "Then do you know anything of Beth at all, or have I misunderstood everything?"

Bran and Anton's glance at each other revealed far too much, but they couldn't help themselves. *We delight in your daughter in ways that are none of your business.*

"We're fortunate to count her as a friend as well," Anton said, politely. "We were helping her arrange Harry's work and organize his papers."

"Is he the one who taught her Arcane Taxonomy?" Clarke, the brother, demanded. "I really thought he knew better. He was always so respectable."

"She taught herself," Bran said, glaring back at him. "Harry encouraged her. She ought to be encouraged, I think."

Clarke, whom Bran thought less of by the moment, gave a harsh laugh. "Oh, encouragement? Is that what they're calling it now?"

Next to Bran, Anton had gone still, cold. It might end up being a race to see which of them punched the man first.

Anton's English reserve saved them. "I beg your pardon?"

"The rumors—" Will Clarke burst out, making clear what he cared most about, and it wasn't Beth.

"Are not our responsibility, I think," Anton said.

At this, Mrs. Clarke broke down. A handkerchief suddenly appeared, produced from some secret pocket, and she hid her face in it. Her next words came out choked, thick with tears. "I would ask her to come home, all forgotten and forgiven, if I only knew where to send the letter! You haven't heard from her?"

"No, madam."

"This is your fault," she muttered, eyeing them both.

"No, madam, I don't believe that it is." Anton's poise—his refined accent, his manner that came right up to the edge of arrogance—demanded that he be taken seriously. It was a marvelous thing to watch.

The brother remained flummoxed, furious. Stoking the pride that might have been all that was keeping him upright. "I've had word from a respectable gentleman that you both were . . . were . . ."

"Were what?" Bran asked warningly.

"Were taking advantage of my sister."

Bran chuckled a little. "I admit, I really wanted to get Harry's chest of specimens from her, but she wasn't having it. She likes birds, you know." He wanted to see her so badly he might start crying himself. He suddenly sympathized with Mrs. Clarke's outburst.

On the other hand, Anton tilted his head, curious, questioning. "Which respectable gentlemen, if you don't mind my asking?" Ah, there, he'd gotten right to the heart of things.

Clarke tipped his chin. "He spoke to me in confidence."

"Montgomery Ashford, is it?" Anton asked, and Clarke's face went a bit red.

"Good God," Bran muttered, scrubbing his jaw. He was getting himself worked up and could feel the tightening in his chest that meant a coughing fit was coming on.

"He's a much more suitable match for her than either one of you!" Clarke said. His gaze studied Anton head to foot, as if to say, *Just look at you.*

Bran couldn't take any more. "Why, you son of a—"

Anton clapped a firm hand on his shoulder, and Bran subsided.

"Suitable by what measure?" Anton asked, far more calmly than Bran would have.

"None of this will bring Beth back!" Mrs. Clarke cried out, waving her handkerchief and glaring thunder at them all.

Bran coughed. Just once, then croaked, "Mrs. Clarke, may I trouble you for a glass of water?"

She rang for a maid, and the water arrived quickly. Bran was grateful. He staved off the coughing fit this time.

"Mother—"

"Will, I forbid you to say another word!"

The brother fell silent and sulked into an armchair.

"What are we to do?" Mrs. Clarke pleaded. "How do we bring her home? Assuming she is alive, and not stolen away by kidnappers."

This family clearly had no faith in Beth's ability to manage herself.

"Call off your detectives," Bran said. "And we'll see what we can do."

"The Pinkertons were Will's idea," Mrs. Clarke said. "Not that it's done any good at all."

Clarke opened his mouth as if to defend himself, then thought better of it.

"Mrs. Clarke, you must know that Mrs. Stanley is sensible, intelligent, and well capable of taking care of herself," Anton said. "But if you keep hunting after her, she'll only hide herself further. Please try patience while we do what we can to find her."

This prompted a distressing image, of the naturalists hunting their prey, treading carefully through the wildest places. As if Beth were a creature hiding away in some cave.

"The scandal of her vanishing is worse than the other," Mrs. Clarke said. "I only want her back, do you understand?"

"Whatever society says about her?" Anton asked, brow raised.

Clarke had the decency to glance away at this.

Anton nodded. "We'll do what we can. But please don't interfere."

Collecting herself, Mrs. Clarke offered belated tea out of obligation, and Bran and Anton declined, to everyone's relief. As the two men fled, they didn't offer to shake hands. Neither did Will Clarke.

They needed the long walk back to their flat to work out their nerves after that encounter. The frozen Arctic was much to be preferred to society. Maybe Beth had fled to Baffin Bay. He wouldn't blame her.

"What can we do, then?" Anton asked. "What can we assume about where she's gone?"

"Someplace with birds."

Anton chuckled. "I have been all over the world, and there are birds everywhere. That's what we like about them, yes?"

"Her contacts, the ones who send her lists for her migration studies. She might have gone to one of them. The subscription list for the *Pinfeather*. See if there've been new subscribers. Publish a letter to her in one of her journals, begging her to come home."

"You'd think the Pinkertons would have tried all that."

"And we've established that the Clarke family, and therefore the Pinkertons, don't know Beth at all. They all think of her as some wilting flower. She might look it, but she isn't."

"And what of our meeting with the Signal Corps?"

Bran stopped walking. "I'd almost forgotten about that." Everything they'd been working toward, practically their life's work, and worrying about Beth had driven it clean out of his head.

"Are we going to Washington, or are we going after Beth?" Anton asked.

Where had they gotten to that this was even a question? Anton's expression seemed neutral. No furrowed brow, no anguish—Bran could feel his own anguish tight through his face, squeezing his lungs.

"What do you think?" Bran asked finally, because he couldn't seem to think at all.

Anton smiled. "I think we should ask ourselves what Beth would want us to do."

THIRTY-SIX

Stercorarius antarcticus

The foyer outside the Signal Corps offices at the Washington Arsenal had a row of windows overlooking the Potomac. The sun was out, the water calm. Would be a nice day to take a boat out. Anton paced, glancing outside, trying to keep his mind on the moment and potentially the most important presentation of his career.

Bran sat in one of a row of chairs against the wall, his eyes closed, hands gripping his knees. "I don't suppose you'd like to stop pacing?"

Anton relented, coming over to take the seat next to him. "You know of any particularly good *practica* that will persuade the committee?" He was only partly serious. He knew the answer.

"I could try, but I think your charm will do better. My tricks aren't always reliable."

"Neither is my charm, I fear."

Bran glanced over. "You have nothing to prove. Your accomplishments, your abilities—they speak for themselves."

He was so trusting and earnest. Such a good observer, seeing without judgment. This all must seem simple to him.

"Oh, but I do have to prove myself. All the time, every moment." Bran's brow furrowed. Anton tried to explain in terms he would understand. "According to taxonomy, what am I? How would you classify me?"

"*Homo sapiens—*"

He shook his head. "Am I British? Bahamian? Sir Archibald Torrance's half-breed son? Mulatto? Any of the half dozen other names we've both heard spoken behind my back? What name applies?" Bran pursed his lips and looked away. Anton followed his gaze to the window, the blue sky beyond. "On the ice, I know what I am."

"I would call you my friend. Lover." Bran touched Anton's hand. A quick brush, hardly noticeable to anyone watching, but in this fraught moment it felt like a strong, long embrace, as if Bran had put both arms around him and squeezed.

"Thank you," Anton murmured. He wanted to kiss Bran but only smiled.

"We've prepared for this," Bran announced firmly. "We know our work. We are the best men for this job."

"We've survived calamities that would have killed a thousand other men."

"We have, haven't we?" God, his smile glowed.

Then he coughed. Once, twice, from deep in his lungs. Bent over, fist over his mouth, trying to stop it. Anton had brought along a flask of honeyed brandy for just this thing, and passed it over. Bran took a quick swig and handed it back.

"This damn cough," he croaked.

"When we get home, you're seeing a doctor."

"I'll be fine—"

The doors opened, and they separated instantly, a well-practiced movement.

An army lieutenant regarded them. "Gentlemen? The committee will see you now."

Planning an expedition to the poles was, Anton believed, more difficult than the actual expedition. In the Arctic, tasks frequently collapsed to the very narrow focus of survival. Of course they had science to perform, milestones to achieve, flags to plant, charts to draw, and all the rest. But survival was foremost, unless one wanted to achieve fame by being a cautionary tale. Forty years later, the Franklin expedition was still spoken about in the furtive tones of a ghost story. The most experienced crew and best-equipped ships the greatest empire on earth could assemble—and they had vanished into the ice. The expedition had become a subject of conquest on its own for those who sought to learn what had become of it. How uncomfortable, knowing that the earth could still swallow up hundreds of men without a trace.

Becoming some sad mystery wasn't how Anton Torrance intended on achieving fame. He intended to be known as one of the greatest cold-weather explorers who ever lived. He would succeed because he would not allow himself an alternative.

The next room was a surprisingly comfortable study, with all the amenities high-ranking officers would be used to. Dark paneling, imposing furniture, paintings of famous naval battles, the head of a bighorn sheep stuffed and hanging on the wall, with a rifle on a rack underneath it, though Anton would bet it wasn't the weapon that had shot the sheep. As masculine as it was, the room was still domesticated. Contained, warm, safe. The beards of the gentlemen gathered were neatly trimmed, the shirts starched, the jackets tailored. A purser brought in a tea cart.

Moving through such spaces took as much skill as surviving in the Arctic. Just a different kind of skill, which most men of status took entirely for granted, so they saw this as natural and the wilderness as exotic. It used to be the other way around.

Bran complained about politicking, but he was better at it than he gave himself credit for. Recovered from his coughing fit, his gaze was up, his eyes clear. Not so much as a drop of sweat on him. As if he walked into rooms to ask for the trust of the United States government every day.

A whole crowd seemed to have gathered in the office of the chief signal officer. Really, it was only six men, but it seemed like a crowd when they were all looking at Anton and Bran with varying degrees of interest or outright skepticism. There were a couple of officers—a major and a colonel, along with the lieutenant who'd announced them. Anton was almost offended that the meeting hadn't rated a general. A representative from the Department of the Interior was on hand. And yes, that really was Spencer Baird, secretary of the Smithsonian Institution. A panel of experts, here to judge whether the army should take Mr. Anton Torrance seriously.

One more expert attended: Mr. Josiah Ellsworth. An older man, he clung to his ivory-trimmed cane, and his eyes were yellowed and clouded from so much sun over a long life, but he still gave the impression of focusing on small details, of listening intently. Of voraciously noting all around him. He had helped map the Northern Rockies into Canada in the '40s; Anton had read the man's book about those days. He had summited peaks that had been declared unclimbable. Landmarks on those maps bore his name. The other men at this meeting were officers and bureaucrats. Ellsworth was the one who would understand, and Anton found himself crafting his speech for him. This was the future Anton would like for himself: to survive long enough to be consulted on the matters he had spent his life mastering.

He remembered Bran's touch on his hand. With Bran beside him, he could do anything.

"Gentlemen, I am deeply grateful for your time and attention here today, and I hope you'll find what I have to say worthwhile—"

The door opened again, and the lieutenant announced the arrival of the last gentlemen invited to these proceedings. Anton was thrown.

In walked Montgomery Ashford.

Bran cursed under his breath.

Anton had too much dignity to demand to know who the bloody hell decided to invite him. Ashford was carrying a valise and a couple of placards wrapped in cloth. Anton knew exactly what was on them. He was here to make his pitch.

This wasn't a meeting. It was a competition.

The major offered an explanation. "Ah, Mr. Ashford, glad you could make it. Mr. Torrance, I hope you don't mind. I thought the group could hear both presentations at once, while we're all here."

Anton must remain polite. He hoped his demeanor showed calm. A total lack of concern because Ashford's presence meant nothing. "Very practical," he said evenly.

"Mr. Torrance, good to see you, as always." Ashford approached, hand outstretched. His gaze held venom. "Mr. West."

"Mr. Ashford." He shook the man's hand as amiably as he knew how. Bran did likewise, managing to keep his expression impassive.

This whole thing had suddenly turned fraught. The stakes suddenly seemed impossible. Forward: no choice but to move forward.

Bran's lips moved silently, shaping Latin words. Anton wished he wouldn't introduce any wild variables. Let Ashford act first; then they'd have a better idea of the ground. The last thing they wanted was an Arcanist duel right here in the office.

The thought occurred to him: maybe that was just what Ashford wanted.

Baird was an Arcanist. Would he recognize what was happening? Would he step in?

"Mr. Torrance, please continue," the officious colonel said. Ashford took a seat and looked on, grinning.

"Thank you, sir." Anton very much wanted to tell Bran not to do anything rash. Bran regarded him with uncharacteristic calm. Smiling, even. He seemed to be saying *Trust me*.

He did, he decided. He must. Anton reassured himself that this was familiar ground and presented no danger.

"Gentlemen," he started off, clearly and confidently. "I'm sure I don't need to remind you of the many scientific and strategic reasons for mounting an expedition to the Antarctic . . ." He listed those reasons anyway. The number of firsts and records waiting to be claimed, which always seemed to appeal to men like this. The pressure—that other nations were planning expeditions and America had an interest in getting there first. He discussed his own credentials, and Bran's as both a naturalist and an Arcane Taxonomist. Last, he presented Bran's—Beth and Bran's—proposed Arcanist experiments involving the use of the earth's magnetic field for navigation and communication. How such investigations necessitated a trip to the poles. Let the panel chew on that.

Buried in the middle of the proposal was the budget, which was hair raising. It had to be, to adequately equip a crew traveling to the other end of the world and back. He didn't leave the budget for the end—he didn't want his audience to believe the number was impossible. He ended with the accomplishment: the United States would make its mark on fresh, untouched territory. Would plant flags on the map and make it theirs; would collect specimens, measurements, knowledge, and bring that power home to American Arcanists.

If either Bran or Ashford had exerted any Arcanist tricks through the presentation, Anton couldn't tell.

"Now, gentlemen, I'll be happy to answer any questions you have." He didn't look at Ashford.

One of the bureaucrats, the man from the Department of the Interior, spoke up. "Mr. Torrance, I admit I'm a little confused. Wouldn't someone of your type be better suited to tropical exploration? Blazing trails through jungles, that sort of thing?"

The first thing Anton did was look at Bran, to see if he had to stop him from launching into a fight. But Bran was only chewing his cheeks to keep from saying anything. Next, Anton indulged in a brief, blissful moment of contemplating murder. Then he recovered.

"Not at all, sir. We're suited for what we prepare for and where our experience lies." He could tell them his father was British, and they'd tell themselves that his affinity for the cold came from him. Never mind that his father had spent his working life in the Caribbean because he hated the cold. Anton wouldn't give them a reason that played on their assumptions. He wanted to make them look at *him*.

Fortunately, the remaining questions were about the budget, the specifications he was looking for in a ship, and the equipment he planned on bringing. All information he knew well, and he effortlessly sounded like an expert.

The panel thanked him politely.

When the major invited Ashford to take the floor, Anton had no choice but to sit quietly. He was on the ice now; the supplies he had were all he would ever have.

Ashford rubbed his hands together in anticipation as he stood. He arranged his placards, removing the cloth with a flourish to display that picture of the great auks.

"Not a word," Anton whispered to Bran, who was fidgeting. "Just let him go."

The man launched into his usual speech, with his sensationalist notions of treasure he could put his hands on rather than the more intangible ideas of knowledge and discovery. He spoke of living fossils, discovering isolated territory where prehistoric creatures lived, stuff right out of Jules Verne. Anton had to admit, he excited the imagination.

Then Ashford paused, turning somber. "But more than all that, gentlemen, my expedition will succeed because I believe I have discovered a means of travel using the methods of Arcane Taxonomy. The old skills of the polar traveler become irrelevant when one has the means to cross distances effortlessly. Instantly, without danger and uncertainty."

"Flight," Bran said. "You're talking about Arcanist flight."

Ashford opened his hands, acknowledging the point. The panel responded with murmuring and exchanged glances.

"*How?*" Bran demanded.

"I believe a certain scholar's studies of the connection between bird migration and the earth's magnetic field offer . . . possibilities."

Anton looked at Bran for some explanation. Was this possible? This hadn't been part of Beth's proposal.

Bran seemed nonplussed and spoke carefully. "As powerful as Arcanist knowledge can be, it shouldn't replace practical skills. Mr. Torrance taught me that. As ambitious as he is, Mr. Ashford has no experience with cold-weather exploration."

Anton could kiss Bran, right there.

Ashford met the argument head on. "Mr. West and Mr. Torrance have accomplished so much, have had such esteemed careers, their ambitions rest on what's already been done. Not on what is possible."

Anton spoke a sentence in Kalaallisut, the Inuit dialect he was most comfortable with.

Ellsworth, who had been silent all this time, perked up and tilted his head. "Was that the Inuit tongue? What did you say?"

"It's one of several Inuit languages, sir. A simple observation that when you've been through a storm, preparing for the next is easier. I merely hoped to demonstrate that I have spent a great deal of time learning to survive the cold from those who know it best."

Ashford scowled. "Of course we can expect one of Mr. Torrance's race to have an affinity for the savage languages."

Anton had heard these jabs a thousand times. Long ago, he'd learned to take a breath and move on. Still, every time, his gut clenched, his skin flushed. *Let it go . . .*

Bran stood, his hands in fists. "Come over here and we'll talk about savage languages."

Anton gave Bran a look, and Bran subsided. Which said something about how often these exchanges happened.

"Call them savage if you like; the skills I have learned from the Inuit people will keep myself and my crew alive in the south polar regions." Anton couldn't express this truth any more clearly. "Mr. West's Arcanism is practical, not fanciful, and will do the same."

Baird, the Smithsonian's man, leaned forward. "Which of you is the better Arcanist, then? Show us. Right here. Ashford, you say you're working on flight. Show us what you have."

Anton had a terrible sinking feeling, as when watching an unexpected storm rise up. He could do nothing to affect the outcome of the next few minutes. This ought to be decided by experience and logistics, not an Arcanist duel.

But Bran was smiling. "I'm game. Why don't you get us started, Ashford?"

Ashford turned away and paced to the window, as if gathering himself for a great leap. He rubbed his hands together, pacing a few more steps. Anton wondered what it would look like, to see a man fly. Would he levitate, floating gently into the air? Would he need to flap his arms like a bird? Or would he vanish from one end of the room and reappear at the other, a true feat of metaphysics?

Glancing over, Ashford held up his hand, giving the impression of a magician about to pull a card from his sleeve. He was murmuring under his breath in the familiar way that Arcanists did, a jumble of Latin, drawing on whatever power he'd woven into the words.

Anton leaned over to ask Bran what he was saying, but Bran shushed him.

An electric charge passed through the air, the feeling of static and brimstone that preceded a lightning strike. Strange, without any clouds in sight and no sign of a storm. The other men glanced nervously and seemed about to dive under chairs.

When the crack of thunder came, it was only noise. No flash of light or explosion of energy accompanied it. Everyone flinched—even Anton, he wasn't ashamed to admit. Everyone except Bran, who must have known what was coming. The rest of them braced. Some other effect must follow, there had to be more, some great demonstration to accompany the spectacle. But spectacle was the bulk of Ashford's trade.

The storm let off a single gust of wind, bursting through the room and fading. Disconcerting, feeling a breeze indoors, but if you spent enough time around Arcanists, you learned it was a common trick. The wind scattered a stack of papers that had been resting on the desk. The lieutenant scurried after them, collecting them, while the colonel frowned with annoyance.

"Well, something flew, anyway," Baird said.

"That's an essential skill," Bran said, with excessive charity. "Sailing ships with an Arcanist aboard are never becalmed. The *Constitution* won some of her battles because her surgeon, Dr. Evans, controlled the weather gauge."

"Yes," Ashford said. "Just so."

Never mind that ships these days were powered by steam as well as by sail.

Bran was slowly pacing now, mirroring Ashford's previous movements. Far from revealing any urgency, Bran might have been taking a stroll in the park. "We want to emulate the flight of birds, but the question for me has always been, Which kind of flight? The hovering of *Archilochus colubris* or the diving speed of *Falco peregrinus*? The effortless soaring of *Cathartes aura*? Flight should have purpose, and that purpose determines its qualities. Not to mention there's the question of physiology. Maybe we're just not built for it."

Ashford pointed. "The arctic tern travels from pole to pole. That's what I am proposing. The power of migration!"

"*Sterna paradisaea*," Bran supplied.

"Just so."

"You've collected them? Have you seen one?"

"Of course I have. They're common." But he didn't list places or times he'd made such observations or noted his first sighting of one. Bran would have. Beth would have.

"There are nesting colonies on islands off the coast of Maine. I recommend a trip. Striking views there." Bran was generating power. Not just his ease with the names, but his familiarity with what these birds *were*. "Ashford. What's your favorite bird?" Bran asked.

Ashford laughed a little. "How does that even matter?"

"Mine is *Pandion haliaetus.*"

"Osprey," Ashford said. He clenched his hand and another breeze came up, as if he wanted to prove a point. Not as strong as the first, but it still scattered the papers that the lieutenant had just gathered up. The man cursed.

Bran smiled a little. Nodded at Mr. Baird, and—

Anton couldn't rightly explain what happened next. He was sure he had been looking right at Bran. Wondering what Ashford would do next. Worried about the men who'd been watching all this with skepticism. Then . . . he shook himself from a dizzy spell. Like he'd blacked out, but without falling over, without losing consciousness.

The room was different. Instead of standing in the middle of the floor, Bran was leaning against the colonel's desk, his arms crossed, brows raised in a question.

Other things had changed: Ashford's placards were covered back up. The lieutenant's pages were gathered up, straightened, and closed in the lieutenant's hands. The lieutenant flinched back, startled, when he saw them. He hadn't been holding them a second ago. Each man on the panel was suddenly holding a packet of papers, the printed summary and budget Anton had planned on handing out at the end.

And Anton touched his cheek, at a sting of recent pressure there. A flush in his skin. He knew *that* feeling well. Bran had kissed him. Right here in front of everyone and nobody knew it.

Bran's hunting *practicum*, but not with just one animal or one moment—he'd frozen a roomful of powerful, skeptical men. Changed the world around them without them realizing it. Now there was a trick.

Baird recognized what Bran had done in the same moment and laughed. "Well, Mr. West. I'm impressed."

"Thank you, sir." The others—even Ashford—seemed to still not understand what had happened. Bran explained. "It's good for hunting. Rescuing someone who's fallen overboard. That feeling when you see a disaster about to happen and wish you could stop time, just for a moment—" He snapped his fingers. "I like to think it's what the osprey sees at the surface of the water, just before he strikes. Time . . . stretching."

"You could rob banks with that," Ashford said thoughtfully.

"I suppose I could," Bran said. "But I'm here instead. Gentlemen, one more thing . . . I owe a great debt to the scholarship of Mrs. Elizabeth Stanley. She's credited in the proposal there, and I'd like her work recognized."

"Mrs.?" the colonel said, predictably skeptical.

"Yes," Bran said firmly. "She's one of the best naturalists I know."

"Well." The men grumbled, but they didn't argue, and Anton grinned. They were exploring all sorts of new territory here, weren't they?

Ellsworth shifted in his seat, leaned forward on his cane, and cleared his throat. All fell quiet, as if a wolf had growled in the dark. "You Arcanists. All flash. If you could get from here to there in an instant, you'd miss all the fun. Mr. Torrance, tell me what it's like on the ice."

Anton could always tell the polar bear story, but he considered: such a well-rehearsed story would sound too easy, too glib. Ellsworth would be familiar with the style and think Anton was putting him on. Brushing him off as just another gentrified audience. So he told a rarer story.

"It's difficult to convey the colors in polar climates. There *are* colors, and not the featureless field of white that is easier to describe, but inaccurate. The snow, the ice, the clouds in the sky—they might all seem white, but there are shades. The gleam of pure crystal when the sun strikes fresh snow, or the dirty cotton of a gathering storm. There's this particular metallic gray of the sea that shows through when an ice floe cracks, like quicksilver. That color often means death, if you're stuck on ice that is coming apart and threatening to drop you into freezing water. I spent some weeks on just such a floe, praying that it would not break up any further, that it would carry me to some spit of land. That churning, opaque surface was all around me, scattered with stark islands of ice. There is mystery in those waters, and I must confess to you that part of me wanted to dive in, to see for myself, if only for a second before I drowned. I have never felt as close to God as I have at the edges of the world, secure in an ice hut while the winds howl outside. The question has been asked if any corner of the world remains that has not been conquered, if there are any discoveries left to be made. I am here to tell you that there are, and that there always will be. I have never made a discovery that did not raise five more questions in its place. I hope to always ask new questions."

"Thank you, Mr. Torrance," Ellsworth said, wearing a smile perhaps inspired by a distant memory.

"You're very welcome, Mr. Ellsworth."

The colonel called an end to the meeting, thanked them for their time, and assured them a decision would be made soon. Just like that, they were finished, one way or another.

They couldn't help but face Ashford on the way out, in the echoing corridor outside the office where their fates were now being decided.

"Clever, West," Ashford said coldly. "Think of all the things you could do. *Pandion haliaetus*, you said?"

"You know very well you have to find your own way into these things."

"Hmm. There's always help to be had, if you know where to look." He winked. "Mrs. Stanley's a charming woman, I think. So nice of you to give her credit, but it won't help you."

"And you think it'll help you?" Anton said. "Do you even know where Mrs. Stanley is?"

Ashford hesitated. The confident patter stumbled. "My understanding is she's gone on a retreat. For her health."

As if he hadn't orchestrated that entire incident. "Try again," Anton said.

"What . . . what do you know?"

"Good day, Mr. Ashford." Anton put on his hat. "May the best man win."

Bran was shaking. Perhaps from anger. Perhaps because he was stifling another coughing fit. Anton clapped his shoulder and steered him to the door, leaving Ashford sputtering behind them.

The coughing fit came not half a block from the office building. He bent over, hands on knees, rattling. Anton wished he could bundle Bran up and carry him home.

"You're not well."

"Just . . . a moment." Bran tried to wave him off. Eventually, he straightened, inhaling carefully. "See? Just needed a moment." But he remained standing stiffly, uncertain.

Slowly, they walked to a park along the river. "Thank you," Anton said finally.

Bran only shrugged. "I've been meaning to try something like that for a while. A whole room. Wasn't sure I could—"

"I mean for the kiss. It was . . . lovely."

"You could tell, could you?"

"Always."

Washington, DC

December 1880

Mr. Anton Torrance:
Pleased to announce contract for South Polar Expedition awarded to you and your team. Congratulations and happy voyaging.
Major Wilson Keck
US Army Signal Corps

Bran insisted he only needed time. Time, a bit of exercise, a determined return to his usual routine. Meanwhile, Anton sent for the doctor.

Bran sat in their drawing room in shirtsleeves, the doctor looming over him, peering through glasses. So this was what it felt like to be a specimen. The man placed a hand on Bran's chest and told him to breathe deeply. He only got in one good inhale before a bout of coughing shook him.

The doctor frowned, and Bran almost argued—let him try again, he was sure he could breathe without coughing if he had another chance, time to prepare—

But he knew. Before the doctor said a word, he knew.

"Do you travel?" the doctor said casually, as if they weren't discussing Bran's future. "You might consider a warm, dry climate. Just for a time, to help ease your lungs. They're quite damaged, I'm afraid."

Bran chuckled darkly, which started more coughing, and the more he tried to stop, the worse it got, until he was bent over and trying to hold his breath. The doctor gestured to Anton, who brought over a cup. Bran hoped for brandy, but the cup held nothing more than hot water with honey and lemon.

"I'm supposed to go to Antarctica." Bran's voice scratched.

"Far be it from me to tell you what to do, but the freezing cold will do nothing good for you. I'm sure Mr. Torrance has seen similar conditions."

Mr. Torrance was very quiet.

"Consider carefully." The doctor packed up his things, and Bran thanked him in a whisper. Anton closed the door softly after he left.

Bran sat still, feeling air go in and out of his lungs, scratching like sand. He breathed carefully so he wouldn't start coughing again. He sipped the honeyed water and hated that it seemed to help. This was a tincture for invalids, and he was not an invalid. He refused to be one.

Anton peeled off his coat and vest, draped them over the back of the chair across from Bran, then settled into it, leaning his elbows on his knees.

Bran spoke first, hoping to cut off whatever he was about to say. Distract him, forestall the inevitable. "I can stay on the ship, preparing specimens, keeping the logbooks. I'll sit by the broiler the whole time. It's months before we're due to leave; plenty of time for me to heal up. It'll be fine—I know it will." Then he coughed, a hideous rattling sound deep in his lungs that couldn't be passed off as simple throat clearing. A child would know something was wrong with him.

Bowing his head, Anton spoke to the floor. "I will not take you to the ends of the earth to watch you die there."

"But I won't. We don't know that will happen. Either one of us could slip on a patch of ice and fall overboard and die. A thousand accidents can happen. You can't prevent either one of us dying, not in this work, so why should this matter?" He wanted to shout, to speak fiercely. To defend his chance. But he couldn't. His voice was a suppressed whisper, to stop that damned coughing. He rubbed his eyes, which had started stinging dangerously.

"Take Heinz with you," Bran forced out after a moment. "He's steady, a good naturalist. He'll listen to orders."

Anton shifted to the sofa and put his arms around him. Bran, hands over his face, allowed himself to be held.

If Bran could not travel to Antarctica with him, did Anton still want to go?

That the question even occurred to Anton was a shock. For a decade, this had been his dream, his overriding plan. All the hardship of the North: the skills he'd learned, the years he'd spent, the toes he'd lost were all to prepare for this southern expedition. Having Bran at his side made the prospect all the better. They were a good team, with Anton's skills and Bran's attention to detail. They would not just succeed; they would triumph. They would stand on the ice shelf and imagine themselves the only two people in the world, who could do whatever they liked, who had built their own destiny with each step they had traveled.

Without Bran, did he still want to stand on that ice, alone?

Slowly, day by day, he realized that the answer was yes. He did. Bran would stay behind—and Anton would come back to him. Bran was insurance that Anton would want to come back home.

Strangely, he never once questioned that Bran would wait for him to return if he was left behind. The ice of the South beckoned; it would be there whenever Anton wished to travel—though he might wish to do so sooner rather than later, to secure a couple firsts in his name, to be recorded on the great blackboard at the Naturalist Society. Bran would be here, waiting. Anton could move between the two realms, confident.

He would tell all this to Bran. Strip him down and wrap him in his arms, cover him with kisses and try to explain how Bran was a beacon to him. How necessary he was. If Anton left for the far reaches of the globe, it was because he had Bran holding the end of his tether.

THIRTY-SEVEN
Cyanocitta stelleri

A more pressing expedition captured their immediate attention: Beth.

They did their own detective work, starting from what they knew of Beth rather than what strangers assumed about her, which meant starting in Harry's study. Ann let them see Beth's correspondence and records, and they wrote to her network of observers across the country. They assumed that if any of them had heard from her, or were perhaps even housing her, they had been instructed to say nothing. So rather than demanding information, they asked simply to pass along messages.

They cornered Teddy, the porter at the Naturalist Society, and promised to name some new species of fish after him if he told them news of any new subscriptions or odd correspondence. Nothing, so far.

Patience, patience. One did not learn what there was to know of an animal from one sighting. It took multiple specimens and observations across the seasons. Bran and Anton wrote a lot of letters with the same intention: to any who might have encountered her, to simply pass on a message that she was missed. That she was loved.

Bran was getting stronger, better. If not for the cough, Anton might have thought him well. But he slept so long and so deeply, sometimes Anton had to watch to make sure his chest still moved.

Bran brought out the skins of falcons, of vultures, farseeing birds that hunted, and took those traits to himself, searching for her trail, yearning for insight. She must be accessing Harry's finances. She must still be using her name to do so. But she must have gone someplace where no one knew her, where no one would question her. Someplace full of travelers, strangers, movement.

Bran said he dreamed of Steller's jays and thought it was a sign. West.

A month after she disappeared, they received a telegram sent from a train station in Missouri, three words only: *She is well.* They had no reason to believe it came directly from Beth; one of her contacts lived near there. It might have been a message passed along secondhand. Anton immediately sent a reply, begging for a location where they might find her, but no further communication came.

If the message could be believed, then she was safe. She was well. They repeated this to themselves, to each other, as if it were a comfort. But this implied that she did not want to see them. That wherever she was, she was happier without them. This was not a comfort.

"She'll come back when she's ready," Anton said one day, eight weeks after she had gone.

"What makes you so sure?" Bran replied, and Anton didn't have an answer. He'd spoken a hope, not a fact. Bran added, "She has found someplace with so many wonderful, fantastical birds, she can't bear to leave."

"Costa Rica?"

Bran shook his head. "Alaska."

"I don't think she's in Alaska," Anton insisted. They'd been able to laugh some at that, a small unfunny joke. But Bran began scouring the journals for bird surveys in Alaska, searching for the flavor of her words.

Then, he found her.

1881
Colorado Springs

The train sped across the Great Plains in a day, which seemed vaguely obscene when just a generation before, the journey took months by wagon. The vast spaces, awe inspiring even from the window of a train, must have been overwhelming and never ending from the seat of a wagon. What was it about people that they insisted on leaving their native habitats and venturing into places that were dangerous and unrelenting? Bran had only ever seen skies this big, a land where he could see from horizon to horizon, in the Arctic.

He saw no bison. Stories told that once there had been great herds of thousands of bison. They were gone, hunted to death like the great auk, and he wondered what Beth would say about that.

In the end, she hadn't submitted any articles to the *Pinfeather*, where they were sure to look. But she had sent some to a newer publication, the *American Ornithology Review*.

In their front room, going through a stack of new journals, Bran had folded back the cover and stared in disbelief until Anton demanded to know what he'd found. He'd shoved the page under his nose, pointing at the byline:

Garden Birds of the Colorado Plains

by Stanley Clarke

Stanley Clarke. Harry and Beth, right there.

It was a standard survey article, describing the habitat in detached detail but adding personal impressions, then listing the species of birds observed, along with the number of individuals. He wouldn't have looked at it twice if it hadn't been for the name, but he did look at it twice now, and heard her voice in the writing. The calm turns of phrase; her occasionally obsessive notations of the weather. When these observations had been made, the day had been dry, clear, and a bright sun had made the air feel warm. *A coat was not necessary, until a brisk afternoon wind started, bringing with it a cold bite and a crisp smell of snow from the mountains. Though this area is rapidly developing, in some places the old prairie remains, along with the grasslands where cattle are raised, and to watch the winds blow through the yellowed winter grasses is to be hypnotized by the air itself.*

Bran eyed the survey with some envy—there were some excellent sightings and several species he had never seen alive. Canyon towhee, black-billed magpie, mountain chickadee. Iconic western birds, and he suddenly longed for a trip. He had been farther north than just a handful of other living men, but he had not seen the Rocky Mountains, and that suddenly seemed like a great failure on his part. It would be an easy enough trip, not like the old days of the frontier. Just a couple of days by train. Colorado had been a state since '76. There would be *hotels.* They wouldn't even need to camp.

He heard Beth all through the article. Then she confirmed his hunch: *White-crowned sparrow. So delightful to see a friend from home. Always a favorite sighting.*

Anton saw it, too, and glanced up, startled.

"I bet she's got them eating out of her hand already," Bran said.

"She's all right, though. That's the important thing, isn't it? That she's safe?"

Yes, but she was still two thousand miles away, and that felt wrong. She could have written; she could have returned at any time. She should have written.

If only he knew what she was thinking.

"I'll write to her, care of the magazine. They'll have to forward it on, and she can write back through them without raising any suspicion."

"Bran. We're explorers. We'll go find her."

They could do that, couldn't they? "A dry climate, the doctor said, yes?"

"I believe he did."

"Well then."

So here they were.

Between the wide spaces were towns. A lot of them, with streets, churches and bell towers, houses and shops, all the amenities of civilization. Those hadn't been there just a generation before, either, and a sudden panic overtook him: They must survey these prairies before they vanished. Catalog it all, every plant and insect—and then what? Put them in cases in university museums to dry out and gather dust? Their drive to explore had many reasons behind it—to be the first in some place or other, to learn, to widen the boundaries of knowledge. To win Arcane power. But there was another reason: to see these places before the trains and towns and houses came to them. Hard to imagine a train stop surrounded by clapboard houses and water tanks in the high Arctic. But someone had once said that about the prairie.

He didn't know what he had expected, traveling west. The old stories of pioneers and battles between the cavalry and Indians. (He didn't see any Indians, but realized he didn't know if he would recognize one if he did. Not if they were wearing bowler caps, jackets, and calico dresses like the white townsfolk were. The identifying traits were not what he thought.) Something resembling the blurry photos from paleontological digs, dusty men in rock-strewn landscapes. The lurid settings of dime novels.

He certainly didn't expect to leave the train in Colorado Springs and find himself in a bustling town full of brick buildings, banks and mercantile stores, ornate houses, finely dressed men and women, very respectable.

One noteworthy detail made the town seem wild: to the west, a great mountain, Pikes Peak, overshadowed all. Nothing like that on the East Coast. This time of year, it was covered with snow, blazing white in the sun.

Beside him, Anton tipped his head back, closed his eyes, and took in a deep, slow breath. "I can smell the ice from here."

For his part, Bran tried not to breathe too deeply. He didn't want to start coughing. "Fancy some mountaineering while we're here, then?"

"Thinking of it."

They could immediately see why Beth had stayed here.

Bran thought he ought to be able to send a thread of his Arcane self into the air, sailing on the wind like a kite, and she would find it, take hold, and he could follow it back to her. When he did, though, the thread dissipated. If he found the eyes of a hawk to see through, maybe—

As usual, Anton suggested a more practical route.

The address the journal corresponded with was a post office nearby. If nothing else, they could wait outside for Beth to come and get her mail. That seemed inefficient. Instead, they merely had to use the skills they had in searching for a specific bird. Know the creature's habitat. Learn its behaviors, its food. Set out likely bait. Beth would need a house. She was used to a certain level of comfort, and they didn't see her abandoning that for some mining-camp tent or isolated cabin. She had been writing and sending letters, receiving publications, which meant she was buying ink and paper as well as checking mail. She didn't cook, or at least they'd never seen her make any gestures toward cooking, which meant she had help. She was in a boarding house, maybe. A limited number of boarding houses would cater to respectable young women. A bit of asking around, they could find them.

At which point Anton wrote a letter and left it at the post office, requesting that if any reply came, it be held for him. He would check each day. Meanwhile, the pair went into the foothills for some simple walking. Some easy observations with no pressure to produce, to collect, to compete. Like being children, when the sight of a new flower or colorful insect was enough to excite, before the child grew into a natural historian. Bran remembered his first notebook and the childish drawings he had made in it, awkward sketches of the turtles, beetles, and snails he found at his family's farm. The small feeling of power it gave him to record what he saw. The drawings represented proof: the vision was fleeting but the drawing remained, and he could remember. Except he didn't know what had happened to that old notebook. After thousands more observations and drawings, he had left that first notebook far behind. All his work suddenly seemed fleeting. Intangible.

The first bit of Arcane *practicum* he'd ever performed was to push the water in a pond away so he could pick up the turtle hiding at the bottom. He'd been young, hadn't quite realized what he'd done. But that had set him on the path to Harvard and Arcane Taxonomy. Just now, though, he missed being the boy with the turtle.

Pine forests settled on a rocky backdrop, along with gray smears of winterbound leafless scrub oak. Rust-colored sandstone layers lifted up by the granite of the mountains underneath them made a striking splash of color. A geologist's paradise here. They didn't make much progress on their walks, stopping to study outcrops, to note the three or four different kinds of conifers. The air itself was shockingly different from what they were used to: clear, dry, and thin. Too early to tell if it would help his cough.

Bran's first sighting of a Steller's jay was almost enough to distract him from their quest. With it came a sense of longing: he would never have time enough to explore all the different regions of the world. This, a mere two thousand miles from home, was all new to him.

Beth was much closer than that. He had an overwhelming feeling that she had seen this very jay. He turned around to look, to search the path behind him. She wasn't there. But she was close.

Anton wanted to climb. He led them off the obvious trails, trying to find a vantage, to get a better sense of the peak and the steep hills around it. Bran had to stop when his lungs squeezed painfully and his breathing turned shallow. The high elevation here was noticeable— he couldn't breathe. He urged Anton to go ahead without him, and Anton continued for a handful of steps to the next set of trees rising up from the stretch of rock, but then he hesitated, considered, and turned around.

"The way looks snowbound up ahead," he said. "I'd need crampons to continue on."

He almost sounded convincing.

They went back down the hill, to their hotel and a warm fire.

They returned to the post office and asked for any messages. Hoping, but bracing for disappointment. A single message was produced: a card in Beth's handwriting with an address and set of directions on it. They took this for an invitation and hired a pair of horses.

They found a cottage near a pretty creek lined with pines, and knew it was Beth's because of the trays and boxes filled with seed and swarming with birds, dozens of chickadees and juncos, with a couple of nuthatches and a flicker darting back and forth. And yes, the jays were here too. A recent snowfall had mostly melted under a warm sun. Patches of snow remained on damp ground, and the sound of dripping snowmelt trickled in the nearby trees.

The place was an outbuilding for a lodge farther upstream, at the end of a gravel path that seemed to be frequently used. So she had company, someone was helping look after her, and this was a relief. Bran wasn't sure what he'd imagined her situation to be—maybe that of some cloistered refugee in a gothic novel. But this was nice. Pleasant.

As Anton found a place to tie up the horses, Bran approached the door, which swung open, and there she stood.

She was nothing like she'd been. Her hair was in a loose, sloppy bun with a straw hat nestled on top of it. Her dress was plain, the coat pulled over it practical rather than elegant. The coat was brown; the dress under it was dark blue. Mourning put aside at last. The society girl was gone. This was a woman who spent her time tromping around outside.

"Hello," she said, her voice familiar, subdued. Her smile flickered, uncertain.

Bran was staring at her middle. She wasn't wearing a corset. Her elegant, statuesque frame seemed off somehow. Hard to tell, but then the coat flapped open and she rested a hand on a slightly rounded stomach.

By this time Anton had taken care of the horses and come up beside him, and he was staring, too, and Bran wondered if they were seeing the same thing.

"Would you like to come in for tea?" As if they were back at the brownstone, as if nothing had changed.

"Why didn't you send word?" Bran burst. "Just a note would have done. We were worried sick!"

The exclamation started a round of coughing to punctuate the statement—he was sick, not a figure of speech.

"Oh, do come in, please." She stepped aside and held open the door.

"Are you . . ." He trailed off.

"Yes," she said simply.

Beth had thought she would miss Central Park, but now she had the Rocky Mountains, a glorious trade. Instead of her little garden she had an entire wilderness at her doorstep, and she reveled in it. It was all new, unfamiliar. The sky was vast; on clear days, its blue was gemlike, astonishing. A bluebird sky, people called it. Wind and storms came out of the hills unexpectedly, and the plains to the east seemed to go on forever. Even the air smelled different here, thin and organic, full of dried scrub and pine trees.

But there were house finches, just like at home. And juncos, chickadees, and white-capped sparrows. Along with the birds that were new to her: western kingbirds, black-headed grosbeaks, vermilion flycatchers, scaled quail. Magnificent, all of them.

She'd had to leave her books behind, but luck was with her, and the newly founded college nearby had just opened their library. Beth presented herself as an author, showing the articles she had written under her own name, the ones Bran had scoffed at, and asked if she might use their collection for her work. She wasn't sure what the response would be—at worst, they would turn her away, and she'd be no worse off. She'd gotten quite brave, hadn't she? But the administrators said yes. Moreover, they asked if she would perhaps like to teach a class on writing and natural history as a guest instructor. The college admitted both women and men as students. Beth had never considered that she might teach. She considered it now, and thought of how she might find girls with an aptitude for Arcanism.

And then the baby. She hadn't wanted to believe it at first; it took weeks for her to admit that this was real, this was happening. A moment of despair—she was alone; this was too much for her to do alone.

Then she thought: Harry's mother would have no claim on this child. Her own mother wasn't here to intrude and command. This child was *hers*. She could name it whatever she liked, teach it whatever she liked. Tell whatever stories about themselves she wanted. Already, she loved her child. It was part of this new life, this new world.

She hadn't worried about whether she should wear gloves in weeks. She'd put away even the half mourning. She was a different person here. Was *allowed* to be a different person here.

All she lacked were Anton and Bran.

Some thread still connected them. Some sort of magnetism that couldn't be muted. Bran reaching out, unerringly finding her. A sense she had, growing stronger, that if she looked over her shoulder, he would be standing there.

It was Anton who left the entirely mundane letter at the post office, and she wasn't surprised. He had a practical, admirable directness.

When she saw them standing in her yard, somehow both bereft and hopeful, about to step forward but still drawing back, unsure, she wondered how she'd gone weeks without seeing them and doubted she could ever let them go again.

She sat them on the sofa in her sunny parlor and set about making tea.

The room doubled as her study and was a mess: her bird logs stacked on one table, a new set of opera glasses resting on top of them, several books the library had ordered for her on another, along with a pile of sketches. They had to move aside books to make room to sit.

With no Ann here, she put the kettle on the fire herself, prepared the teapot herself, set out the cups and the half a cake left over from yesterday herself. This was so very different from how she had been before. They must be shocked. She kept unnecessarily busy because she didn't know what to say.

"You seem well," Anton ventured finally.

"Do I?" She abruptly sat on the armchair across from them, clutching her hands together in her lap, around her belly, which seemed to be expanding every day. "It's mine. Do you see it? I can do what I like, when I like, with no expectations and no sense of obligation."

"Why didn't you tell anyone?" Bran said, accusingly to her ears, but it was only his emotion getting the better of him. His passion. "We could have helped, we could have protected you, we could have—"

"Placed a sense of obligation on her," Anton said softly, and Bran slumped.

She had worked it all out weeks ago, or she thought she had. She didn't know if it would make sense to them. "I couldn't risk my mother and brother finding out. They would have dragged me off and locked me up. I was so afraid. I'm sorry you were worried, but I was so afraid." She rested her hand on her stomach. A spreading gesture, as if to contain it. "Here, alone, I could tell whatever story I wanted about myself and the baby. I could be whatever I wanted. And you could do what you needed without worrying about me. You have so much work to do, and you shouldn't trouble yourselves with me."

"We've just traveled halfway across the country for you," Anton said. "We want to be troubled!"

Bran licked his lips, hesitating before speaking. "But if you don't care so much for us—"

"I love you," she said. "I love you both dearly. You saved my life." She blinked and patted her eyes to stop the tears. She still cried, but didn't mind it as much. "Or at least you saved me from Ronald Benson."

Bran's brow furrowed. "Who on earth is Ronald Benson?"

She laughed a little. How would she ever explain to them? She poured the tea, and they drank silently, awkwardly. So much still to be said.

"You won't be coming back to New York?" Bran ventured.

"Not right away, no. I think . . . I think this would be a good place for a baby, don't you?"

"I do," he breathed.

Anton huffed. "If you really wanted to hide, you could have picked a better name than Stanley Clarke."

She smiled more easily than she had in months. She felt lighter than she had in months, even with the pregnancy weighing on her. "It would have made Harry laugh."

Bran chuckled. And coughed. The rattling, worrying noise seemed to come from deep in his lungs.

Beth pushed over a small crock of honey. "The honey helps. It's so dry, everyone gets a sore throat when they first get here."

Shutting his eyes, Bran held a hand spread over his heart. For a moment, he seemed not to be breathing at all, and Beth started to panic.

"Bran is ill," Anton said quietly. "He won't be going on the expedition."

No, she couldn't take this, she couldn't sit at another deathbed—except she would, for Bran and Anton, if she needed to.

Bran argued. "The doctor said if I stay in a drier climate, if I can just get myself well." Another cough broke through. He sat with his lips pursed, as if he could swallow it.

"No," Anton said, and that was that.

Bran nodded, relaxing. Relieved, maybe. Willing to let Anton decide, because if it were up to Bran, he'd go get himself killed in Antarctica, and she'd rather he didn't. A drier climate? He could stay here . . .

"Oh, Bran, I'm sorry." She leaned over to touch his hand. He took hold of hers, like it was a lifeline. If not for her, he wouldn't have stormed off; he wouldn't have fallen through the ice; he wouldn't have been in Maine at all. "This is my fault."

"Beth, stop it," Bran said. "It's no one's fault. My own damn stubbornness. Like Harry. We're all such *men*, aren't we?"

"Well, yes," she agreed.

Anton bent his head close to Bran's, rested his hand on both of theirs. A connection, a circle between them. "It would give me great, good comfort knowing you two are looking after one another while I am gone."

Grief, but comfort also. Yes. Bran whispered, "Name a bird or two for us, won't you?"

She couldn't stand it anymore, being even this little ways apart from them, and with a wordless exclamation she flung herself at them. They weren't expecting it, but their instincts were good. She had meant to land between them, but they caught her instead, diverting her so she sprawled across their laps, and they clung to each other.

In the early years, theologians and church leaders considered declaring Arcane Taxonomy to be heretical and pressured for its criminalization. But when the potential for commercial, political, and military applications emerged, they relented and instead declared it a manifestation of God's will. Questions remained. Did Arcane Taxonomists work miracles? Did that make them conduits of God's power? Were Arcane Taxonomists a kind of modern, industrialized saint—or was their power a temptation, a sin of pride, a work of hubris? The real difficulty was navigating a world in which religion no longer had a monopoly on miracles.

Many Arcane Taxonomists, while unwilling to declare themselves outright atheists, were not religious. Charles Darwin wrote of his growing agnosticism—he did not see the hand of God in a brutal natural world that followed its own laws, and a natural history that did not follow the history laid out in the Bible. He did not see divine presence in what was, essentially, genealogy.

But Darwin also saw great wonder in the natural world. There was no need for the divine when nature itself provided no end of awe. He concludes *On the Origin of Species*: "whilst this planet has gone cycling on according to the fixed law of gravity, from so simple a beginning endless forms most beautiful and most wonderful have been, and are being, evolved."

The Arcanist and naturalist John Muir believed that no contradiction existed between belief in God and the practice of Arcane Taxonomy, which he felt had a spiritual aspect that was rarely acknowledged. Nature offered the most direct connection to the Divine. At the heart of Arcane Taxonomy is the sense of connection it grants to those open to possibilities. "When we contemplate the whole globe as one great dewdrop, striped and dotted with continents and islands, flying through space with other stars all singing and shining together as one, the whole universe appears as an infinite storm of beauty." This philosophy led Muir to advocate for the preservation of wilderness and the creation of the first of the US's national parks.

Arcane Taxonomy is a skill that will never be mastered because it is always changing, as the world it draws on is always changing.

—Excerpts from *A Common History of Arcane Taxonomy*, by Ava Stanley, 1925, San Francisco, California

EPILOGUE

Aves

1883
New York City

In the summer of 1881, the three of them said their farewells the night before Anton and the *Wayfinder* launched on the South Polar Expedition. They didn't see him off at the pier: Bran was too melancholy, and Beth was round and ponderous and ready to burst and didn't want to face the excitement. Anton gently told them he preferred it this way, leaving with embraces they couldn't share in public rather than watching them get smaller and smaller on the pier as he sailed away. Bran and Beth almost believed him.

When he was gone, they got to work. Bought a globe and marked his route. Tricky—the continent of Antarctica was barely charted, the ice sheets changeable. One of the expedition's goals was to make detailed maps as well as measure currents. Gather information to make the journey easier for the next expedition. Discovery was a staircase, each step bringing one closer to the top.

The *Wayfinder* left its last port of call in Argentina, the expedition's last chance to send word home. Bran was able to send a telegram to tell Anton that baby Ava had arrived. Anton was able to send back love and congratulations.

They didn't hear from him again for over a year.

If something had happened to Anton, if some tragedy struck and the ship vanished, like the Franklin expedition in the North, would they ever know? Would they face the rest of their lives wondering?

Beth gathered knowledge. Books, papers, essays, nearly every word that had been written on the topic of migration. From the logbooks of a hundred years of whaling ships, she traced the movements of *Megaptera novaeangliae*, the humpback whale, that traveled north and south between feeding grounds and birthing grounds. Two great circles, Arctic and Antarctic, like the currents of the oceans. Bran pored over forty years' worth of weather reports from naval vessels to get a better picture of what Anton was sailing into.

And the birds. Birds were the greatest travelers in the world. The arctic tern, *Sterna paradisaea*, migrated between the two polar regions. The bar-tailed godwit, *Limosa lapponica*, was said to do likewise, but this hadn't been verified by naturalists. How could one know that the godwit one saw in Alaska in summer was the same one that arrived in Australia six months later? This was a great problem in need of a solution, to find some way to mark birds and follow them. One problem at a time, Bran decided, and the immediate problem was how to help Anton from nine thousand miles away.

The arctic tern spent summers in the north to breed, then appeared in the south, in the southern summer. A journey of almost ten thousand miles, twice a year. A tiny little thing, only a few ounces. It ought to get pummeled by the elements; it ought to be vulnerable. Yet it survived, adapted to its world, to flight, to survival. To journeying in polar lands.

In the fall, they bundled up their new daughter and traveled to the coast of Maine, consulted dozens of ornithological surveys to estimate when the terns would fly south, and watched and counted the birds and sent wordless messages along with them. Strength, love, resilience, and a sense of wonder at all Anton must be seeing. Safety: may he and all his crew come home safe.

A couple of nights, they saw the aurora borealis, a rare sight so far south. Bran had seen it often on his expeditions, but this was Beth's first time. The ribbony pale light evaded comprehension. It was the same light she saw in fireflies, in the bioluminescence that touched waves rolling onto a nighttime shore. They could hardly sleep after watching it. Just as well; Ava was fussy and kept them up, and they didn't mind at all. In the Far South, the aurora australis lit up Antarctic skies, and they imagined Anton watching it, as unable to sleep as they were.

A week later, the terns would arrive where Anton was. Bran woke up in the middle of the night with that dizzying vertigo, looking through the eyes of a creature that soared and banked, cold wind sleeking over dense, streamlined feathers. Below, ice floes dotted a metallic sea, forming a constantly shifting archipelago. A ship plowed through, churning a white wake behind it. If the bird veered slightly . . . there, a tall, fur-coated man standing at the prow, spyglass in hand.

Did the man look back, meet the tern's gaze, see what watched through the bird's eyes?

Bran dreamed. Pure fancy.

But maybe . . .

A month past the expected date of the *Wayfinder*'s return to South America, the longed-for telegram arrived. Restoring contact with the wider world, Anton sent word to Bran and Beth: *I saw so many arctic terns and thought of you.*

Two and a half years after leaving New York, the *Wayfinder* returned.

The pier turned into something of a festival. Men from the Naturalist Society, students from Columbia, curators from the American Museum of Natural History, dozens more: all came to have first look at the returning expedition. Telegrams had been sent, and the *Wayfinder* had been sighted entering the harbor, on its way to the pier on the East River. The expedition was reported to have been a success, but then Anton Torrance would report it a success in any case, wouldn't he?

Well, no one had died, so in that sense it was a roaring success. Torrance and his party had made successful landings, collected samples, recorded charts and measurements and a thousand other observations, and they had returned. There'd be books and lectures and parties and medals and accolades. The true importance of the expedition wouldn't be measured until years later. But right now, several hundred people wanted to be able to say they had been there to meet the ship when it finally came home.

At the front of them all were Elizabeth Stanley and Brandon West, who was lifting up a very small girl to see over the crowd. She had a finger in her mouth and seemed nonplussed. Ann stood with them as well, the girl's small coat tucked over her arm, craning her neck along with the rest for the first glimpse of the ship.

"Can you see anything?" Bran whispered to the girl in his arms.

"No," she said in a small, confused voice. "It's loud."

"Ah, poor thing." He held her, and she put her arms around his neck.

"I'm so nervous," Beth said.

"Me too."

The crowd grew, pressing in behind. Bran and Beth hardly noticed, shading their eyes against the midmorning sun to see better, and at last Bran pointed. There it was. Slowly, slowly, the ship eased closer. Dockhands appeared with mooring lines, and they seemed to move far too leisurely; it was all moving so slowly.

Finally, at last, the ship came close enough to make out details. To Bran's eyes, the vessel looked battered and beaten. He could make out scars where ice had smashed into the hull. They must have been frozen in for at least some of the time, and his heart dropped, thinking of the danger they had been in. He knew that feeling of being on a ship as the sea ice closed in, wondering if it would break apart long enough to slip away before they all froze or starved. One of the masts had been broken and repaired. The steam engine had a rattling pitch to it that it hadn't when they'd left. The deck seemed tired, sagging. The damage told a story.

Part of him would always be disappointed that he hadn't been there. Part of him was glad to be here instead.

Many of the crew and expedition members, most of them stripped to shirtsleeves as if the brisk autumn weather was balmy to them, pressed up against the railing, looking down.

"There he is!" Beth spotted Anton first.

He was half a head taller than everyone around him, his strong hands gripping the railing as he leaned out, searching the crowd. His shoulders didn't seem to be as broad as they should have been. His whole frame seemed too thin, his face too gaunt. His hair had a dusting of gray that it hadn't had before. He wasn't smiling. He seemed tired. None of this should have been a surprise, but it was.

The crowd astonished Anton. He hadn't been expecting it, even though his younger self would have reveled at the attention. Now, he just wanted to be home, and the hundreds of people—shouting, arms waving—seemed like a barrier. But then he saw Beth and Bran, grinning madly, holding up between them a little girl with brown curls, wearing a yellow dress, hands clapped over her ears against the ruckus. Even Ann was there. Oh, they were all so beautiful.

Then he smiled.

Bran let Ava slip out of his arms, made sure her hand was firmly in Beth's, and then ran for the gangplank that was still being moved into place to finally link the ship to shore.

Bran was the first one up, and Anton shoved past his own crew to be the first to meet him. However exhausted he was, he moved fast for this.

They crashed together at the top of the gangplank, for once unmindful of whoever saw them. They hugged fiercely, fingers digging into shirts, gripping hard, holding on to never let go. Bran was laughing. Anton held his face against his lover's shoulder and kept it there for several long, deep breaths, as if reminding himself of what the world should be. They drew apart finally but kept hold of the other's arms.

Together, they turned back to the pier, to the base of the gangplank, where Beth and their daughter stood.

Beth held the girl close. "See? There's our dear Anton."

"Did he bring me a penguin?" Ava asked.

"Let's find out."

AUTHOR'S NOTE

This novel went through several versions before taking on the form you hold in your hands. It's a better book thanks to the patience and efforts of editors Adrienne Procaccini and Clarence Haynes, as well as my agent, Seth Fishman. Many thanks also to the team at 47North who helped along the way. Thank you all.

Thanks to Daniel Abraham for reading the manuscript and talking me off the ledge a couple of times. Thanks to my weekly dinner crew, Max, Yaz, Anne, and Wendy, for keeping me going. And as always, thanks to my family—Mom, Dad, Grandma, Rob, Deb, and Emery—for being there from the start.

Thanks also to everyone who said, "Hey, you like birds. When are you going to write a book about them?" and got the ball rolling.

A few more notes: While Beth, Bran, and Anton are fictional, I drew on some real history for inspiration.

Florence Merriam Bailey is credited with writing the first field guide for amateur birders, *Birds through an Opera-Glass*, in 1889. By advocating for watching birds in the wild rather than killing and collecting them, she basically invented modern birding. She was also active in the early Audubon Society, which worked for the protection of birds, including lobbying for restrictions on hunting them for feathers.

Matthew Henson was an African American explorer who accompanied Robert Peary on his expeditions for over twenty years and was part of the group that reportedly reached the North Pole in 1909. (Note:

Peary's claim to have reached the pole is disputed. Henson's contributions to Arctic exploration are not.) His memoir of the experience, *A Negro Explorer at the North Pole*, was invaluable background reading.

Of a Feather: A Brief History of American Birding, by Scott Weidensaul, is where I learned about Florence Merriam Bailey, the early conservation movement's efforts to ban the feather trade for hats, the transition in life sciences from collecting birds to observing in the field, and lots of other good tidbits.

While writing *The Naturalist Society*, I read a lot of great books about polar exploration, Antarctica, the history of the life sciences, and the culture of the nineteenth century, as well as biographies of pivotal figures. Thank you to all those authors for their efforts and for getting their work out there. Any errors, inaccuracies, and liberties taken are my own.

If you're interested in learning more about birds and getting into birding yourself (if you're not already!), I recommend the Cornell Lab of Ornithology's website All About Birds and their Merlin Bird ID app. I track my birding activities via eBird. Find me there to check out what I've seen recently!

ABOUT THE AUTHOR

Photo © 2020 Lucy Tuck Photography

Carrie Vaughn is the author of more than twenty novels and over a hundred short stories, two of which have been finalists for the Hugo Award. She's best known for her *New York Times* bestselling series of novels about a werewolf named Kitty, who hosts a talk radio advice show for the supernaturally disadvantaged. In 2018, Vaughn won the Philip K. Dick Award for the postapocalyptic murder mystery *Bannerless*. A graduate of the Odyssey Fantasy Writing Workshop, Carrie is also a contributor to the Wild Cards series of shared-world superhero books edited by George R. R. Martin.

Vaughn survived her nomadic childhood as an air force brat and managed to put down roots in Boulder, Colorado, where she currently collects hobbies.

Visit the author at www.carrievaughn.com.

For writing advice and essays, check out her Patreon page: www.patreon.com/carrievaughn.